Anders Flagstad's

Circles
and
Wheels

ALSO BY
ANDERS FLAGSTAD

Spare Parts
(Book One of Principal Parts)

Thad Says Parts Is Parts
(And Thad Is Right)
(Book Two of Principal Parts)

The Chaotic Pendulum

...It smelled like a refinery up there. Whoever was throttling it was going to town with it, the diesel smoke was as thick as fog. Three guys were yelling at each other, pulling on the bumper, trying to steady it, Red, Shaved, and a new guy with a baseball hat. There had to be a fourth guy trying to unjam the accelerator (maybe?-why was the truck racing forward like it had a mind of its own? I'll never know) – the door was open on the driver's side, so I couldn't see much of anything up in the front. But I could see the license plate now, upside down, over my head - California 9845BTRS - and I could see we were apparently on some high, curvy bridge thing which overlooked downtown maybe a mile or so away. I got up onto my one knee, off the pavement. I pushed myself onto one leg. I edged away. There wasn't another car or other person in sight. Just the yelling men, me hopping on one foot, and the possessed delivery vehicle.

You know, the odd thing was, the bridge curved up high, almost unnaturally, and in a circle, as if it were a boomerang propped up on stilts in the middle, ready to boomerang itself away from this crazy city and make its own way off into the starry unknown and a new, exciting, city-free life. Weird. And it sloped. Boy did it slope. It's a good thing San Diego didn't get much snow, huh? We were at the top.

The truck was doing a slow pirouette towards the water, a long, long, long ways down...

Night Streets, p.174.

Circles and Wheels

Short Stories by

Anders Flagstad

Bubble Eyes Publishing
www.BubbleEyesPublishing.com

Illustration page 3
"Woman at the Beach"
Oil on canvas, 2005
Jose Ivan Ibarra
Photo: Jose Ivan Ibarra

Bubble Eyes Publishing

Copyright © 2015 Anders Flagstad

Copyright © 2015 Kenneth Anderson

Library of Congress Catalogue Number: 2013936379

ISBN: 0-615-79325-8
ISBN-13: 978-0-615-79325-2

Illustrations and Design by K.P. Anderson

for
L. S.*(as always)*

CONTENTS

FOREWORD

You wouldn't notice it unless you were consciously looking for it (which perhaps was the intention) but once you realize what you've found, when you're standing on the buckling sidewalk, looking up at a Niagara waterfall of concrete embellishment rearing above you, well, let's just say it's a little hard to miss. But what is it?

Look at it. A new, poured-concrete apartment block, a sort of Spanish Baroque Special Units Architectural Assault Force of massive pediments, heroic architraves, triumphal arches, fountain-filled patios, faux bell towers, rivers of red ceramic tile roofs pouring down from every direction, all of it, every wildly ornamented piece of it, firmly fastened together with six story colonnades wrapping around the entire complex. This California retro newcomer recently arose a couple of blocks away from me and my very modest house. Color me surprised.

Our neighborhood of tiny Deco bungalows from the Twenties and Thirties didn't have a chance. Yes, that frothy bubbling concrete apartment block is, in fact, architecture you'd expect to see at a World's Fair from the turn of the last century, not something you'd want to find in a politely decaying inner city suburb, but somehow it squeezed by the zoning boards (and the rest of us – where and when were all the neighborhood meetings? - all the citizens group's input committees? - all the petitions and notices? - we were, all of us, obviously asleep at the wheel), and it sprouted like a stucco-covered fungi.

The Beast (that's what we call it) appeared as if out of thin air a couple of years ago, at the end of a rainy winter, just at the beginning of a foggy spring, on a lot that had hosted a bowling alley – a mostly-abandoned, once-popular, round-cornered, neon-festooned Deco concoction that had been politely decaying for so many, many years in that spot, that no one who lived here could remember it not being randomly open at various hours of the day, on that same corner, in exactly that same condition. We thought it immortal. We were wrong. Nothing is immortal.

But why bring all of that up now? It's in the past, isn't it? What's done is done.

Yes, now we have to learn to live with it, somehow.

We have a Spanish Renaissance gateway ponderously and authoritatively dancing over our heads every morning. In the light from the rising sun it looks as if it were a door to another dimension.

It is a beast, truly. Untamed. Beautifully wild. It is life. It has its own agenda. You wouldn't want to turn your back on it. But I'm being silly, aren't I?

The Beast has, of course, proper setbacks, xeriscaping, and a modest, self-effacing presence on the corner of a busy boulevard and a quiet side street (the last sentence, of course, is from the sales brochure for the condos being sold there). But it is true to some extent – maybe the city made them do it - you really don't see The Beast because they left a lot of those big Eucalyptus trees standing everywhere, up and down both blocks of the corner it sits on.

In other words, it hides.

What is it hiding?

Well, I had to stop by, just to check it out. So I went. Carefully.

In the elevator lobby, I saw 12 pictures, all in a row, all on one wall. And beneath it, on a shelf, many copies of the same small book containing reproductions of the 12 pictures with 12 stories to go along with them. I took one. It was some kind of promotional literature. Later that day, I wrote this note to the management telling them how I felt. They thanked me (The Beast is nothing if not polite) and said they might include my note in future printings of their little book, if I would give them the permission to do so. I did. And they did. So, if you're reading their book, and reading my note, it (and I – frightening thought – how did I let this happen?) must be a part of The Beast now, in a manner of speaking, and, well, now you're seeing the same pictures I saw and now you're reading the same stories I read too.

So, you tell me. What is The Beast?

Circles
and
Wheels

WOMAN WITH YELLOW UMBRELLA

Jolene never told anyone the first time she saw the angel.

There was a scratchy towel. It had a hole in it. Just big enough to put her small hand through. And there was sand. Squirming through the hole. White and slippery. It ran away when you grabbed at it. She listened and she looked and she pushed the sand away from her, when it crept out of its hole, she pushed it back, way back, where it was supposed to go. It was a lot of work. But someone had to do it.

What else could she do? She was just a baby, but she still had responsibilities, even back then. It was, maybe, her first memory of this earth – that globe spinning through confusion, suffering and delight we all cling to in fierce desperation although we'd be hard-pressed to say why exactly. The earth, the globe, it all fell on her, all at once, all at the same moment. And she remembered it.

Air. Brightness. Gold. Green. Warm. Grassy dunes, foam-flecked, blue surf stretching long and wide in front of her, laid out as if it were a gift, pulled tight in front of her admittedly unfocused eyes, an empty, expectant landscape of blurry, shimmering morning light – and all it for Jolene. Just for her. She was smiling to herself. She was alone. But she couldn't enjoy it. She had to work at the attacking, squirming sand problem. There was no one else to do it. She didn't complain. She didn't fuss. She worked.

Her mother had to have been nearby, surely. But Jolene swears to herself (yes, she could be mistaken) that her mother wasn't there. Jolene remembers it very clearly – feeling uncomfortable, curious, bored, irritated, patting at the aggressive sand, tumbling over here, twisting over there, finally she fidgeted clean off her beach towel right into the floury piles of sand grit crouching everywhere along the towel's edges, ready to spring, fixing to eat the towel and gobble up Jolene up in their entirety. Abruptly her towel work ended, right then and there and Jolene found herself face first in an angry white hell and that's where she stayed.

Dirty grit up her nose, even more in her mouth, she didn't like it - who would? - she opened her mouth to yell for her mother – a technique that had always worked in situations like this in the past - and more powder poured its way in. That puzzled her. And made her afraid. She wasn't crazy afraid yet, but she was getting close. She coughed. She opened her mouth to yell. More sand found her and choked her. Now she decided to panic. Jolene didn't often yell, but this time she was going to do it, yes she was. She tried to suck some air in, preparatory to a heroic scream of fear, and more sand found its way inside instead. She spit and gasped and tried again and again and again and - no luck for Jolene. She threw her head around, backward, forwards, to each side, it did no good. She felt dizzy, funny, she didn't feel happy. Not at all. There was plenty of air out there, she could tell it was there, but none of it was getting to anywhere near where Jolene needed it to go. Funny how you don't appreciate a thing until it's gone, huh?

A shadow loomed over her. It went away. It came back. Jo didn't notice it much at first. She was too busy trying to breathe. Above and behind here she felt (more than heard) a whispery flutter of soft, supple wings, she coughed and wrinkled her noise at an unexpected smell of sappy, sweet spice. Then the light left her, gone completely, and gray soft feathers tickled her above, behind, below, from every side. There were everywhere at once. Something changed. Air pushed its way into her lungs again, her mouth surprised itself at being wet and dustless. She laughed. She breathed and she laughed again. She dug her fingers into soft cotton toweling, found the hole again with her fat fingers, rested easily on it, neatly on her back – she was athletic even back then - and balanced herself exactly in the center of a field of friendly, clean, yellow cotton stripes. The sun was shining. The breeze was warm. She wasn't afraid at all anymore.

Later, other hands, familiar hands wrapped her favorite blanket, the one that smelled sharp and clean like wash day, around her tubby legs and tucked her dimpled chin in and nibbled at her ears with the sound she loved the best – "Jo Jo Jo."

And that was that.

It wasn't anything special. It just was. It was hers. The wings, the feathers, the spice, the tickles. Jolene's. So she didn't talk about it. You've got to have some things that are secrets that you can keep all to yourself, and not blab first thing you did to every person you met and so that's what Jolene did with her first experience with an angel and that's all there was to it. That's it. Everyone saw angels, Jolene was pretty sure about that, it's just no one, apparently, wanted much to talk about them. So neither did Jolene. That's how Jolene saw it. It was a plan. It worked for her. That was her memory of her first angel.

The second time with the angel, well, she kept that a secret too.

Afterwards she could never look at a pair of mittens again. And the winter, it became a season that was spoiled for Jolene Ann. Utterly destroyed. Truth is, she tried not think about any of them all too much. Angels were becoming something unavoidable. She didn't like it. It made her feel oppressed by a constant plague of immanent divinity. She read something like that someplace. Jolene thought it applied to her situation, especially.

Angels were different. They weren't like us. They had their own ways. And Jo had hers. And the two did not mix very well. She was finding that out the hard way.

The second angel, well, Jolene was older then. And the older Jolene got, the less Jolene said. All manner of secrets were coming easier and easier to her. Secrets were as natural as breathing. To Jolene's way of thinking, the more you talked, the more people had hooks to snag you and drag you off to places you didn't want to go. Jolene wasn't about to let that happen. Jolene saw what they were doing. She was too smart for them. She kept angels to herself. She kept generally to herself. She kept quiet.

Yes, Jo was silent and calm as she grew up, allergic to fusses, arguments, and loud voices, vigilantly navigating her simple days in wide circles around and away from the bounding people surging about her. She spent a lot of time each day trying to squeeze her small self in between their ricocheting bodies trying to find a place to go and rest easy. Brothers and sisters, moms and dads, aunts and uncles and cousins popped up everywhere. Busy, loud, rough - it was just too much for Jolene. Peace was best. It just made sense. That was just Jo's way.

"JoJo, now you just stay put up there until supper's set, you hear?"

That from her ma downstairs in the warm, red and white kitchen, but nobody had to tell Jolene twice to stay put. No one had to tell her to settle down in one place and get comfortable and feel safe. She knew how to do that. She was patient. Not like her siblings.

A brother and a sister or two - or maybe three - would rapid-fire fly past her – resembling kid-sized rocks discharged from a six-foot tall demonic slingshot – and they would yell harshly as they flew "Ma, Bobby hit me on the arm again", and "Give it back! Give it back I'm telling!" and "You best bet you'll be sorry!" In situations such as those, Jolene could only shrink into the corners, disappear into the faded, orange wallpaper, evaporate and turn into tongue-less dust, sprinkled in a breathless Jolene-shaped pile, deposited in a forgotten closet and wait. That was a lot of her life - waiting out the fury and bluster of the latest family storm – hoping it would pass entirely over her and move on – listening to it distantly, bursting onto another unsuspecting room of their house, bringing only torment and disorder to all who sat there and didn't have the sense to hide like her.

So Jolene learned – you blend and wait, blend and wait.

And it worked.

In a second everyone would be outside or downstairs again, and Jolene would be back to smiling into her large rectangle of sunlight warming her little wedge of afternoon, pushing her fingers carefully into the frayed carpet and squeezing the fuzzy pile gently in and out of her small fists. Quiet was her best friend back then, as she remembered it.

But that wasn't where she saw the angel.

No, it wasn't. As she already mentioned, Jolene still didn't like to think about it. Although Jolene for the most part liked to sit and think quietly to herself about all kinds of things. Maybe more than was needful. Maybe more than was healthful. Still she did it. People noticed her doing it. "JoJo, why you just sit there all the time, all silent and still-like?" one of her loud siblings would ask in a hurry, going (once again) from some important place in the house to another, leaving before Jolene could even answer with her quiet voice and short, but careful explanations.

They noticed. But they didn't notice a lot, and they didn't notice for long.

It got lonely sometimes for Jolene. It did.

And yes, Jolene may not have talked much, but when she did, she made sure it counted. She made sure it meant something.

You see, when Jolene was doing some explaining, Jolene always imagined she was talking the way her dad did, when he was doing some explaining. Dad said you had to be mindful when you described things. Dad said one wrong step, one sentence put wrongfully in front of another, even one word uttered out of place, and the whole thing would just fall apart, right in front of your eyes - fall to pieces and you'd be days getting it back together again, orderly and correct and understandable. Dad was serious about talking. So Jolene didn't say too much.

Jolene and Dad were the quiet ones in the family. The careful ones. The ones you could trust to get things done right the first time. Not like the others. Especially not like her ma. Ma was always commenting on some thing or other and was doing a hundred things at once. Of course, with a big family, there was always a hundred things to do, every minute of every day, and ma was the one who had to do it, that's true. Still, her mom was a little too active and talkative for Jolene, and she loved her quiet, sad dad and their slow, measured, and infrequent conversations. A person had to know what you wanted to say before you said it. You had to be careful. She knew it. Dad knew it. They were a pair. Two peas in a pod.

In fact, it was not unknown for Jo to stumble at, over, on top of, and through an important explanation in front of her dad, just so he would get another chance to do his crooked smile, his arching eyebrows (Jo loved to watch her dad maneuver his bushy eyebrows around his face), and start up that wrinkling thing he did with his big nose, telling her to slow down, start at the beginning, think about what she wanted to say, get him interested. She knew what she wanted to say. She wanted to tell her Dad that she loved him, bigger than the sky was blue, she wanted to stay in that house forever and take care of him and love him and be loved and that would be enough. But it never happened. The appropriate time didn't occur. While she waited for the perfect moment, Jolene made do with saying it all with her bright blue eyes. She telegraphed it, from her irises directly into his. She hoped he got her message.

But back to the angel.

She had red hair. Jolene could still see and accurately describe to this day that living, joyful kind of hair flowing backwards and upwards, flipping over the angel's shoulders spilling over her front and splashing off to either side of her face. Jolene couldn't really remember the color of her skin, or the exact color of her eyes, but if you looked into those angelic eyes long enough (a second would do) you would feel as if you were falling, falling, falling deep into a something – usually not a scary something – no, it was an entirely different something - a kind of meaningful, strange and comfortable, yet uncomfortable something. And this something that was waiting there, it was waiting especially for you. Just for you and only for you. You just knew it. You did. As soon as you saw those eyes.

The angel had wings of course. The wings were broad and covered the whole sky and were colored in patches – some parts gray-blue, soft and pure as a dove's chest, and some other parts fluffy white, bold and terrifying as a summer afternoon's storm cloud. You expected to see lightning, hear thunder. Her body was some transparent color, but her hands were warm and lined and used to hard work, same as Jolene's mother's. In fact, they looked a lot alike, the angel and Jolene's mother. Their hands, that is.

The angel appeared over Dalton's Department Store downtown one December morning before Christmas, smiling conspiratorially at Jolene and putting a single finger to her lips, her bottomless eyes twinkling (Jolene remembered the twinkling especially, she hadn't ever considered angels as possessing a sense of humor before, especially in the eyes). The angel swooped down upon Jolene and her mother and a couple of brothers and sisters on the wind-swept corner of Fifth and DeLaporte and Jolene naturally reached up to touch her hair and see if it was as soft and silky as it looked. Her collar pulled back, she remembered that, the cold scraped against her neck and ears - a frozen nail file, frosty sandpaper, it hurt to be honest, she'd forgotten her scarf again. She remembered that too. Jolene stepped a few feet forward, letting her new yellow mittens with the puppies on them drop into the dirty ice-and-salt-crusted gutter, keeping her eyes up on the swooping angel as best she could.

She remembered two familiar hands twisting and yanking her backwards with as much gentleness as you would handle a sack of potatoes being thrown into a dark corner of the pantry on Big Shopping Day, and really loud horns and a high whining, whistling sound, and a wall of metal and color coming towards her and her ma, magically at her side, no, maybe in front of her (or was she in back of her?), yelling, screaming something in a voice Jolene had never, ever heard her use before. Her brothers and sisters told and retold the story, but no matter how many times they told it, Jolene couldn't ever remember exactly what happened next. She couldn't. It was true. No matter what anyone else said. That was where the story in her head always stopped. She couldn't recall. No matter how hard she tried. She couldn't. She couldn't. It was the truth.

Jolene was in the hospital for a month and a half. Everyone visited her. Even the bus driver visited her. But her ma didn't visit her. She never saw her ma again. She missed the funeral. She didn't even hear about it until she got home.

And she never, ever forgave the angel.

9

That was over forty years ago. Forty years. Two words. Such tiny drips and drops of words – how could they hold such a flood of time? They couldn't. It was too much. It was all too much.

I will not cry. I won't.

And whatever had happened to her, to happy, trusting little Jo? How did she go from the corner of Fifth and DeLaporte to where she was (wherever the heck was she anyways?) right here, right now?

Her head felt buoyant. It bobbed. It bounced. She was dazed. Sand was in her clothes, in her hair, in her face. It made no sense.

No. No crying.

"How did I get to here?"

She whispered it, she asked, she begged, but would there ever be an answer for her, for Jo? No. No one would answer. She was alone. That's what alone meant. No one answers you, Jolene, if you're alone. When will you ever learn that? When?

Jolene blinked and wiggled her eyebrows and tried to get the sand out of them. No crying. None. Forty years and fourteen rounds of Chemo ago (not to mention round number fifteen about to start), and there had been more of the red-haired angel, more than once, and that was too many times really, but nothing ever changed did it, and Jolene had never, ever really wanted to talk about it - well only to one person, maybe two, but she was still pretty sure she didn't want to talk about it - and who knew, maybe there were more angels to come, maybe more unplanned, random life changes ahead of her, so why complain now? Who could possibly know how to conduct their life with angels on the loose in the middle of it?

And what would she say, really, if she started unburdening? If someone actually listened to Jolene's trials and tribulations? What? What? How unjust it all was? How unfair? Don't make her laugh.

She spit sand out of the side of her mouth.

Look, the world was unfair, no getting around it, you just made do with what you got, improvising some kind of dance that worked, worked with whatever you had and whatever they sent your way - including the occasional angel, of course - until there was nothing left to dance around or about, until there was nothing to make the inevitable pain stop.

And after that, well, after that, when there was nothing left, well then, well you… what? What do you do Jo? You did something else. Something else to make the pain stop. Something else so that you can get through the day to get through the night to get through the next day. Something less like a band aid and more like an amputation. A slicing off. A pain-ectomy. Cutting off the pain and the nothingness, and well, everything, entirely. A more permanent something. A something that worked, that gave you results. That kind of something. A permanent solution. That's what she needed. A lasting, permanent solution. A pain-free, permanent and lasting solution.

She found herself shaking her head forcefully back and forth trying to jar loose a raw and throbbing (but increasingly familiar and bittersweet) train of thought. She succeeded in getting herself even dizzier than she already was. After a while, she stopped shaking her head. She looked around her, a little embarrassed by her twitching and jerking.

She was alone, of course. She whispered that to herself, small words, weak and lost in the wind blowing between the dunes.

"No, that's never any good either, pretending life is all pain and broken promises. It's not always that way. Not always. Some promises are kept. Now, you know better, Jolene. It's just the chemo talking, that's all."

"Just the chemo talking."

"It's the chemo."

"You know that."

"No, no use talking about it. Absolutely none."

"Won't change a thing, Jolene."

"It certainly won't change the fact you might be lost."

Well, Jolene didn't want to think about that. She didn't want to think about anything. She was tired of thinking. And compensating. And waiting, and wondering, and wanting. She'd thought too much and too long lately. She'd decided to give herself a think-vacation.

No thinking. None.

Because just now Jolene was not happy. Not at all. She was lost. Better to admit it. She was tired. She was cold. No, she was hot. Well, both. No, she was irritated with herself, with life, with everything and everyone really, and anxious and feeling a little nauseous – well, more than a little - and, to top it all off, knew she was about to start crying. Again.

"I am not going to do it, I am not going to start bawling, not here, not because of a walk from a parking lot to a beach." She talked out loud. She talked clear and careful, in order to make it true. It order to fix it. Tight

She said "No. I won't. I will not cry."

At least she thought she had said it, clearly and carefully. Had she? She couldn't tell anymore. Was she talking to herself? How could she know? She couldn't, that's how. How could a person, alone, ever know? They couldn't. That (of course) made her want to cry.

"I can't, - don't even think about it. No. No. No. I won't."

But then she did. She felt hot liquid tracks betraying her, softening and washing away her resolve and willpower (as they always did) and sliding their purposeful way earthwards down both her sunburned cheeks. They melted her. She dissolved. Right on the spot. A very familiar feeling, especially lately. Jolene was left gasping, standing, swaying and waiting for the short, welcome feeling of calm release that these crying jags brought her. And it came, blessedly. Like it usually did. And she felt release. For a moment. She did.

And it felt good.

Then she started hiccupping. And the realization that crying was one of the few times nowadays that she felt anything approaching hope or happiness made her even more miserable and that brought on stronger hiccups, and then the hiccups brought on more tears, and the tears stopped the hiccups, but the tears also made her more hopeful. And then that started up the hiccupping again. And Jolene was off and running. Round Number Two.

Smiling lopsidedly, she looked upwards, closing her eyes and rooting herself to her sandy spot, twitching her flip-flops off and pushing her toes and heels into a puddle of warm, floury white powder at her feet. She waited. She was good at that. The emotional storm raged on, and Jolene felt a warm sun bake her gently and softly dry, smoothing out her tear-lined face.

Quiet.

It felt good.

Except for the wind – which slapped at her unmercifully and slung sand at her.

You know, chemo was one long (well-known to her by now) hormonal rollercoaster of anger, then tears, then exhaustion, then back to anger all over again. And she was always tired. Always. She was a walking, one-woman mood-swing lately. She ought to sell tickets. Or better yet, bottle the wild rides up and down, and hawk them on the streets as the latest designer drug, the new cocaine. What would it look like? Like small plastic bags of tears, of course, Jolene tears.

That started her crying all over again.

Jolene, really!

The breeze continued to pester and needle her mercilessly, she turned and turned mechanically, wiping away her tears and trying to get out of the wind's way. Both actions were pointless. She began to wonder if she'd have enough energy to cart all her stuff all the way to the beach and back to the parking lot again – or even get it back to the car from here if she decided to give up this National Geographic Expedition to the Atlantic Ocean.

The more she thought about it, she really didn't know if she had the energy or not.

Could she get back?

Could she? What if she couldn't? Then for a moment, squeezing her eyes shut to concentrate on this situation, she couldn't remember what in God's creation she was doing in the middle of a bunch of sand hills on this particular afternoon, dragging piles of things around here and there.

Why was she here?

Why?

There had to be a reason.

But her mind was a total blank.

Where was she?

Another vicious whip of the wind, and Jolene had just about had it with the wind. That did it. Enough was enough.

Lurching into action, she swatted violently, but precisely at the sly, obnoxious blasts of fine, white particles of mineral which seemed determined to gum her eyelids together and give her exposed arms and face a thorough, impromptu dermabrasion, - as if she, Jolene, were a paying customer at a fantastically malevolent outdoor spa.

She swatted backwards, flinging both hands around her head.

And then again, forwards and to the right, across her nose and her eyes.

Anyone looking at her would wonder who this crazy, crying lady was, and why she was being attacked by angry beach-bees. Or maybe beach-wasps. Well, at least some kind of dangerous stinging insect, but probably not annoying gusts of beach-wind. They'd never guess the wind. Only mentally-imbalanced people did that. Only deranged people, people who saw angels, people who talked to themselves and didn't know it, people who had terminal diseases – only those kinds of people did things like that.

She swatted and snuffled and shook her head back and forth, felt the dizziness coming on and stopped the shaking, squeezing her eyes shut and willing herself to a state of calm.

"Don't think. You're on a think-vacation. Breathe in, breathe out, breathe in, breathe out. A think-vacation, think-vacation."

It wasn't working. It was hard to take herself seriously when she was making the same sounds a cartoon steam locomotive did, pulling up a steep pastel-colored hill. Her head was spinning.

Jabbing at the wind was obviously not a helpful response to the situation at present, but there was an aspect of it that was becoming immensely satisfying to her - no matter where she punched, she hit the air every time, right on target. She couldn't miss. She was a non-stop success, totally in control. It was wonderful. Breathing hard she tried out a few more experimental jabs. The wind ignored her.

Where was she again?

Let's see... This beach path she was shuffling down curved to her left, branched about a thousand times and continued winding its various ways right out of her sight, in every direction. All she could see were dune tops ahead. That's all she could see to either side also. She thought she could hear surf futilely pounding away at some much-abused, but distant shore, but then, it could have just as easily have been her heart pounding in her chest, self-righteously complaining about this last-minute impulse to hike into sandy wastes.

So it's a beach. How did she get here?

She looked towards where the car might have been, but couldn't see a parking lot. Sand, fence, and emaciated grass greeted her on all sides. Paths twisted and recombined merrily in back of her, in every direction. Her footsteps were already being erased.

She continued jabbing absentmindedly, straining to see

14

something, hand on her forehead shading her eyes, her bright orange-striped beach bag swinging awkwardly from her elbow, squinting to see some landmark that would at least get her in the general direction of safety and her parked car. But safety was invisible, hidden now, off by itself, tucked away in a sandy corner in a far away, sand-dune-surrounded lot, screened behind devious, mind-numbingly complicated labyrinths of moving sand hillocks.

She was lost.

Lost.

She tried to feel sad about it. But she couldn't. She didn't feel anything about it.

That actually felt good.

She touched her cheeks. Oh. She was crying again.

The wind scooted behind her and wrapped around her ankles, circling her - a cat with sandpaper for fur. Twisting to the left, in what she thought was an especially energetic, and totally unexpected move on her part, she began a wild upward swat, truly heroic, and then thought better of it (she was actually getting tired of the swatting), but stopped too late, way too late.

She managed somehow (it was just her luck too) to trip on her ridiculously heavy umbrella - the one that she had been doggedly dragging for what seemed miles - and to topple over dramatically and finally. She disappeared from sight. Not without a prodigious grunt of surprise first, and not without a spectacularly theatrical crash. It was a good imitation of a great oak being felled in a medieval forest of long ago. One second the massive she-oak was there. The next second, she wasn't.

Her majestic arc downward was arrested by a crumbling, sun-blanched, slatted fence - a fence that slowly, and with a certain amount of grace and generous consideration for her un-athletic frame, crumpled and shattered into dozens of pieces, depositing her carefully, face-up on a pillow of warm, sloping sand under the bright, open September sky.

Suddenly it was very quiet.

The wind died down immediately, and a heavy hush, an almost abashed silence fell on her and on the dunes. The indian summer heat was a heavy blanket bundling her up for a long winter's nap. She blinked for a few moments, breathing heavily. She frowned. She started mentally feeling around her body for broken bits and pieces of herself, eventually coming to the conclusion that the majority of her middle-aged parts were in as good a working order as they had been thirty seconds earlier, and started laughing instead of crying – a thing which surprised her.

How long had it been since she'd really stopped and let the constant buzzing in her head evaporate and allowed a stillness to condense inside her instead? It felt to Jolene that it had been a long time. Years. Decades. Centuries. A very long time.

She closed her eyes and lay in the sun – for just a few more minutes – her belongings scattered about her in the dunes - an explosion in the beach supplies department of a drugstore with one female mannequin lying motionless in the center of it all. Quite the sight.

She stretched and lay and breathed.

It felt right, somehow.

She still didn't know where she was.

Her eye was twitching, and there were sand flies buzzing in her wig. She thought she could hear footsteps approaching. She ought to get herself up, she definitely should.

But she didn't.

She was hopeful. And that was odd. The thought came to her, (it was crazy, but she already knew she was crazy) that if she stayed very, very still, what she thought might be possible, what she imagined she was struggling to be hopeful for, well, it might all materialize, right in front of her face, and then Jolene could make a grab for it. She might still be saved. Safe at least. Safer. She'd settle for that. Whatever form it took. Assurance. Surety. Protection. Really, Jolene didn't want much. She didn't want a lot. She'd settle for even a little. She assumed an appropriately expectant mental attitude, and waited for the dews of peace and quiet and salvation to rain down abundantly upon her.

But that's not what she got.

Instead, as usual, random memories bubbled and boiled on the surface of her consciousness. It wasn't dew. But it was better than weeping.

Sometimes she remembered the farm. When she could. Those impossibly light-filled, boundless summer hours. Days and days of them. Crumbly smells of old wood, cool iron smells of pump water. The prickly smell of fresh baled hay, stacked in unlikely towers of scratchy green blocks in her grandpa Dunne's barn (her mom's father). Heavy country air soaked to slopping over with a syrupy, spicy smell she could taste all the way in the back of her mouth. Languid summer days, purple-shadowed afternoons, long comfortable evenings, loud crickets, silent spiders catching frantic moths by the back door light over hushed porch-conversations with her gram Dunne after supper. It was special. It was hers. Shelling peas, shucking corn, and whatever and whatnot and all - and oh, everything - all of it – every bit of it was pure, unadulterated heaven. Heaven. Always.

Anyways, that's how Jolene remembered it, it was her life, she could remember it any way she wanted to.

Jo had a secret self back then, back there, only Jo could see her, and she was Jo-Esmeralda (Esmeralda for short), that was her name, you see. There was this person, named Esmerelda who lived on the far away Dunne farm, green and bright as an emerald, a being who lived at a location where it was always summer and it was always humid, hot, and life was tremendously interesting. Esmeralda stayed there always, just because she wanted to. And Esmeralda liked her situation. Esmerelda led a loud, confident life out under the hot, yellow sun each day and every day and Esmerelda explored and worked and took a bath every night and had muscles and got brown as a berry, brown as a nut, so much her freckles almost disappeared and everyone loved her. Even Jolene. And that was something because Jolene was hard to please. Jolene was picky. Esmeralda wasn't. Esmeralda didn't have time for picky. Esmeralda was too busy getting happy.

Jo-Esmerelda was not at all like Jolene. She wasn't like the Jo that left each spring and returned each fall to the city, quiet and pale and skinny, who lived with her family overflowing with excess and excessive people in their small red brick and white-porched house. Esmeralda lived a free life, a safe life, a connected life, life with a direction to it. Esmeralda lived where there was room enough for a person to stay out of every single other person's way, all day long, if Esmeralda wanted it that way. But Esmerelda also got watched over by people, and was noticed and not lost in a crowd of brothers and sisters. In fact, Esmerelda was never lost. She was never confused or tongue-tied. Esmerelda knew things, and knew she knew them, and wasn't afraid to say she knew them. Esmeralda was heading places. She had plans. And she was going to take Jo along with her.

Yes, that was Jo-Esmerelda.

Later, life was different and things changed - much to Jolene's misery, things have a tendency to do that in this world - and the plans and places and direction and knowledge faded and faded until you couldn't hardly tell they'd even existed before. Jolene watched it happen, hating it, helpless to change it or slow it down.

First, all kinds of things shifted, all together, abruptly, one year in the spring. Everything. All at once. Her body changed. Her complexion changed. Her moods shot off in random directions at just the wrong times, and people started acting different towards her. Expecting new things. Frowning at old things. It was complicated. It was perplexing. It wasn't fair.

Second, Jo-Esmerelda just up that summer and moved away. Far away. As in never-speaking-to-you-again so far away.

Last year Esmeralda was running free - a wild thing - all over the farm. This year, she was missing, gone. A memory. Where? How? Why? Jolene didn't have a clue. Esmerelda skedaddled for parts unknown and left Jolene holding the feed bag so to speak, all summer (and for the rest of her life, by the way), confused and wary and worried and overworked. Her confidence and self-reliance were all a thing of the past. The new Jolene learned – she had to, right? – the hard way - how to be Jolene all over again – just Jolene, just her secretive self, shy and scared and alone, and angry as all get out with a new, half-grown-up body to boot. She learned how to be alone with the Jolene newness, and learned she did not like it. She did not like it at all. It was not something she would've asked for. No. Not that anyone had ever asked her at all. Where was an angel when you needed one, huh?

And Jolene learned to loath all those familiar smells, all the farm odors, and her boring life, and the endless work on the farm during summers and how it got too hot and how much she sweated and how it got too quiet and how lonely she became and how embarrassing it was to be so, well, rural. She spend more and more time up at the farm. Less and less down in the city. At some point it became a year-round thing. She didn't know why. It just happened. The farm was always the same, all the time, all day long, every day. Sweet day in the morning! – as her granma Dunne used to say – her life was coming to a complete stop. When would something finally happen to Jolene? When would life happen to Jolene? When?

Well, Jo ought to have been more careful about what she wished for. Yes, it was true, too true.

She graduated from high school, a graduating class of nineteen, from her enthusiastic but tiny rural school and no one even asked her if she wanted to go to college. In fact, being the youngest child, she found herself politely shoved into a spare bedroom, staying at home and helping out her aging parent. It all happened to fast. She can't exactly remember when and how she agreed to it.

And everyone said it was for the best. Jolene even said it was for the best. She said the words. Out loud. But inside she didn't say them. She hated them inside. Jolene hated even more that she was the only one who ended up choosing to stay home (well, home at their granpa's farm house - they'd had to move somewhere, didn't they, after dad got cancer? - after they lost their old red brick house in the city? - yes, they did – and guess who did most of the moving? - one guess who did all that work – just one). It was hard, of course. But it wouldn't be forever, right? And she thought it couldn't get much worse. But she was wrong.

Granpa Dunne died. Granma Dunne died. And that was how Jolene got left high and dry up in the hills living alone with her dad with a big farm and a big house to take care of. No one even asked her if she wanted to help out. No sirree. They just shoved Jolene in the direction of work and said – there you are girl, get at it.

That's how it goes for people who are quiet and keep to themselves. People do a lot of your deciding for you.

For months and years afterwards, sometimes, lying in the tall grass, exhausted from another long day of farm chores and nursing chores and managing tenant-farmer chores and whatever other chores the farm and life would saddle her with, Jolene would will the angel to descend to her. Just for her. She'd frown and she'd concentrate on a specific patch of blue above her and focus a powerful beam of "please" at it and then she'd bite her lip and close her eyes and will it six more times (for a total of seven, which was her lucky number), and then she'd open her eyes and she'd just wait.

That is, until the rain hit, or the light faded, she would wait. Jolene would watch for the angel to appear (why wouldn't she appear? – she'd done it before), looking for a speck of color wafting - angels do that, they waft - the angel would waft graciously, towards Jolene, downwards from on high, down, down through the late afternoon thunderheads piling and spilling and rumbling over the blue mountains in the distance, and Jolene would see her and wait for her.

Jolene was sure that was how it would happen, that was the direction from which she'd arrive – from the west. It was a feeling she had. So she went with it. She would watch for the angel, who would drift over, fluttering towards Jolene with her ever-twinkling, humorous angel eyes of indeterminate color, darting here and there, tenderly motioning Jolene to come, come, and finally floating Jolene and herself off, swiftly and softly, to a new life, a life far, far away from farming and nursing, somehow leaving everyone, including Jolene, happy and content with their divinely instigated new living situations. The sun would set, and that would be that.

Unfortunately, that never happened.

Which brings up the awkward question - what exactly, then, is an angel good for?

Jolene would really like to know the answer to that.

Anyways…

Other times, of an afternoon, lying in the grass in the lower pasture, she'd stare at the blue sky and hate it. She hated the clouds above her and the grass underneath her and the old house on the hill and sometimes that felt better than willing the angel to descend. It was certainly more dependable – the hating that is. It always got her riled up. She didn't know how much longer she could take it - staying there, taking care of a sick dad, scraping by on their tiny pension, doing the necessary things of daily life without going absolutely, positively mad.

She would, you know. Insanity was just around the corner. It was just down the hall, a short trip away, a few footsteps really. Stark, raving, bonkers, cuckoo mad and she felt she was going to explode and then they would be sorry. Wouldn't they? Huh? Wouldn't they? You bet they would.

Lying in her bed at night, tossing and turning, thinking, unable to sleep, she felt she could sympathize completely with a fox or a wolf or mountain lion that got its leg caught in a hunter's trap and gnawed it off during the night to get themselves free before morning. It all made sense. A gnawed-off leg during the night was the smallest price Jolene would pay to get the chance to start her life over in the morning for real. A very small sacrifice. Tiny in the greater scheme of things.

She felt, deep in the ocean depths of a sleepless midnight, if she didn't get away from this farm and this house and her family soon she'd start screaming and screaming and would scream so loud and so long she wouldn't be able to stop screaming. That would show them. That would show everyone. Then they'd wish they would have listened to her. The clean, white padded wagon with the burly, but handsome attendants would pull up, she'd be carted off in a bright white strait-jacket with the siren screaming and Jolene screaming and then they'd all visit her on Sundays and she'd be yelling in a muffled, strangled kind of way (she'd be hoarse by then) and everyone would be crying and carrying on and apologizing for how insensitive they'd been to her, and then they'd regret it, probably for the rest of their natural lives. But, by then, of course, it would be too late, way too late, wouldn't it?

Oh, if only they'd listened while there'd still been time. If only…

Then she'd let her eyes close for only ten minutes or so and right away light and flies buzzing would be waking her up, and it would be morning already and the sky would gleam a distressingly bright pink in the east before the sun came up, and the predictable, non-stop busy-ness of her life would overwhelm her again for another day, drowning all her pathetic internal cries to be saved until the evening hit her smack between the eyes as if it were a screen door some laughing someone had slammed deliberately into her surprised and confused face.

That was her new life.

And, as it turned out, Jolene didn't go crazy.

Yes, life stumbled on, one, long day after another.

And Jolene complained a lot.

And she watched the skies.

Then, that last day, she was in the green hell of farming life - the humidity had to have been 170 % - her head hurt, it was stuffed so full with cottony, woolly non-thoughts, and the light was so bright outside it hurt the insides of her eyes, and she felt sick.

The whole day she felt teetering on the brink of throwing up. It was useless. It wouldn't work. No matter how often she ran all the old debates she'd had with her dad over the years again and again in her headache-filled head, she never got him to understand, ever. She fanned herself in the heat, making dinner, and thought furiously. She fought for herself, by herself. And she lost, of course. She had to leave. She was going to leave. She would leave. She was an adult. She had a right to choose.

No, the truth was, she was going to live on this farm for the rest of her life. She'd probably die here.

Mashing the potatoes (viciously and furiously – she admits that), she tried to get them (the points in her arguments, not the potatoes) to line up, but they refused. As she cut the green beans, the logic congealed, lumped together, jumbled itself up and came out sideways, backwards, every which way but forwards. It was the opposite of orderly - so much so that even Jolene didn't understand what she was trying to say or why she was trying to say it. When she was frying the pork chops she tried talking to him in her head. It hurt. That's all she understood. It hurt to leave. It hurt to stay. It hurt. All the time. Something has to change, papa. I have to change something. Help me, papa, help me.

But that was not how you explained things to her father, to her hyper-organized dad – cool in his careful approach to life's troubles, appalled at self-imposed chaos based on sentiment and feeling. He was one man that was not going to be afraid of calling confusion for what it really was – just plain laziness, pure and simple, an unwillingness to work.

Well, that was the old dad.

The new dad didn't say much, he slept a lot, sat up in his chair staring at nothing, it seemed as if he was trying to will himself somewhere else, he rarely held her hand as she read the evening paper to him, he held his body still and stiff and correct and he avoided her eyes if she looked his way one too many times in one night.

She wanted her dad to let her go. She wanted him to say "Go on, live your own life, I've lived mine it's your turn." She wanted him to look Jolene in the eyes with strength and fierce pride and… what else? Concern? Worry? Love? – and say "Enjoy the time God's given you. I'll be fine. I'll be happy. Don't worry about me, do what you think's best for you. Go on, live!"

That's what she needed.

That's what she thought she needed.

Well, it was what she wanted anyways.

She climbed up the barn's steep stairs that afternoon, bringing him his supper, the stairs almost a ladder, and she hated the stairs, sincerely, as she usually did. She had to use both feet and hands and watch vigilantly for splinters and balance the glass and covered plate and twist and squirm and hop her way, up, up to her father's room, and it was never easy. As usual, she carried a book to read to him pressed painfully between her arm and one breast. Today, the climb up the long ladder-stairs seem to stretch higher and higher, much higher than usual, ridiculously far above even the attic platform where they stored hay in the winter. She rested for a moment, a third of the way up, blew at some hair that had fallen in front of her face, jammed her wiry body between a pair of two-by-fours for support. She looked at the rest of the stairs, bit her lip and she concentrated on a tiny piece of hay or dust floating in the air up the stairwell. She balanced and she observed. She didn't want to move. Ever. Not ever again. She breathed and she balanced until that little piece of hay floated its way up, up and out of her sight into the anonymous evening shadows. So. What was she going to do? Stay here on the barn stairs forever? She started hopping and twisting again. It was always such a struggle for her.

For the thousandth time she asked herself - why? - why did he stay alone up here so far away from everything and everyone? Sometimes she thought it was a punishment for her, or maybe it was a lesson, or maybe he'd forgotten about her entirely and didn't care anymore what amount of trouble he was to Jolene. Who could tell?

She made it, this time, only spilling a little bit of the milk. And she hadn't even dropped the book!

You know, Jolene had never liked this room. But as she'd mentioned, her dad refused to lie down anywhere else, lately. She avoided it as much as she could, with the dolorous and melancholy quality of its silences. It reproached her and shamed her – the solitude up here felt like that - and it was broken only by an irregular and nervous ticking – the unsteady gear sounds of an ancient clock that had been salvaged (when any sane person would have thrown it away in the garbage the first chance they had) from the sad old brick house dad and ma used to have back in the city.

The clock always reminded Jolene of her mother. Her mother used to call it her pride and joy. It was a curvy, brass-edged mantel clock, complete with angels and all sorts of divine personages sprinkled here and there, now black-green and unrecognizable in their corruption since no one had polished them in decades. It was made of all kinds of darkish, layered wood, some of it peeling away now. It rested precariously on a splintery two-by-four her father had painstakingly nailed to the sloping underside of the roof. The board slanted slightly. It looked as if it were about to dump its contents on the unwary at any moment. The clock itself didn't work very well. It was ugly and lazy. It always had the wrong time. It was not a clear nor a careful clock. All of which hurt Jolene. Her old dad would have hated it. He would've fixed it, all of it. The new dad didn't seem to notice anything was out of the ordinary.

The shelf hung in a shadowy corner next to where her dad's small metal bed lay, with his one table, and his one old kitchen chair, painted three colors. Everything (including her father, yes it was true) had this peeling, paint-flaking, dry-rotted, badly-patched look of neglect and well, loveless-ness that poked at her at odd times. As if someone had strapped a rusty knife into her chest, and then decided to twist it in her insides at random intervals. It hit her now. Not the most pleasant feeling in the world.

The room was long, very long, the whole length of the barn. She started across it. The wood of the floor was soft with age.

Old bits of tools, odd shreds of leather and stray assemblages of amputated equipment from machinery long ago disassembled or sold for scrap, all of it lay heaped and piled randomly throughout the first half of the space. It was a kind of wall, a protection maybe. Maybe it was just despair. Her father was buried on the other side of it, in the other half of the room. There was a narrow, twisted path cleared through the clutter. She started down it.

Holding her breath, (it smelled alternately sweet and stale, felt cool and hot as she crossed different air currents rising through the gaps in the floor boards) she scanned the room for her father. She allowed herself a quick breath. The dust always made her allergies worse. And yes, smoking probably didn't help much either, did it? She should stop. Her father said it wasn't ladylike. Well, he used to, back when he had opinions. Now why didn't Jolene didn't see anyone up here? Her eyes only gradually adjusted to a dim, late afternoon light streaming in the lopsided window cut at an angle into the far wall.

"Dad?"

"Are you up here, Pa?"

"Dad!"

Oh. Twenty feet in front of her, she could just see him, asleep, a grayish mound of clothes and blankets on the his cot in the corner. His red and white checked handkerchief was tied around his neck. He was turned towards the wall. All she could see of him was his bald head. He looked pale even in this reddish light. The table was covered again in piles of books. Everything was messy. Is he sick? He usually didn't go to sleep this early.

He's going to win again. They aren't going to be able to have a discussion. She'll never get to leave here. It's starting all over.

No. It won't. Not this time.

Think! Think about what you want to say and say it. It's not that hard. That's what Dad always said. Think. Open your mouth. Move your tongue.

She stopped in front of the bed and table.

She set the milk and plate down on the uneven floor, let the book drop softly onto dusty boards. Nothing made a sound. Got to clear off the table. I suppose I'll have to wake him up. Yes, of course I'll have to wake him up. He's got to eat something. But he's breathing so easily. Isn't he? Isn't he? Dad? Dad? He doesn't look good, does he?

The books were open, spines broken, pages fluttering to the floor. There were circular brown marks, water stains, on the covers. Why does he live like this? Why do we have to live like this?

Maybe she didn't.

Maybe she wouldn't.

How very quiet it was in this upper room of his. Jolene used to like to sleep up here when she was just a little girl. Great crossbars of syrupy golden sunlight slammed down in front of her, outlined in floating chaff. A shadow or two moved outside in the light. Owls? It must be later than she thought. The window darkened, got light, darkened again, then it was light. It was too quiet for Jolene, as always, quiet that is, except for the wheezing arthritic clock. She hated that clock. Yes she did. It should have been in a real living room, with a comfy sofa, and real chairs and a big front window looking out on a proper front yard. It shouldn't be giving mice a place to live.

You know what?

Never again.

Never again would she settle. Yes, it would be tonight. Tonight she would do it. Tonight she would declare her freedom. Freedom day for Jolene. One of her brothers or sisters would have to take up the slack. Yes, tonight. Now. Open your mouth. Talk.

She would explain everything to her dad.

He would listen just like he used to do.

And they would sit together quietly and calmly decide what was best. It would be like it used to be. He would understand. He couldn't not not understand, could he?. No. This was her dad, her pa.

She was crying. And she was sneezing because of the dust. It was hard to see. She'd need a light soon. She moved to shake his shoulder. She touched his shirt.

"Dad?"

He'd understand. Wouldn't he?

"Dad?"

And then Jolene caught the merest glimpse of an oddly familiar grey and red blur, light and dark feathers the color of heaven, it streaked, it made a long banking turn outside the window three times and then it was gone. She saw it all through the disturbing, wavy old glass of the barn window, true, but she and the gray flyer knew what was going on. Jolene knew, knew it with a certainty. Her Dad's shirt was cold, His shoulder was cold. He wasn't moving at all. Not one bit. Nothing was moving in this room except her.

There wasn't a dad up here for Jolene to talk to anymore.

The humorous old angel had fooled her again.

Was it all an angelic joke? What did angels laugh about anyways? What or who did they laugh at? Obviously, in this case, what they were laughing at was Jolene.

So.

She'd been wanting to be let go for the longest time, and all along she was going to be free anyways. Very funny. She'd been wanting to worry about herself for a change and here she was, finally, all alone, on her own, and not responsible for anyone else's happiness except her own. Such a good joke. So glad to have been so amusing.

Yes, it was finally her time.

But now all she could do was cry.

She'd never hear her dad's voice again. It staggered her. She was a little astounded by the amount of pain a person could feel all at once, in the tiny space of a second, and still go on living.

After her father's funeral, a long time after, and after she'd been back in the city again for way too many years, and after she'd started working professionally and coughing professionally as any young professional smoker, and after she'd landed her position as first assistant accounts-receivable manager in an unbelievably dusty, smoky, sunless back office of (ironically, angel-wise that is) Dalton's department store, it was only after all that, after she had gotten the life she'd been wanting, that it began to dawn on Jolene, painfully, that maybe this being alone stuff, well, maybe it wasn't everything it was cracked up to be.

Wanting was more complicated than it looked.

She wondered what it was she really wanted.

She wondered why everyone else seemed to know exactly what it was they really wanted.

She wondered why an angel would dupe her into wanting something she wouldn't have wanted at all, if she'd known what it was she was wanting, before she wanted it. Weren't angels, maybe, possibly supposed to be on top of things like that? Yes they were. Jolene was sure of it.

Yes, Jolene wondered a lot of things.

You know, maybe the angel hadn't fooled Jolene. Maybe Jolene had been fooling herself. No. That's not the way life worked. That couldn't be right. Could it? No.

Later, she stopped wondering so much about maybes and possibles and ceased agonizing over thinking and wants and might-have-beens. That's because later, Jolene met the unforgettable Robert.

It took most of the middle of the afternoon for Jolene to make it out of the dunes and onto the beginning of the beach, one hand on her head, gripping her inexplicably large hat and her slightly inappropriate wig, the other hand stretched out behind her, dragging a sled made of knotted towels containing the sum of her multifarious and many beach-ly possessions.

A few people passed her. She tried to appear normal and harmless. She felt she met with some success. No one woman-handled her into a waiting police car. That was success, wasn't it?

She had to stop a lot. Almost every three steps. She pushed forward, stubbornly, weakly. The wind fought at her the whole way.

She dug in and pulled with her complaining calves at every step, as would a veteran, middle-aged (and foolish) husky in the long middle bits of the Idatrod dogsled race in Alaska. It was a Jolene trip of heroic proportions, of monumental efforts, of tough decisions made and hard triumphs won, of monumental willpower and of stark determination. Yes, it was all of that. But what else was new? Really, that was about par, nowadays. That was how Jolene lived her daily cancer-ridden existence, her everyday life, her every waking moment – the simplest things required a hero's dedication.

Or a dog's.

Take your pick.

Frankly, Jolene could use a dog right about now.

Yes, kind of lonely out, it being a week day and all and this odd September starting out a boiling scorcher but winding up tepid and lukewarm and pathetic and nothing special really. Only a few fellow beach goers on her slow, detour-ridden way in. Every one going home. Which was good, of course. Very good. All the more beach for Jolene. That's how Jolene saw it.

She smiled, keeping her lips over her teeth, which were a little yellow, since she hadn't been brushing hard lately, what with the chemo and all. Her gums bled at the drop of a hat. Or a wig.

And Jolene didn't much feel like indulging in a wide smile. She was nervous. Jumpy. She'd had to take some anti-nausea stuff, and it always made her excitable and prone to anxious moments. Well, nervous at first, then blurry and indistinct, later. It was always something, huh?. Always interesting. It never stopped, did it?

And the beach itself was cold-ish and empty. What a surprise, huh? Until two young men in black pants and white business shirts in red ties arrived and helped her truck her pile of stuff the last ten feet to this mostly level spot in a gentle feminine-shaped valley wedged between two bulbous dunes which opened out halfheartedly onto wide, deep, blue-hearted waves shooshing industriously below them.

What these two young men were doing on a beach dressed for a church meeting Jolene had no idea. They seemed just as puzzled by Jolene as she was of them. Puzzlement was in the air, everywhere. No one was sure of anything. It was all a muddle. All of it.

They asked multiple times why she was there, and where she lived and all kinds of other details Jolene didn't want to think about. Jolene answered with multiple silences and winning smiles, adjusting her new wig every time the wind blew it and her hat sideways. Which was often. Eventually they got the idea. Alone again, the truth stared her in the face, lopsided hairpiece and all - Jolene wasn't sure she could answer any of their questions. Why was she here? Why? Did she have to have a reason? And she'd have to think a little bit about where she lived. They called it chemo-brain, right? Memory loss. It was just the chemo. Short term, medium term. A gently descending, mercifully effacing fog of zen-like, involuntary living-in-the-present. She was here. She knew that. She was alive. For now. What else did she need to know?

She watched two black-white dots, red ties winking on and off as they looked back down at the beach at her, disappear down the edge of the dunes in curtains of salt spray billowing off the surging surf. The spray was cold, but it felt good in the sunshine, which was a little stronger now for some reason. Two upside-down exclamation points, the dots wavered, appeared, got closer, then receded, and eventually evaporated into the sandy distances. It took a few minutes or so. The dots. Why was she watching the dots? The dots looked familiar. She was certain she'd seen them before. They seemed helpful somehow. Helping dots. Strange, huh?

Her stomach or her intestines continued to signal her that something was deeply and desperately wrong. Jolene knew already. Yes, she'd taken poison. They called it infusion, at the chemo center. Hang in there you guys, she patted her middle-aged white torso, decently hidden behind a swimsuit underneath a wildly leaf-patterned yellow mumu, the anti-nausea cavalry are on their way. You just wait a minute. You'll see. Peace is just around the corner. Just a little patience. The drugs will kick in. They will.

And the drugs did kick in. She felt hazy. Pleasantly. Not painfully. A little like she'd been drinking. As if! Maybe a sip of wine with her nephew Johnathan. Maybe. Years ago? Months ago? Yesterday? Well, now, she wasn't sure. Did it matter? Of course not. But she couldn't explain all that to total strangers. Why should she tell strangers about her private life? Why?

Who was she thinking of? What strangers? Who would she be talking to? Jolene looked around her. A few seagulls. Lots of grass, Sand. Hazy cream-colored clouds. Sky. Jolene was alone. Who was

Anders Flagstad

she talking to?

No one. That's who. And that was exactly how she wanted it.

Enough with the thinking, Jolene.

Think – think-vacation, Jolene.

She watched the waves. The tide was coming in. Or was it going out? You could never tell by watching. You had to look away, pretend not to watch, look back a half hour later. Watching never did anything.

"It's funny…", she thought (or maybe she was talking to herself again), and while she was doing that she adjusted the straps of her swimsuit, under her mumu, (not the easiest thing to do while sitting down in a low slung beach chair) so that they didn't bind quite so much, then she had to re-arrange her towel, then her chair. The wind picked up. She could smell rotting seaweed, corruption, death, decay. She felt sick again. Oh, darn. Her neck was a bright red – she could feel a scratching against her collar and the swimsuit straps. Waves of heat rolling off the back of her neck. You know, Jo, honey, you really shouldn't be getting sun if you're in the middle of doing chemo – not the best idea, really.

More wind. Her face sandblasted. She moved her hat down one side of her face. It didn't help.

"It's funny…"

She watched the dunes. She watched the waves. She watched the sky. Nothing moved. Well, the sun crept up towards her feet. She kicked and fussed with her legs and pushed herself back, deeper, deeper into inky shadows under her enormous, braid-fringed, banana-colored beach umbrella spread royally above her – a rich, ribbed, goldly luminous Persian carpet pulsing with heavy sunlight and glowing over her head, surrounding her body with all the different variations of her favorite hue, (yellow of course, hadn't you guessed already?) a rain of lemony goodness. She felt good for a second, which was a rare feeling these days. Oh! Yes! She felt as if she had been eaten by a dream of a sleeping color, and that was O.K. by Jolene.

She dearly, dearly loved her sun-colored umbrella.

Even if it did weigh a ton.

The waves gurgled and whooshed at her. They wriggled their foamy fingers in her direction. She wriggled hers back at them, giggling.

"It's funny" she continued "how everything goes in circles."

30

She waited (for a response?), looked out, over empty (well, almost empty) beach and blinked at a shocking bright line of light – mottled greenish ocean stretched clean and taut against a horizon of flat, white-blue skies. The blue light was so strong. It hurt. White dots - plastic bags blowing in the wind? - she blinked - no - she blinked again - no, they were seagulls, floated down towards her. Her eyes teared up and she couldn't see the birds anymore.

She stopped and waited again, for what, this time, she wasn't sure. The seagulls apparently hovered away and drifted out of sight. She waved her hands at the surf, and discovered a lone seagull earthbound and staring at her and hopping purposefully towards her left foot at the edge of her towel. She waved at it repeatedly. Nothing deterred it.

"Circles?"

"No, that didn't quite make sense, did it?"

"That's not what she wanted to say. What was she trying to say? What was the point?"

The seagull cocked its head at her. It hopped. It hopped again, closer to the towel. It examined her. Closely.

She frowned directly at it. It shuffled two webbed feet forwards in the hot sand. It seemed to be staring at her head, no, at her hat. She decided to ignore it.

"Yes. I see. The point. Uh, well. I guess I don't have a point. Do I need a point? Why does there always have to be…"

The gull lunged forwards. She glared at it. The gull opened its bright red mouth and gave out a strangled cry and that did it, she kicked some sand at it. It cocked its head. It flapped up, spread its great dirty white wings in the wind, hung for a moment, perfect and motionless against the painful blue, flapped back down and landed in the exact same spot. It cocked its head again. She refused to acknowledge it. It hopped. She looked the other way. Pointedly.

"O.K. Circles. Circles, then. You start out on one part of a circle. You journey long and hard, turning, moving through new experiences and places, learning, watching, struggling certain that you'd accomplished something, anything, thinking you were going somewhere, anywhere, and then bam! you have to face up to the fact (since you are, in fact, going in a circle, my dear) that you've ended up right back where you originally started. The same place. Like none of it had ever happened."

The bird squawked at her, three times in succession and hopped sideways once or twice with its mouth open. Its head jerked back and forth. It still stared at her sun hat. As if she'd stolen it.

"You're very impolite to stare like that."

It hopped and jerked. She tried to stare it down.

"Look, it's not that hard. It's a circle. Birds do it. People do it. You're going in circles. I do it all the time. I've been doing it all my life."

"Get it? Circles?"

"Maybe you get it, but you just don't care."

"I used to be like that."

"I..."

But, even Jolene was tired of talking about it. She sighed, closed her eyes, listening for approaching webbed feet, and lay back imitating a limp, over-cooked, expensive piece of spaghetti draped over a designer beach chair. No one expected pasta to have a backbone. It felt good to be boneless. Hot air smothered her. She was suddenly too tired even to work her lungs. She just wanted to stop. Completely stop. So tired. So peaceful. So restful. So familiar. So...

So freakish. So frightening. And in a twisted way interesting. It shocked Jolene how quickly (and unpredictably) her body lost energy these days. As if someone had stuck an enormous shiny faucet into her side and cranked the valve open, and spilled out all her strength, all of it, out onto the ground in a big puddle, leaving Jolene weak and hollow and defenseless and blank. Mostly blank. And everywhere weak.

How was she ever going to walk away from here? She wasn't. If she kept this up.

She riffled through one of her bags, without opening her eyes, found and ate some melting chocolate she found, which, of course, got all over her towel, and interested the staring gull to no end. She could hear it clucking to itself, jumping around in a fever pitch of gluttony in front of her, not knowing what to do. That is, until she threw out the rest of the gooey bar with its gooey wrapper off into the dunes behind her starting a monumental gull riot that took a surprisingly long time to calm back down again.

She lay there and listened, eyes closed, forcing herself to breathe slowly.

She lay there, and she felt a little less weak as each minute passed and the sugar hit her bloodstream, and more oxygen surged through her lungs.

She lay there, with waves thundering irregularly in front of her – as if they were the ticking of a slow, malfunctioning clock, or maybe, a pump - water being sucked and tossed, pulled and pushed, moved back and forth against its will – she lay there and it all started to make her feel a little unbalanced.

When did it ever stop?

She felt herself falling. She didn't like the feeling. But instead of throwing up, which is what she normally did these days, she started to fall asleep, which was not a normal activity, insomnia being a constant companion of hers lately.

That was good, even if surprising.

Bright drops of afternoon sun burned her ankles, pushed against the top of her umbrella, cascaded down the slopes of the enveloping dunes and she swore she felt each and every photon of light – every one – impact, burrow and lose itself in her body – this struggling, doomed structure – she felt them spreading recklessly, heedlessly, heaving their way into every corner of her, exploding in dazzling bursts of every color of blue imaginable in their own private, miniature rendition of an atomic-level Fourth of July deep inside of darkest Jolene. The light filled her, filled her to overflowing, carelessly, foolishly, negligently. It teased. It tickled. Then it didn't do anything at all.

It never ceased to scare her how much she needed to feel Robert's hand in hers.

His hands – they were necessary. An implacable compulsion. An unavoidable force of nature – she needed his palm touching her the same way she needed to breath oxygen or relied on gravity. It was necessary. It was basic. It was essential. It was horrible. Robert's fingers had to be in hers, his bodily presence demanded her bodily presence. Yes, quite naturally once Jo meant Rob, Jolene had disappeared off the face of the earth, as had Robbie, dead as a doornail, and a new composite being – a Jobert or a Roblene had taken their places and lived their lives in place of them.

It had hit her hard and it had hit her fast and the old Jolene hadn't had a chance in hell of surviving it.

Robbie was quiet, sometimes, yes, with a devious smile, and a more than slight tendency to stretch the truth in some situations and an ability to make a person feel like, well, like they were the most important person in the world, and he had the shoulders and arms of a lumberjack and the smile of a preacher. And he had the tongue of an angel. Or a demon. Robbie liked to talk, when the mood hit him. He was good at it. Very good. And when he did talk, it was normally about Robbie. Well, who didn't like to talk about themselves? Everybody did it. But in Robbie's case, since Robbie was fascinating, endlessly fascinating, Jolene didn't mind it one bit. You wouldn't have either. He was a joy to listen to. He was unusual.

Robbie was a phenomenon.

He was finishing up a business degree and working two jobs and had bumped into Jolene one windy night on the fateful corner of Fifth and DeLaporte (now, their corner) and Jolene had been very suspicious of him at first, distant and frosty to his apparently warm and sincere invitations to coffee and later, to the movies, and later to other things. She didn't know why he was so interested in her.

She worked, and stayed at home nights reading, she talked on the phone with her friends, washed dishes after supper, did laundry, sewed her clothes, worried about the new clerk not making reversing journal entries for the year-end financials at Dalton's, but gradually, mostly, she found enormous pieces of her head devoted to Robert and what he was doing and why he was doing it, and who he was doing it with. Soon she didn't have to wonder. Most of Robbie's time was spent with her. He was always there. She loved it. She hated it. She thought she was going crazy. She didn't care.

And she still wondered, but it was a little different now - why was he doing this?

Why?

She thought about it at work, and got her cross-footing wrong in the General Ledger (which old man O'Connaghy didn't appreciate at all, he made her stay until two in the morning once getting it right again). She thought about it on the bus going home at nights and missed her stop. Five times one week. She thought about it walking to the grocery store and found herself in front of her own front door, hours later, hands empty, with empty cupboards to boot, and so she had to make the trip all over again. It was very disturbing. She was positive he was a bad influence on her obviously weakened mental state.

She thought about it, babysitting for her oldest sister two days a week, watching her four boys - the oldest boy Johnathan, doing most of the babysitting actually, even though he was only six - which was a good thing since she was so distracted, as she'd already mentioned, and she thought about it as she walked home. It (the question – why?) echoed through her head meaninglessly, ricocheting off anything she tried to think about, a song from the radio you couldn't get rid of, a simple, maddening tune that Jolene couldn't or wouldn't shake off.

Yes, that little question remained. Why? Why Jolene? Why her? What did he really want? Her girlfriends kidded her about Robbie, and her insecurities. Jolene laughed with them. Yes, she had a man. Yes, he was a good man. They told her to be happy she had anything at all. And she was, sometimes. But mostly she was scared. And that wasn't a good feeling. Love wasn't supposed to feel this way, was it? Jolene couldn't be enough for a man like Robert. Something was wrong.

She knew how to be alone. That was easier. Being with someone was harder. It was as if you'd loaned your legs out to somebody. You never knew where your legs would take you, now that you didn't control them anymore. And you had to be in control. It was crazy not to be. Anyone would say that. So Jolene had come up with a plan.

Which brought her, for good or ill, to where she was now.

It was winter. People looked as if they were ambulatory sausages. Jolene waited, scanning well-wrapped faces passing in the crowd near and far, but not really seeing any of them, looking intently for Robert's sincere, square shoulders pushing through the hurrying commuters. She stomped her feet. She squinted her eyes. She blew on her hands in the November chill by habit, as if she could really feel the cold. She couldn't feel it. She wouldn't feel it now if they froze solid and fell right off.

Why had she told him that she thought she was pregnant?

She bit her lip to keep from crying and turned her face away from the people pushing past her on the icy sidewalk. She pretended to look at the store windows.

He was obviously slipping away from her. She knew it, could

feel it, he'd be there breathing sincerely beside her all night long and she'd stare unsleeping at the cracks in her midnight ceiling and she could feel him sliding away from her into someone else's midnight and she'd cry and cry. She couldn't help it. Who wouldn't? It was all so hopeless.

Yes, she was talking herself into a worried frenzy, a frayed, unraveled Jolene bundle of not-enoughs and never-will-be's. And yes, she couldn't stop herself (or wouldn't, no she'd tried, she had). Yes, it was crazy. Yes, it was wild. It was horrible.

It was as if she were watching someone else.

She had to do something about it. She had to do something now. She needed to be more. More than Jolene. And quick.

She consciously began deleting little pieces of her life before she told him about it. Pieces that just would not fit the Robert mold. Not entire pieces, but irregular knobs, cracked parts and sharp bits that needed sanding. Well, anybody would do that, anybody. They were never big things, not at first (well, did she ever talk about anything important to Robbie anyways, and really Robbie didn't really ask questions, that wasn't his style), but the little details grew more and more elaborate, and it just kind of all got away from her. It was work. It was exhausting sometimes. Keeping it all straight.

It was worth it, though. It was all worth it. Robbie was her big chance. Robbie was going to be living. Robbie was going to be happiness. Robbie was going to be the rest of her life. Jolene had to make sure that her life happened. That her happiness happened.

Only a small problem now. Jolene bore little or no resemblance to the girl she talked about to Robert. This other-Jolene was interesting and daring. She was popular and funny and serious and worldly and sincere and loyal and well-educated and... well, everything. All at the same time. Robert's girl was a life-contortionist, a personality pretzel shaped only to please. What a woman! After her, who would want just plain accounts-receivable Jolene? No one would. Certainly not Robert. He wouldn't want the real Jolene, ever. Jolene knew he wouldn't. No use pretending, none at all. He would walk away. And you know, Jolene wouldn't blame Robert at all if he did

What was she going to do?

And, yes, it had gotten way out of hand. So, Jolene had come up with this plan. And then she was crying again. And then the telephone conversation last night. And then the wait at the corner today.

This corner of DeLaporte and Fifth was a torture. Why did she meet Robbie here all the time?

Jolene looked up. And immediately regretted it.

The angel was right there, right there – as if all that time had never happened, and maybe it hadn't - and Jolene was still a kid, or still just out of high school, or still living her predictable, quiet life B.R. (Before Robbie). She, the angel, was hovering, lingering in back of her this time, and Jolene saw her red-haired, gray-winged self, all of her, reflected in the biggest of the Dalton store windows, full length and in dazzling color. Jolene saw the angel out of the corner of her eye as Jolene was pacing back and forth on that cold corner, careful not to slip on the ice, and she stopped in mid-pace.

The friendly eyes bottomless as usual, seemed glad to see her, maybe a little confused, maybe hurt, Jolene couldn't say for sure. Angel's faces were hard to read. This time her hand wasn't over her mouth, it was palm to the side and outstretched - she seemed to be wanting to pull Jolene back up to wherever the angel went to for years at a time, or maybe she was reaching to touch Jolene's shoulder, or maybe she was wanting Jolene to reach out to her. Who could say? Then the angel looked sad. Jolene forgot to breathe. She was there, right there, and Jolene turned herself slowly around, she twisted and corkscrewed her neck and looked behind her, blushing, mouth open, tongue-tied and she felt a rush of air and a wash of perfume flow over her and the air over her shoulder was conspicuously empty. The store window was empty. No one was there. At least no one with wings. Panic bubbled up and out of her of nowhere. She didn't have to think, she knew, she knew.

Oh God! It's Robert! Robbie's dead! Robbie's dead!

She should have met him on campus, then maybe they could have gone to that Italian place with the big blue platters of spaghetti and sloppy, overflowing bowls of meat sauce and that cheap Chianti he likes and he could have told her about his job interviews again, and his last semester at the University, and she would have listened to his each and every word, making sure he didn't drink too much, making sure she didn't drink too much, and asking the right questions at the all appropriate times, and then he would have pushed his chair back at the end, balancing on two legs, and smiled his satisfied, head-shaking, eyes-downward smile and exuding sincerity, would've wondered out loud again how he'd gotten so lucky as to have Jolene in his life.

And she'd blush, and she'd look down, the way she usually did, but this time she'd finally tell him the truth. She would. She would tell him. Tell him everything, slowly, carefully, leaving out no details, but stating the facts simply in the correct order and slowly so as to be understood completely. Sure. She'd explain. No, she was not pregnant, not really.

And he'd understand. He'd be puzzled at first, - of course, who wouldn't? - but in the end, he'd understand. He had to understand. Then he'd say everything was OK. And they'd stay here, in town. Or they wouldn't stay in town. They'd go to another city, or, no, maybe they'd even move to another state, and Jolene would go. She'd say that. Out loud. Anywhere he was, she'd go. She would say that. Anywhere. As long as they were together. Anywhere. She would say that.

She was crying openly now, sobbing and pacing in circles on a downtown street and making a spectacle of herself and she knew it, but she couldn't help it. The angel had come and gone. Another piece of herself was going to be taken away. She wasn't sure how many pieces there were of Jolene left to take. When would it stop? Little by little she was disappearing - just the pieces of a jigsaw puzzle pulled off a table falling forgotten onto the floor, too jumbled up to salvage, good only for the trash, and soon there'd be no Jolene there at all, none. She'd be gone. No pieces left. Gone.

The longer she paced and circled - a trapped animal - the more certain she was that Robert was lying in a street someplace under a bus, or under a pile of bricks, or electrocuted, or poisoned, or stabbed, or shot, and it kept on getting worse and worse, and she felt herself being wound up tighter and tighter until she wasn't sure how she could stand it anymore and then she felt a hand on her shoulder and turned around.

She turned around slowly, expecting to see a hard-faced policeman tell her to move on or to ask her if she were waiting for a man named Robert Hutchinson and would she accompany him to the morgue and identify the body – but no, it was Robert's face she saw looking into hers with an astonished, worried look, and she fell into his perplexed arms laughing and crying and hiccupping, all at the same time, and Jolene realized she was found. Jolene was found. She existed. She was alive. Yes, someone had found her, fished her up out of oblivion, saved and treasured her and remembered her. Jolene was protected. Jolene was visible.

It took her a while to calm down, even longer to talk.

Robert's voice floated over her right shoulder the whole time, murmuring "It's all right now, everything's going to be all right, just take your time Jo, it's going to be fine, just fine. I'm here now Jo…" And on and on. Looking back, despite the furious storms of sobbing, it was one of the happier moments of her life. She took a deep, shuddering breath, and dove in, not looking up, not even trying to see what Robert was thinking. She had to do it. She had to do it now. She wouldn't have the courage or foolishness to do it again, do it later.

"I haven't told you the truth, Robbie, not all of it. I'm, I'm…" she couldn't go on, but the image of red hair, gray wings and worn hands flashed in her head and she wobbled rapidly through the sentence with more strength than she thought she really had "I'mnotreallypregnant" She waited a heartbeat, then two, then three for some reaction, tried to judge what he was feeling by the grip of his hands on her back, or the sound of his breathing, pr the pressure of his chest on her head, but she didn't dare twist upwards, didn't dare look up. She couldn't. She was paralyzed.

Rather than burst or collapse or both, she started to babble. Into the awful silence over her right shoulder. She poured out bucketfuls of words and tried to cover everything with something else before anything could happen inside of her, or inside of her Robbie. If she just talked enough and rapidly it would all be O.K. She could make it O.K. It just took work. Jolene wasn't afraid of work. She knew what work was. You can do it, Jolene. Do it. Do it.

"I was going to tell you, I don't know how, I thought you wanted, I mean it seemed like I wasn't… I didn't… I thought I wasn't enough, and it just happened and I could see how happy you were when I told you and oh Robbie, I love you, please say something, please forgive me, I love you Robbie…"

Bucketfuls. At some point, during all of this, she'd been, not-ungently, released by a set of strong arms, just one hand remaining, sitting awkwardly on her shoulder, and she wasn't sure what she should do. She allowed herself one, just one small glance upwards at his face and saw what she thought were tears and a look of disbelief and (what was even more shocking) defeat and hurt and some other emotions she couldn't name. Or maybe she was just imagining it all. He must have seen her look up, because he turned his face away, (that made her crazy to see it) his voice a soft baritone rumble, every word swallowed before it was spoken. She could still see his face in the reflection of the window at Dalton's. It was horrible.

"I don't know Jo, I don't know, I'm going to need some time, I don't know Jo…"

And then, well, then he let her go.

That was the last time she saw Robert she got a letter from him later, but never looked inside the envelope, she never actually opened it. She didn't have to. She knew what it said. She kept it though.

She kept it – it was her first tumor, not necessarily benign, and she had carried it her whole life, a faded bundle of paper wrapped around a lump of pain, hidden in layers of foolishness and she'd stuck it in the backside of a forgotten drawers someplace, somewhere, where she wouldn't ever have to see it unless she really wanted to see it. Unless she really needed it

Well, it wasn't quite that forgotten. She always knew exactly where it was. She did. Actually, she took it with her whenever she went on a long trip. In fact, it was, this very minute, in her yellow and orange striped beach bag right beside her on the beach, safe and sound and unopened. Just in case she needed it.

A few people she'd been sharing the sand with apparently, (mysterious individuals she hadn't seen or heard the whole time she'd been there) had been packing up and filing off into the dune-maze behind her for a half hour or so. Jolene had woken up, looked up and watched them disappearing with a strange feeling of disinterested kindness – almost as if she were blessing them. She wished them well, all of them, and she hoped they were happy. The waves kept up their patient pounding and grinding for Jolene's benefit alone now. Even the seagulls had abandoned her and were thieving and bullying elsewhere on the coast.

Shadows of grassy sand hillocks lay stretching out towards the water, the beach seemed to be getting narrower and narrower, and in an orangey-gold light, it seemed as if Jolene were looking at the waves through a pair of binoculars – they were closer and closer, maybe her eyesight was going, or maybe it was her mind that was going, but most probably it was just that the tide was actually coming in, after all.

She was comfortable and resting for once instead of being uncomfortable and unrestful, and she liked the unusual feeling. She wasn't going anywhere. No decisions to make. No doctor's appointments. Nothing to do. No one to see. She wondered, briefly, if the sea would continue its march up the beach and eventually just carry her off, but even that – as a possible disaster scenario - didn't penetrate her heavy armor of tiredness and calm. No, the vast, pounding engines of anxiety and despair she used to negotiate her life were motionless and cold and dead. She was staying put. She was staying here.

Jonathan flipped back, with an efficient, characteristic jerk of his head, what might have appeared to the anonymous observer as a large and long patch of shimmering, blond-colored grass hanging over his eyes. It was in fact his hair. And he opened the door even farther. Simultaneously, he smiled and bowed to Jolene, and grandly motioned her forward into his small apartment with both hands, his forehead almost touching the floor, doing some twiddly thing with his fingers while he did it. Jolene dimpled her chin, smiled and curtseyed, elaborately, bowing her head and almost cracking her skull against Jonathan's when they both struggled to straighten up at the same unfortunate moment.

As Jolene tried unobtrusively to adjust herself and her clothing - so that what she had intended to be covered in public stayed covered in public - she caught Tobi's eye as he chopped energetically at some poor, defenseless vegetable in front of him and stirred a furiously boiling pot on the stove to his left. Tobi fastened his eyes on Jonathan, then on Jolene, and rolled them (his eyes) as usual in big circles of exasperated affliction. Jolene decided tonight was the night, (she had been thinking of doing it for a long time now) to bewitch Tobi with her patented, Jolene, pan-dental smile-of-death She initiated the smile. At first nothing happened. Tobi's face remained absolutely blank. She increased the dazzle-volume. Still nothing. Then, a moment later, he fell to pieces. He smiled back, pointedly showing all his teeth, in a fair imitation of a shark, and shaking his head, in a sad, world-weary way, reached behind his back to open the refrigerator. The dinner with her nephew had officially begun.

Jonathan and his partner, Tobi ("now remember, that's Tobi with an 'i' Aunt Jo with an o") had made lasagna (Jolene's favorite). Tomato, basil, and a multitude of other spices warmly surged over her in a pressure wave of humid cooking smells. It felt so good and so soft on her skin she wanted to lie down right there in the apartment's hallway and let it bundle her off to sleep. Instead, Jolene took her shoes at the door and trailed little white sand streams onto the worn brown carpeting, collapsed into a waiting sofa, and waited, hand outstretched in mid-air, for the glass of wine already poured and sitting for her on the far-off kitchen counter.

This was the day of The Call, although she didn't know it yet. The three of them had been to the beach earlier, and Johnnie (he hated it when she called him that) and Tob had left early to make dinner. She'd let them. Tobi (who was also mysteriously called Gustavo by Jonathan, mostly when Tobi was in trouble, which seemed to happen quite a lot) was a good cook, as Jolene had found out through long experience with these après-beach soirees as Johnnie liked to call them. They were a pair, Jonathan and Jolene, and after Jonathan had met Tobi, they'd become a trio. Jolene was never sure exactly what Tobi thought of her, he was a mystery, that boy. He did a lot of traveling, something to do with his job, computers or phones or something. She didn't see him all that often. And he was hard to get to know, when she did see him. Ah, but then, Jolene could be a mystery herself, couldn't she?. It wasn't altogether a bad thing, mysteries had to hang together, they had to look out for each other. So that's what Jolene and Tobi did.

Johnnie and Jolene had started to call themselves J and J, and had met down at the beach. Well, met as adults. Jolene had been babysitting him for most of his young life. Still, one weekend, tramping across the sloping upper part where people stretched out and baked in rows of people-shaped loaves of red flesh she'd almost tripped over a couple of bodies angled (in her opinion) a little too close to one of the paths, and was about to offer some helpful, loud instruction when she was startled to recognize the general outline of the brown-as-a-nut carcass before her (under an oddly science-fiction-like, bright white, wrap-around set of

sunglasses) as the body and face of her nephew.
All ancient history now.

She'd been going down to the beach on Saturdays, and often finding Johnnie at the same spot, christened it JJ Point and she would pitch her tent-like umbrella, and Johnnie and Tobi would scoot out for more sun, and come in when they were too hot, and they'd spend the afternoon dozing and talking and listening to music.

She was careful and cagey at first. She still reserved for herself the right to be a little ornery. She also reserved for herself the right to love them. She just didn't go and spill it all and tell them everything about the Jolene world and what she was feeling. She was selective. At first. And later too. And cautious. Yes, Jolene could be silent and possibly irritating. It was something she gave herself permission to be. But the relationship had worked, somehow, shakily and tentatively, and then more easily. To her surprise.

She didn't explain how she was feeling. She didn't feel she had to. Not the way she would have had to when she was younger and she did more random, compulsive explaining. She was voluntarily enigmatic. She just did it. And it made her happy. And that was that. They made her happy. She seemed to make them happy. That just about seemed to be the sum of it – that was all she needed to know at present. It was enough.

And now here she was, sipping some unpronounceable wine from some small mountain town in Northern Italy (or was it Croatia?), watching the two of them watching her. If she didn't know better, she'd say she this had been a good day – she'd mark this day with a white stone. She guessed she'd say that.

The windows were covered in condensation from the cooking and the couch was facing away from the window when Tobi, bringing crackers or some little salami slices or something else small and intricate and edible stopped in midsentence – as if he'd seen a ghost, just as he was setting the plate on the big block of wood that served as their coffee table. He just stopped and stared over her shoulder for ten seconds, until Johnnie came over and touched him on the arm. Yes, he looked as if he'd seen a ghost. Then he told a joke or something, something to make people forget and made some excuse about getting back to the kitchen, where he and Johnnie talked in low voices for a solid thirty seconds. Actually none of that was unusual, was it? The rest of the evening was full and warm as it always was and when Jolene got home, she saw she had a message on her answering machine.

Was that the angel again? She never asked Tobi about it. She figured she knew the answer already. The call was from her doctor. Then she saw the doctor. Then the next appointment she made was with an oncologist. That was a year and a half ago, no, it was almost two years ago.

So the angel had come again. Jolene hadn't seen her. What had Jolene lost this last time? She was the angel of lost things, wasn't she? Or was she the angel of things that were taken? What did she take this time? What did she steal from Jolene?

Innocence?

It couldn't have been her innocence. The many years after Robert had taught her the hard way (sometimes that's the best way, sometimes the only way) that while it was important to want and need, what was more important was just to move and live. And learn. When you stopped all that you'd stopped living. Right, Jolene?

Moving and learning and living.

That's what was important, right?

Well.

Maybe.

But, it wasn't just the living, the important thing was the giving. Giving out and not looking for what came back. That'd always been the hard part, for Jolene – the not looking for something in return part. Everyone wants something back. And the crazy thing was, not wanting things back gave a person a kind of safety, a kind of secure place, that you could live a decent life out of. A place no one could take from you since it was a place you yourself gave to yourself. Giving without the expectation of return. Safety. Well, that's how Jolene saw it. It made sense to her. It made you innocent, in a manner of speaking.

No, she'd gotten back her innocence a long time ago, and she wasn't about to give it away again.

Why had the angel come?

No, it was a loss, she was sure of it, the angel, her angel, was always about loss. She took. Jolene lost.

Loss.

Well, yes, losing could be painful, but shedding the extra weight made the walking afterwards easier. She just wished there were some other way to do it.

Such brave words, Jolene.

And now cancer.

Cancer.

Cancer.

Even the word sounded hateful.

Cancer.

So Jolene wasn't immortal.

O.K.

Maybe, Jolene, it was time to start living more. It was time. It had always been time. It's had always been a good time to live.

O.K.

We can do this.

Me and my angel and myself. With a lot of help. And a lot of patience. We can do this.

Just breathe, Jolene.

Maybe it wasn't so strange. Maybe it didn't matter. Maybe the angel was there all the time. Maybe it was all good. The wanting, the having, the losing, maybe she just watched it all and it was all good and it will always be good and Jolene just had someone walking alongside her as she wanted, had and lost. An angel hiking companion. Maybe Jolene just didn't notice her. And then again, maybe not. Who knew? Anything becomes ordinary after frequent repetition. Anything. Even angels. Even angels with messages. Even the occasional angel with red hair, bad timing, and a flair for the dramatic entrance.

The beach was deserted.

It was getting cold, well, cooler at least, and Jolene was feeling content, but vaguely uncomfortable, she needed to move around, or needed to finish something, or needed to start something. She needed to get up, at the very least.

The thought of getting all that stuff back to the car should have been discouraging, but it wasn't. Probably because she had no intention of lugging it back. She'd take care of it tomorrow, maybe ask Johnnie to get it. He'd do that for her. She knew he would.

In the meantime, the beach was a show she had all to herself. The sun was starting to catch the top of the dunes with a halo of light behind her. Long, lumpy, ribbony clouds far out over the ocean were aflame with pink and purple fires, and she felt a cool mist, prickly with salt and sand blowing in over the breakers and pushing her and the yellow beach blanket she was rolled up in – pushing it into a saffron sail – up, up, and away - pushing her away from tiredness and immobility and peace and away from thoughts of endings, pushing her back towards her car and back towards the tumbling, raucous world of movement and change.

The sea was helping her. It was trying.

Jolene was scared.

It scared her to death, all those ups and downs, lefts and rights, and she didn't know if she had the energy to do it any of it anymore. But she didn't see what else there was to do. Besides, what more could happen to her? Yes, a loaded question, best not to ask, but third time's a charm, so she'd blunder through it all one more time and see where it took her.

One more time, Jolene. You could do it. With help.

Just because change isn't pleasant, doesn't mean it's not good, huh? Oh, just stop with the thinking Jolene. She grunted and groaned her way to a standing position, and turning her back to the sea, looked out at the wilderness of dunes before her, a kind of a future – whatever it was going to be.

But first she had one more thing to do, and she reached down.

"Aunt Jo!" "Aunt Jo!" Now Jonathan was getting worried. He didn't bother to push back his shock of blond hair, he wasn't even noticing his heart beating rapidly and painfully under his blue-striped dress shirt. Jonathan jogged down the winding path to his and Aunt Jo's beach with a sense of strangeness. Nothing looked familiar. It was early Monday morning, he was late for work, but she hadn't come over on Sunday like she said she would, and calling and leaving messages hadn't gotten any response. He knew she went to the beach at the oddest times, and seeing her car in the parking lot, a little ancient Volvo, dusty and lonely, all by itself in the corner had made his head spin. Her car was in the parking lot, but she wasn't. "What in the heck could Aunt Jo be doing out here so damn early?"

Seeing sunglasses of hers lying on the sand and her yellow umbrella wedged upside down in a shock of tall, spiky grass, its handle sticking up at a crooked angle into the early morning sky, brought Johnathan skidding to a halt. His heart was trying to pound its way right out of his chest, his head was rotating helplessly to the left and to the right and back again, his breath was coming in and out in ragged coughs and painful barking sounds.

"Aunt Jo! Aunt Jo!"

"Where are you, Aunt Jo?"

"Aunt Jo let me know where you are."

He ran, faster and faster, afraid of what he might find, sliding around a bend, tripping on some saw grass and a rolled up towel (yellow and orange) and nearly doing a somersault, wind-milling both arms and sliding to a stop in front of half-buried beach bags, more yellow towels and miscellaneous pieces of paper trapped under more bags, tubes of sun block, crackers, chocolate, bottles of water. It was a mess.

He looked up the beach, and then down, but he was alone. Entirely alone. He started calling out again, anxiously whispering to himself in a cold, humid morning breeze coming off the ocean as he put all her stuff back into their various bags, the sun just rising, a perfect golden circle, balanced on a perfectly flat blue horizon as clear and obvious as a mathematical proof.

"She had no business out here on her own, no business."

Why he was cleaning up he didn't exactly know.

"Aunt Jo!"

He couldn't just leave all her stuff laying out on the sand like that. It wasn't respectful.

"Aunt Jo!"

He stuffed in and called out, stuffed in and called out.

"Aunt Jo! Answer me. Aunt Jo!"

He saw a weathered, yellowed envelope, falling apart with age, and a note stuck in it. It was a short note, creased in the middle and folded in two - it almost fell to pieces in his hands. It said "Meet me at our corner next Monday and we can talk. It will be all right. You'll see. Love R." That was it. And there was one long red hair stuck in the middle of the note.

"Aunt Jo" he said again, he tried to talk (who was he talking to?) but it came out more a breath than a whisper.

The wind gusted around him, shoving him towards the parking lot, Jonathan heard something or someone, and he looked around in wild amazement, expecting to see her appear out of nowhere. But all around was air, brightness, gold, green, warm, grassy dunes, foam-flecked, blue surf stretching long and wide in front of him, laid out as if it were a gift, pulled tight in front of his unfocused eyes, an empty, expectant landscape of blurry, shimmering morning light – and all of it was for Johnathan, for him alone.

Alone.

He was by himself. The light was everywhere. Where had the morning come from so quickly?

STILL LIFE WITH FRUIT

Friday 6:23 PM

"Shit. Shit. Shit."

His thighs pumping up and down, his breath getting raggedy and thin, David pistoned the pedals of his bike in and out, back and forth, any way he had to, anyway he could, sliding powerfully under the peeling Eucalyptus trees, slower and slower and slower as the hill got steeper and steeper. He wrinkled his nose and squinted between gasps and grunts. The air reeked of rotting plants. Gravel hissed under his tires. Car bumpers played tag with his left foot and its whirling steel pedal. Fluorescent, late-fall sunlight, avalanches of it, slammed into his face, his arms, his thighs slantwise, alternating with heavier, colder shadows. David was late. David was in deep trouble. But David was alive. He smiled into the sun and the heat and the cold and let the columns of light beat him up.

David told himself they were search beams. Dried leaf and dust-filled cylinders of bright, deadly light chasing him down. Sensory tentacles of a celestial police helicopter strafing the road with a single-minded, white-hot purpose. Find him. Find the ducking and weaving bicycling dot that was David Hirscher. Yes, they hunted him, they nosed about, they reached earthwards, they tried to, at least. Seeking, touching, grappling onto this lone escaping man, trying to force him flat, trying to silence him, trying to shove him facedown onto the cracked, black asphalt and beat him into a final, bloody submission. Yes, they would try. But they would fail, of course. David was on the run. Nobody caught David when he was on the run.

Except for the car going for the right turn lane that missed him by centimeters.

Another right-turning car almost hit him, and David bellowed and swore at its retreating bumper, but of course, no one heard. No one ever hears. If a bicyclist fell in the forest (or on a city street), they never made a sound. Bicyclists were invisible. They didn't exist, formally.

David grunted. No. Respect. No. Respect. No. Respect. He continued his rhythmic whining (just because it felt good) and with each foot's downward stroke, said it louder. Not looking, of course, to see how much closer he was coming to the top of the hill because David had given up simultaneous bike-riding and hill-top-watching years and years ago. A watched hill never ends. There are only pedals and quadriceps. Lowly biker's treasured hill-wisdom.

Fuck! Fuck. Shit. Shit. Shit.

His lungs ached with a stinging fire. It felt good. His head hurt though.

Strobing sunlight wasn't bothering him. Neither was the distracted truck driver gaining on his muscular biker's behind. He wasn't really interested, maybe he should have been, but he wasn't. No, David hadn't really even noticed. He was somewhere else. He was worrying. And he was laughing. One after the other. Worrying about what? Laughing about what? He didn't want to think about it. He was tired of thinking about it. He just wanted to feel for a little bit. That wasn't too much to ask.

So. He giggled and chortled and his head hurt, his neck hurt, his eyes hurt, there was angst somewhere inside of him, but something else was there too and it was going to pop any minute. He whistled to himself (even though he was lousy at it, Elizabeth always begged him to stop whenever he started it) and inhaled carbon monoxide like there was no tomorrow and he pumped.

Well, chortling is what Elizabeth called it. David called it laughing. It was not the same thing.

Yes, he'd been winking at the birds, getting high on this beauteous San Diego afternoon, pushing his dopey, smiling face up into the sky and feeling the wind wind-burning his cheeks – basically just a dog flapping his tongue out of the side of his snout and hanging too far into the slipstream of southern Californian air sliding past him. Yes, David admitted to all that. David had attained that zen-dog-being-present-being-here-now state and he hadn't even been trying to do it.

Until a few seconds ago.

Now, well, now there was a certain amount of pain. These dramatic emotional pendulum swings from omnipotent giddiness to bankrupt desperation (and back again) were killing him. They'd kill anyone. They were even worse with a headache. He was obviously losing his mind. But in his own gnarly, twisted way David was enjoying them, and he would keep on enjoying them, (yes he would, Elizabeth), no matter what anyone had to say about it. He was alive. And he was living. Which sometimes wasn't the same thing.

He wasn't' lit or drunk. There wasn't really all that much monoxide flowing his way. His consumption of Mountain Dew had been practically nonexistent this morning. No, he was free. And he felt like laughing. So he did.

O.K. He wished Elizabeth next to him, right here, pedaling, squinting into the sun, shaking her head of long brown hair at him. He imagined his right hand running down the side of Elizabeth's face (somehow miraculously, the two of them, riding their bikes in a straight line, avoiding clueless car drivers, and gazing deep into each other's eyes, all at the same time). They would struggle to climb to the top of this hill. They would laugh. He would trace the soft mound of skin along her cheeks, drop back over her chin with the knuckles of his fat, knobbly rock-climbing fingers, rest the back of his hand gently, carefully, just for a second, in that small valley tucked neatly into her slim throat. She liked that, usually, and uh, then, well, trailing his little finger lightly across her neck, yeah, maybe, feeling a trembling in her muscles as he brushed along the arch of her shoulder, then her back, then losing his fingertips in her dark hair, brushing her brown eyes, well, she'd have to close her eyes for that, right? They couldn't be riding bikes for that. Maybe they'd stopped and were resting at the top of the hill by that point.

He wanted her. Didn't he? Yeah. Of course he did. Who wouldn't? A girl like Elizabeth? He wanted to tell her how he felt. He wanted to share his dog freedom with her, his dog day, his dog life. He wanted and wanted and wanted it. But he couldn't have it.

He couldn't?

What was happening to him?

Yeah, right, he could never tell her about all of this, about any of this. Ever. What exactly was there to tell? Elizabeth didn't even like to ride bikes.

But he had to tell someone, somehow, there had to be some way of getting it out of his head or his head would burst into pieces and his heart would jump out of his chest all on its own. It could get pretty messy if he didn't do something quick.

But who?

Oh yeah, David wanted to shout, wanted to yell, to eavesdrop, to overhear, to rubberneck, he wanted to be everywhere at once, listening in on everyone and everything.

O.K. He wanted Michael (his best friend) next to him. Cool. Right now. Yup. That would work. He wanted to share the hot pressure of open falling sunlight pushing on your head and arms, the cool weight of a sluggishly approaching evening rolling over you, sounds of pedestrians blabbing, radios blaring, friends guffawing, kids and parents and grandparents asking about each other's days and not listening to the answers. He wanted all of it. All the usual stuff.

He wanted life and living and people living their lives all around him, and by him, and through him and on top of him and underneath him. He wanted all that. All at once. Right now. Right here.

He saw himself and Michael, Michael with his aw shucks

expression, shaking his head, watching David dance around a stop light on his bike – one-wheeling it.

Yeah. That's how it would be. That's exactly what he'd be doing if Michael were here.

But Micheal wasn't.

And where was this Michael anyways?

Who cares?

David was free. He was crazy, yes, and like all good things there was bound to be a morning after with all kinds of consequences, all right, he gets it, but he just couldn't take tomorrow very seriously just now. Not now. Not today. Most definitely not today.

Doesn't he deserve a few hours off from worrying? A break? A little one? Everybody deserves a break, right?

He stopped laughing for a second (why was he laughing?- he couldn't remember – and his forehead ached) still pumping away uphill, still not watching for the top and started humming to himself, off-key, as usual, as was his David-custom.

But the sun was hot on his legs which felt good, and the laughter wouldn't stay shut, locked away like it was supposed to, and he started honking out his happy-laugh maybe a little too enthusiastically and scared the shit out of the guy driving the big white pickup sitting next to him waiting for the light to change, who hammered on his horn, bawled out some injury in Spanish and accelerated off in a shower of gravel and exhaust up and over the ever-nearer top of the hill. David could hear Michael's patient but entertained voice in his head "Pedal on, bro, pedal on" that was what Michael's advice would be, and David would have to admit that, yes, that was good advice, as was usual, from the Great Miguellator, so on David went, pedaling on.

He balanced on his bike at a stoplight, bouncing up and down, letting his bike oscillate between his knees, glanced at his wrist and he saw that he was more than an hour late.

How in the hell had that happened?

Well he knew, yes. But no, he didn't want to think about it.

David, boy, you know Elizabeth will not be pleased.

Shit. Shit. Shit.

Actually, David just needed to talk to someone - Fuck, he was in a mess – he and Michael, they always told each other everything, well, almost everything, well, a lot of stuff, a lot of shit, but, well – nah, Michael was his co-pilot, his sidekick, a great guy, who wouldn't think so? - Michael was his good bud, and he had been a more than reasonably adequate guy to share an apartment with, before David had found his own place, before David had met Elizabeth, before David had all this other stuff start happening.

Nope, not going to think about it.

Yeah, even if Michael DID leave dishes in the sink for days at a time supposedly "soaking", it was nice to come home to somebody, have someone to hang with. He could hang with Michael. He could talk to Michael. He could call right now. Right this very minute.

But no, David couldn't talk to Michael about all this. Not this. Not what had just happened. Could he?

Could he?

No.

You're thinking about it. Stop.

But...

He could talk to Tobi about it?

Nah. Not even. He could hear Tobi's embarrassed silences as clearly as he could the ambulance siren racing up the hill behind him, clearer even. No. No Tobi.

You're thinking again. No thinking. None. Especially about Tobi.

Tobi.

He pulled himself vertical at the thought, or the non-thought, standing on his pedals, a little too enthusiastically and swerved and jerked (so surprised he forgot to put is feet down) almost hitting a parked car and stupidly careening out into traffic, which caused a small cascade of car horns to erupt, crescendo, and die away and also caused a traffic jam behind him as cars slowed down and abruptly made way, detouring around this suicidal mountain bike rider in the middle of a hill waiting for the light to change.

That was stupid, David. That's how dead happens. That, dear audience, David reminded himself, was the quickest way to transform a living biker into a memorial of flowers and lit candles on a street corner some night surrounded by a bunch of really sad biker friends. Besides, he barely knew Tobi, he'd just met him today at the gym.

He started across the intersection, got partway up the next hill. Then his cell phone started ringing. It was an odd ring, a new ring. His cell was obviously dying. But that was the least of David's problems, right?

"Shit (that had to be Elizabeth) Shit. Gotta think. Gotta be sharp. Shit."

In one motion, he dropped into a sub-walking gear with a thumb-click and reached into his sweatshirt to pull out his cell knowing full well he ought to pull over and stop to talk, but rationalizing he really, really needed to make up for lost time and fast and get home pronto. Dead and fucked. Dead and fucked. But wasn't he in enough trouble as it was?

Yeah, but... Actually he was too keyed up to stand still right now. He wanted his lungs to fill to bursting and his legs to cramp. He needed something to do, something to feel, something to move towards, something to hit hard, something to ricochet against. He also wanted everything finished, now, all at once. Let it all happen. Let's get it all over with. Let's do it. He wasn't asking for all that much. The back of his head hurt. He realized he was glaring at a stoplight. Furiously.

Then, David chuckled (great! the giggling again), and he smothered a laugh into the receiver as he held it up with his right hand, balancing upright on his bike one-handed, going uphill again and entering a turn lane at the next crowded intersection. He was going to get arrested, for sure.

David (foolishly, casually, he didn't really want to know, did he?) glanced down at the caller ID, and promptly let go off his front wheel, barely catching himself as he started doing a header over his handlebars onto the trunk of a parked car on the corner.

It was a call from himself.

"Hello?" he said maybe a little too loud, frowning, not moving forward anymore, feet pressed onto his pedals, balancing the bike back and forth, right and left, and alternately holding the cell to his ear and then holding the cell out in front of his disbelieving eyes to see if his own name and his own number were still flashing encouragingly back at him. He vaguely heard cars honking in the background. He backed up, bouncing halfway onto the sidewalk. He heard sounds that sounded like something resembling words while he was doing all that.

"What the fuck are you playing at?"

An irritated, very small (but tantalizingly, strangely familiar) voice bubbled up over the sound of cars speeding to get past David, a long line of cars revving up the hill to make the light before it changed. Well, at the very least, David wasn't hearing his own voice calling himself. That was a good start, Right?

"Check your fucking pockets dude, shit! Ain't you got any brains at all?"

David's frown got deeper, then disappeared, replaced with a broad shit-eating grin (he knew that voice) as he pulled his bike up over the curb, onto the sidewalk and under a particularly large and delaminated Eucalyptus, reaching into the pocket of his black hoodie (wait, this wasn't even his black sweatshirt, it was really kind of a dark, dark purple and it was supernaturally clean) and pulling out a strange, fluorescent green-yellow, not-David-owned wallet. His smile evaporated. A worried, nervous frowning expression began to take shape on David's face.

He stuck a dangling cord (the phone's headset/earbuds) into both ears so he could get cussed out properly (if it was going to get done, it may as well get done right – something David's dad always said, well, years ago before he disappeared leaving David all on his own, to sort out his life's problems all by himself), and David started looking at the glowing, trendy sport-wallet in his hand. What the fuck? Did David sleep-snatch? Was he an involuntary wallet-magnet?

A license showing through a scratched plastic cover on the top said Gustavo Gutierrez, the rest was in elegant, official Spanish, and the photo was so fuzzy it could be almost any guy with spiky black hair in his early 20's, even David himself. Hmmm.

Yeah. He knew the score. It definitely was exactly who he thought it was. It was him. Him. David found himself smiling, against his better judgment. Him. He started laughing again. His head hurt.

The voice was Tobi. The picture was Tobi. It was all Tobi. Tobi. Tobi. Tobi.

A memory of smooth, olive skin, hard back muscles, round buttocks, a devious, evil-looking smile under two disconcerting, innocent coffee-colored eyes washed over David and swamped him, pulling him completely under and burying him. The scenes playing in his head hit him and had him the way one of those unexpected huge waves gets you. You know, the kind that sometimes a guy gets in a set at the beach on a day you thought was calm and a total waste, surf-wise, which surprise and amaze you – a monster wave you can climb out onto and snap into and ride for what seems like hours.

This wave carried David away. He let it. It was the second time Tobi had done that to him. Tobi was the guy David had just spent the wildest 120 minutes of his life with, the guy whose phone number was in his back pocket. That Tobi. The Tobi.

The 1,000 watts of pure David happiness beaming out through his incisors filled a smile that hurt David's face. It was actually kind of embarrassing. But he couldn't stop it.

"How you gonna get my stuff back to me, huh, Jimmie?" said Tobi – it sounded as if he was in a big echoing metallic place, the insides of a forty-foot high tin can. But David remembered, his cell never did pick up very well.

"That's David, the name's David, Tobi. And who's this Gustavo dude? You told me your name was Tobi"

David wasn't smiling anymore, the frown was back, the headache was worse. Yeah, maybe it had been too good to last.

Then bam! Something exploded right next to him, literally right fucking next to him.

The headset tore at his ears as he jumped at least three feet into the air. Athletic, even for David. "Shit! Fuck!" Some scrawny, young, buzz-cut guy with a skateboard had run quietly up behind him, thrown down his board right next to David with an echoing crash - a gunshot - and rolled like hell downhill, a short, blond bullet crouching and laughing, disappearing neatly at the bottom (with a whooshing sound as he skidded sideways on the gravel) into an alley on the left. David flung his hand up to give him the finger and neatly tossed Tobi's phone into oncoming cars in the process.

Part of him was cool as a cucumber. That was interesting, David. How did you manage that? But he didn't stay cool for long. No.

He wrenched himself sideways, desperately managing, just barely, to slap the cellphone with his other hand towards the street curb (missing the windshield of a surprised and irritated Fiat driver) imitating a volleyball professional punching an invisible ball over an invisible net in a spectacular save at a Pacific Beach All-Pro Invitational tournament. The driver wasn't impressed. She was actually quite angry. David realized he was pointing his middle finger directly at her. She gave him the finger back, as did the woman sitting next to her, and the two of them accelerated on into the rest of their lives.

The earbud's wires snapped his head upwards and backwards – the wires, of course following the phone's rapid course changes. David ending up stumbling downwards and forwards, falling over and through his own bike, skipping lightly and desperately on his tip toes, trying like anything to keep from crash landing on his own face in the gutter (and looking, he supposed, to the random citizen pedestrian on the street, to be a scruffily dressed, attention-loving, wannabe diva ballerina choreographing with mountain bikes for some kind of performance art). It wasn't easy. It wasn't pretty. But David wasn't trying for pretty. He was aiming at living. And no surgery.

He continued, stumbling, falling completely over the sidewalk, and loudly deposited himself at considerable speed into a trash-filled bed of scraggly, city-maintained ice plant, in which he promptly skidded to a long, lubricated, sliding stop on his knees and his face. At that point he fell backwards, and with a few choice obscenities, plopped down on his ass.

The phone was gone. The headset was nowhere to be seen. David's ears ached, as if he'd had some kind of impromptu ear canal elective surgery. On top of everything else, someone couldn't stop laughing behind a garage halfway down the hill. The laughter sounded blond and young. David tried not to listen to it.

For a moment everything was quiet (well, as quiet as a busy city intersection during the daily evening gridlock could be, even with a laughing garage in the background). Then, David noticed what seemed to be a talking weedy plant standing in the aforesaid city-funded landscaping sticking upwards into the evening sunlight in green prickly defiance. There were sounds coming out of cracks in the sidewalk.

"What the fuck? You still here, bro? Jimmie? What the fuck?"

David, grimacing and squinting, navigated his way on all fours towards the sound, echo-locating it - a bat hunting a moth in the night – swerving his head this way and then that way and then this way again. In the distance, downhill, he heard more of the faraway laughter. A bleating cube of metal found its way into one of David's bleeding hands and he placed it carefully on one of his throbbing, bleeding ears. His hand felt wet. He wiped it off without thinking on his pants and left a long red-black streak on his new cargo pants. He closed his eyes, shaking his head, trying to concentrate.

"Yeah? Tobi? Gustavo? Gus-tobi? What? Motherfucking what? What do you want?"

"Hey, pues Jimmie, you know man, you gotta do what you gotta do – I mean, it's all me man - Gustavo, Tobi, it's all good man. I'm called Tobias, dude, named the same as my father's brother. Gustavo's the ID I use up here in the states, but Tobi's the real thing. I told you true, man. I didn't lie – would I lie to you Jimmie? Would I? Why would I lie, Jimmy? So, dude, you know, I'd love to sit back and shoot the shit and all, boss, all day, but I really need to get somewhere quick and I really need to get my stuff back, man, so, how soon can you …"

David put the cell down for a second, down by his waist. Distant laughing was intermittent now, punctuated with an amazed mumbling as if someone was telling a really funny story to another someone who really wanted to hear it, and the story was turning out to be too good to be true, and then… Then, there were two people laughing, no maybe three or four.

Cars swooshed by. David was kneeling and bleeding on the sidewalk. He sighed and looked at the phone, and then inexplicably, he felt happy. Out of nowhere.

O.K. All right.

David was talking to Tobi again. It was exciting. O.K. Tobi's voice was exciting. The fact that David was holding Tobi's cell was exciting. That round behind of Tobi's was exciting. No. This was too much. Loco. That's what it was. That's what Tobi had been whispering to him, sometimes yelling in David's ear, over and over again an hour ago or so ago – mi juero loco. David wondered what it meant exactly. It had to be a compliment, right? He shook his head. *Loco.*

A tiny Tobi rattled on and on, somewhere down in the vicinity of David's kneecap.

"…and I've got no money on me, and I mean no money, bro, none, nada, zero and by the looks of your wallet bro, you're as broke with a wallet as I am without one, not saying you're…"

David opened his mouth to say something. Then it dawned on him. Tobi had his wallet.

"…and all, so yeah, so when can you get my shit back to me? Bro? Hello? Anyone there? Jamie? I need my junk back. And vice versa, man. You need yours. I told you I got someplace I gots to be boy and right now. So, without you, dude, I'm up the fucking creek without the fucking paddle. No way of getting there. So what do you want to tell me, boy? Huh? Hello?"

Tobi started hearing a laugh. It was a laugh, a dangerous laugh, that David had just heard under entirely different circumstances a half hour before – a laugh which had gotten him into all kinds of trouble. It was a kind of knowing, beckoning, welcoming, low and sexy rumble that made David's knees go all watery and his eyes glaze over and his breathing go all funny. The feeling a hypnotized bird gets faced by a hungry snake. Yeah, David was fucked. Just fucked. As usual.

Tobi continued to kind of laugh and talk and laugh and talk all at the same time (something Tobi was especially good at, David couldn't get enough of it) and David couldn't put the phone down even if he'd wanted to – which he didn't.

"And you must be a popular boy – you've gotten like three phone calls in the last ten minutes - someone named Elizabeth keeps on calling you, and a guy named – wait a sec, here it is - Michael. He your boyfriend, Jimmie? You got a boyfriend you not telling me about, Jimmie? Ha! Hey, live and let live, that's what I say. You do what you gotta do, right? But back to me, Jimmie boy, we gotta…"

Fucked. David took a deep breath and started talking.

"Look, I'm David OK? And I don't have a couple of names the way some people do. It's David, just David. D. A. V. I. D. David."

It was babbling, he knew it, but he couldn't help it.

"And don't answer my phone. OK? Never. As in not ever. Especially Elizabeth, all right? All right? Toe bee? (Tobi was still laughing, he didn't stop, he always had a great a time, apparently). David tried to sound severe and angry. It wasn't working. David could not get enough of Tobi's voice. He loved it. It was honey dripping into his ears, as his brains oozed out at the same time. He was smiling his idiot's smile. He was. He could feel it from the inside. God help him.

Wasn't he supposed to be doing something right now? He couldn't remember. Well, for one, he should get up off of his knees and stop imitating a coffee table. Where was his bike?

"Yeah, Tobi, yeah, look I know, but…"

Tobi, of course, interrupted him as if he wasn't even talking.

Maybe he didn't hear David. Maybe the chain lubricant that

David had dropped the phone into that morning had finally lubricated its way into a critical cellphone chip location and his phone was drastically if not terminally ill. Maybe.

Or maybe Tobi was an unstoppable force.

"Right, right, Davy I got you – no boyfriend, a girlfriend. It's cool. I'm down with that. Swing both ways. Got it, bro, got it. But I have to say it, man, I gotta say bro, when you swing you really know how to swing. I mean, I'm going to be sore for a week. Ay! You something else. The gift that keeps on giving. But I'm sure you hear that all the time, huh? Davy boy? Anyways, I bet, Davy, I bet you want your phone back safe and sound, don't you?. We both want our phones back. Yeah, we got that in common, yeah, that and a whole lotta other things."

The last comment started Tobi up laughing again. This time it didn't stop for a while. David hung there waiting, miserable, face blushing, wanting to hang up, but unable to stop the flow of sweet Tobi out from the phone speaker, through his bleeding ears, into David's waiting brain where the poor neurons were being continually massaged into a hormonal mush the likes of which he hadn't thought possible before. Yes, he was fucked. Well and truly. It was scary, actually.

"You want to get your phone (which is kind of crappy bro, I gotta say it - you need a new phone man), so do I, Davie, so do I. I mean I want my own phone back as well. I like my phone fine – you ought to look at getting one just like mine – I got it cheap, man. I can show you where you can get a cell half off every day of the week. Anytime. There's this store. My cousin's the manager. Your wallet, your hoodie, I want all my shit back as well, so bro, we got a deal, huh? Davy? When and where stud? When and where?"

David was distracted (if it were possible for him to be even more distracted than he already was) by the sound of rifle shots, which were actually approaching skateboard wheels on uneven sidewalk, pushing, apparently, energetically and heroically uphill. He didn't dignify the sound by turning around. He did, however, keep his peripheral vision on Level Red, Full Alert - just to be on the safe side.

After a quick agreement to meet back at Tobi's hotel room, the earlier crime scene of the two hour long "swinging" session, David pedaled, thoughtfully, back down the hill, observing the city life around him, and pumping his wiry body steadily and purposefully towards downtown and the hotel.

His back, his neck, his shoulders were both relaxed and tensed. It was a weird feeling. Whatever it meant, it felt good. But, David was definitely fucked.

He rode. He stopped. He dialed his voice mail. He started riding again slowly, partly watching for buzz-cut kamikaze skate boarders, unconsciously eagle-eyeing it for the occasional but deadly flapping-driver's-side-door (eager to open and slam him into the emergency room), but mostly he was thinking. David spent what little mental energy he had available on trying to whip together a reasonable explanation for his being a couple of hours late for dinner with his Elizabeth.

Nothing came to mind. His mind was nothing. It was empty and it echoed. Not good.

He stopped and called Elizabeth, (what the hell?) figuring on winging it like he usually did (even though it usually sank him almost irretrievably into even more trouble − but David was an incurable optimistic), he got her voice mail multiple times.

Then a figurative pitcher-full of ice water poured down his figurative back, right in the middle of sliding through an intersection.

And what about David's phone? Why was David using a stranger's cell phone, some guy named Tobi - or Tobias - or would it show up as Gustavo? - of course it would - what was he going to say to Elizabeth? What? What?

Fuck! Shit. Shit. Shit.

He had so much explaining to do in his near future. So much. Too much. Way too much.

The first person David had to explain all this to was David himself. Explain? Explain what was going on? David didn't know. David didn't know what was happening to David anymore. And if David didn't know, how would he make anyone else understand it, so they'd know? Did anyone else know? Did they understand it? Did they? If someone did, please, tell him. As soon as possible. Please.

Bro. Bro. Calm it down. Twitch the old stress-volume knob down a notch or two. A little slower, now. A little easier. Smooth. Comfortable. Right. Like that. The very first thing to do, bro, the very first thing is you've got to do is figure it all out. Figure what you think it means yourself. Get it straight. So to speak. Yeah.

Whatever. Whatever that is. He had no idea anymore.

What do you want, David? Where are you going, David? What in the fuck do you think you are you doing, David?

Nothing. Nothing came to mind. The universe, apparently, wasn't going to go all soft and slow and comfortable for him. Not for David. Not today.

And David's night was just about to begin.

Friday 6:41 PM

David hadn't gotten very far down the hill, going back the way he'd come, before messages on his voice mail he'd dialed into had him biking in slow circles, one-handed, in a 7-Eleven parking lot. The more he listened, the slower he felt himself pedaling. Slower. And slower. So slow, eventually the slow pretty much became a stop, and he was standing still. A car waiting to park eventually honked at him. David didn't hear it. He was staring sightlessly straight ahead of himself (he seemed to be doing a lot of that today), moving jerkily backwards and forwards, balancing on his bike, bouncing his front wheel once a second against a pink, graffiti-covered wooden fence on the far side of the store's parking lot. He closed his eyes.

Above the messages, David could hear a kind of scuffling going on behind the fence every so often. It sounded adolescent and malevolent. No. Not again. He didn't particularly want to know at the moment, just what surprises the fence might have in store for him. And because he didn't, he wouldn't. Besides being inconvenient, paranoia was exhausting. Instead, he listened carefully to small, tinny, urgent voices called to him plaintively from what was fast becoming a glass and plastic oblong David-torture device.

For some reason, new messages for David were showing up on Tobi's cell phone preceded by a tiny trumpet fanfare, the sound of a large number of insanely energetic snapping fingers and what sounded similar to a Russian Men's Chorus chanting "Ha! Cha!" in a kind of Forties Swing Beat. The car honked at David again. From the perspective of the many and frequent shoppers at the convenience store, it looked as if David was doing some kind of spontaneous Urban Public Performance Art, bouncing and dancing his bike against the pink fence. Most shoppers didn't look very much as if they were enjoying it.

David ignored their shaking heads. He did move his bike a little farther down a pothole-filled alley, away from the parking lot and their pointed stares, and the inconvenienced honking, and continued bouncing satisfyingly into the fence over and over again with an audible ka-chunk, sometimes in time with the Men's Chorus, sometimes in a kind of syncopated beat, as he ducked and flinched his way through his unretrieved voicemails.

A familiar voice hit his eardrums. It startled him, he jerked back, and the new scab on his ear started bleeding again.

"Baby, this is Elizabeth, Could you pick me up a little sooner than we'd planned? I need to stop on the way and grab something at the drugstore – like maybe 5? See you in a couple of hours, Baby.

"Davie, this (static) your dad. I know it's been a couple of years, well, more like, well, - fifteen maybe? – shit, that long? Well... (long pause) (static) fucking small town airports (static) cell towers, never (static)."

"Davie, dad. I don't know if this thing is recording or not (static) but (static), I have (static) and, so you have (static)."

"(static) what do you mean, hold my hand out the window, fuckin' ridiculous every single time you need to (static)."

"Dave, it's Elizabeth. So tell me, just when were you thinking you'd pick me up? I've been waiting out here for half an hour. Can we even get there by 6? I'm getting worried. You've got me worried, Baby. It's, let's see, it's 5:36 now. Dave? Are you OK? I hope everything's all right. So, I'm outside in front of my apartment. Waiting. Like I said. God! I hope nothing's happened to you. OK. Well, all right. Looking for you. Is that you? Dave? No? Well. I'll see you soon, right? I hope. Call me. As soon as you get this. Well, Bye."

"Like this? Over here? Yeah. O.K. All right. Yeah, there's one bar. Fuckin' crazy. Hope you can hear this, Davie, I flew in from Vegas, and have a layover in San Diego for a couple of hours (static) need to talk to you. Face to face. I'll (static) past Security in Terminal 3 around 6 tonight. That's today bud. See (static) there (static) fuckin cell (static), my arm's only so long, (static)."

"All right Dave, what's going on? I walked over to your

apartment, and your car is here, but you're not. Your phone works. Your friend Michael says you were on your way home. So where are you? We're all here. Where are you?"

"(static) FUCK (static)."

"Dave old chum, old pal of mine, Sir Michael here. No biggie, just thought I'd give you the heads up. I don't know if you know, but Elizabeth's been buzzing your door and mine for a few minutes. She's sitting down on our front steps. Exactly, precisely, right in front. Sitting there. Blocking the front door. She doesn't look very happy. Not a happy camper, D. I'd buckle the armor on if I were you, maybe wear a fire-proof suit. Just a friendly F.Y.I. dude. Good luck man."

"End of new messages."

"Shit. Shit. Shit."

And just like that, David was pumping out of the parking lot, heading back towards the hill again, faster, much faster this time. The street and the hill were nauseatingly familiar. Maybe it was just that David felt nauseous. It was all starting to feel Obsessive-Compulsive. A young David, doomed by his inner (and outer) demons, is forced forever to ascend and descend the same San Diego hill, day after day, year after year. Can no one stop him? Does no one care?

He breezed through intersection after intersection. He hardly saw the intersections, to be honest. Sure, he was heading in the opposite direction of Tobi's hotel and the waiting Tobi, and sure, it was the wrong direction for his long-lost, forgotten waiting parental unit, sitting in an airport cell-phone hole somewhere at San Diego International, but it was in exactly the right direction for his car and for Michael's apartment, and his apartment, and the waiting Elizabeth.

One out of three. That was the best he could do for now.

When was it all going to stop? When would it slow down? When could he figure out what was happening to him and at him and to him? Was a little clarity so much to ask?

A familiar, buzz-cut head peered out from behind a garage on an oddly familiar alley as David swung by. David cut a fat tire track across some anemic grass, jumped a curb, and hit the next street flying, missing the alley entirely. The head had a surprised, disappointed look about it and David saw what resembled a pail of water sloshing about in two hands thrust suddenly back behind the fence. He heard yelling and a metal bashing sound. Mr. Buzz-cut stared yearningly after him, shirt and pants wet as David propelled himself spectacularly out of range. David gave him one cool backward glance, and allowed himself the smallest of victory smiles. This period: Bikers 1, Skaters 0.

And he pedaled on.

Friday 6:49 PM

David lived in a converted bowling alley. It's last name had been The Turquoise Desert Family Recreation Center, and before that something about starlight and blue moons (you used to be able to see the burnt out neon signs hanging from the roof), but it had been semi-abandoned for years, sold to condo developers and turned into a mixed-use project with signature, genuine, predistressed hardwood floors, courtesy of the ex-bowling lanes. People said it was haunted. But people said a lot of things. Parts of it were fussily fancy. However, David (and Michael) didn't live in the many-and-large-windowed condos facing the inner courtyard with Plaza De Taos ornamental balconies and pleasingly cracked adobe-like colonial arches with genuine Tuscan columns and heavy, red, ceramic roofs running everywhere over every possible roof-like surface.

No, they didn't live there.

David and Michael lived in the low-income section set aside in the third floor efficiencies over the alley facing north in the shadowy backside of the former bowling lanes that the condo developer had been forced to offer for the financially embarrassed. Basically their whole section of the building had the appearance of a structure that had been constructed hurriedly from miscellaneous contents of returns and discount bins at the local Home Depot.

Except they did have gorgeous blond hardwood (pre-distressed) floors throughout their tiny floor plans. But really, David wasn't complaining. It was a great place. And the price was right.

David wheeled his bike slowly along the back alley, threading his way on a path through the cacti and the xeriscaped stony desert garden at the back of the condos and held his breath as he neared the side path that led through the elaborately sculptured Alhambra Gate into the courtyard. He started to cross the open space, and froze (luckily) when he sensed a distant gravel path crunching under an impatient foot some distance away. He peered carefully through a round, rod-iron, flower-encrusted hole on one side of the gate and held his breath.

He could see Elizabeth pacing, back and forth only ten yards away. He'd never seen her pace before. Although, to be honest, Elizabeth looked great – pacing and stopping and looking around, her dress kind of clinging to the various ample curves on her body in a wet t-shirt kind of way. Or more likely, David thought on closer observation, clinging in a bent-out-of-shape-beside-oneself-sweaty-just-run-a-number-of-blocks kind of way. But still, Elizabeth looked great.

As she stepped four times and turned, stepped four times and turned in a hazy golden sunset wash of light, David was able to admire and enjoy her – what a lucky guy he was – the crushed rocks on the path crackling underneath her angry feet, her constant spinning and strutting really setting her dark hair whipping back and forth, her hair cascading actually in long waves over her shoulders in a movie-sexy way all in slow motion each and every time she spun on a high heel and reversed direction. Yes, it was beautiful. She was beautiful.

She was going to kill David. He knew it.

He lifted up his bike and held both wheels so not even the turning gears would make a sound, and padded across the open space in front of the gate, still holding his breath. Nothing. The crunching continued, and although he couldn't be sure, he thought he could her Elizabeth muttering something (probably un-ladylike and certainly uncomplimentary to David) to herself now and again as she walked and turned, walked and turned. David let out a little air. He took a little in. He tensed and got ready to act.

He pulled out his (well, Tobi's) cell, and quietly dialed Mike's number, pressing his back against the back wall of the apartment, but before he could connect, the phone practically jumped out of his hands lighting up with some kind of neon display on its side and blaring out (with pretty decent bass) "THAT'S the way uh-HUH, uh-HUH, I LIIIIKE IT, uh-HUH, uh-HUH, Yes, THAT's the way UH-HUH, UH-HUH" He jammed the phone into the front of his pants and with horror and despair heard footsteps come to a determined stop in the decomposed granite some thirty feet away.

A small voice complained into his crotch "Jimmie, I mean Davie, I mean, David, boss, you coming? I don't have all day, dude. I told you, where the fuck…"

Fumbling in his front pants with both hands to silence the damn phone, he noticed he'd gotten the attention of a couple of his neighbors (the retired couple, Ed and Marie) looking out their condo's corner back window through the black leaves and vines of a wildly exuberant rod-iron balcony overlooking the alley. They were looking at David. They were shaking their heads. Ed stuck his head out the window and was about to speak when David finally found a significant button (of some sort) and the voice on the telephone cut off in mid-profanity, allowing David to pull his hands out of his pants with a diminutive flourish and a great deal of what he hoped was wide-eyed innocence.

David smiled and waved to Ed who said something harsh back over his shoulder to Marie and then promptly closed their window with a bang. After the crash of the window, David heard gravel shifting and footsteps approaching. He threw himself and his bike behind the condo-wide communal dumpster, eclipsed by an enormous spray of almost iridescent purple-red bougainvillea. A bougainvillea thorn caught his pants and quickly, efficiently, almost surgically sliced most of one leg off of his shorts. The phone began to slide out of his pants. David froze. He heard a voice from across the courtyard.

"Davie is that you? Davie it's Elizabeth. You remember, *your girlfriend*. The one you were going out with tonight. The one you've been going out with on Fridays for the last year. David! David? Are you there? David! Am I talking to myself? David?"

David punched his crotch repeatedly, finally managing to hit redial through the fabric of his shorts, and held the phone in his fist, bunched up with the slashed fabric in his shorts, trying to be still, to be as one with the alley, existing merely as an extension of his bike - just another piece of junk metal leaning against the smelly steel of the alley dumpster waiting for the good waste management people to carry him off to a new recycled life.

He constantly had to adjust his pants, trying not to let the Tobi's cell drop onto the scrupulously clean concrete apron under his feet and shatter into a million pieces. He chanted every prayer he could remember, every mantra he could think of as the footsteps began a hesitant, but obviously purposeful trip through the front gate, across the flagstone courtyard, past the gaily splashing lion-encrusted fountain and towards the back gate of the apartment (and David's certain doom).

Another voice, small but welcome, drifted upwards from his disarranged shorts "Hello?"

A window flew up with a kind of exultant disgust and Marie's head appeared this time, looking through the window screen with a cocked head, a set of frowning eyebrows, and a mouth in a perfect "o". She was motioning Ed with her left hand to come quickly to the window, and pointing with her right down at David, gripping and un-gripping his pants, shifting the weight of his bike on and off his shoulders, and just incidentally, talking to his crotch.

"David? David? David Edward Hirscher, why won't you answer?"

Elizabeth's voice drilled back through the intervening air - a laser beam – aimed definitely and directly at David from somewhere halfway through the courtyard now. Elizabeth had started using his Full Name, and that couldn't be a considered a good sign, even a laid-back Southern Californian boy like David could see that. He briefly wondered how she had gotten past the heavily guarded gates and the elaborate security precautions of the Turquoise Desert Development Corp, LLC., then he remembered Michael.

The footsteps scuffed the flagstone angrily, closer and closer. David could just hear Ed far above talking over Marie's shoulder in a rising, rolling retired-person's growl of righteous indignation "…not in public, not in my neighborhood, I don't care if he does live here – I don't care, Marie. Give me the phone Marie, I'm calling the police. No, Marie, give it here…

And from below a tiny Michael bleated upwards from the center of his pants.

"Helloooooooo. Anyone there? Who the hell is Gustavo?"

That, followed by a sudden acceleration in the scrunching flagstone-footsteps effectively jolted David out of inaction as if he'd tripped over a 500 megawatt high-tension power line and grabbed onto it with both hands and couldn't or wouldn't let it go. Grim-faced, David snatched the phone out of its lovingly-protective, sound-absorbent bundle of ruined pants and hissed a

near-soundless "Michael" emphatically into the receiver
Nothing.
"Michael. It's Dave."
Still more nothing.
Then a loud "Daaaavy boy" needled its way into his wounded ears.
"For the love of God, Mike, if you were ever my friend, keep it down, and just buzz me in the side door! Now! No questions, dude, just do it!"
"So dramatic, dude, what in the hell's up, huh? Oh, yeah, the buzzer…"
And not waiting for any more non-responses, David sprinted out and up and along the other side of the building, bicycle held in front of him - a shield - slamming through lantana, tearing around (and being torn by) agave, bounding through the David-high ornamental grass (David now in a rough imitation of a drunk bison), catching the side door just as it stopped buzzing, and then running up the stairs, three at a time with his bicycle wrapped around his head – as if he was demo-ing the new Olympic Sport, Urban Mountain Bike Carry and Stair Climb Steeplechase.
Michael's door opened and closed and David spun inside slamming into the wall in front of the door and bouncing into Michael's living room/dining room/kitchen/bedroom and onto his bed. The bike rebounded, a thing alive and kept on bounding, jetting into the kitchen, landing abruptly upside down, and hanging from the sink by its ergonomically perfect seat. Dish soap and a couple of broken plates now decorated the floor and walls. The sink had been (surprise) full of "soaking" dishes – emphasis on the past tense – had – but, unhappily was full no longer. David jumped to the window. Michael jumped to his sink. Micheal sadly surveyed his (now ruined and scattered) Corellware, casting dirty looks back at David. David didn't see him doing this, though.
David peeked down, hiding behind Michael's stained vertical blinds, out and over three stories towards the other low-income, back alley side of the building. Michael's window was cranked wide open. Elizabeth was right there, underneath him, David could even smell Elizabeth's perfume bubbling furiously upwards into Michael's open window.
Elizabeth was firmly entrenched, looking up and down the alley, looking up at the back of the apartment building (forcing David to

duck for cover repeatedly.) She seemed to be talking to herself. There were two of her. A gently, concerned waif-like Elizabeth and a wrath-of-God Elizabeth. There was an argument going on. The gentle waif was not winning. Not good. Not good at all.

David, jumping backwards, jumping forwards (seeing himself as the cocky-about-to-be-killed sniper in a cheesy WWII movie - what could he say? – he had a lot of imagination), saw her scowl at someone on the other side of the courtyard (he assumed Ed or Marie), saw her look at her phone checking the time yet again, saw her look left, look right, frown with her entire face, search her environs with that Elizabeth serious-as-a-heart-attack-all-hope-should-be-abandoned expression that David had only seen once before and had hoped never to see again, and place her hand on her hip. Something was about to happen. She snapped her phone into the air. She jabbed her finger at the screen. She put her phone to her head. She jerked her other hand violently away from her ear. She stared straight ahead. She made a call.

David glanced first at the open window, then back at his phone, then back at the window, then at his phone and momentarily had a brilliant idea, an urge (it seemed an eminently reasonable plan to David at the time) to throw the fucking cell forcefully into the newly-created pile of shards of broken plates and cups and water David had just created at the back of Michael's apartment where it could short out and no longer endanger, threaten and aggravate him in any way. Such an easy plan. And so simple. So elegant.

But then he thought better of it. With a look of male resignation at the inevitability of (justly, he had to admit it was true) female righteous indignation, David winced, held his phone at arms-length, watched and yes, cringed, closed one eye, waited, then waited some more for the inescapable. Michael watched David, fascinated. But nothing happened.

Of course, somewhere, probably in a certain hotel room, a snippet of tasteful house music (not finger-snapping Russian Swing) was playing and Elizabeth's name was flashing up repeatedly upon an impatient (but handsome) Latino's face. Of course, of course. David smiled, then stopped smiling, then gritted his teeth. The thought of Elizabeth and Tobi meeting, even as accidentally and as distantly as through a cell phone call made his whole life appear even more unreal than it had been just a few seconds before. And that was saying a lot just now. David's life was getting pretty unreal, pretty quickly.

Who said change was good? It was fucking, stupefyingly, entirely terrifying.

He took a deep breath, laughed (quietly, so no one, anyone - read: Elizabeth - nearby might catch even a hint of his distinctive honking) and closed his eyes. The laugh was more than half a sob. The laugh had been a better choice in David's mind than just groaning and moaning loudly for an hour or two in his friend's apartment and thrashing about helplessly. Although that (the groaning, bitching, complaining, thrashing, probably drinking) was definitely going to happen anyways. He was sure of it. He'd just do it later. After all this was over. Probably in the waiting area of the nearest emergency room, after Elizabeth was through with him. But that would cut out the drinking part. Yeah. Better do it somewhere else.

His chest heaved. He chortled silently. His life, as he knew it, was over. Yup, done, fried, fricasseed, and set out on the dinner table. He was toast. He was yesterday's breakfast (was that even an expression?) He was also starving. He looked down. Elizabeth was gone, apparently. He secured his (well, Tobi's) phone, replacing it back in a still-functioning pocket of his raggedy pants, and looked around himself for the first time. Maybe Michael had something to eat. He was starving. He'd eat anything right now. Even Michael's funky tofu meat-less loaf.

Crunch. Crunch. Crunch. Someone, invisible, around the corner, thirty feet below them was starting to pace back and forth, in the darkening twilight of an inner city alley. Elizabeth was nothing if not consistent. David liked that about her. A lot. Michael listened and looked over at David from his collection of (now) broken dishes and just stared. That's all he did. Stared at David. You know, David was no expert on human behavior. He'd be the first to admit it. But if you'd have asked David, David would have been forced to admit that Michael didn't have the look of a person who was going to offer David a free dinner anytime soon. Nope. Not likely. Not in this lifetime.

David opened his eyes wide in a kind of expectant welcoming expression. He smoothed his worried forehead. He also tried smiling. Michael didn't stop staring at him exactly, but he didn't look away either. Michael spoke to him. It was a start.

"Sooooooo, Big D, I expect you've had quite the afternoon,

huh?" said Michael, moving to his bed (three feet from his kitchen), trying not to glare (but failing) at the long greasy skid marks (left from the bike chains and gears) trailing over his blankets in a direct line from the front door to the kitchen. David tried to keep it cool, serene, everything was going according to a well-thought out, carefully executed strategy - yes, condition: copacetic - everything coming up roses, as per plan – nothing untoward to report. He tried, he really did. David's master plan, his overarching strategy obviously included (for a very important reason) trashing Michael's apartment and breaking up his stuff. David talked and talked. He never actually talked about this afternoon. Michael noticed. David paused. Michael glowered. David talked some more and kind of choked. His throat was really dry. David paused. Michael stared. David kind of shambled to a full stop and fell silent. David cleared his throat. He did it again. And again.

Michael raised one eyebrow.

"Michael..."

Yes, that was still more a toad croaking more than a human-David voice. One more time. David cleared his throat with elaborate care. He couldn't think of a thing to say. All he could think of doing was re-booting his monologue, once again, starting from the beginning. If no one stopped him, he'd be in this loop for hours.

"Well, Mickey, O.K."

Michael raised the other eyebrow.

"Yeah, uh, well, where to start?"

David actually wanted to talk. He REALLY wanted to talk. Actually David wanted to explain to another human being about how confusing it was to be lying to Elizabeth about a guy he'd slept with (a guy!), how he had felt physically ill (physically! ill!) deceiving his closest friends (and those friends included Elizabeth, he LOVED Elizabeth for Christ's sake, and that included Michael, they were best friends weren't they?), about how this was the first time something along these lines this had ever happened to David, and about how he didn't know what in the fuck he was doing anymore. Michael! It was a first time being unfaithful to Elizabeth and a first time being with a guy. Help me. He wanted, needed, yearned for a chance to talk.

He hated himself right now. He wanted someone to tell him

that this was deep shit, serious relationship stuff, and he was really living man, living the wild life (he, David! the wild life!), and how it was all going to be all right, it was all going to be fine, man, everything was going to turn out great.

It wasn't supposed to hurt this much. He wanted someone to hold him and tell him his world, and all the people in it hadn't just evaporated in one afternoon of wild sex. Probably that would be have been the cue for his family to step in, but David didn't have family. David had David. And he was still the old David, goddamit. He was still the careful one, the cautious one, the one you could depend on, right? He was still David, after all. He was still here. Right here. Standing in Michael's oil-stained apartment. Well, he was here somewhere. He was sure he was still here. He'd been here a moment ago. This morning. Maybe if he looked around a little bit, he'd find himself. Hiding under the bed. Peeking out from the closet. No. He was out of the closet.

Help!

And what about his father?

You know, you can't even think about that one right now.

And Tobi?

Tobi?

The matching hoodies, the joking at the gym, the trip to "try on a weight belt to see if it would fit" back at Tobi's hotel room (hah!), a piece of David had known exactly what he was doing, a piece of David had been whispering all kinds of things so incessantly in his head that he'd been amazed he'd heard a single thing Tobi had said during the long walk from the fitness club to the hotel (or had it been just a block or two? David really couldn't remember anything about it- nothing at all). David's head had been a spinning mess.

Dizzy. Buzzing. David hadn't been able to think. It was as if there had been a million mosquitoes buzzing in his head. It was as if someone else had been walking his legs besides Tobi, and then once up in the room, when Tobi had put his arm around his waist to tighten the belt it was as if someone else had stepped into David's body and efficiently spun him around so that he faced Tobi, lips a half inch away from each other, hot breath maddening the skin of each other's face and neck so he just had to do something, anything to get it to stop.

Or make it go on. And on, and on, and on.

It wasn't until he'd been biking home, laughing and scowling, loving and hating the world, that he'd realized who had stepped into his shoes that afternoon.

Admit it.

It had been David.

It had been himself.

He'd come home. Only he'd erased himself entirely out of his old life in the process. He was a ghost. What a joke. It turned out that this old bowling alley was haunted after all. David was the ghost of the Turquoise Desert.

Michael watched David standing there. David's mouth hung open. He had all this shit to say. Nothing was coming out.

David gave up. He couldn't do this now with Michael. He couldn't. Maybe he could later. But he couldn't now, could he? No. He couldn't.

"Dude. Really, I want to make a full confession. I promise. I mean, that's what I want to do, but what I need to do, need to do this very minute is get a hold my spare set of car keys."

Michael pursed his lips. It was his thoughtful look. Also his doubtful look. This time it looked doubtful and what? maybe a kind of hurt? Maybe even angry? David hadn't really seen Michael angry at him in a long time, not since 4th grade, and that business about Michael and Lucy and David's birthday party. Guess this was David's Great Day of Firsts (or Seconds). Lucky, lucky David.

David assumed a look that he was sure was commanding and rational, then tried for just friendly, then tried for don't-punch-me-I'm-really-harmless, but Michael was having none of it. A raised set of eyebrows again, and a nodding head was all David was going to get for an immediate response. That was followed by a rapidly fired, exceptionally (and unfortunately) accurately aimed set of keys that managed to hit him right where the cell phone wasn't protecting him anymore in the front of his pants. Yeah, David probably had that coming, he did.

It was a minute or two before David could speak. After he could stand up again, he only saw Michael's back. He was cleaning up his sink. Washing. That's when David knew it was bad. Really bad. Between them. He'd never seen Michael washing dishes before.

A few minutes more, after moving his bicycle off of Michael's kitchen cabinets, leaving it locked to a water pipe in the wide hallways outside Michael's efficiency, and David was barreling down the front stairs, four at a time, running out the fancy front doors and running over their neighbor Howard on the landing outside.

Howard, aka The Lady, aka the drag queen - Chick Chick a Dee Dee - gave David a furious, then a puzzled, then a sympathetic expression. What? What was that for? Did gay get branded in burning gaydar letters on his forehead as soon as it happened? Was this just the beginning? When would it ever fucking let up? When would he get a break? A chance to breathe for a second or two? When?

David flashed a smile at Howard which prompted an even deeper, more puzzled and frankly sympathetic look and Howard leaned forward, obviously poised to ask a question David couldn't possibly answer, when David fled the scene of the crime while he still had the chance.

David ran the two blocks to his broken-down car, an ancient, asthmatic Corolla, tumbled into his sagging driver's seat, and mapped the route in his head so that he could speed over to the airport, then speed over to the hotel, then speed over to Elizabeth's to see if he could convince her he wasn't a total fuck-up, then speed home to see if he still had a best friend.

Friday 7:03 PM

He called Michael as he waited at the light around the corner from their building. It went right into voicemail. He wasn't sure, but he thought he passed Elizabeth walking home to her place, under the dramatically exfoliating Eucalyptus grove, on the hill of the sadistic skater dude. She looked abandoned. He almost stopped. He really did.

He was hitting every fucking light all the way to the interstate. It would be just his luck to totally miss what looked as if it would be his one and only chance to find out why his dad had evaporated - why his dad had vaporized and vanished before David had a chance to even know what a father's face would look like – why his dad had left David and his mom all by themselves, deserted, fucking abandoned to make their fucking way alone in life. David wanted a face-to-face explanation. He wanted to know why. Why did his mom have to die alone? Why was David alone, holding her hand at the end, uselessly, no one mentioning the obvious, where was he? Dad was a big fucking emptiness to the very end. He still was. David deserved an explanation. He deserved that. David deserved to know. He deserved to know why.

His eyes were tearing up again. David hated that. He wiped his eyes and his nose with the back of his hand. Honking behind him told him the light had changed.

Fucking O.K. I'm going, I'm going.

How many times had his dad, or the memory of his dad, turned him into a crying mess? Too many times.

Yeah. Too many fucking times to be doing this shit all over again.

Well, maybe he didn't want to know why. Maybe he wouldn't get the chance. David didn't even know what his dad looked like. How in the fucking hell was he going to recognize him in a swarm of cranky jet-lagged strangers at a jam-packed luggage carousel?

And what difference would it make, anyways? Hey Dad! Why did you leave me? Guess what, I'm gay! How's life been treating you these last two decades? And by the way, fuck you!

Seeing his dad. What or who in the hell was he doing all this for?

For David?

Who was that? David didn't even know who he was anymore.

He thought about Elizabeth, he thought about his mom, he thought about his dad, he thought – you know – I'm just like him. I'm a miserable bastard. To myself. To my friends. To everyone around me. I use people then I disappear.

His life was breaking apart. David was shedding. All over the place. David was a reptile, a chameleon in the embarrassing and uncomfortable position of shedding layers of useless, brightly-colored skin in a very public manner. And for what? More useless, brightly-colored skin? What was it all for? Why was it all so painful? Who cared? Who wanted it? He wondered what happened when you shed the last layer and all that was left was a bleeding skeleton and strings of muscle and an extra wide smile.

What a pleasant thought. What a pleasant life. Sign me up for more, yes please.

Sunday 11:45 AM

A dull, steady booming jerked David awake. He sat bolt upright, his ears spun, his head spun, his eyeballs spun, - he was a fish in a fishbowl taking an unlikely ride on a dangerously unsafe rollercoaster. Ominous drumming on the inside of his head, in sync with an unfortunate and consistent, all-powerful hammering outside, coincided with the wild complaints of his stomach. Something apparently large and indigestible was sitting in there. He realized (with understandable panic) he had no idea where he was, how he got there, why he was there, and oh yeah, he was blind.

Not the most auspicious start, huh?

Shrill screaming to his lower right, which he identified after a few moments of agonized, slow-motion thought as a phone, prompted him to throw out his right arm spasmodically, raking it in clumsy circles across some flat surface near his head, (which accomplished nothing – he heard a tinkling, breaking sound exactly as if thin glass were hitting an unprotected marble floor). With his other arm and hand, he rubbed at his eyes trying to loosen up his puffy, gummed-shut eyelids and let a few illuminating photons in.

"Mr Hirscher, Mr Hirscher" a male voice floated in above the booming and ringing. At the same time, David felt the back of his right hand ricochet across some irregularities that felt suspiciously the way buttons would feel. He heard clicking, humming noises start up. It was at that point, David remembered later on, that all sorts of interesting things began to happen, all at once, all .in David's vicinity, all for David's benefit.

A blast of white-hot sunbeams – an admirably solid, permanent-looking block of light, deposited itself on the floor in a fair representation of an eruption of molten lava - fascinating in a kind of vomit-coaxing-inducing kind of way - burning oddly hip after-images of green, purple, and gold onto his retina. Apparently he wasn't blind.

This wasn't helping. Somewhere, someone had thought this an opportune time to crank up an Opera sung in a petulant and overly-confident Italian, and he became aware of a nude man, sprawled across a teardrop shaped white bed, on a teardrop shaped white platform under two gilded moose heads with white mink fur coats staring squint-eyed at him (balefully is how he would describe it later) from across a sea of the whitest carpeting he'd ever seen. And calling out to him by his last name too. That was odd – even by David's standards – as David was a person who's capacity for attracting oddness had increased logarithmically in the last few days.

Curtains were opening, tasteful, understated LCD lights were playing about him, a screen emerged out of a wall to his left and began to display something that looked suspiciously as if it were an invoice, and he noticed all the furniture in the room around him was moved towards the walls, away from floor-to-ceiling brushed chrome, tinted glass monstrous bay windows, windows that jutted (to David's discomfort – he hated heights) out over a precipice hundreds of feet high at least. As if it were the chin of Superman just asking for someone to take a jab at it and knock it off. Except, of course, he, David, was lying in the chin of this Superman. Well, within his head. Would that make sense? Would that make David the teeth? Within something, at least. He was in something, whatever that something was, and it was HIGH.

The nude guy looked back at him and continued to stare. Really impolite. So David stared back. He was young, a little thin, with jet black, spiky hair, green puffed-out eyes, bags under the puffs, bags under the bag, he didn't look too hot - well, to be honest, it was him, David, obviously, David in a mirror in someone's chin.

"Mr. Hirscher."

Someone was standing next to his bed now, a door was open, maids were looking in, carts were blocking the hallway, maids were looking away (whoops! naked man here!). He was momentarily disoriented, then realized he was having a conversation with a man in a suit, any number of women in uniforms, and he was sitting upright in a bed without blankets, dressed only in his tan (and he didn't have much of a tan at that).

With what he thought was great foresight and dignity, David carefully (his head was about to explode so he had to move very deliberately) gathered a white, fluffy duvet that was apparently his only covering (and also the only textile within reach) from a more distant pile of white on white coverlets, spreads and comforters folded in a neat pyramid under a nearby floor lamp. The duvet made him look as if he were being devoured by an oversized albino python, but he didn't care, and he laboriously wrapped and covered and tucked himself until he at least had the appearance of something approaching modesty.

After all the arranging and tucking, he tried to stand and turn in the direction of the be-suited voice, stepping down suddenly (and unexpectedly – his spinning, overinflated head made sure he understood how completely unexpected that step really was) and skidding to a stop on well-polished white marble. He maneuvered off the generous platform of stairs surrounding the oddly-shaped bed, waded and stumbled through the vigorous Italian singing, tried not to imagine he was giving an impression of a drunk Victorian lady in a particularly expansive wrap entering the glittering and crowded foyer of the Metropolitan Opera for a solid night of Tannhauser and gossip.

One gay experience and now he was doing drag. Just one. At this rate, what would he be doing by tomorrow night?

He'd had the strangest dream, that his dad had appeared out of nowhere on a Saturday night, that they'd driven to Las Vegas and spent a day and a night gambling, girls, lots of blackjack, poker, crazy late night talks, coffee shops (he wished he could remember it all more clearly, well, actually he wished he could remember any of it at all), clubs, dancing, more talking, more blackjack more alcohol, girls, boys (?) (that couldn't be right - could it?), and a lot of black suits and shiny square-toed black shoes and girls and blackjack and coffee shops and...

"Mr Hirscher."

The more he looked at the room, the bigger it got. He could see a staircase made of clear acrylic leading to a mysterious set of doors and a hallway. He could just make out another set of rooms beyond, suspended from the ceiling by huge nautical looking ropes tied in elaborate Japanese-like knots. That had to be the kitchen, although the slight asynchronous swaying of the refrigerator and the sinks and range were causing a sympathetic swaying in David's intestines that was threatening to turn first into a tumble, then gain momentum and result in a total collapse.

David looked away and made the mistake of peering left, across an expanse of white carpet and out through a brilliant wall of windows into the uninterrupted air again.

David hated heights – had he mentioned that already? – he

hated them with a personal, firmly-planted loathing that he cherished deep in his heart. There was no reason for heights. None. None that David could see. The only reason he'd gotten the apartment in San Diego on the third floor was because there were absolutely, positively no other cheap efficiencies available. That was the only reason. Well, and the fact, Michael helped him get the place. David moved a few cautious inches closer to the maids-and-carts side of the bed away from that Grand Canyon of steel and suspended glass towers stretching away from him towards the cactus-covered horizon. The endless, brightly optimistic wild blue yonder of what was apparently the sky of Las Vegas just outside his window beckoned him. Well it could go on beckoning. David wasn't coming. David wasn't interested.

"Mr Hirscher."

Was that even a window? Or was it just... open? David's insides did a few casual flip-flops, then some more serious ones, and David was anxiously scanning the immediate vicinity of the massive suite(?) for anything resembling a bathroom door.

He inched towards a likely door. There was a crowd of people between him and the door, but that wouldn't stop him. He was young. He was strong. He could do it. The blue sky blazed in.

There had to be glass didn't there? Weren't there laws about that? He didn't feel any hot, desert air blowing up at him, yet...

"Mr Hirscher or should I say Gutierrez?"

David looked up and over at the suit, sadly taking his attention away from the bathroom. He held his breath. Tried to think of something else other than his gastro-intestinal tract.

"There is a matter of thirty one days lodging, plus incidentals, also the required gratuities and various purchases charged to the room during the last month. I've left the bill on the desk by the door." There was something the size of a phone book sitting on the desk, printed on heavy stationery paper with a lot of small print and even more numbers on it. It was about 10 feet away. It glowed with a strange supernatural glow. It looked radioactive. It looked expensive. David didn't want to get any closer to it than he had to.

He bundled himself up a little tighter in his wrap and backed up towards the bed, keeping an eye on the suit and the maids, reaching and feeling his way behind him with his right hand, holding the fluffy white thing up to his chin with his left. He tried to smile, even laugh. He tried to look rich.

He was going to jail. Where was his dad now? Missing in action again. Typical. Well, typical David luck, huh?. What had he expected anyways? What?

Flailing about trying to find the bed, he pushed a couple of pillows off and smacked his hand into something heavy and oddly envelope-shaped. It was, surprisingly, an envelope. A heavily packed envelope With a note sticking out of the top.

O.K.

Now what?

The suit-voice broke in on his scattering thoughts, making sure David got none of them corralled and put into any kind of order. Apparently the suit was of the school: when in doubt, hyphenate. It worked for David.

"Sir, Mr. Hirscher-Gutierrez, I'm afraid check-out is in 5 minutes, and the credit card on file has been declined. Management would request your attention to the settlement of an outstanding balance of $43,627.18 and they ask you respectfully to find accommodation elsewhere as their efforts at contacting you these last two weeks have been so - let's just say unrewarding - for all parties involved. Understandably, they feel an amicable separation would be very much in both of our best interests, at this point. Mr. Hirscher-Gutierrez…"

"Mr. Hirscher-Gutierrez?"

But David wasn't listening. David was reading. The note was from his father. Short. Well, short-ish. A short-ish note from a long lost father that David couldn't ever remember.

> Davie –
>
> The money Davie, well, what can I say? What's in the envelope – it's all yours. Keep what's left after they squeeze the turnip, so to speak, it should get you by. I would say sorry for staying away so long and staying out of your life and your mother's, but you know what? You've turned out O.K., better than I'd hoped for.
>
> Sorry about your mother, I loved her, and she loved me, but sometimes, well, I'm not going to say that love is not enough, because,

you know son, it is. Love is always enough. I just thought I needed more than her love back when I was young and you were very young.

I was wrong.

And now for the inevitable fatherly advice – which is still my privilege. No, don't say anything. Just listen, and read on, all right? Good.

Life is like a car (yes, keep on reading David), some people buy it and spend all their time polishing it and changing the oil and planning trips but never go anywhere. They have a perfect car, in perfect repair, just in case of emergencies. And then they turn the car in for a new one. Other people buy one and use it up, driving from Niagara Falls to Cincinnati, to Seattle, to Alaska, to L.A. and St. Louis and the Yucatan and the Everglades. They get into trouble, they have accidents, they dent the car, they spend more money than they should have on it, and eventually, yes, they turn it in for a new one. But they have memories - blizzards on the Great Plains with only an 18-wheeler's tire tracks to guide them to safety, thunderstorms bursting on them in Death Valley and the valley doing its once-in-a-century blooming thing – and.. well... you get the picture, David. They've seen it. They've done it. They were there.

Yeah. They were there.

And Davie, it's possible to love honorably, and still love and live. It is.

Don't do what I did.

Look, just find out for yourself. Live your life. Use your life up. It is, David, in the end, your life to use. It's up to you what you make of it.

So...

You'll be seeing me soon (yes, you will, stop shaking your head)

Love (I mean it),

- Dad

Sunday 2:07 PM

David hurtled (at 60 mph) south, down I-15 towards San Diego and home, in his faded, beat-up and boxy '91 Corolla, which used to be silver, but was now a kind indeterminate, transparent color. He called her Cora — Cora Corolla. She wasn't a sprinter clearly, she was barely a marathon runner. But she did run if you asked her to. David was asking her to. She was running.

Shirtless, windows open and furnace-hot air blasting his hairy chest (David was kind of proud of his furry pecs — he got them from his dad, as he'd found out this weekend), David shifted around in his seat. He bit his lip, he thought about Elizabeth and Michael and his life. Nothing fit anymore. It was all random now. It was useless to try and get it to make sense. He tried to get his stubborn driver's seat to stop poking its sprung springs at him. That was a an absolutely useless struggle too. Shit.

Although… It was kind of comforting (he thought as he squirmed back and forth, left and right) to feel the lump of his dad's note, folded a couple of times, stuck in his wallet, and wedged deep within the one undamaged front pants pocket David still had left. It was also comforting to feel the pancake of Tobi's phone number in his back pocket, now crumpled in a wad, sandwiched between the cracked car seats of Cora and his uncomfortable rear end. Yeah, neither made much sense. But both of them were his. They were David's.

The two of them, they were a kind of set of bookends. They framed his future. Or his past. Or some shit like that. Maybe they didn't frame anything at all. Maybe David's life was wide open and frameless. David smiled to himself, grimaced as his brain sloshed unpleasantly and painfully in his skull, took a deep breath, did not think about his stomach, shifted into second gear, and braced himself to see if he and Cora could make it over the next punishing Mojave incline baking under the undiscriminating, desert sun.

UNTITLED #27

Howard glanced backwards, casually, walking to the front of the restaurant along the countertop, balancing three plates on each arm, and motioning to Etta in the back with his eyebrows to bring up the rest of the entrees for the 7 spot at the far end. In the process he nearly missed it, barely catching sight of it out of the corner of his left eye.

One tanned, well-manicured hand snaked across the mirror-bright nickel-onyx countertop Howard was currently walking on top of, detouring around the obstacles of a messily overturned wasabi plate and a psychedelically pink pile of wilting pickled ginger strewn over a considerable area. The hand accelerated directly towards Howard's left foot, preparatory for a surprise-attack grab at one of Howard's jet-black stiletto heels.

A bad move. A very bad move. This was not happening. Not again. Not tonight. Not to Howard.

Howard gauged where the white (now, soy-stained) cuff with the oversized cuff-link was attempting to intersect with his right foot, neatly swiveled one muscular calf 20 degrees counter clockwise and brought a steel-tipped high heel down with a murderous click that neatly impaled the wet and stained designer fabric on the counter and effectively halted the progress of the furtive guerrilla-hand.

"Now Dee…" said a bleary, sake-soaked voice below him, as a pair of slightly bloodshot (but still dreamy) blue-green eyes peered hopefully up in an unfocused attempt at innocence. Beneath it all, a wild mop of uber-glued blond hair, and a solid, substantial, square-shouldered frame sagged towards him. Howard always thought he looked Belgian for some reason.

"Shhh! Stop. Not another word, Randy. Not. Another. Word. And that's Lady Chick Chick a Dee Dee to you."

Randy continued to look up, smiling crookedly. Well, smiles, alternating with scowls and cursing, then smirks and joking. Except for a modicum more of irritability and jumpiness, it was all pretty much routine Randy. And Chick was tired of it. Especially tonight.

"Randy. Do you know how much pressure I can bring to bear with just one of these knife-point mothers? The weight of three elephants, you heard me, three, and we're not talking runts, we're talking bull elephants here. Google it and check the math yourself. I could press pennies out of copper with these heels, baby."

Howard started handing plates to Etta who had run to the middle of the restaurant in response to additional vehement eyebrow-summons.

"What do you think would have happened if I had aimed just two little inches to the right, huh? Sugar? What would've happened? What?"

Randy looked and stared blankly up at Howard, content to be getting so much attention, then realized he'd been asked a question and smiled because now he had something to do (for some reason he couldn't move his left hand anymore). Randy thought. Thought some more. Then, Randy frowned. He shook his head no. He didn't know.

"You'd have a one-sided stigmata, that's what you'd have, and…" But Randy wasn't listening - he was reaching up with his right hand (this cuff sans link) and moving it up and down Howard's right calf. "Stockings" he said over and over again, "silk stockings."

Howard directed a murderous (but useless), look downwards. It eventually turned, reluctantly, into a patient look. Randy always had that effect on him.

"I had them knit special for me in Bruges. The right leg is a scene of Lord Hill inviting the French Imperial Guard to surrender at Waterloo, the left is a scene of the Apotheosis of the Emperor Vespasian, that's him down by my heel, sighing that he is about to become a god."

Randy looked up at Howard for second or two blinking slowly. Then a few seconds longer.

"Vesp... Vespay... Vespash.."

"They're just fishnets, honey. Just black fishnets. Sometimes a stocking is just a stocking, darling. Randy we can't keep on doing this." Randy wasn't listening again, he was tugging at one of his soggy sleeves, trying to remember why it was stuck to the counter.

That's when Etta screamed.

David popped the top off a cold one, a sweating Flat Tire this time, and chugged for a full five seconds as he dropped in free fall in Howard's flat. He fell, or rather collapsed between the point he had been standing vertically by Howard's front door and the point he landed, stretching horizontally on Howard's dilapidated purple velour couch.

Lady Chick – not armored in drag this time - was the less combustible, more prosaic Howard tonight – slim (ish), tall, untamed, mousy brown hair, but compelling gray eyes – "like Athena" Howard liked to say. In another life, Howard had almost become a professor of Classical Studies, but that was another story for another time, muffins. It was midnight. Howard was too keyed up to sleep and full to bursting with news, and David liked to hear his stories, especially if beer were involved at some point.

An unquiet, rolling sound rattled briefly through Chick's small efficiency apartment. Neither of them paid it any attention.

So Howard talked. And David listened – asking sometimes serious, sometimes silly questions as he usually did, both of them pausing if they couldn't be heard over any low rumbling sound that echoed from time to time throughout the building. Some said it was a ghost. Some said it was a cheap, improperly installed HVAC system belching and violently burping, when it should have been humming and gently blowing. Most agreed it was annoying. Then, after a time, it was ignored - as best one could ignore a sort of low, thundering crescendo of a basket of bowling balls being released joyously in an upstairs hallway. Except, for Chick, and this was the truth, there *was* no upstairs hallway – being on the top floor of the Turquoise Desert Building already – which had been the Turquoise Desert Bar and Bowl at one time, but long, long ago. So maybe it was ghosts after all. Or maybe the consequence of lowest-cost contractor bidding. Or both. Or neither.

The sound hit again. They both paused in their conversation, not even realizing they were doing it anymore. Really, it wasn't even annoying. It just was.

"Child, you're going to lose your front teeth, sucking on a beer and doing back flips like you do. Just don't hurry those full, round lips off of that bottle neck too quickly, or you'll have beer overflowing all over my couch. Like last time. Like always. Are you listening to me, Mr. Hirscher? David?"

Sometimes to David, Howard sounded as if he'd just jumped off a showboat from some mythical Mississippi river town only found in Broadway musicals. Well, if people ever had come by showboat to San Diego from mythic Mississippi. Had they? Had boats left Gulfport or Biloxi by the score, making for the scrubby desert of San Diego in a mania for dry air and easy access to the Mexican border? David had only the faintest and most fleeting of grasps on the basic facts of history. Unlike Howard. David thought vagueness made life more mysterious. Howard thought it made life more idiotic. Each thought – to each his own. Which is why their relationship worked as well as it did.

Pondering modes of emigration, David continued to chug, waiting and watching Howard, arching his eyebrows almost into his spiky black hair, humming an expectant hum into his beer and making rapid round spinning/twirling motions with his free left hand (which he knew would drive Howard crazy), trying to get him to speed up and talk about the strange events in the life of Howard in the last couple of hours. David chugged, twirled and hummed, chugged, twirled and hummed. Chick finally gave in to the inevitable. He always did.

"All right, all right already, enough with the moaning and the ASL." David ceased all motion and sound, gratefully sank fully into each sagging cushion his body was touching, carefully disengaged his mouth from the bottle beforehand. A second later, beer came bubbling forth in imitation of an alcoholic Old Faithful, up, over the top, and frothing madly down onto his clean sweatshirt. Beer always did that to him. It was as if his shirts were beer magnets.

Trying to keep the beer bubbling onto him, and not onto the furniture, David whined upwards from a contorted position on the edge of the couch.

"Chick, I don't know. I just don't know how I do it. Really. All I do is…"

"It's a gift, Davie, a gift."

Howard interrupted to stop the traditional long explanation he had heard already from David many, many times in the past. Howard had the speech memorized. Word for word. He'd even typed it up and printed it out on a card, for David to use and possibly save himself and everybody else conversational time. It hadn't worked. David finished what was left of the bubbler and made an empty hand gesture pointing towards the kitchen to which Chick responded (after only a few second's hesitation, looking at his couch and the floor)

"In the Frig, the bottom drawer, sugar" and David disappeared for a second – a man on a mission. Chick looked upwards at the ceiling again, one slim but capable forefinger placed on his lips.

"Where to start…"

Howard wasn't sure exactly what had happened tonight - it had started out the same as any other busy night, with Howard observing the usual hypocrisy of humanity at very close range in the restaurant.

Howard (or rather Chick - black stockings, a minuscule, almost non-existent bombazine cocktail dress, and a top hat with an extravagant veil) watched Fumio, or rather Mr. Nakagawa (the name you used depended on exactly what quantity of trouble you were immersed in at any particular moment), her lord and master, co-owner of the Volvo Volcano, peering out over the top of his fingerprint-covered eyeglasses, straining to stretch his eyeballs over the sushi counter, across the entire restaurant, and catch his wife's eye thirty feet away at the cash register.

Clearly he was mumbling to himself - possibly more homemade

haiku, more likely Chargers-cursing as he listened to the broadcast of yet another losing football game (were they even playing tonight?), or (that was it, yes), Mr Nakagawa was talking to Rin Nakagawa, his wife, the Ice Lady, on the flashing Bluetooth stuck in his right ear. Or maybe not. Possibly. No. Well, for whatever reason, his lips were moving and small sounds were coming out rapidly out of his mouth in no particular direction.

The masters Nakagawa talked constantly on their headsets, for hours on end, back and forth – muttering spells under their breath and manipulating and weaving new destinies for those around them, all night, every night, for as long as Chick had known them. Chick figured, mostly, (knowing the Nakagawas) it was an ongoing monologue of Rin's, an endless list of Fumio's character flaws and his lack of business sense, punctuated by Fumio's closely reasoned rebuttals.

Howard noted with alarm a pause in the mumbling as two pairs of hostile boss-eyes swung in his direction - this was usually a good indication that the topic of conversation had changed to Chick himself. Well now, all right, probably the present would be a good time for the Lady Chick Chick a Dee Dee to get her lazy behind back to work, and hit that runway and be the loyal, sushi-serving fool she'd always been and could yet still be for the rest of the night.

And by the by, just where the heck was Herr Georg? (pronounced Gay-org – he was a German from Deutschland), who usually came dressed as a penny-pinching vampiress? Georg – also called Lemon Joose because of an elaborate joke having to do with disappearing ink - it probably sounded a lot more hilarious in his native language – anywho, the punchline was Zit-something in German, and yet another name stuck to him - Zit. So, yes, Zit-Goerg-Lemon Joose rejoiced in his many monikers often and with great energy, but sadly, tonight, Zit and all of his names were missing in action. And Chick was not happy. Being down one person would make this Friday night into a Night of Horrors for the rest of them. It would be complaints and catch-up and sparse tips the whole shift. That girl should have been here already, strutting her many-splendored, multiply-named Teutonic stuff ages ago.

The Volvo Volcano (or as it was affectionately known to its employees – the Vulva) was a strangely tall, thin rectangular space (it had once been an electrical substation back in the 20's, you could still see where they had bolted the transformers to the floor by the front doors). It had paneled floors, walls, and ceilings done in a fuzzy Lucite, backlit and pulsing with buzzing celestial waves of various shades of whitish, grayish light. Can you say "trendy?" The ceiling was a circus tent in shades of muddy beige and rusty blood-red. One of the narrow sides had the front-end of a 1990 Volvo 740 4-door Sedan (gray/white of course) protruding from the wall, the Volvo doors were flattened out underneath, as if they were wainscoting, and moderately priced sushi appeared out of the rolled down car windows at frequent intervals. That was the front end of the hors d'oeuvre and appetizer machine that was the Vulva.

In back of the front end, was, surprisingly, the back end. You went through a narrow hallway to the right of the Volvo doors, and were (progressively) ushered through four swinging doors: first, one to the kitchen, then one to the storeroom/dishwashing room, then third to a unisex and very compact (one of the tiniest rooms Chick had ever seen) bathroom, and fourthly and finally (if you were keeping count) a heavy metal door at the very end which opened directly out of the bathroom onto a triste looking back alley with a strong but familiar smell of old urine and decaying grease of unspecified origin. The back alley door, by the way, was a door that Chick had never found unlocked - how trash exited, or food entered the restaurant, she had no clue, and really, if pressed, she had no desire to know.

Back inside, flowing out from the mashed wall of the Volvo was a sinister, meandering rough black counter - a solidified tube of lava - which looped and twisted and curled the length of the entire floor, providing the only seating/tabling for guests, and having a dark sidewalk set down the center from beginning to end. Various pieces of what had to be other Volvos protruded up from the floor, out from the ceiling and were embedded in a melancholy fashion directly into the counter.

At times, projections of angry flames played menacingly on the bottom half of the Lucite walls, in time to a disconcertingly slow rendition of classical Balinese and/or Gamelan gongs, wind chimes, and brass cymbals and a mournfully hesitant House beat.

It could take some getting used to. Maybe it was an acquired taste. But Chick hardly noticed any of it anymore.

The part everyone noticed right from the start were the girls (as it should be, thought Chick). Drag queens walking down the counter, serving and taking orders – that made the place. Chick (Lady Dee) was usually very aware of them (besides the fact she was one of them), because these people could either make her life each night a paradise of mutually helpful, friendly foodservice labor or an orgy of hellish, catty, bitchy backstabbing. Sometimes it was hard to tell which was which, what with all the bitchy help and backstabbing friendliness. But it was home.

So. Back to her night.

Tonight, she had perused her fellow employees, standing on the runway, viewing the night's crowd so far. Putting her finger up to her pursed and pondering lips, (pursed was a good look for her, she had to admit it was true – she did it as often as she could get away with it) Lady Dee had tried to predict which kind of night this night would be

Hmmm… Let's see… The augurs looked good. It looked to be a decent tipping night, possibly low in the diva drama department for a change, which would be welcome. But, oh! Man-o-man Davie! Did the Lady Chick get it wrong tonight, baby. Not something she is comfortable admitting in public, either, just so you know. But there it is. Lady Chick made a mistake.

David hummed sympathetically upwards at Howard from a fresh Flat Tire he'd snagged from the kitchen a moment before. He thought the humming might be encouraging to her. In the narrative sense. He wasn't too far wrong.

Howard had frowned at David (wondering if he was paying proper attention to his beer and his foaming tendencies)(he was), but, as usual, the boy hadn't caught the frown, so it went wide and winged its way right out the window, lost in the sultry San Diego night. Howard rolled his eyes (which David also missed), clicked his tongue (really, why did he even try?) and continued telling his story. David thrummed and listened, alternately.

Howard began with his usual Review of the Ladies of the Night. Hi Fi, Rustie Naille, Pedro One and Pedro Two, Jose, Monica, Etta, everyone was there in their usual inimitable form.

Hi Fi – also known by some, principally his mother, as Thomas – showed up in a new platinum blond wig which resembled a small, run-over hubcap. Chick was not impressed. But before he could bring the subject up properly, Rustie Naille – known on his birth certificate and to the DMV as Stephen – whipped out a larger version of the same platinum hubcap hair out of thin air as soon as he arrived and the two of them (Hi Fi and Rustie) were off and running, loudly discussing each other's character traits - as usual – with anyone who would listen.

They started in the front, worked their way to the back by the locked door to the alley, and then fought (walking backwards) through three doorways to the front doors again. For a small restaurant it had a surprising echo. Chick knew if it wasn't corsets, it would be lipstick, if it wasn't lipstick it had to be shoes, tonight apparently was wig night. Eyes flashing, hands waving, as former lovers (very former) they knew all the weak chinks in each other's armor, and they pried them open every night as often as they could.

Chick called them the Evil Aryan Twins. They hated that.

But what could Chick do? It was the truth.

Then there was Pedro One and Pedro Two (rechristened Pedruno and Pedrotro by Hi Fi – Hi Fi who spoke a unique form of broken Spanish that invariably caused all kinds of unfortunate misunderstandings among Spanish-speakers, some funny, others, well, not so funny sometimes. Well, both Pedros, the two tight-shirted Mexican busboys, pretended to be busy cleaning and re-cleaning an already sparkling section of black, shining, lava-tube countertop, as Chick wandered in off the street, early as was his custom. The Pedros worked hard, Chick had to admit it, yes, but you had to watch them. Why? They liked to play games, and their favorite game pieces were the Ladies. In brief, they started tip-wars amongst the servers – vigorously helping one while neglecting the others. The resulting maelstrom often sucked Chick into its all-consuming vortex of Diva Passion, no matter how he struggled to stay free of it. It had happened last night. Chick was damned if it was going to happen again tonight.

Then there was Jose. Living in a world of steam and water and thundering dishwashing closets, the perpetually moist dishwasher, Jose was nowhere to be seen for once that night, undoubtedly busy in the back scrubbing - a crazy goal - trying to get a little ahead of the early dinner rush. Usually before opening again for dinner, Jose liked to hang around the front, seeing everyone enter and arrive, each server passing into the Vulva as if descending the gangplank from the Queen Mary after a grueling transatlantic voyage.

Yes, Chick admitted it, there was dramatic potential in one's entrance to the Vulva. Jose was there to see it. He would lean against the wall. Standing. Observing. Looking. As if he were watching his usual afternoon cable show. You know, Chick liked Jose. He listened, he never interrupted, and he never talked about himself. He was very attentive. Quiet. A gentleman. Or maybe Jose just didn't understand all that much English. Regardless, Lady Chick a Dee Dee had decided for herself a long, long time ago, she approved of this one. He was a keeper, as dishwashers go, and as men go. Men should be seen, and not heard.

The grande dame of the Vulva was "elderly" Monica - Mon Kay Glande (known to the world as Daniel) and he was just coming on shift at the same time as Chick, when Chick pushed the heavy front door open a crack and proudly insinuated himself in after him. Monica of course stopped abruptly, looking in his large man-purse, and Chick ran straight into his backside. Monica did not deign to notice. Monica, well, he was indeed a trip, in fact he was any number of trips. Chick was not going to mix it up with the venerable and vicious Glande again tonight. Monica would have to exercise her considerable and expert verbal surgical skills on new patients this shift. Chick had had it, and had enough, for two nights running. Respect for the aged can only go so far.

And then there was Etta.

Etta, dear, hardworking Etta Horse (as in "so hungry I could'da")(Ralph), a rather big-boned girl, and a little touchy about it, but by far the best server in the Vulva, had two huge parties she was dealing with already tonight from a late afternoon rush earlier. A third one (was that a bachelor party? Chick would probably end up having to help her out with that one – damn! drunk young men, either heaven or hell), yes, there was a third one, and they all looked to be angling to sit in poor Etta's section, so Chick had started out his night as a runner. After the first hour, Chick's section was still almost completely empty. Barren. A wasteland. It didn't look like it was going to be his night tonight. Damn. And double damn.

Rin the merciless (previously introduced - one of the whispering owners) was the hostess and cashier. As fierce and loud as she was with the help, she was quiet, shy and retiring at the cash register. Rin could never remember in whose section she had seated the last herd of customers, especially when they pounded towards her, as they liked to do, piling in one on top of the other as would large groupings of thirst-crazed Wildebeest scenting water for the first time on the dry and dusty plains of the Serengeti at the hind end of a particularly nasty dry season. They would throw their emaciated, thirsty bodies fiercely at Rin and stampede. Rin would vaguely motion in a pathetic attempt at self-defense to the entire restaurant with some menus she held in front of her - a shield - and let the guest-chips fall where they may, which meant, of course, pretty much anywhere.

Random seating. Chick and the ladies would pick up the pieces. It worked. Mostly. Well, not really. It was hell, if you really wanted to know the truth. Not the seventh ring of hell, but something quite close to it, location-wise. You had to admit though, it kept the nights interesting.

Zit, the last of the Ladies was missing in action that night. Zit was late. Had Howard already mentioned that? Howard paused, David made a non-committal hum into his beer and shrugged his shoulders, Howard looked at the ceiling and counted to five. Yes he had already mentioned that, David. Did David remember? David nodded, a little unconvincingly, a trifle uncoordinated, it was after all, the child's third beer. Howard sighed. Manfully sucked in a large amount of air. He ploughed on.

Zit was late, very late.

Something was wrong. Chick could feel it, a tingling in the tips of his fingers and (he would never admit this to anyone except David) he felt it in his nipples. His nipples never lied. Zit was the most punctual German Chick had ever met and that was saying a lot.

The funny thing was, Chick had found himself wondering what exceedingly reasonable argument Zit (he was mind-numbingly rational as well as punctual) would construct to explain his leaving all his coworkers in the lurch that night. It was going to have to be a good one. He and everyone else knew what Chick knew - it was going to be a wildly busy Friday night (there were three conventions in town including the Shriners, and some kind of Naval maneuvers in progress, and – what the hell - Comicon was starting next Thursday). It was big. Very big. The market for raw fish delivered by scantily-clad men would be unbelievable in the next few days. Chick was ruminating on Zit and his arguments in fact, just as Randy was grabbing futilely at Chick's footwear. At that moment Etta bellowed plaintively for help from the back of the restaurant. Chick scowled.

Zit agonized over cause and effect. He had an exact calculus of maximizing pleasure and minimizing pain continuously operating with clockwork efficiency under that methodically shaved head of his, behind those deceptively mild, blue eyes, over his pair of curious, thin, compressed lips Nothing was left to chance. Even when he showed up, rarely, under Marlene Dietrich curls (Marlene, Zit often said, by the way, was not nearly so racy in German as she was in English proving once again that Americans live in a pathologically fantastic, lust-driven world of their own choosing), yes, even as the divine Marlene, Zit was more daunting than dashing. Chick had to admit Zit was formidable. The effect was even greater when he sported a beehive. He made you want to sit back down and re-examine your life-decisions right then and there, as soon as you saw him glancing in a calculating way in your direction. He oozed clarity. He radiated willpower. And for some reason he seemed to get a lot of tips. Consumer guilt? Gestalt confusion? Weltanschauung shame? Who knew? It worked. Whatever it was. He should have been a cult leader.

The rub, the real difficulty with being around Zit was that his pleasure-mathematics hardly ever took into account any other person's pleasure/pain but his own. Never, in fact. If he could move some pain onto the people around him, without increasing his own, so much the better. In heaven's name why the hell not? Who wouldn't do the same if he were in his shoes? Act don't analyze, get yours while the getting's good. That was Zit's categorical imperative.

And Zit was infuriating to argue with. He always won. Why would someone willingly choose pain, for the uncertain hope that someone else's pleasure might increase? Why make the effort? Why even try? By the time Zit was done with you, you were pushing old ladies in front of busses as a matter of course in order to cross an intersection ten seconds faster.

But back to the scream.

Chick did mention the scream, didn't he?

Yes. Well. There was a scream. It was Etta. Chick and everyone else (even Randy) had all huddled around the storeroom/dishwashing room door, trying to get a clear view around Etta's rather large, and now sopping, light-blocking silhouette. Steam was everywhere. Etta was nervously bunching and un-bunching her tiny, bulging signature leather purse, the purse she usually had swinging from her clothes (well, pinned, so that she could wait tables – you had to see it – it actually looked very pert and cute the way she inserted it cleverly into her the flowers spreading graciously over her ample cleavage). The famous purse was no longer gracing her blue-black ruffled push-up top (she was going to ruin that purse if she kept that up, the ruffled top was, unfortunately, a wet disaster already). No, the purse in her anxious hands was now a twisted mess, resembling a well-loved chew toy an obsessive-compulsive terrier might have been gnawing on for many a contented hour and only recently, reluctantly, released.

But back to the dishwashing room.

Chick could see Etta staring in confusion at Zit's torso, arms, and legs. That was all you could see. His head was buried in a steel tub, overflowing with greasy suds and oily water. His tie (he was Marlene as a man tonight) was wrapped around one of the rollers of the washer's conveyor belt. It had dragged him in. Zit wasn't moving. Chick couldn't get over the fact that you couldn't see his head. The tub was sunk into the counter in front of a noisy conveyor belt on an ancient, arthritic dishwashing machine (still running with squeals and grinding jerks, its gears unmeshing suicidally, shaking itself into oblivion).

Chick remembered (irrelevantly) the day the Nakagawas had bought that same dishwashing machine - second-hand for Jose's predecessor to speed up the overall sushi plate turnaround. It had been (on the face of it) cheaper than buying additional new plates, probably because there would've been no place to store them, except maybe on the roof. The machine took up almost the entire room as it was. Now Zit's body was draped across the dishwashing counter, as if he'd been overly inquisitive, crawling on all fours to puzzle out the machine's operation and had stopped along the way to wash his hair first.

Jose was nowhere to be seen

It wasn't until later someone thought to ask where Jose might have been. But to no avail, Jose had simply disappeared. He hadn't ever re-appeared - at least to Chick's knowledge - and Chick sympathized with him on this one, entirely. Explaining yourself to agents from La Migra were one thing, explaining yourself to detectives from Homicide would be another thing entirely, altogether. Only a madman would do both at the same time.

Unlike Jose, everyone else was stuck there for hours.

Periodically answering questions, anxiously watching each other, generally excited, annoyed, and angry and sad, they waited and fretted and cried and complained. Zit was dead. Between police interviews. Rin and Fumio kept to themselves mostly. Randy was talking (or slurring) at Ms Glande who was pointing to Etta who was absolutely tearing what little was left of her little purse apart - so tightly was she twisting and wringing, twisting and wringing. Etta must have completely and absolutely lost it. The purse and her emotional balance, that is. Which was odd, wasn't it? Later Chick found the purse empty, torn and abandoned on the floor as he was being called forward to the cash register area to be questioned. He gave it back to Etta, who promptly collapsed again and melted into a crying heap. From out of nowhere she was wearing a long gray raincoat. It was wet. She was wet. But it wasn't raining outside. Oddness trailed Etta that night.

The Evil Aryan Twins (Hi and Rustie - whom Chick had passed on the way up to the Official Inquisition during the long journey to the cash register) were gliding slowly back into the main room after their little individual tete-a-tetes with the detectives. Both Hi and Rustie were looking a trifle grim, Chick thought, a little too preoccupied if you asked him.

Ms. Monica Glande attempted a smug look of self-satisfaction (unsuccessfully, Chick might add), and was holding something (knowing her, probably her tips in ones and fives) firmly in one fist. The other fist held (with a white-knuckled, grip of death) a semi-hidden, nearly full bottle of Tequila, not the bright amber well Tequila (Chick called it Instant Headache in a Bottle), but a nearly colorless bottle in the shape of a stallion's head that usually sat in regal solitude on the topmost backlit shelf, graced with its own spotlight, noble, unattainable, high above and behind the main bar and its more plebian alcohol.

Now, why would the owners Rin and Fumio have given him that? Hmmm…

Chick made a mental note to visit Monica, the matriarchal Glande, if the bottle was still out and about after Chick's upcoming official grilling was over and done with. By then Chick'd need a drink, right? But, of course, Chick never got the chance.

On emerging from his close encounter with the police, which was relatively short, painless, and uneventful (why was it so easy?

very suspicious) suddenly it was all over.

Ambulance gone, police gone, Zit gone, everyone scattered into the night, Rin was locking up and disappearing last of all. He pushed Chick out, shaking his head, no, he didn't want to talk. Chick was left with his mouth open. Baffled. Tired. Thirsty. And the evening was young. Not a position Chick was used to being in. Not a comfortable position for him at all. He stumbled out onto the sidewalk and headed east into this City of Night.

Thomas (Rustie Naille) walked ahead of him, ambling down the boulevard. He appeared out of the gloom, his metal dress shining in pinpoints as would a starry constellation. He flashed brightly and proudly in all directions whenever he walked underneath a pink-orange cone of streetlight. Chick had to admit, it worked for Thomas. He glowed. With celestial magnificence. Thomas would blaze under a sodium lamp, then, Thomas would disappear, sinking back into mystifying blue-purple darkness as he hit yet another stretch of shadowy sidewalk. It was hypnotizing to watch.

Yes. It was theater. Effective and engaging. Flashing and sinking, Chick watched Thomas make his way up the street. Sometimes walking fast. Sometimes walking slow. And then, Chick realized. Thomas was watching someone else. Thomas was following someone. But who? Chick peered more closely into the dark avenues ahead.

Thomas was following Randy. The dear, drunk man with the wandering hands and the deep, deep, blue eyes. And Randy wasn't walking home, either was he? He seemed to be heading back towards that tiny Pawn Shop on the next block (which wasn't unusual, Randy owned the shop, after all, Randy was, as Randy put it - a part-time pawn broker – a full-time Diva Worshipper). So Randy was going to work.

Hmmm…

It appeared, to Chick, that Thomas was walking a trifle more soberly than he usually would at that time of night, bright blond wig perfectly vertical on his head, steps firm and deliberate, head held confidently erect. He seemed very - what? – aware, that's how he seemed. All of Thomas's antennae were out and tingling.

And it did seem a tad late on a Friday night for Randy to be weighing gold chains and dispensing twenties – of course, every server at the Vulva had, at one time or another, used Randy's services to help out between paychecks – Chick included, but, still, it was a very odd hour to be doing it, just now.

Maybe someone needed a quick financial tide-me-over. What a hard worker Randy was! He had a gorgeous body and an even more gorgeous working ethic. Husband material if there ever was one. In fact, speaking of tide-me-overs, Chick, could've used a tide-me-over this very minute. He was, at the moment, as they say, financially embarrassed. Rent was coming up, quick. He had a shit-load of sequins and rhinestones on layaway. Lots of forgotten things were begging for attention. Repeatedly. In a snarling tone of voice that was difficult to ignore. Fortunately, Chick was good at not hearing what he didn't want to hear. Unfortunately, Chick couldn't think of a single thing he possessed that Randy would be interested in lending him money for on the spur of the moment. Not one. Sigh.

Well, there was his refrigerator. Could Howard borrow it for a bit? Would his landlord notice? Would his landlord care? Even if it was technically owned by his landlord?

Hmm…

Well. No. Not this time. Maybe another time.

Randy disappeared around a corner. Thomas disappeared after him.

You know, Thomas was a dear, and he was stable, and he was financially secure – so of course, Chick wasn't interested in him at all. There was nothing going on in the romance department for Chick and Thomas. No electricity there. No sparks. No Disney-level fireworks. Nada. Nothing. Zilch. Friendship, alas, was all there was. That, and only that.

Randy, well, that man was another matter entirely.

Unfortunately.

Cue the expressive sigh.

Yes, it was complicated. Wasn't everything? At least all the good things are, aren't they? But back to Thomas.

Chick and Thomas were at an impasse. Chick knew that Thomas had obviously already taken the tumble for Chick. Thomas wanted Chick and Chick did not want Thomas. It did not make for a good working relationship, at the Vulva every night. It made for a hair-raising relationship, sometimes literally.

It had been the story of Chick's life. Someday, Chick would be mooning over Thomas, with sad puppy eyes and Thomas wouldn't remember Chick's name, even if he were staring straight into those sad, brown Chick irises with a magnifying glass.

Yes, as with so much in life, it's timing. It's always in the timing.

But back to Zit, the dead man.

It was odd, and in a way beautiful, thinking back to the dishwashing room. Yes, dishwashers and dishwashing could be beautiful. Don't be a snob. Immediately after Etta had found the defunct George-Zit, Chick remembered it as being preternaturally quiet. A kind of meditative motionlessness, despite the machine crying and rattling itself apart. There was a stillness there, a dewy hush.

No one had said anything. No one knew what to say. Then a soothing voice, unlike one Chick had ever heard before at the Vulva washed over the sweating, sobbing, wilting (Chick had to admit to it) bodies packed into the narrow back hallway. It was Fumio, talking on his Bluetooth calling the police, with the calm voice of a Buddhist monk patiently explaining (or not explaining as the case may be with a Buddhist) an opaque koan to an even opaquer acolyte. Fumio didn't have his usual caustic whine. He didn't have the bumbling hesitation of a small business owner reporting the brutal murder of one of his employees. He was soothing. He was harmonious. It surprised Chick. It surprised them all.

Then Chick was surprised that he was surprised. And that surprise caused more surprise. Surprise cubed. Then squared again. A strange feeling. But pleasurable.

It was actually good to find gentleness where you expected none.

Chick paused.

David peered.

Chick stopped for quite a while. His hand was in mid-reach for the frig. David waited, sitting on the edge of his sofa cushions. David slurped what was left of his beer. Slurped some more. Waited some more. He didn't know if it would be polite to talk to Chick just now. He didn't know if it would be polite just to stare at Chick while Chick stared at the refrigerator. Eventually he ran out of beer.

"So, Dee, You think Jose did it?

Chick gave him an odd look. Very odd. David tried to look innocent and non-threatening. He yawned. He shifted his beer-stained torso to one side as his cell phone vibrated and chirped out a sad, romantic ditty and he looked up at Chick in a harassed but stoic kind of way as if to say - I'll let it go, if you say so, I wouldn't mind if you did, whatever you want, Chick.

"Go ahead, lover" Chick shook his head, shook himself out of his trance, and treated himself to a Manhattan (what a night!). He pulled a chilled glass out of his refrigerator (yes, the refrigerator was definitely too big to get down the stairs, even with two people), but lacked vermouth and bitters. And whiskey. Oh well. He did have maraschino cherries. And Tequila.

He had a shot, then another. They went down too easily, too fast and they didn't begin to stop the inevitable questions (why? where? how? - Chick was starting to sound as if he were writing dialogue in a low-budget, made-for-cable movie). Actually Chick needed to get ready for bed. Baby was tired with a capital B and a capital T. It had been a big, long day. Time to put an end to it.

He'd thought he'd try and give dear David a little privacy, David often got these complicated phone calls, it was the least Chick could do. Coming out is never easy, is it? Although, Chick could not remember a time when he wasn't entirely himself - out and fierce, everywhere he went.

David obviously saw Chick returning, and climbed over and behind the couch. Privacy was apparently called for. David was whispering furiously. A difficult compromise was being forged. Sipping rather than tossing his next tumbler of Tequila, Chick had to bite his lip and think. Had he ever been that young?

No. He hadn't.

Exasperated David-sounds shot upwards and bounced off the ceiling from behind the couch. The bubbling and murmuring hit a crescendo and broke. A rebellious silence reigned. David did not re-appear from behind the couch, not right away.

The poor dear.

Chick waited for a moment, looked down at his scarred, blond wood floor (which always looked suspiciously to Chick as if people in ugly shoes had rolled heavy balls down it for many decades and perhaps they really had) and wondered. The Tequila actually helped the wondering.

Who would hate Zit enough to drown him in soap suds? Certainly not Jose, Jose never spoke to anybody, ever. Never to his fellow employees at the Vulva. Quiet and gentle, Jose could not, he would not, raise his voice (or his dishwashing machine) in anger.

Zit could hardly have offended Jose, could he? If Jose had been angry, how could such a diminutive, well-behaved young man have manhandled the Zit? You'd have to be pretty strong to get that bundle of wiry musculature that was Zit near the machine long enough to get him caught in it, and stuck in it, and asphyxiated in it, all at one time. Only a gymnast-contortionist-sociopath would be capable of doing all that. Certainly not anyone working at the Vulva?

Yes, you'd have to be strong to hold him down. Strong and tall. Yet it was supposed to appear as if it were an accident wasn't it? Wasn't it? He'd have to think about this tomorrow. Something wasn't right. Something didn't add up. But he'd be up all night thinking about those somethings unless he thought about some something else soon.

Chick shimmied back into the kitchen, and poured a little more Tequila into his "Manhattan." Then he realized it wasn't Tequila, it was Gin. Then he realized that the bottom of his (extra-large) shot glass (O.K. it was a wine glass) was littered, absolutely covered in half-bitten cherries. That gave pause for thought.

Chick added an extra maraschino cherry, for luck, then another one, for more luck, with a satisfying plopping sound. He spied an empty Tequila bottle, no it was the missing whiskey bottle, peeking its head out of the trash under the sink and thought - how *did* they drip that wax so elegantly on each and every bottle? What a strange job that would be – wax dripper – where would you get the training? He dropped another cherry in his glass. Gin slopped over the sides.

But everything was done by machine nowadays. Wax dripping. Conversations. Dishwashing. Even killing. David's voice rose up again in a grumpy. self-defending, moaning sob from behind the indistinct purple shadow of Chick's couch. The back of the couch faced Chick's miniature hallway. There was a pink bean bag chair resting in the hallway, behind the couch. Chick thought he could just about hear the sound of tiny kernels of Styrofoam squeaking and complaining as David shifted mountains of them here and there trying to get comfortable and help him think and maneuver his way through his amorous pacts/accords/treaties/ententes more clearly. It wasn't working.

Getting comfortable. That's always the trick, isn't it?

Just then, comfortable sounds resembling goodbyes swam in

the lazy evening air from behind the couch cushions. Always a good sign, for David and his intricate conversations, something was possibly going David's way for once. Chick was provisionally happy for David. He sipped some more. His eyelids drooped. Chick really needed seriously to hit the hay.

Outside it was getting colder, the buzzing of traffic, muffled and unclear. You could smell fog unfurling itself over the city. Yes, it was getting late. Chick sipped and sipped, nibbled on his cherries, cocked his head, nodded his gratification and enjoyment, then shook his head (again) ruefully at the confused young man behind his couch a few feet away from him. Desperation and retreat hung on his every word.

So much living to do.

Then it was quiet.

Chick waited a moment or two after silence fell again.

Still no David jumping up from the sofa's far side. It was getting pretty calm back there. Chick knew what to do. He popped a beer and left it cradled on the sofa arm a few feet away from the rustling of the bean bag chair. Then he sat back to wait.

Chick had known David for only a couple of months, but from the look of it, David and his girlfriend were involved, pretty much without interruption, in a series of delicate negotiations that got more and more detailed as the days wore on. Chick had to smile, he didn't know where David got the stamina.

David was negotiating just as hard with a new boyfriend he'd just met too. His name was James, although Chick had never met him, or heard his voice, or even seen his picture. David was being a little secretive. Which was fine, really. Everyone deserves a secret. Or secrets. Tonight it was the boyfriend's turn apparently, for emotional wrestling matches.

David thought if he just talked enough, long and hard, to everyone around him, all the time, without stopping, that everyone would finally understand him and give him the break he so richly deserved. That wasn't Chick's experience, especially when you're just coming out, but hey, Master Hirscher (as Chick liked to call David) wasn't asking Chick's opinion, and he apparently wanted to live a very complicated life. Chick made a quick trip to the little girl's room, adjusting the untouched beer resting on the sofa on his way out so it wouldn't get knocked onto the floor.

More power to him. He'd learn. Boy would he learn. When

Chick returned, the beer bottle was gone. A few seconds later, a frowning David draped himself over the back of the couch and started talking, long and hard, as expected. Chick slipped out to get more refreshments, making all the appreciative noises he could at all the appropriate intervals. David had forgotten all about Zit and Jose and murder and mystery. All David could talk about was another word beginning with "m".

As Chick slid back into the living room area with his glass half-full, he entered with a properly receptive expression on his face. So our little Davie was off and running. As usual. David worried and fretted, picked at and pulled on everyone else's unreasonableness. He was trying to make everyone come out happy, all at the same time, including himself, and it wasn't coming easy. In fact, it wasn't coming at all.

Although Chick was dead on his feet and had heard this rant on many occasions before, and could barely keep even one eye open at a time, he braced himself against a sturdy wall, squinched his shoulder blades, raised his drink, smiled and tilted his head in attentiveness. David wound himself up and let loose.

What was it with monogamy? Why the fetish about exclusive relationships? What ever happened to love? Chick briefly exited, to return wearing a stunning silk lounging robe with a tiny cape done in a gold on blue print based on ceiling plasterwork found in the Petit Trianon in Versailles. Chick yawned once or twice. David hardly noticed.

Where was the trust? Why were people so strange? Why didn't anyone understand me? Chick listened, nodded, listened and pulled on another small loveseat sitting opposite the sofa and out popped a neatly made bed, white and blue polka dot sheets and a matching queen-sized pillow and pillowcase on one end.

This time David got the hint, visibly pulled back, simmered down, then came to a full and complete stop. Chick went out, wordlessly, to get another pillow, leaving David staring into a corner of the ceiling, biting his lips, running one hand through his cow-licked, messy brown hair, and trying to work out, painfully, in his head, some complex calculus of love involving rights and responsibilities.

He was so cute.

When Chick returned, David was a limp body, an open mouth drooling just a little, a slow and steady, heavy breathing that was making even Chick sleepy listening to it, and he was beautiful. It's hard not to be beautiful when you're in your early twenties. You'd have to work really hard at it not to be. David was something. In a mixed-up, young-man, self-absorbed kind of way that is, yes, he was a formidable something.

Hmmm... But what exactly was David? What kind of something? Obviously, a work in progress kind of something. In the uncomfortable position of realizing he wasn't what he used to be, and wasn't yet what he would be. Well, aren't we all?

Chick plumped the extra pillow, punched it deftly beneath David's wild hair, and smoothed it out. Chick turned off the lights.

Tucking a blanket around the unconscious form in the darkened room Chick tilted his head and brought a slim hand up to cover his rueful, tightly closed mouth. Yes, Chick had a lot he could say to David. Chick had a lot of stories he could tell. But David hadn't ever asked, so Chick hadn't ever told. And Chick wouldn't start telling. No he wouldn't. Not yet. He smiled and frowned at the same time, cocked his head a little more and watched David drool for a second.

They always look so innocent when they're asleep.

Yes, David would ask Chick someday. When he was ready. And Chick would tell him. Yes, Chick would tell him. He'd tell him everything.

Which would be... what?

Classic gloves like classic automobiles should either be black or white? High heels can never be too high? A tan and a large hat cover a multitude of sins? Well, yes. All of that. And... possibly... Rely on yourself, Go with what you know. Believe only what you see. People will lie, cheat and steal to get what they want. People will let you down, yes they will, just when you need them the most, every time. When it got right down to it, the only thing you had at the end of the day was you. Your very own self. That's who you had an 'exclusive' relationship with – that's who you were monogamous with – you, yourself, and yourself alone.

O.K. That's what he'd say.

No that's not what he'd say.

Was that it? Bitterness and anger. Anger and bitterness. Was that all? Of course it was. And of course it wasn't.

Actually Chick just didn't know for sure anymore. Who did know, really? Only fools were absolutely sure of anything. Only a fool refused to learn.

Yes, too true, that. But not being sure wasn't something Chick was going to tell a single other living person about for quite some time yet. Chick was no patsy. Chick's mother didn't raise any fools.

Maybe Chick wasn't as convinced today of the horror of the world as he had been yesterday, or had been even last week (or last month, or last year for that matter). The older he got, the softer he got. It was frightening. It was strange. It was life. Chick was just a chocolate bar melting in its wrapper in the hot summer sun on a long summer's day. At some point, the day would be over and so would Chick. His destiny – to be a puddle.

And yes, soft was dangerous. For a draq queen. For a gay man. For anyone barely scraping by, for anyone trying to make a living in this city - a city which, frankly, didn't give a damn – for anyone looking for a little love along the way. And now, sweet, opinionated things such as David were sleeping, blissful and content on Chick's couch, buttoned up and snug in the knowledge that Chick's crib was a place of safety. They lived happier lives, knowing Chick could be counted on to be their guiding light and their strong shoulder when the going got rough at any point in their young futures.

And the going would get rough. Chick knew that – it always did get rough, didn't it? – Chick knew that all too very well.

Oh, if only David knew. Chick had a strange impulse to shake him by the shoulders and wake his sleepy self up and tell David everything - what the world is really like, and how lonely a person could get, and what it felt like to lose your way, lose your dreams, and how many times…

Oh, give it a rest girl. Let the boy sleep, Chick. Let it go.

Yes, the gentleness was gaining on Chick. It would overwhelm him at some point, dissolving his resolve, inch by painful inch, till all the bitterness and anger were just sharp-edged holes in him and Chick was left totally unprotected. A sitting duck. For the next crazy. Chick shook his head. And that was O.K. too. The way Chick was starting to figure it, if you had to go, gentleness was a great way to do it.

He closed the blinds, the light from the streetlight outside faded into thin pinkish bars of horizontal light scratched into the far wall of the apartment, and Chick retired (yes, he did not retreat, not yet, not now) into his gold and white French Provincial boudoir to meditate, eyes gently closed behind his matching gold and white silk sleep mask, on the past day's events and the surprises of the new day to come.

There was still a murderer out there, after all, gentle dears, somewhere in that big, bad city of San Diego.

Chick had a couple of voice mails on his cell the next morning, and a text message that had come in the middle of the night from a number that looked vaguely familiar. There were four unanswered calls without messages. What could he say? Chick was popular. It was hard to keep track of it all, sometimes, but service to his public was a burden Chick was proud to bear.

The first voice mail was from Hi Fi. He left a long, gassy rambling description, dripping with spiteful glee, of how, as he left the Volvo Volcano, after the police had stopped questioning everyone, he, Hi Fi, overheard Rustie (Hi Fi's old boyfriend, you remember – Chick asked himself – how could I ever forget if you never stop reminding me?) telling Rustie's new Florida-born 22 year old fling (Jamie) to leave town for a while – just until things cooled down.

Just until things cooled down. What about that? What do you think of that, Chick? Huh?

Well, yes, what about it?

Chick wasn't about to be taken in (yet again) by Hi Fi. In another week the two (Rustie and Hi Fi) would be cuddled in a powwow in some corner cackling over someone else and plotting the annihilation and ruin of anyone who attacked the united front of Hi and Rust. It had happened many, many times. Hi Fi must think everyone he knew had Alzheimer's to think they'd take him seriously. Still, he called Hi Fi back.

Chick got voice mail, which was odd, Hi Fi always answered his cell phone, his Bluetooth was surgically attached to his earlobes. Hmmm. Chick thought he'd try again later. Or maybe he'd just stop by un-announced and see what that would get him. Shake the rug a little, and see what fleas fell out, that sort of thing.

The second call was a hysterical wail from Etta, so Chick saddled up, leaving sleeping beauty where he lay, pieces of David twisted tightly around his blanket surrounded by random piles of purple velour cushions, and Chick made his exit, stage right, from the apartment, striding out through the elegant Moorish gateway onto the cracked sidewalk in front of his building.

Having donned a pair of faded patched ELZ jeans sporting at least a dozen extraneous zippers about his hips and knees, a loose fitting white linen Guayabera shirt with wide white on white Baroque stitching down each side of the front, and oh, a pair of white curvy sunglasses (he was too tired to even try and pick out a hat), Chick the P.I. (that's private investigator to the un-initiated) was on the case.

He'd only gone half a block before he walked, no, ran back for his topless, floppy sun hat. What had he been thinking? He felt naked walking the streets hatless, and not in a good way. It was indecent. It was uncivil. It was cruel. No one should let themselves appear in public so un-accessorized. Not if you still had breath in your body to change it, and the taste to do it right. Luckily, Chick had both.

Launched a second time into a dim day of weak Spring sunshine, made even weaker by a low-lying, army-blanket-gray ceiling of fog sanctimoniously sealing this Saturday morning into a state secret, Chick wetly shushed, sweeping down the elderly buckling sidewalks in front of The Turqoise Desert with his customary grace and aplomb, rapidly putting his apartment complex far, far behind him. Chick could walk fast if he wanted to. He glanced at his phone again. A glyph, telling him he had an unread text message, flashed obligingly and obnoxiously in one corner.

Oh, well, if he must…

He peered at the message (and watched his footwork on the tricky rolling slabs of 1920's era concrete stretching in front of him), he coolly brushed the delete button, and he walked on. Maybe his hands were shaking. Maybe they weren't. In any case, Chick had things to see. People to do.

The deleted message had been from the dead man. He wanted more money.

Etta dripped agitation. She exuded it and, yes, Chick had to admit it, her becoming aura of desolation worked for her. But it always did, didn't it? She was miserable. Desperate. Overwrought. Overcome by fate, destiny and life itself. It was quite impressive. Chick watched it play out in front of him, mostly appreciatively. Probably, much of it was even sincere this time.

And while Chick usually performed equally well, observing all the rules and etiquette of offering sympathy and expressing the emotional and physical support necessary to the situation whenever the occasion offered itself, in this case, well, there was just no time for it. Chick didn't have a week or so to get Etta calmed down. At least he didn't think he had time now. Chick was in deep shit. Chick himself needed a little (no, scratch that – a lot of) support thrown his way and quick.

And he sure as hell wasn't going to get it here.

"Oh, Dee, Oh Dee, what am I going to do? How will I live?"

Etta forgot to look up at Chick (out of the corners of his eyes) after he announced this, causing Chick to experience the tickling of, the merest beginnings of a fear that maybe things were actually much, much worse than he thought or knew.

"He was my everything, Dee, he completed me. And he was a two-timing bastard on top of it all."

With that, Etta had taken the mostly damp Kleenex he'd been wiping his eyes with, and tore it efficiently and rapidly to shreds, muttering and frowning at each shred as he deposited it victoriously into a nearby trash basket, still forgetting to look up at Chick to see how he was reacting to Etta's every syllable. Not good. Not good at all.

"You, Etta, were seeing Zit? The same Zit? The one we both argued with, hated, and knew all too well, the same one cooling on a slab in the City Morgue even as we speak?"

Somewhere, deep in his psyche, Chick knew he shouldn't be asking questions with just that choice of words, but, after all, Zit had been blackmailing Chick for nine months, and Chick could only fume when Zit had driven up to work in a new (well, admittedly, old and used but still serviceable) car – using money

Chick could have used for the very same purpose. It was natural. Anyone would have felt the same way. Anyone.

Wait, did Etta say "two-timing?"

Etta opened his mouth. He fastened his eyes on Chick's. He seemed about to answer that question, seriously, and in the affirmative, with exemplary detail, and with a certain crescendo of exploding feeling, when Chick stopped him in mid-opening-breath and said three little words.

"With who, Etta?"

Etta looked a little miffed at losing his opportunity for an extended period of self-righteous, inspired monologue, but with great effort, calmed himself long enough to say simply –

"Jamie, of course."

Chick did a double take, just like they do in the movies. Etta enjoyed it. To Etta, it was worth being cut off in mid-rant. One seldom saw Chick quite so speechless. Chick's mouth hung open. Then he closed it. He frowned and tilted his head.

"Steve's, I mean Rustie's Jamie, Etta? Is that who we're talking about?"

Etta froze and peered at Chick with a wide-eyed look of respect and admiration. This was new information. The two-timer was being two-timed. Well, and he was dead to boot. Etta began to think maybe the scales of justice in this one were evening out.

The two of them talked on a tiny bit about Jamie's unsavory habits and where he liked to hang out (he had a caffeine habit, but who didn't?), and why he never wore yellow, and how he got that strange scar on his groin and then Chick made a hasty exit to allow Etta to process and reprocess the whole thing all over, again and again with the next person she chose to leave a hysterical voice mail with.

Hmmm.

Chick made an abrupt right turn as he left Etta's and by judicious jogging, just made it on the Number 321 headed out west towards Kensington.

Next stop Tom and Steve's - that is Hi Fi and Rustie's. They still lived together. And yes it was a war zone, and yes, U.N troops had been called in on more than one occasion to keep the peace (although even the Secretary General must have understood by now that The Twins were one cause he was never going to win – as in the "lost" variety). And yes, if anyone was asking, it is hard to run and catch a bus with a large white summer hat on, and even harder to keep it clean on public transportation nowadays. If anyone was asking.

Chick found Hi Fi at home, watching T.V. Rustie was out shopping. Hi Fi indifferently opened their conversation with a kind of combination stammer/mutter as usual, keeping one languid eye on an antediluvian rerun of Survivor, and the other on nothing in particular. Chick had no idea what Hi Fi had just said. But before Chick had a chance to say "boo", Hi Fi was mumbling again. This time Chick was luckier.

"I got it wrong."

"You got it wrong, Hi Fi?"

"What? Did you say something Chick?"

"No. Yes. I mean, what, exactly, did you get wrong?"

"Wrong? What's wrong? What are you talking about? Oh. Yeah. Jamie. Jamie wasn't seeing Etta. Jamie was seeing Zit."

"Is that so?"

"Yes, I believe it is."

Hi Fi glanced out of the side of his eyes at Chick, watching his reactions – quickly, yes, but Chick caught it. Chick merely stared back at him.

"Oh, Chick, and as it turns out – look at that jungle, do you think it's real? It screams Pasadena backlot – anyways…"

Hi Fi looked at Chick again. He frowned. He was bored. He was miffed. Somewhat. Clearly he saw he was going to have to up the ante a little bit, just a little, to sort of keep himself in play here. This wasn't as much fun as he thought it was going to be. In fact it might turn out to be work. Work. Hi Fi's frown deepened a tad.

Chick maintained a helpful blankness in his eyes and prepared to wait. Hi Fi watched T.V. for a few moments, then seemed to realize Chick was still sitting there. Yes. This was, actually, turning out to be strenuous, demanding, exacting work. Bother.

"Oh. Jamie. Jamie was seeing Monica as well, Chick. Our ancient Ms. Glande had Jamie tied around his little finger."

"Really?"

"Really."

Chick's facial features remained motionless. He could have been posing for Mount Rushmore. He could have been ON Mount Rushmore. Stony wouldn't begin to describe what Chick's face looked like. It was a gift he had, what could he say?

Hi Fi could see Chick was going to be a difficult house to play to. More? O.K. Hi Fi could give him more. More than he could handle. Two could play at this game.

"Oh, and Zit was blackmailing someone, I don't know who. I think Etta knows who it was though. Etta and Zit were pretty close."

This time Chick spoke not a word. His face however, spoke volumes, for a millisecond, just the tiniest millisecond.

Hi Fi nearly gasped. Seeing Chick finally about to crack and react, Hi Fi could not resist rolling on majestically, pouring as much gasoline on this fire as he could along the way, everywhere he could, as rapidly as possible, while he had the chance. It wasn't pretty. But it was effective.

Chick wasn't fooled. There was something else going on here. Something had gone wrong. Chick could see gears working furiously behind those Hi Fi irises. Heat was building up. Massive amounts of energy were being expended. But to what purpose? And for whom? Chick had to find the answer. He raised one corner of his upper lip slightly.

That's all Hi Fi needed. He took the plunge. "You know, they weren't close in a romantic way, not at all. Not Etta. Not Zit. At least that's what everyone says. But everyone knows Zit was getting extra money from somewhere, and it certainly wasn't from the Vulva, or from that thin, pimply 22 year old Floridian. Jamie, who, if you didn't know it already, doesn't have two nickels to rub together. I should know. I do know. I know all too well. I went out with him for three months last fall"

Chick had no response to that. Neither did his face.

Hi Fi commented (nervously looking at Chick's information-less visage out of the side of his left eye) on how you almost never saw it raining in the jungle lately – have you ever noticed that? – and suddenly directed both eyes carefully and slowly over in Chick's direction. Yes, he was right. Nothing. No reaction. And it had all seemed to be going so well. Something had gotten under his skin. Briefly. Then it had gotten right back out again. Now. This. Nothing. And nothing is nothing but boring. And boring was work. And what was the fun in that?

Hi Fi waved as Chick left and devoted his full attention to whatever happened to be on the screen in front of him, when it suddenly started to rain cats and dogs on the television show. He gasped and pointed at the screen and turned around to mention it to Chick, but there was no one left to talk to, which was just his luck. He was always a day late and a dollar short. Always.

Chick found Jamie at the coffee house, just where Etta had hinted he'd be. This was Jamie's idea of laying low. Jamie would be in jail before noon, or dead before that, if Jamie had managed to cross someone emotionally labile who had access to a gun in the last 24 hours. Chick had to move fast if he was going to talk to him before Jamie was in a hospital and in a coma.

Jamie was texting, watching a movie on his I-Pad, playing a game of Angry birds and thrashing pigs on his cell, talking to two friends at the next table (who were doing pretty much the same thing), all of it, all at the same time, and all of it badly. Chick was impressed Jamie wasn't trying to text the Angry Birds and beat the crap out of his two friends by mistake.

Jamie did have a pleasant southern drawl, although Chick wouldn't know a South Floridian accent from a Northern Maine one. Chick had never been to Maine. Chick wouldn't know.

Chick heard David's voice. Clearly. Chick looked at his own phone. Did it just answer itself? Did it call David by itself? It had a tendency to do just that, in the middle of the night, as Chick groped his way to the bathroom and ran his hand over the night table with his cell charging neatly and quietly on one corner. It had something to do with waving his hands over the screen or some such foolishness. Why would anyone in his right mind make a phone that reacted to hand waving? Hand waving was a universal Diva motion. It occurred continuously 24 hours a day, 7 days a week, even more often (if that were possible) on holidays.

But no. It wasn't Chick. It wasn't his phone. His cell had a huge fluorescent image of a rose made out of rainbows and rhinestones, rotating in interstellar space, around a particularly good face pic (recent) of himself, just as it usually did. Chick looked at it fondly (he always loved roses and rhinestones, and the two together never ceased to take his breath away), and then scanned the nearby environs. He looked about. Again and again. He heard David. He was sure of it. That was David's honking laugh (tiny, yes, but Chick would know that laugh anywhere) and then he saw it.

David was calling Jamie.

How

Why?

Where?

No.

NO.

NO!

Could this be David's mysterious James? The new boyfriend? Oh Davie. Oh, Davie, my boy, my dear boy, you really need a guardian angel. You're going to learn about this world very, very quickly, very, very soon.

Yes, that certainly was David's friendly voice cutting through the sound of traffic outside the coffee shop. Chick heard it through the open window of the coffee shop, as he hid nearby, slouching behind a conveniently placed lamp post and holding onto his stylish, but enormously aerodynamic hat for dear life. Chick hated hearing David's voice coming up from Jamie's cell, but hear it, he must.

The conversation was short, the voice was there, the laugh was there, and then it was gone.

And Chick's phone went off as would a banshee wailing and descending upon those who are about to die. It literally screamed in his pants.

Chick really needed to change his ringtone. Hi Fi thought it was too funny, when Hi Fi loaded it up on Chick's phone on the sly. Yes, Hi Fi, very amusing.

Jamie looked up in dismay (who wouldn't?) but Chick was too quick. He squeezed against the lamppost, positioned his large hat behind a basket of geraniums hanging from said lamppost, and slid his hand to his waist, wrapping his fingers around the phone, doing whatever hand waving was necessary to answer it, inching the phone back up to his ear. All without Jamie being aware he was being stalked (he hoped). Chick was good. Very good.

"David, what a surprise!"

"Chick. Hey. A guy named Randy keeps popping up on your

caller ID. He's called about five times this morning. James is being a real dick this morning. He won't talk to me. What do you think is going on with him, Chick? Oh, and by the way thanks. Thanks for the couch and the blanket. And, uh, Chick, uh, well, you know I have to ask you something. Uh, Chick, uh, did anything like uh, happen last night? I really don't remember much after that 4th beer. I just woke up on your pull-away-out thingy and I, well, I mean…" Chick looked at the phone, gently shaking his head and looking down demurely at the sidewalk (for no one's benefit really, except for Chick and the moment itself - Chick was, after all, talking on a cell for Heaven's sake), the geraniums knocked his hat off, but he managed to catch it before it hit the bubblegum-pocked cement at his feet.

"David, dear, you were a little worse the wear last night, and there are rules about these things."

Chick knew full-well that David probably hadn't seen The Philadelphia Story. But Chick had always wanted to say that to someone. And that had been his chance.

Ah Well. David generously added in a gentlemanly addendum after a loud honk of laughter.

"Not that I would have pushed you away…"

Chick interrupted him as if the they had had a bad connection (too busy, too scared, and yes, too vain for even well-meaning back-paddling just now, from confused beautiful young men).

"Thanks. David. Really."

David made a hurt, perplexed humming sound, and Chick quickly promised him a longer verbal reaction to his indecent proposal in the future and with cell off, made his silent, deadly way towards the unsuspecting Jamie. Jamie being a popular man, a man who was, obviously, the center of a vast ring of interlocking relationships, an entire shadowy social network, heretofore unbeknownst to Chick, but encompassing practically everyone Chick knew and loved or had ever loved or probably ever would love, Jamie, here, was the man to question. He was the man with the answers. He was the center. It was diabolical. It was stunning. It was pathetic.

"So… Howard, I mean Chick, I mean Howard, I mean…" babbled Jamie on seeing Chick rise up out of the coffee house's concrete floor directly in front of him, apparently out of nowhere, as would a ringwraith, one hand already magically resting in

Untitled #27

authoritative splendor on Jamie's left shoulder, gripping Jamie's substantial shoulder muscles, said muscles being clenched tight (as probably were Jamie's more posterior anal muscles also) in fearful anticipation.

Anticipation, yes. But of what? Chick must find this out. Chick must know.

Chick quickly surveyed the table and the man in front of him.

He noted the usual. Sloppiness. Lack of forethought. Inattention. Yes, the consequent, occasional nasty surprise being one of the many disadvantages of rampant, habitual multitasking – Jamie was totally unprepared for the nasty surprise named Chick when he actually appeared. Entirely and absolutely. Jamie was unreadiness personified. That much was obvious from the start. Chick sighed. He wouldn't last an hour on the streets at this rate.

Disappointed squawking gurgled up from Jamie's cell, the Angry Birds must have been most severely disappointed. Jamie tried to cover up his IPad, on which appeared a Greyhound Bus website with different times and ticket prices for Fresno. Also his face was blushing a bright shade of fire-engine red. Chick used to have a nail polish that very same color.

Yes, little Jamie had been a very busy boy. And very indiscreet. Chick cocked his head and made tch-tch'ing sounds as Jamie squirmed. Jamie was in quite the state. Well, well, well. The game was afoot, as Mr. S. H. used to say - or had it been Mr W.?. Either way, Chick decided he may as well have some fun with the poor, confused Jamie – Lord knows Jamie had had fun with everyone else.

"Hey. Dee. Howard. Chick. Lady. Dee."

"Just pick one of my names and stick with it, Young J."

"Uh. O.K."

"You can call me Chick."

"Uh. O.K. Uh… Chick."

"So. James. I can call you James, can't I?"

"Uh. Yeah. Sure thing, uh..."

"Chick."

"Uh…"

"You can call me Chick."

"Chick. Yeah, uh, sure thing, Chick."

"So, James, am I to understand I am the only person working at the Volvo Volcano that you haven't slept with?"

117

"Now, now, Chick, why do have to do me that way…"

Jamie gritted his teeth and tried to smile – it wasn't a very successful, or pleasant set of simultaneous facial expressions.

"Why?" he said and glanced at the Greyhound schedule, gasping a little.

"Why?" he continued, as he closed, turned off, wrapped up, and gathered into his arms, all his many personal belongings.

"Why? Yes, why Chick? Why?" He murmured as he pushed himself out of his chair.

Chick stepped in front of him.

"Chick, you don't believe every tale you hear out of school, do you? Chick? Chick?"

Jamie started edging backwards, feeling his way with the heel of each foot, carefully, cautiously, inching bit by bit towards the front doors and sweet, sweet freedom.

"How about dead-men's tales, Jamie?" bantered Chick, sidestepping Jamie, and opening the screen door at the front of the shop for him. Jamie halted, awkwardly, halfway in and halfway out of the coffee shop, hands full and juggling a half dozen awkwardly shaped objects, jaw dropped and still dropping, eyes as big as, well, coffee cup saucers. He whispered back, jumping out of the way of another exiting patron.

"I don't know what you're talking about Howard."

"The name's the Lady Dee, J-boy" said a low, familiar voice behind Jamie.

Both of them (Jamie twisting his neck backwards and upwards, Chick glancing over the top of Jamie's head – the owner of the voice was tall) interrupted what they were doing to look at a substantial, square-cut body blocking the orphaned rays of sunlight struggling to make their way around a large, well-built, male form. Randy, the drunk foot-grabber from the night before at the restaurant, in all his bulging Belgian muscularity had placed a hand on Jamie's shoulder. This was turning out to be quite the day for Floridian-shoulder-touching. Jamie jumped. That was gratifying to Chick, he wasn't ashamed to admit it.

Then Chick was surprised. Which didn't happen very often. Or at least it hadn't happened very often before last night.

Jamie gulped and said "I was just coming over Randy, just now. Really. Really, I was, Randy."

Still hand-on-shoulder, Randy scowled down at Jamie, then,

Randy looked over Jamie's cowering head and threw a few dazzling, hopeful grins in Chick's direction – Chick, in turn, was confused, not ungrateful for the attention, but not about to encourage it either. This was neither the time nor the place. He was not going to be picked up by a hunk in this way. Not standing next to an open screen door in a public food establishment with a potential murderer stuck between the two of them.

Maybe later though. Chick would have to think about it.

Seeing no reaction to his impressive incisors, Randy resumed his more successful Jamie-frowning. Chick started to say something, (like – get lost Randy) then thought the better of it, uncharacteristically stuttering to a stop in mid-first-word. Randy waited for Chick to say something. Chick waved his hand at him. Randy bowed in Chick's direction. Chick bowed back. This was obviously going to go on for quite some time. Chick cleared his throat to get Randy going again. Chick would probably get more of the full story out of Jamie if Randy was doing some of the encouraging. Being big, bad and Belgian had its advantages.

Jamie gushed on, ignoring all the bowing and smiling going on. He spit and spouted the way a leak would in a failing kitchen faucet, trying to persuade Randy to allow Jamie to wriggle sideways and get free of Randy's ever-tightening grip It wasn't working. But you had to give Jamie credit for a fascinating, unrehearsed, impromptu monologue.

"Uh, here. Here you are, and here I am, and well, here it is. Ha! Ha! Ouch. Ouch, Randy. Here. Just like I said, Randy. It's right here. You know, Daniel, I mean Monica, I mean Mon Kay Glande, Ms. Glande, well you know who I mean, don't you? I knew you did. He found it last night. I don't know when she found it. I mean he found it. And Ouch, I don't know where he found it either, I swear. Ouch. Really. Ouch. Stop it, man! I don't even know why he gave it to me. I don't know. I don't know anything. Ouch. I swear. I'll even forget my own name if that would help. Ha! Ouch. Ouch, that hurts. Stop! Really. I was just heading over to your place. Really. Look. Just heading over. Ouch. With this..."

And as the hand gripped the shoulder more and more strongly, almost as if the pressure had squeezed it out of him, a piece of gold dropped from Jamie's hand into the outstretched and waiting hand of Randy. It rapidly disappeared in Randy's front pocket. And with that Jamie shot free as fast as a beebee out of a third-grader's gun, spinning backwards and sideways, clutching his various electronic communication devices to his chest, barreling down the street to try and catch the Number 105 bus (he just made it) pulling away from the stop on the corner. That was the bus to downtown. To the Greyhound station.

Now it was Chick's turn to stare open-mouthed.

Randy linked his arm in Chick's, said "hungry?" and pulled Chick towards a trendy patio restaurant/wine bar just down the block past the X-rated Video store, across the street from the Chick's favorite shoe repair shop. What could Chick do? It was a sort of forced strolling. Chick made the best of it. He wanted to know more. He was hungry. He didn't have anything else to do. And he was broke. So, he strolled.

It was late, very late. Low lights were on here and there in Chick's apartment. Rumbling filled the hallways for a few seconds. Damn ghosts. It couldn't be the heat or the air conditioning. Nothing made a sound like that. It was loud. It was low. It was thundering. And always ended in a kind of exultant bang. You could almost hear cheering. But you could never be sure it was actually happening within the building. It was more of an echo. Or a mirror-image of an echo.

Damn ghosts.

It was a typical weekend night. David had stopped by after going out with his friend Michael. Chick hadn't heard anything about either girlfriends or boyfriends yet from David. All was quiet on the western relationship front for the moment. David held his hand up. Chick tossed a bottle at him.

David started sucking on his beer as Chick started talking and was nearly smothered by the towel Chick threw across the room. He sucked. The beer overflowed. David managed to get most of the overflowing beer on the towel, only a little got on his jeans, none of it went on the couch (he was getting better at beer drinking) the majority he slurped off the side of the bottle, then he took another swig. Chick's eyebrows went up. He saw them, saw the warning, wrapped the towel tightly around the bottle. The bubbling over didn't even reach his jeans this time. Yes, he was definitely getting better at it.

David looked up, a self-satisfied, proud look in his eyes. Then he swallowed, burped, laughed, honked, excused himself, and tilted his head. He took another gulp, and talked with his mouth around the bottle.

"So, Chick, Etta did it?"

"Did what, Davie? Drinking and talking at the same time are probably not the best combination for you, David."

"I'm not. I'm not. So. What about Etta?"

David had to call out to Chick, or rather to a wall, because Chick had disappeared. Chick was busying himself with a red-wax sealed bottle he'd purchased recently and some maraschinos and some bitters in his kitchen. It was exacting work. David could hear the clinking of glass rods, crystal, mixing canisters and metal measuring spoons all the way in the living room.

"Chick. Can you hear me? Someone killed Zit. O.K., so not Etta, then who? It's always the most unlikely suspect. It must be you, then."

That earned a strange glare from Chick, as Chick strode back into the living room, a half-full glass of amber colored liquid at his lips. David shut up for a second.

"You should be a detective." Chick took a slow swig from his artfully-filled glass.

"Or a comedian."

Chick set down his drink, and stared at David. David hummed for a moment. Then Chick ruffled David's spiky hair with one free hand, and with the other dabbed with a wet dish towel at some wayward beer that had found its way onto the carpet despite David's best efforts. Chick shot a reproachful look upwards at David, but David was preoccupied with another long slurp. Chick sighed.

After a moment, David looked questioningly at Chick over the top of his beer. Chick put down the towel, put his hands on his hips, looked back, cleared his throat carefully and began.

"Etta found the body, and in a fit of hysteria she tried to get Zit out of the water, but only succeeded in getting herself incriminatingly wet, and she managed to pull up a heavy piece of gold jewelry out of the suds. She thought it was Zit's and wanted to hold on to it as a, I don't know, a kind of keepsake, I suppose. Etta's always been sentimental that way." Chick paused for a second, looking for more stains, waving the towel over the carpet.

David motioned impatiently with eyes to continue. Chick sighed again.

"But, unfortunately, or fortunately as the case turned out, the perpetually poor Ms. Glande saw Etta shaking and taking – the body and the gold that is – and observed her dropping the gold jewelry into her purse, which she gripped closely to her, and kept next to her body the whole night, all during the police questioning. When Etta accidentally dropped it, later. Ms. Glande was there to swoop down and pick it up. At least that's what I think probably happened."

"Oh."

"Yes, oh."

"So. It was Glande who did it. That was his gold jewelry. He's the murderer."

David suggested this to the open air above him in the couch, moving his free hand in a theatrical way that mimed someone pointing his finger at heaven and disclosing a divine truth, recently revealed. Chick rolled up the towel and swatted him with it. It was wet. It hurt. It was meant to hurt.

"No, it wasn't Glande's, David. At least not for long. Ms. Glande ended up giving it to Jamie."

"Jamie? Who's Jamie?"

Chick ignored the question.

"Glande always had a weakness for honest greed. Poor, vicious, and a little on the stupid side, that was his perfect man. When will she ever learn?"

"Who's Jamie?"

"Anyways, Davy, Jamie needed Ms. Glande. When Jamie took the gold cuff link to Randy to pawn it, something happened, and Jamie ran out on Randy."

"Who is Jamie?"

"I think you know Jamie, David. I'd say you know Jamie in a biblical sense."

"I would."

"I'd bet my false eyelashes on it. The ones with the diamond dust permanently affixed at the end of each lash. The ones I bought in Bangkok."

"Are you saying what I think your saying?"

"I don't know hon, what do you think I'm saying?"

"Is my James your Jamie? What does my James, my boyfriend, a nerdy computer programmer, have to with anything or anyone at your wild restaurant?"

"David, I don't know how you're going to take this, but your James is not only your James, he's our Jamie. He's not a programmer, he's a hustler. And in fact he wasn't your Jamie or our Jamie, he was everyone's Jamie. Jamie was sleeping with every man, and probably every woman who worked at the Vulva, ate at the Vulva, or was waiting at a bus stop in front of the Vulva. He was a very busy beaver, our Jamie."

"Oh."

"Oh, indeed."

They both maintained a respectful moment of silence while they meditated on this fact. Thus passed David's second gay boyfriend relationship. He'd have to find some other male for those long, intense, emotional phone conversations he'd had late at night (at Chick's place of course), find another guy to exchange those endless, intimate texts with at every possible opportunity, seek out someone else to perform those other necessary and vital functions Jamie had performed for and with David. Yes. It was over. But David didn't look too awfully crushed. Chick was sure his cellphone had an ample supply of male phone numbers stored in its contacts to supply him with a substitute. David wouldn't be so very lonely for so very long.

Chick opened his mouth and David jumped to interrupt him again, his hand in the air, his finger raised, until he saw the threat of another towel-slap and he ceased and desisted in time. The towel was put away. David watched Chick throw it back over his head neatly falling next to the pile of dirty linens in the laundry basket by the kitchen sink.

Then David said it anyway.

He ducked behind the love seat as he said it though.

"So it was Randy who did it, then, huh?"

David waited a second, felt no slap, heard no rapid footsteps, no under-the-breath cursing approaching his hiding place. In fact David heard nothing at all. Cautiously, oh so cautiously and carefully, David poked his head out from behind the love seat.

What he saw made him hold his breath.

He saw Chick staring out the window, off into space.

"It was Randy?" said David, unbelievingly.

"It was Randy" said Chick calmly.

"Uh…"

"And if you ever say a word, David Hirscher, just a single word of this to anyone… Well. Don't. That's all I'll say. Just don't. There's no proof, Davie. None. Just the lump of gold Jamie dropped into Randy's hand yesterday morning. It had an RW inscribed on it. I knew it was familiar somehow when I saw it, it just took me a day to remember. The night Zit was killed, Randy had been missing a cuff link, towards the end of the night. His cuff link, it must have come off when he shoved Zit into the dishwasher. I gave him those cuff links…"

David waited. And waited. But Chick wasn't talking anymore. He was staring into the wild blue yonder again. Except that it was the wild black yonder, since it was long past sundown by now. David waited for what he thought was a decent interval, and then waited some more for good measure, then he had to speak.

"But, why? What could Zit have done to make Randy so mad he'd want to kill him? Huh? Chick? Chick?"

David resumed his place on the couch, crawling out from behind the love seat, confident that he was safe from towel-battles for at least a couple of more minutes (Chick would have to run to the kitchen to re-supply if he wanted to mount another wet towel attack anyways). Actually David was more than a little concerned about his friend. Chick did not seem to be himself. He was someone else. Someone David had never met before.

"I don't know. I don't know I just don't know. Maybe…" said Chick, apparently not really listening to David right now. He was doing the staring thing again.

"Maybe…" said David softly.

"Maybe…" said Chick after a second.

"Maybe…" said David, again, hoping to prime the pump.

"Oh stop it, David. Maybe… Maybe Randy thought Zit and I were seeing each other. Maybe Randy was jealous. Maybe he got drunk and did something stupid. Maybe Randy's not the safest person to be around when he's drunk. Maybe he bench-presses Volkswagens in his free time. Maybe he has poor impulse control. Maybe he does stupid things even when he's sober. Maybe he's not sober all that often. Maybe love makes him stupid. Maybe it makes all of us stupid a lot of the time. Maybe that includes me. Maybe, maybe, maybe…"

There was a long silence after that. David went to get another Flat Tire out of the refrigerator. He picked up Chick's empty glass out of Chick's unresisting hand on the way there. Chick didn't even notice. David sighed. Chick sighed. David thought to himself – well, there's a first time for everything – let's see if I know how to make a Manhattan. He retired to the kitchen to try.

"He's Belgian, you know" said Chick from the other room.

"Really?" said David, pouring miscellaneous amounts of bitters and bourbon into Chick's glass. It was already half-filled with maraschinos. This was going to be a mostly fruit, incidentally alcoholic drink.

"They're famous for waffles. And chocolate. And bringing their dogs into restaurants."

"Is that so?" said David, taking his index finger and swirling it around to mix everything together. He'd washed it first, of course. His index finger, and the glass. In that order.

"That's Belgium for you. What in heaven's name are you doing in there, child?"

David ignored that question. He looked at his creation. It had a slight resemblance to a Manhattan, didn't it? Chick would probably not even notice the difference. Pretty decent effort. If he didn't say so himself. He walked back out carrying it casually in his right hand.

"But, Chick, why would he think that? Why would Randy think that you and Zit were together?"

David, grabbing yet another beer (the last one) out of the bottom shelf of the frig on the way back, peeled off the label from his sweating beer bottle, one-handed, with his left hand, and folded the sopping paper with only his fingers into a star shape, still all with his left hand. David was good with his hands. It came in handy at times like this. And on other occasions.

He handed Chick the glass with the fresh Manhattan (a la David), dropped the origami label onto the floor by his feet and flinched, just a moment too late, as another towel aimed for his shoulder. Where did Chick get those towels from? It was like they materialized in his hands out of thin air. It snapped a millimeter away from his shirt. He looked up. But he didn't jump. He was used to it. Chick was a good shot. And Chick hadn't ever hurt him yet.

Chick had a horrified expression on his face. He was looking at

David's newly-made Manhattan. He looked at the glass. Then he looked directly at David. Then looked at the glass again. Then he almost smiled. But the smile didn't quite make it all the way out of him. It got stuck somewhere. But it was close enough to a smile though, for David. Chick liked it. He liked it a lot. Obviously.

"You're sure full of questions tonight, Master Hirscher. That's for me to know. And for you, well…",

Chick paused for a second, then the pause got longer, and soon (to David) Chick seemed to be shocked to find David still standing in the room with him. David picked up the label, its multiple folds unfolding wetly in the middle of the floor, gathered his empty beer bottles together and started to make his way to the kitchen. He put one between his legs and gripped it with his knees. He was a little unsteady on his feet. He was holding a lot of empty beer bottles, empty of beer courtesy of David. David, on the other hand was full of beer.

Chick watched it all, and he wasn't watching it all – his body was there, but Chick wasn't. David duck-walked his way to the kitchen. One of David's bottles slipped to the floor. Then another. Then another. Then the label disintegrated in his fingers and another bottle fell out of his slippery hands..

"You better not be thinking about leaving that strip of waterlogged whatever it is on my clean floor, and those nasty bottles, they better be headed for the recycling bin and hey, Davie, Davie, look here – David, listen, no, listen to me - give them here, yup, all of them, even that one, no, I can see it, even behind your back - you're hopeless, Davie, you know that, don't' you? - Davie, you're just hopeless."

David collapsed on the sofa and smiled at Chick's retreating back. He felt safe here. It was a place you could let your guard down some. Maybe more than some. Maybe a lot. A kind of home. A kind of a lot of home. He scanned the floor for more bits of paper or puddles of beer. When David looked up, he caught Chick watching him. Chick was examining him in a resigned, weary, patient sort of way. His eyes were frowning. But his lips were still smiling. Almost. No. All the way now. He was totally smiling David was sure of it. Yup. Home. It was all home. Totally home.

PERSIAN MINIATURE

Marie hated the light. From the very beginning she did. She first saw it depositing, filtering down, mounding, layer after layer, into glowing snow drifts in cupboard corners - shapes of graceful inward-looking arabesques and delicate beckoning curves, all under a crosshatching of exquisite connecting filaments. It tried to look decorative. It tried to look harmless. It gathered into little piles of softly glimmering, dull luminescence that increased and extended no matter how often she brushed at them, poked and prodded at them, attacked them with every cleaning implement she had available.

She watched, day by day, as more little pinpoints of sparkly white clumped together, way under and towards the back of beds and dressers, behind the refrigerator and underneath suitcases in storage. She noticed (how could she not?) the twinkly bits that clung like cobwebs in her closets and shoeboxes, bits that began to coalesce into larger and larger bits - steadily and alarmingly bright masses that began to take over random areas of her house. The light thought that it was being sneaky, doing a little here, a little more there, it thought that it was fooling her. But it wasn't. Marie saw. Nothing was getting by her. She saw it all. And she didn't like it. She didn't like it, not for one second.

Ed never seemed to see them, the lumps of light sprouting around the house as if they were electric mushrooms, but Ed wasn't paying much attention to anything anymore. Since they'd made the big move from their old house (oh, how she missed its familiar, comfortable wallpaper, its friendly exhausted floors, its tired, accommodating steps - here, everything in this new condo was sharp edges and bright white, anonymous paint, flashy steel appliances and plastic everything, lots of plastic, so much of it – everywhere - where was the feel of scratched and loved-to-death wood? – what was there left to polish in a place like this?), well, in any event, since the move, Marie just couldn't sit down, sit down and feel settled. She was only a guest now. A guest in her own house.

Ironically, it had been Marie who'd insisted the two of them move - partly because, well, for the last ten years or so, they'd just been rattling around in that big old house in Kansas as if they were a couple of forgotten beans in an empty pantry bin, and they had both just about had enough of the winters, sure, more than enough, but it had mostly been because Ed had gotten worse, and now they were closer to a hospital, and it was less humid here, and Ed's oxygen was easier to get delivered in a city like this (although she still had to argue with the driver about where and when and how to leave the canisters – who would want to store heavy machinery in their living rooms? Californians did apparently), but still, despite everything, she just couldn't get herself used to this San Diego condo. She couldn't let go and relax - she couldn't get comfortable no matter how hard she tried.

And then the thing had started with the light. Light! Of all things! As if she needed another thing to worry about.

Marie had first suspected it might have designs on Ed one evening when Ed was lying down with his eyes closed and Marie had been having a hard time getting her heart to calm down herself, and she had been sitting up with Ed by the bed, Ed trying to drift off to sleep, the oxygen hissing quietly in the background snaking down its clear tubing and inflating Ed's poor shredded lungs. The pump was laboring away into the silence and Ed was still having a hard time of it (breathing and all) and he had reached out to grab her hand (something he didn't do all that often) letting it drop over the side of the bed, and she had gripped it, letting him know she wasn't going anywhere and she had thought she was going to cry. It would have been O.K. to cry, she knew sometimes it helped, although once or twice it had distressed Ed some, and she felt her heart flutter in her chest the way a butterfly might trying to escape a cocoon and then the room had seemed to brighten. She could tell the light in the corners was getting brighter. And then she knew.

It was waiting. Waiting for Ed. It wanted him. And it was coming for him. Coming for her Ed, to take him away from Marie, forever.

She had forgotten to breathe for a few seconds after that. But, then, that's when she'd made her decision, holding Ed's hand, in a puddle of lamp light, sitting by the bed stand with a couple of half-read books stacked haphazardly on top of it, determined and scared in the early evening as Ed labored to breathe and the oxygen machine did its patient work grinding away in the easy evening shadows. Yes, she'd decided. She would fight it. Fight it with everything she had. She would fight for Ed and she would win.

She gripped Ed's hand more tightly and tried not to notice the tears steadily falling onto her chest, puddling in the reading glasses she kept on a chain around her neck. She stayed that way for quite a while. Longer than she had anticipated. But she was right. The crying was doing her good. And Ed seemed to be quietly sliding into a marginally less-painful nap, a nap that might turn out, if they were lucky, into a good night's sleep.

But how to do it? How do you fight the light? How could she defend Ed? She started crying harder, in spite of herself. She didn't know. She didn't know how. She'd have to think about that one.

Did she have time? Ed rolled a little to one side and started snoring softly, and Marie, leaning back in her chair, sighed and tried to let her heart calm down, leaning stiffly into her chair, a thin pained smile on her face, her cheeks wet and her heart racing to beat the band.

Slow. Easy. Quiet.

Her heart didn't have to be a scared rabbit running under the shadow of a hawk, as usual – no, but instead it could rest, patiently beating and watching - a wise and wily cat sitting hidden to one side of a mouse hole, ready and alert and determined.

You hear that, heart?

Fifteen long minutes later, she felt better.

She could beat it. She could beat the light.

Couldn't she?

Yes.

She would figure it out. She could wait. Wait and watch. She'd be the cat not the rabbit this time. The light would make a mistake and she would be ready for it. The light would never know what hit it. It should never have come into this condo and messed around with Marie's Ed. Never.

Marie hadn't met many of her neighbors yet, even though they'd lived there for a year or so now. She thought of herself as being cautious, quiet, self-contained. All of which was true, she supposed, but lately that hadn't seemed to be - well, she wasn't sure - it just didn't seem to be enough for her. She felt half-empty. She wanted more. Somehow. But she didn't know what the "more" was that she wanted. A sort of unformed longing for anything else other than what she had. Kind of silly, really. She didn't want to be a burden to anyone. But in the last couple of years, Ed had gotten her worried and flustered and she found that it took all of her energy to keep the house going and Ed going and her life had constricted down to a single point. And that point was Ed.

In the end, it was just easier, living alone. Alone with Ed that is. Besides, she was none too strong herself, with her heart and her arthritis and all the rest. But she wasn't complaining, she wasn't the complaining sort. They had food, a roof, and Ed has his good days as well as his bad days. She and Ed would muddle through it all somehow. They always had. But sometimes she just felt awfully small and well, thin and used up. She wasn't going to call it loneliness, she just called it being tired. Tired and old. Part of the aging process. Nothing you could complain about - and what would happen if you did complain? What good would come of it? Better to get supper ready, make the bed, dust the house, do the laundry. Simple, small things that needed doing and got your mind of your troubles. And there was taking care of Ed - that wasn't simple or small but it needed doing. And she was determined to do it as long as she could, light or no light.

The one person she knew better than anyone else in this strange, new place was a someone she'd met accidentally the first day after she and Ed had moved in, and the person was unlike anyone she'd ever known before. That first day, feeling more and more disconnected and unreal, she'd wandered around outside the condo complex, somehow managed to get herself lost trying to get back in, and had been found and saved by a slow and steady talking Benjamin Xavier (which he pronounced Bane-Ha-Mean' Ha-Bee-Air') - which delighted Marie - sounding exotic and a little risqué and maybe a name you might choose for a neon-spangled, sparkly night club located in some romantic city - Rio De Janeiro maybe - in a crazy, big budget MGM Thirties musical. It was that kind of name.

Actually, Xavier (or Hobby - the nickname in English he insisted on) said – "as in most things in life – he and his name were all actually both more simple and more complicated than dancing sambas next to the Amazon." Marie had been quick to agree. Although she had no idea what he meant. Hobby was good at explaining things. And Marie was good at listening.

Hobby was a former Jesuit priest from Argentina, with salt and pepper spiky hair, a soft, singing, almost Italian accent, and sharp eyes that missed nothing, but seemed democratically to be viewing each and every thing that life and God paraded before him - observing and learning - all from under thick eyebrows behind two thick bifocal lenses in a ring of even heavier and thicker black eyeglass frames. He had long, careful, aristocratic hands that looked (to Marie) like they would be very comfortable authoritatively handling ancient, gold-encrusted manuscript folios just as easily as those same hands did what they were usually doing in front of

Marie - which was: mowing and trimming, planting and raking, weed-whacking, and leaf-blowing – "doing all which is useful and necessary to the vegetable kingdom in the place delegated to my care" (as Hobby described his work) or as Marie would say - gardening around the condo complex.

Even though he was Catholic and believed in the pope (she had never asked him, she thought it might be impolite, but she felt sure that was what being a Jesuit had meant), Marie had still decided to like and trust the quiet, diligent, and attentive Hobby from the very start. And he seemed a man of mystery to Marie, somehow, with a sad and dusky, dimly reflected past, curiously stuck here with her in the bright, relentless sunshine of Southern California.

He was an Argentinian iceberg, unmistakably bumping his way into Marie's new life here among the palm trees, in a land that never knew winter - he was out of place, but strangely more at home than Marie here, passionate but respectful, intelligent but humble, there was just so much more to him than the small part he allowed to be visible to the casual eye. Most of him was under water, hidden from view, all the interesting parts. At least that's what Marie liked to think.

One day, her mind on dusty drifts of heaping light spreading deeper and wider throughout her condo, Marie worriedly exited the shortening almost-noon-day shadows of the second courtyard of their complex tucking her green re-usable grocery bags under her arm and waved to Xavier, whom she could just see working in the third courtyard. Of the three elaborate courtyards in her complex – a complex called the Turquoise Desert - a renovated bowling alley now a mixed-use – and they had a certificate to prove it - retail-low-income-luxury-condo development – well, of the three courtyards, she liked her own courtyard (number two) the best. The only bad part was its closeness to a noisy, busy street off an even noisier, busier main street in the big city of San Diego. But all the stores, all within a few blocks of the Turquoise Desert made her shopping easier. That was always a blessing.

"Buenos dias, Senor Hobby" called Marie across a narrow strait of blue-green tile with a wavy pattern on it like the sea, surrounded by sandy, gravelly xeriscaping filled with agaves and spindly smoke trees which obscured her view of him, Hobby that is, who was bending over a section of flowering ice plant, talking softly to it, and digging out stubborn grass clumps that insisted on growing where they shouldn't. Over his head she could see what she called the cheerleader pom-pom flowers bobbing like big blue-white fireworks on the end of their long stems. At the sound of her voice, a large bird (was that a hawk?) with brown and white checks and a disturbing expression in its arrogant, condescending eyes abruptly took off from one of the upper branches of the smoke tree, startling Marie twenty feet away, but discomfiting Hobby (right next to it) not at all.

"A pleasant morning to you also, Dona Nebraska" Hobby called back playfully (she was from Nebraska originally) "a beautiful light this morning, isn't it? A good light for the growing things of the world."

"Light, yes, very nice" grimaced Marie, mumbling a little to herself as she made her way out and up towards the big supermarket on the corner. Xavier stopped and watched her thoughtfully as she ambled out of sight.

"Goddamit, Marie, where's dinner?" growled Ed, that evening, Marie's heart fluttering about her chest as if it were a lost duckling, then settling down again to a steady beat, Marie wasn't sure which were worse, Ed's silences or his yelling. By the time she brought the tray into the bedroom, Ed had sat back down on the bed, not staring anymore out the window and not grouching at the crazy stuff that went on sometimes in the alley behind the condo complex.

His eyes looked red and watery, like he had allergies, but Marie knew it wasn't allergies. "It's getting later and later every night, be goddam breakfast soon" Ed said, tossing his covers around on the bed he was sitting on and looking at the far side of the room. Ed sighed, (a sound he didn't used to make) and threw his hand out over the side of the bed. She set down the tray and sat down, in the chair by the bed, taking and gently holding the proffered hand.

"Marie, it's not you" he said, about to add something else, then just closing his mouth. He never used to like being held much, almost never used to speak, thought it was weak to talk about himself or bring attention to himself or his needs. She wasn't used to all this new talking and complaining. She wasn't sure what she thought about the new Ed. It was as if she were getting to know this Ed person for the first time, despite having lived with him for most of her life.

Then Ed started talking again, talking like he was conversing with someone floating just outside their bedroom window somewhere over the dumpster in the alley "Don't listen to me, I'm just tired." Ed was rolling and unrolling the blanket lying over his lap. He looked scared. That was new too. It pained Marie to see him like this. "Why's it always so fucking cold in here?" Ed mumbled more to himself than to anyone in the room. Marie watched his busy hands and they looked raw, red and cracked, large hands that had once built skyscrapers and run ten-story cranes in Kansas City fumbling awkwardly at twisting a piece of bed linen. She almost jumped up to close the window, get him some lotion for his hands, turn on the electric blanket - but stopped herself just as she was rising. In this mood he'd just yell at her and wouldn't let her help anyways. She'd wait till after supper. He'd be quieter then.

Later, the sunset outside the window spread a garish, recklessly prodigal show of purples and oranges across the evening sky over the alley. Gradually this faded like all things do, and night fell upon the two of them, a night like any other. Sometimes Marie dreaded the night, long and painful, full of crises to get through, sometimes she welcomed it – a chance to get knocked on the head and blessedly forget about the world, Ed, and everything else for a little while. Tonight, dinner and cleanup, bathing and bathroom stops finished and done with, they were back in the master bedroom early. Marie was glancing anxiously over at Ed lying down under the covers, next to her in her ratty old armchair, he was staring out the now black-and-street-light-sulphur-pink window, his eyes roaming about the night, trying to find something that wasn't there.

Marie didn't like what she was hearing. He wasn't breathing so good, tonight. Ed hadn't eaten all his supper, either. Her own chest felt a little out of sorts. She felt odd, like the tightness and the racing were going to hit – kind of the electric calm before a summer thunderstorm broke back in Kansas – and it always made her edgy. She knew Ed could sense she was feeling skittish and she was just waiting for him to say something. "For Chrissake, Marie, stop fidgeting" he would say "It's making me crazy." But she couldn't get comfortable and didn't know why. Sometimes she worked so hard to make things right for Ed and he just didn't seem to notice. She was in no mood for it tonight. No mood at all.

He looked over at her, his face a mask of anxiety, and instead of berating her, just dropped one hand again over the side of the bed, and she took the hint and grabbed on to it. She liked their new habit of handholding as if they were back in college again. His hand was a little greasy from the lotion she'd put on earlier, but it looked a little less hamburger-ish when she did it, so she was glad she had. Now she was about to cry. Ed smiled for a moment at her. Ed was turning into one big surprise. His grip lessened a little and she blinked back a few tears and looked him over. He didn't look like he was sleeping, was something wrong? And was the room getting a little brighter? Her chest began to hurt, ever so slightly, when she saw what she was sure were corpuscles of light clumping energetically under the wall by the window.

And, (now that she scrutinized the room around her with a little more attention) webs of light were clinging in the corners of the ceiling, spots were gathering furtively behind her chair, in the closet, and under the bed, they all seemed to be gathering strength in a very business-like manner this evening. With a quick intake of breath (which thankfully, Ed didn't hear) she felt a wave of panic roll over her – her chest was throbbing - a wristwatch wound one wind too tight – maybe on the point of snapping – and she realized she had to think, and think quickly. Just for a moment, just in the corner of her eye, something caught her attention for a second. She didn't know if it was a sound, or a flash of light, or a furtive movement of some kind. She glanced over at the tiny, spindly, bedstand by Ed's worried face.

There. In the middle of the stack of books. Something ribbed in leather, printed with golden letters, now mostly rubbed off, pretty much hidden under an atlas of the United States almost fifty years out of date. What was it? Why would she notice it now? She carefully removed this ancient book from the barely-balanced stack and gently opened it to the middle, where a purple ribbon lay wedged and creased - a bookmark, the faded pages brittle and spottily gilt-edged, the binding threatening repeatedly to crack as she pressed on the pages to force the book all the way open. She knew then what she had to do. She had to read. She had to read out loud.

She could feel the pressure of the light all around her intensify, it was a physical thing, it got harder and more aggressive, as she moved her reading glasses back onto the end of her nose, brushing back the chains, smoothing the water-stained pages so she could decipher them better. The light was afraid! It didn't want her to read. It wanted both of them miserable, not comfortable. Well, this time the light was not going to get its way.

Shakily confident, and provisionally more hopeful, she looked over at Ed, made a decision, cleared her throat a couple of times and settled herself back in the armchair by the bed to read the text aloud. The chair and the book both complained, loudly, snapping and popping, and then fell silent. Readjusting her glasses with one hand and holding the book open with the other, she began. It was easier than she'd thought. Her voice got louder the more she read.

>Amal greeted the rukh, a cold and proud-staring eagle larger than a hundred eagles saying "I crave your pardon Lord Rukh Bekhrad, who waits for none and no one, I place my head between my hands and beg you accept this slight gift" and Amal took three of the six silk-hair mice the King of the Hind had given him from out of his pocket and gave of those to the rukh to eat. One, two, three gulps and the mice were gone. Amal leapt up onto great Bekhrad's back, a back big enough for a Caliph's tent, between wings wider than a city, on feathers softer and whiter than the snows that ever-bury the mountains at the end of the world.

>And holding tightly onto the tiny gazelle with the silver chain and the seven keys, they flew east for a month and a day, through the heat of the seven red deserts (each broader than the one before it), over the cold of the seven blue mountains (each higher than the one before it), and to the edge of the ever-encircling Sea that girds and guards the world (Allah be praised) and landed on a lonely and lonesome stretch of white, white sand as the sun set and the shadows stretched out from the last blue mountain of the world towards

the wild and restless sea.

Amal jumped off and into the purple twilight, holding the tiny gazelle with the seven keys, whereupon the rukh Bekhrad, who waits for none and no one, flew high and away far into the westering sun and was gone. The light began to fail, and Amal stood, cold and alone on the furthest edge of furthest Ocean, under a sky filled with stars that were strange to him.

She looked up and took in a long, shuddering breath. She felt as if she'd forgotten how to use her lungs, as if they'd sat forgotten in her chest for a very long time. Where was she? What was she doing here? Who was she?

Yes. Who was she?

Her hand strayed to her forehead to wipe off the stinging, salt sea-mist before it had a chance to drip into her eyes, but of course, silly, she first had to shake her hand in the air, (probably both of them) to make sure she got off all that annoying powdery, dusty, white sand. Sand and salt together would not be fun to get into her eyes either. The sweat was bad enough. Oh. And it was probably all over her face too. No, she'd have to set the gazelle down, and do this right. What a bother. Naturally, it would buck and jump and try and get away again. It was such a fearful creature. Always nervous, always worrying. She'd have to hold it between her legs, which was not the easiest thing to do, still it had taken forever to catch...

But the gazelle was gone.

And her forehead was dry, and her hands were clean. None of it made sense. She looked about her – she was someone who'd been dropped in a strangely familiar room, trying to place exactly where and when she'd been here before, but she wasn't coming up with any answers. What an odd shelter she was in. Where was the ocean? Where was the rukh? Relaxed slow respiration was the only sound in the room. A man was asleep next to her (that was Ed, now she remembered) - and then with an almost audible click, the room fell into focus and the far away beach by the blue mountains in the purple evening became unreal and Ed became real.

Ed's hand draped across her knee which was wedged into the folds of the bedspread falling off their bed. The pinpricks and drips and drops of malicious light seemed to have fallen asleep also, mingled and unconscious in ragged strips about the room, disarmed apparently – a spent time-bomb - as Marie's voice had intoned the words of this disintegrating book.

Confusion and even the memory of it ebbed away quickly, after a while the only thing Marie was feeling was sleepy. Ed was doing well, Marie was doing well, the light was curled up someplace sulking. Marie smiled the quiet smile of someone who'd fooled a particularly crafty opponent, softly closed and replaced the book in its pile and got ready for bed, careful not to disturb a peaceably snoring husband, looking younger and less troubled than he had in years, adjusting his oxygen tubes so they didn't get tangled in the blankets and sheets.

As she drifted off herself, she felt an unexpected but pleasant sense of safety. She dreamed of cradling something in her arms, something small and precious and nervous, something the size and weight of a cat but with tiny hooves.

The next day, Ed slept in, they had a doctor's appointment in the afternoon, so Marie tiptoed around the house, doing odds and ends, dusting the condo's white, shiny, plastic surfaces clean again and pushing and pulling on things whenever it seemed like it was glowing or glimmering too much for its own good. But for the most part, the house was strangely empty of the noxious creeping light. Maybe, just maybe it was giving up on Ed.

Marie did a load of laundry, made them both some lunch, got Ed ready for their big outing and made their slow way down to the car and over to the clinic. Afterwards, with Ed safely back upstairs with his football game on, Marie snuck out to do some serious coupon shopping at the mall. It was a gorgeous fall afternoon. Marie felt better than she had in years. Even the traffic wasn't bad on the way back to the condo.

She parked carefully in the alley. On the return trip in, over in the second court of the condo complex, she noticed the brilliant blue color of the stones of the fountain and the silvery sheen to the tiles on the patio and more iridescent blue in a long strip along the first couple of feet of the wall. Why hadn't she noticed before how beautifully done they were? How the lines in the tile curved backwards and forwards, in and out of themselves like an enormous elegant knot, so complicated only God could know how to untie it? The pattern seemed familiar. Where had she seen it before?

Errands finished, her mind on supper and Ed's next doctor's appointment at the end of next week, she caught up with Hobby, as she walked around the second courtyard. He was putting away his tools in the maintenance shed (why hadn't she noticed before how tall and broad the wood doors to the tool shed were? And how the metal walls looked as if they were a rusted, antiqued iron jewelry box? It must have cost a fortune. She shook her head. How they spent money here at the Turquoise Desert! No wonder the homeowner's association dues were so high...). She realized (for some reason, upon seeing him) she hadn't worried at all for almost the whole day. She'd completely forgotten to do it. In fact she hadn't worried about much of anything at all since she'd woke up that morning. She had a strange feeling in her chest. It felt odd. It felt like hope. It had been a long time since that had last happened. She couldn't remember how long. She realized she was standing there in the courtyard, staring at nothing and smiling for all the world to see – acting the crazy lady. Hobby was observing her, not impolitely. She blushed.

"You look lighter Mrs. Hodges, freer, like you ought to have someone following you with a string tied around your ankle to make sure you don't float away."

Hobby finished stepping out of his overalls and folding them away on a shelf above him. It looked like he was wearing some kind of baggy pants, and a puffy, transparent kind of shirt underneath an embroidered vest. Were those silver and gold threads? Was that silk? Washing his hands in the utility sink, he smiled, extending his now clean limbs in a courtly gesture of service towards the various and numerous bags she was carrying, saying "May I?" He seemed to be glowing in a miniature nimbus of purple-violet light. Gathering the packages and bags up in his arms, he smiled quizzically at her as she wrinkled her brow at him.

"Is everything all right, is there something I can help you with? I mean besides the bags..." he asked, closing the door of the shed behind him with his foot and waiting to hear the double click of the locks engaging. Marie was about to answer when light burst out from a low bank of foggy clouds in the West as the two of them were crossing the first courtyard of the condo complex, flooding it with curtains of shimmering gold light, instantly glazing all the brightly reflective tiles, blushing all of it a deep red-orange-yellow, and causing the fountain in the center to blaze up in coruscating liquid fire of streams of overlapping sprays of red-gold flame. For a moment the water hung still in the air, unfalling, and she could see everything very clearly.

Looking at Hobby again, she suddenly saw him plainly wearing a pair of shorts, some plastic beach sandals, and an indifferent t-shirt of gray and blue stripes. But just for a second, she could have sworn she saw a sheet of fire wound round his head and his legs ending in churning clouds of smoke and his eyes made into twin ingots of white-hot metal.

She felt faint. And when had it gotten so hot? She brought her hand up to her forehead, this time expecting nothing, but the back of her hand came back wet and gritty with small specks of sooty black. She didn't turn around on the stairs to see what Hobby looked like now. She was happy with the steady flip-flop of his sandals following here, ascending the heavily stuccoed stairs with her as she fumbled in her purse to get the keys out for her front door, all the while wondering why her skin was red as a stove.

Later after dinner, she settled in to the lumpy (but lumpy in all the right places) armchair, and watched Ed, who was facing up to the ceiling with his eyes closed, after having a rougher day of it breathing-wise and pain-wise. She lay the back of her hand against his forehead, and stroked it back and forth, then let her hand slide to his shoulder. He shifted and grunted and drew in his breath, crossing his right arm across his chest and grabbing on to her hand, then he sighed. She sighed too. They sat there holding hands for a while. It felt good.

The light, as usual, was spreading slowly around the room at their feet, rising in slow-motion as would floodwaters in a horror movie around them. It would never let up. It would never stop. It wanted Ed the way a heroin addict wanted his next fix.

She put her hand down towards the floor at the edge of a growing pool of dripping light and watched the blue-white reflections of the waves on its surface wash over the back of her hand. The light wasn't hot. But it wasn't cold either. It was adamantly neutral, in color, temperature, everything but intensity.

Well, intensity and amount. The light was becoming clearer and brighter, and in some ways finer-grained somehow. And it was starting to spill over the doorway of the bedroom, in an aggressive fashion spreading down the hallway to the second bedroom (her sewing room). She could swear she heard it splashing as it hit the wall at the bend in the hallway and began pouring industriously down the shallow stairs into their small, sunken living room.

Did it think it could drown Ed, and Marie would just stand by and watch? Well, she could put a stop to this. Two could play at this game. Adjusting her eyeglasses one-handed with a business-like air, and then balancing the aging leather-bound book one-handed with a menacing gesture over the rising and now slightly hysterical water-light, she moved her bookmark and began to read out loud in a clear voice.

> Alone in the purple twilight, beyond the reach of waves breaking on the white, white beach at the world's end, Amal spied a wall of iron with a door of diamond mostways buried in the white, white sand, and in the door was a plate made of diamond, and in the plate was a hole that glittered with a golden light. Hanging above the door was a diamond sword that moved and jumped as if restless to begin its cutting and hewing of a trespasser's limbs.
>
> Amal led the tiny gazelle with the seven keys around its neck to the door, and the diamond sword fell with a killing stroke but hesitated at the last moment, resting lightly on the back of Amal's shoulders, twitching and tickling his neck hairs, while Amal struggled to open the door with the first of the seven keys, the diamond key.
>
> And opening it, the diamond sword fell harmlessly at Amal's feet, the diamond key melted into the air, and picking up the sword and pushing it through his sash, Amal descended a set of iron stairs deep into the earth that led to a golden door, this time with a gold plate, and a gold sword, and a hole that

sputtered with silver sparks.

Using the tiny gazelle's second key, the golden one, and opening the door, and grabbing the now fallen golden sword, he descended another set of iron stairs deeper into the earth to a third door and a sword, this time of silver. Repeating what he had done before, this opened onto more iron stairs and a fourth door, of copper, and then a fifth one, of glass, and finally a sixth one, of wood.

Beyond this door, in the center of a room of iron walls was a basket made of grass, with a chain of grass and lock of grass upon it. On entering the room, a net of knotted grass fell heavily on Amal's back and covered the room, Amal, and the tiny gazelle, and became heavier and heavier the longer they rested upon them. Quickly, using the seventh and last key, this one of woven grass, he undid the chain and the basket fell open and a leathern bag fell out, and the grassy net fell at his feet, neatly folded, and as small as his fist.

Inside the leathern bag was a fistful of bright, transparent powder. In deepening dark, taking the tiny gazelle, the basket, the net, and the six swords, Amal ran back up the stairs, each door closing behind him, and placed the last of the three silk-hair mice the King of the Hind had given him on a flat circle of hard-packed sand on the beach at the end of the world. Then he sat down.

Waiting and watching, hidden secretly behind the iron wall, a thundering flap of wings announced Bekhrad's arrival, and with one gulp, two gulps, three gulps, the mice were gone and jumping up on the great eagle's broad, white-feathered back, Amal flew for a month and a day, back through the red deserts (each one narrower than one before) and back over the blue mountains (each one lower than one before) to the Emir's palace where Amal had left the daughter of the Sultan imprisoned, waiting to be wed or be beheaded by the scheming Wazir Zalam, the Wazir being still master of the genie Isfaq of the brass chest.

At the palace, Amal thanked and salaamed goodbye to Bekhrad and carrying the tiny gazelle, the net, the bag and the swords, he set out to begin his search for the daughter of the Sultan. He entered the palace, drew his diamond sword, and ran searching through the silver court with the sapphire fountain, diamond sword held high in front of him, and none could stop him.

But the Sultan's daughter was nowhere to be seen. So he continued deeper. He ran searching through the golden court with the ruby fountain, diamond sword held high in front of him, and none again could stop him.

But the Sultan's daughter was still nowhere to be seen, so he continued deeper yet. He ran searching to the very gates of the diamond court, diamond sword held high in front of him, and none could stop him. But here Amal had to pause before the white blazing doors of the diamond court, dazzled by a river of light pouring through the half-opened gate, and he could not see.

Not holding his sword high in front of him, but shading his eyes he struggled just for a moment to see through the waves of white flame, and prepared his soul to dash through them, praising Allah's name with his sword flying in front of him. But before he could even suck in his breath, a poisoned knife of blackest black flew out of the resplendent radiance, past the diamond sword, past the gazelle and pierced him directly through the side of his neck and shoulder, pinning Amal to the gold-chased tiles on the floor of the golden court with the ruby fountain that lay before the blazing white doors, half-opened of the diamond court. He knew the time of his death had come.

For a moment, Marie was blinded, she was surrounded by a white light that was deep and wide, and she was sinking further and further, faster and faster, and her useless eyes were covered by something opaque and heavy and wrong, and her mind hung in front of her, dazzled by buckets of light pouring down from overhead, slashing and ripping all before it into gleaming shreds, ribbons and strips, breaking her into smaller and smaller and smaller pieces so it could more easily dissolve her into motionlessness and nothingness and pure transparency.

Then there was a streak of wedge-shaped blackness, and she felt herself being ripped upwards and sewn together all at the same time, with a weird sucking sound that resembled her ancient Hoover vacuum cleaner (sitting this very minute in the hall closet) struggling to clean the largest, dirtiest carpet ever made, and she was whole, and the light was suddenly gone, and she was back in her broken chair, and her right hand still lay on Ed's shoulder clasped tight in his right hand and she was breathing and it was night.

The aged book was on the floor, the front cover slightly askew, its ribbon bookmark sticking out from somewhere in the middle. She looked at Ed's face to see if she could see any pain, any bewilderment, but he was quiet, even more peaceful than he'd been last night. The light now was nowhere to be seen, only the homely circle of lamp light hesitantly illuminating the armchair, the bed, the book, Ed and Marie.

All she could think was "that was a close call."

"Wake up, sleepyhead" Marie felt agreeable, amiable prodding on her left shoulder. She was sitting up. She must have fallen asleep in the armchair. Heaven only knew what tortures of aching joints and throbbing muscles awaited her today for all her sins of wrong-sleeping last night.

And was that bacon she smelled? And coffee? Ed was up, wheeling the oxygen on its little cart back out of the room, dressed in an old pair of shorts and his t-shirt covered in seventeen different colors of paint and primer he used to wear back at the old house when he did his house projects. What she needed was a shower. She could hear Ed doing something with the toaster and humming to himself far off in the kitchen. She hadn't heard that in years – or had he ever done that? She couldn't remember. She certainly wasn't going to ask about it, she thought she'd just let herself enjoy it. Even the morning sunshine seemed determined to be cheerful today. She exhaled, and at the same time pushed herself up and into this unusual day.

Ed was pretty tired after lunch later on, so Marie grabbed her checkbook and went out to get some supplies for dinner tonight. For once, the stairs weren't a challenge - she was the new Marie - a well-oiled, newly-purchased walking machine and not the old, cast-off, broken-down appliance ready for the Goodwill bin or worse. It was a good feeling. Yes, her heart was making her chest grip on her with that uncomfortable tightness, but that was pretty much par for the course these days, and Marie wasn't about to start complaining about something like that. She was alive. Life was good.

Hobby met her at the entrance of the second courtyard, moving forward out of the shade of one of the courtyard walls and into the sun in the plaza center where Marie was crossing towards one of the huge ornamental gates. She could see he was handing her three orange, red flowers from one of those tropical-looking bushes that she could never remember the name of, the ones near the front entrance he was always having to trim back so they didn't hide the entire doorway.

"I found these growing where they shouldn't, hidden from view" offered Hobby smiling, "and rather than throw them in the trash, I thought I would give them to someone who would appreciate their beauty."

Marie felt herself blushing again. She stepped back into the courtyard to take them and thank him and the sun must have caught her straight in the eyes because they were watering something fierce and for a few moments she had a hard time seeing anything, let alone a bouquet or a friendly South American. She also must have been coming down with something too, because her throat felt strangled and for a moment she couldn't speak properly. She was, in summary, a mess. But she was strangely happy. The unusual day was continuing, well, unusually.

Hobby looked dismayed and distressed and (fruitlessly) looked and patted himself for a clean, not soil-or-grass-stained handkerchief or cloth or something, anything with which he might help her coughing and her eyes. She looked as if she were rapidly dissolving in front of his eyes into a candidate for an emergency ambulance call - except she was smiling. Crying and smiling.

"Unless I am acting inappropriately - I am sorry for bothering you" he added, letting her lean for a second on his arm, and pulling the flowers back towards him and downwards into the shadows. Marie found some Kleenex in her purse and dabbed her eyes a little and coughed a lot. Trying to smile brightly and encouragingly, she talked through the large frog caught obstinately in her throat

"No, no, no bother, Hobby. No, they're very nice, thank you very much for thinking of me." Hobby smiled back at her in return, and brought the flowers up into the light again for her to admire.

"But, Hobby, if I could pick them up when I come back, after I've gone shopping, I really do like them, really - then I could take them upstairs with me. Really, thank you" and with that she rushed out the gate, Kleenex working her eyes, clearing her throat, blushing as if she were fourteen again. With an uncharacteristic quick step, she rapidly disappeared down the block and around the corner. Hobby watched her, holding the flowers down at his side, his face calm as usual, a gentleness and compassion in his eyes.

Much later, she returned through the back-alley gate, the back way, and the whitish tiles and the blue-tiled fountain shone blankly under the hot afternoon sun. Marie felt tired now, and weak. Her heart felt like it wanted to race. It wasn't happy. It was a little unsettled. But it was nothing serious, nothing she hadn't been through many times before.

She fumbled with her keys, and got in the first gate, she walked a little unsteadily towards the next courtyard, with the goldish tiles and the red fountain and saw the maintenance shed was already closed up, and Hobby was gone, but the flowers were in a small vase, only chipped just a little, by the door in the cool shade of the archway. She struggled up the stairs, carrying the groceries and the flowers and collapsed in the condo, closing the door with an unsteady hand that shook a little. There. Safe and sound.

She could hear the sound of the T.V. broadcasting some sports program from the living room. Ed was talking back to the sports announcer, like he used to do. She smiled for a second, then reached out haphazardly for one of the dining room chairs, plopping down into it with grunt, dropping one of the sacks of groceries on the floor beside her. She rested for a second, scared of her own fragility and of the uncooperativeness of her own body - but Marie was being patient with it, as you would with an old shoe that just needed adjusting a bit before you put it on and got it comfortable. After five or ten minutes or so she was fine. Good as rain.

That night, Ed was tired too, mostly dozing on and off as they talked back and forth like they used to. Like the old days. A few words, carefully chosen. Making a little go a long way. Marie could barely keep her eyes open, sitting up with him. She was so tired. So tired.

The light rose much more quickly, and emphatically, around her aching feet. It had a kind of insistent, mean pointed quality to it, like it knew it could bully her tonight, persistently, and she'd have to work hard to get around it. It even looked, now and then, as if it were trying to lunge at her. And at Ed. Well, she still had some fight in her. She managed to get her glasses on and the book out as the waves got prouder and sassier, as they sloshed higher and higher. She started reading, looking around their bedroom with a grim smile, speaking loudly and clearly with her best speaking voice.

Dimly, through a mist the color of a fog on a summer's morning, Amal saw the Wazir approaching, surrounded by five monstrously large, heavily-armed Mamelukes, leading the Sultan and the Sultan's daughter blindfolded (she had been charmed by the Wazir's sorcery so that any who looked into her eyes fell hopelessly and violently in love with her, because of that, she no longer had the use of her eyes).

In his hands, the Wazir carried the brass chest, which smoked and boiled and fumed with black, incandescent flames so bright it hurt the eyes to see it and so hot it burnt the skin to feel it. Amal looked about him for his swords, but they had disappeared. He looked for his net, but it too was gone. He looked for his basket, but it had likewise vanished and was nowhere to be found. The bag with the bright, sparkling powder rested in his left hand, and the tiny gazelle stood by his right watching Amal with great, sad eyes as Amal's heart's blood drained out of him into a bright red pool on the golden floor.

As the Wazir exulted and leaned over Amal, Amal swooned, his eyes unseeing, his limbs without movement, and a single tear from the tiny gazelle fell from one soft and gentle eye down, down, down upon his bloody, ruined body, which touching him sealed up his wounds as water falling together, making Amal whole, and the gazelle laid herself quietly down, pushing the leathern bag towards Amal and breathed no more.

The Wazir waxed wroth, his face terrible to behold. He drew back, preparing some worse mischief. Amal thought quickly and opened up the leathern bag and threw the bright, sparkling powder from the Seven Doors at the End of the World onto the smoking and rumbling brass chest, whereupon the Wazir and the chest disappeared in explosions of smoky soot and flaming fire, and the Sultan and the Sultan's daughter fell back onto the floor, and the pieces of the brass and wooden chest fell at Amal's feet reforming themselves into their former form.

Out of the smoke, the genie Isfaq arose, fuming and roiling as would a thunderstorm of fire and he tore the roof off of the diamond court just for the joy of doing it. Laughing, Isfaq stood mightily above them, legs like smoking mountains, a mouth like a bottomless cave, teeth like gray and blackened houses, eyes like burning foundries, nostrils like great iron cauldrons and hands like grasping, broken trees.

"You have released Isfaq from the brass chest, so therefor I give you three wishes, and then I must slay you", said a voice rolling over them like the greatest waves of the sea, pounding them into the ground as those same seas break crushingly on hard sand, "and there is no helping it, for I have sworn by Allah and His Prophet to slay whomever holds the chest after I grant his three wishes, I must do it and I will. You have bested the Wazir Zalam. You hold the chest. You now have your wishes, then Isfaq must slay you."

Amal thought for a moment, then thought again, then thought some more. Then Amal said "I am only a humble porter, what do I know of the might of genie's and magic wishes? My first wish is to give the chest and all my remaining wishes to the Sultan." The Genie Isfaq clapped his hands, a fire raged, and lightning struck and the chest was sitting, bubbling away at the Sultan's feet. The Sultan was not pleased and glared at Amal with a fierce glare, with something other than love and something other than gratitude in his heart. But the Sultan did not do anything, and neither did he say anything.

"Come, decide, you have two wishes left, O Sultan, O Holder of the brass chest, and then I must slay you" rumbled Isfaq, a laughing mountain of shadow and flame standing above the palace. "O my Lord, If you would allow your base servant to approach" offered Amal, who walked through a sea of sabre-armed soldiers to the angry Sultan.

He whispered into the ear of the Sultan who nodded once, then twice, then three times and then the Sultan said "As for our second wish, we ask that our daughter's sight be restored as it was before, to its former state." And before the Sultan could finish speaking, the genie clapped his hands, a fire raged, and lightning struck and the Sultan's daughter stood, no longer blindfolded but veiled, and blinking her green eyes in the smoky light of the ruins of the diamond court. "As for our third wish, we ask that the brass chest be given to Isfaq the genie" - and with a clap, and a raging of fire, and a striking of lightning, Isfaq bellowed and disappeared along with the brass chest and the smoke and with the little that was left of the roof of the diamond court.

Afterwards, the Sultan reflected that anyone so clever and so brave as to outwit demons and wazirs would be a useful help in ruling a kingdom, and so decreed Amal his heir and made Amal his son-in-law, marrying him to his veiled daughter, and thus Amal lived in joy to the end of his days and the kingdom prospered as never before under Amal's wisdom and justice.

And that is the tale of Amal ibn Halamah and the Gazelle of the Seven Keys, although the tale of the Three Blind Merchants of Samarkand is even more wondrous and worthy of being told.

And so begins the tale of the Three Blind Merchants, I have heard that once, in the Great Souk of Samarkand there were three greedy brothers...

Marie felt the book slide from her hands, and noticed a piercing, but not painful, glare all about her, her eyes had suddenly been opened, but they were not opened onto her white-walled bedroom and her lumpy chair, they were opened onto a hall of crystal walls without a ceiling, bare under a blue, blue sky.

Except the walls were light. And the sky was of more light. And there were waves (of light) lapping just under her chin, and far off she could hear Ed happily snoring into the night (the light was leaving him alone, it had never been after him, how had she missed that?) and her heart raced and raced under that cloudless sky in the peaceable light, the light that came for her, to her, with her, the restful, gentle light that softly, simply overwhelmed her mouth, then her nostrils, then her ears and eyes, and finally surged over her the top of her head and she was falling, upwards, higher and higher, drifting contented away and beyond and above her home (she and Ed's home), moving towards another home she was just beginning to remember from a long, long time before.

NIGHT STREETS

I want you to imagine this. Concentrate. Actively. Listen to my words. Try to anticipate what I am going to say, ask yourself - how would this make me feel, if I were in his shoes? - what would I think? - what would I do? - what would I say? Try it. Push your emotional ectoplasm out of its fleshy shell and attempt to wriggle your new pulpy, insubstantial, spiritual fingers around and about the pale and flickering, living flames that are, after all, the entirety of what we dimly see of the extraordinary bonfires surrounding us, every day, every hour.

Yes, the flames I am so awkwardly waxing lyrical about are, of course, people - the people around you, the people you see, meet, ignore, despise, laugh at, laugh with, love, imitate, and praise every day. Try and feel the miracle of a multitude of extraordinary souls wandering companionably next to you as you make your daily walk through this wilderness of sensations and ideas. Try it.

I'll stop for just a moment, and give you the chance to exercise your mind's exemplary empathy muscles.

Good. In fact, very good.

Now, try and see just one - one other single jet of light trudging, head down, feet dragging, breath heaving beside you, another being sincerely trying to make sense of it all, just the same as you. See it.

Go ahead. You can do it. Try it.

O.K.

Good.

Now look at me.

Try and see me.

Really see me, (yes, you'd probably already guessed it, all this extravagant language had a purpose, an agenda – yes, it was directed towards something and someone – yes, that someone would be me).

So. Try and see me.

Imagine a foggy stretch of asphalt, swept regularly every few seconds by sheets of mist and rain. It's night. Look at the unhealthy reflections of pink-orange street lights in the puddles in the gutter. Feel the cold humidity seeping through your sable silk shirt, your thin, black pants, and in and around the cast on your right foot. Look at your watch, you'll see it's past midnight. Feel the uncomfortable friction and bunching of your new crutches under your armpits. Swing your body out into an unknown street and try and cross it, as quickly as you're able, - you're a twitching piece of future roadkill, helpless before the challenge of an empty stretch of cross-able pavement – see if you can make it. The world is a dangerous and difficult place.

A car screeches around a nearby corner and accelerates wetly towards you, bass booming ominously, as would a fog horn in a lighthouse, warning off pedestrians from a dangerous, moving metallic reef. That's me, not the car driver, the guy on crutches, scrambling to get back onto the sidewalk, cold, wet, angry, confused, determined, terrified, depressed, self-destructive and more than a little lost - that is, if anybody, anybody I trusted implicitly (and that list was so short it had no names on it) had thought to ask me what my feelings were at that exact moment. The truth, surprising as this may be to you, was I was quite alone - utterly, absolutely, and predictably alone - but all that comes later in my story, as you'll see.

Yes, you'll see. You'll see me. That is, if you want to see me. It's hard to see a person sometimes. It takes work. I'm hoping you're willing to do the work. I'm betting you are.

Anyways…

Blah. Blah. Blah.

Well, that's what I should have said. All the cold, wet, angry shit. It sounds so poetic. But honestly, if anybody had asked me how I felt, I'd probably have looked at them like they were a crazy person and responded "I'm great, fine, couldn't be better, having the night of my life, thanks for asking, now could you tell me where the party is and point me towards the bar?" That second response, that's what I probably would have said, and you know what? - I don't know if I would have been lying, either way. Poets want to get smashed too. It's never clear cut, it's always a spectrum, and I wanted to get drunk.

I backed up rapidly, with as much dignity as I could muster, imitating an arthritic, six-foot, black praying mantis dancing woodenly in the rain, shouting "Fuck you" repeatedly at the retreating form of the car, imagining I was hearing aggressive laughter over the phat rap music that briefly enveloped me. I flailed my way back to the curb.

I didn't want anybody looking out an apartment window, say from a party I might be heading towards, seeing a soggy, uncool cripple pathetically trying to "cross the street" - it all sounded like a bad joke, the kind I would probably like to tell (hey guys - come here, come here, you gotta see this), looking out a window at a guy on crutches in the rain jaywalking, me standing on the safety of a dry faux-bamboo floor, wrapped warmly in a loud party, behind the courage of a full martini glass. Yeah, I'd do that in a heartbeat.

Breathing heavily and jerkily, I listened for more cars, heard them this time, paddled backwards, ended up pole-vaulting sideways and spun myself out onto the sidewalk, far, far, from any tempting, rainwater-filled, eminently splash-able potholes. I wasn't going to make it. Ever. I'd never get to any local gatherings. I'd never get across the street. I'd stay here for the rest of my life. More cars hydroplaned by me. I whipped out my phone and called my dad.

Why - you might ask, and if you didn't, well, I'll ask for you — why would a son call his father at 12:07 AM on a Saturday night on his way to a party? My dad had similar questions. You'll just have to hang around and see for yourself, the same as my pa did that night.

"Kevin, is that you? What's wrong?" said a relaxed voice, probably a little more relaxed now than it had been a couple of hours and a fifth of scotch earlier that night. Well, maybe not a fifth. He still knew my name. But, seriously, I didn't even try to keep up with my dad anymore once he rolled out of the station on his happy train and got serious about his drinking for the night. More than just drinking was going on. It sounded as if some ancient, colorized World War II movie was bouncing along noisily in the background on the T.V. - either that, or my pa was in the middle of a late night, suburban strafing run manned by modern kamikaze Japanese pilots (probably formerly punctual, hardworking, now-laid-off-redundant-and-mad-as-hell salary-men) in their museum-quality, restored zeroes drumming up consumer spending by machine-gunning random consumer possessions into little piles of plastic and metal bits. I could see it. Clearly. I know. I have a very vivid imagination.

Everyone tells me that - the thing about my imagination. Although not everyone who tells me appreciates it or enjoys it, at least not the way I appreciate it and enjoy it.

I understand that. I really do. To each his own. For the un-appreciative, I have just two words. Fuck and you. So, what was I talking about? Oh, yeah, dad. The pater.

Dad, by the way, was pure, unadulterated, retired Gunnery Sergeant Marine, with various ribbons for actions and service that I swear were visible, pinned to his left pec whether he was naked in the shower or encased in a tuxedo at a wedding. I knew all about them, because he used to have me hang his clothes when they came back from the cleaners, and he taught me the arcane science of where, how, and in what order to pin those marine ribbons on his newly-pressed marine chest. It had to be exact. It had to be done right. It had to be done right the first time. My father. Literally a drill Sergeant I guess.

Dad and his opinions were reinforced, missile-barrel steel - reliably inflexible and tenaciously unyielding. He was big on action, crushingly disdainful of hesitation and not a big fan of fear. At least he never acknowledged he was ever afraid of anything or anyone. Not out loud. At least, never to me that is. If he saw a problem, and saw a solution he wasn't shy about not exploring a myriad of alternatives. I swear my first words were "lead, follow, or get the hell out of the way." In his world, the connect-the-dots pictures always had only two dots - A and B - he could never comprehend exactly why no one else but him (and his Marine buddies) could figure out all you had to do was connect the two. A, B, add a line – that was the secret of life. What's the big deal?

An imaginative son must have been a trial and a puzzle to him. I can see that. It makes sense. I know my marine father was and has always been a trial and a puzzle to me. There's a certain symmetry to that. But back to my phone call.

"Nothing, nothing's wrong, pa. You know, I was thinking, thinking about what you said earlier" I started out, reasonably enough to my ears, but quickly hit the first of many roadblocks, or should I say troop movements? Discussing things with my dad routinely took on all the features of a full-scale Department of Defense War Game - advancing your center, watching for flanking maneuvers, protecting your supply lines and scouting your rear for un-looked-for ambushes. Planning, subterfuge, murderous intent, that was the stuff of ordinary conversation. I'm not complaining. Really. I'm just saying that's what it was.

"Do you have any idea, sport, what time it is?" An armored division moved toward my right flank.

"Uh, late?" A feint, a weak counterattack on my part to buy time to get him to reveal the weakest point in his line.

"Bingo! Let's talk about you buying my old Honda Sunday, tomorrow, O.K.? - you'll get a better deal out of me sobered up and my mind on something other than Iwo Jima. Iwo Jima and bed that is." Dramatic charge from his center, expected to be overwhelming.

"Dad, I wasn't calling about the car, I was calling about mom."

Flanking maneuver and murderous intent (on my part) That got me about ten seconds of silence. I took that as an admission of defeat, at least for this round, and a sign to continue.

Now I ask you, and I'm genuinely, candidly interested in an answer, any answer at all - now, why would it be inappropriate to talk about vehicular parental purchases late on a Saturday night, but perfectly O.K. to ask about my dead mother? Or maybe I know the answer to that one. Maybe that was the reason I'd called. Maybe I'm just a bastard and a bad son.

"So, Kev" dad's voice sounded briefly and then stopped, I imagined I heard the sounds of a tiny T.V. crowd frantically yelling battle cries to encourage my dad to ignore me more pointedly as usual, or maybe they were encouraging him to fight harder - I couldn't decide which. Anyways. the echo in the silence from my dad's big barcolounger sounded bigger and bigger, less and less the kind of silence that could actually be filled.

I heard him breathing. He knew I could hear it. He must be staring at the ceiling – he did that when the old brain gears were straining to grind and mesh or when he was mad - or maybe he was just pouring himself another drink – he did that too when he was mad.

"What happened that night, dad? The night mom died. What really happened?"

That wasn't what I wanted to ask. Dad was two time zones away, and I'm sure he was wishing he could see my face, see what I was up to. He wasn't sure if he should ignore what I'd just asked or answer it yet again, or hunker down and begin slugging his way through my defenses to see what in the hell I was really after. Or maybe he was just tired. Or maybe just overwhelmed by memories. What I really wanted to ask was - Was I the reason they had been getting a divorce? But I'd asked that so many times since I was in 2nd grade, in so many different ways, verbally, non-verbally, written, by looks, by fuckin' crazy stunts I'd pull and force my dad to bail me out of - so many fucking ways that the sum-total of answers to that simple question would have filled entire series of Encyclopedia Britannicas - the cross-indexing alone would have taken up a whole bookshelf. Anyway, he didn't answer. He just sighed (which in a retired Mar. Gun. Sgt. etc. sounds more like a growl). He sighed and he said "Why are you doing this, Kev? Why?"

"You know why" I replied and clicked the end button with my thumb. It was abrupt and satisfactory, hanging up on him, and I was glad - glad that it was raining, glad that no one observing the chill guy in the black in the middle of the block was crying like a kindergartner, glad no one was watching me staring this way and that, arguing with myself, biting on my bottom lip, practically fuckin' sawing it in half.

So there we were, my pa, with an ancient, scabbed over wound a couple of feet long, bleeding again in the early morning hours in a den in a comfortable suburban house somewhere in the Midwest courtesy of his youngest, and me trying to pretend I was like everyone else (however *that* was), with a matching four-foot wound, newly opened, bleeding genially and freely into a night raucous with parties and experimentation.

Yes. Envelope-pushing, boundary-breaking, crazy-as-batshit life-research, wasn't that what being 23 was for? Why did I call him? Did I just want company? Someone to bleed with me, or just notice me bleeding, and the only one in the entire world I could hurt as deeply as I'd been hurt was my dad. Maybe. Probably. Yeah. So I called him, just to share the pain. Something like that. Maybe. Probably. I don't know. I was a fucking idiot. A piece of shit son. No wonder no one wanted to be around me.

That's what it felt like. That's what I was thinking as I pushed out into the river that was 35th street, poling my way across on crutches as if I were a fucking Venetian gondolier, snuffling and wiping at my eyes so I'd look at least halfway normal when I got to wherever the hell it was I was trying to get to. I wasn't even looking for cars that time - and of course, because I wasn't even looking, there were no cars, none at all. God watches over fools and children and drunks. I was two out of the three, I guess. Working on number three. I poled on.

Are you still trying to feel me? I'll make it easier for you. Watch very carefully. See me two days before on a Wednesday night up in L.A. getting a call from my friend Eddie and calling in sick to work to head down to San Diego for a quick night of illusion, delusion, and rank amusement.

Wednesday stretched into Thursday when I was kicked out of a very blond girl's apartment early in the morning (well, early for me, 10 or 11 A.M) . Me - in a red-limned, hung-over, low-energy, bored rage sadistically making off-color jokes about bourgeois, protestant-work-ethic value systems that included jobs and punctuality and reliability. She, hurt and surprised - bundling me off and out of her life as you would a gallon of milk you'd thought the night before was reasonably bearable, but with just a single morning sniff understood was unspeakably spoiled.

So. Eddie wasn't answering his cell, or his doorbell, That meant I took my margarita-stained black-clothed self to a seedy, local sports bar, had a few beers and a basket of onion rings and passed out for a few hours behind a potted plant in a booth in the corner. Charming picture. I'm sure that's what management thought as they escorted me out and deposited me on the sidewalk half a block from the bar in the painfully accurate glare of later afternoon light.

I was halfway to homelessness. This time Eddie was up, and after a shower and some rubbing with stain remover got my clothes and myself back into a reasonable facsimile of cleanliness and responsibility. The rest was a blur. It involved shots, beer, more shots, me wrecking my car, an overnight visit to an emergency room for my cast, a 24 hour stay in jail for a DUI which mostly involved vomiting, sitting and sobering up, and now me hobbling on crutches to one of Eddie's friends (a guy named Michael). By now my job as an accounts receivable clerk was in the past tense. But maybe that had been my unconscious plan all along.

So what are you thinking? How does it feel so far?

The apartment complex was an architectural concoction from the fevered mind of an Aladdin-fixated set designer, maybe something Rudy Valentino would have requested (and been denied as too expensive for the production budget) in the Sheik, or the Son of Sheik or the Return of the Son of Sheik. Except, yeah, those Sheik sets were all tents, tents and carpets and dunes - this was more an Arabian castle, something you'd see a flying carpet flying out of. It was a place. It had a party. The party had alcohol. I didn't have anywhere else to go.

A good part of my education, my formative years you might say were spent planted in front of a television set, which were in turn (the two of us, the set and myself) planted in front of my pa, sitting through afternoon reruns, evening prime time, into late at night infomercials and classic Hollywood. My older siblings were grown and gone. I was mid-life crisis surprise. Guess what? You're a dad again. After mom left the family was just me and dad. Me, dad and the T.V.

Our father-son conversations were usually directed at an intermediary - the T.V. screen - I don't think either one of us were ever sure if the other was talking to the incessantly blathering idiot box or to his living, breathing relative sitting five feet away from him. We slept together, conking out around 2 or 3 in the morning, me on the floor, him in his chair.

I used to nap a lot at school. I didn't get a lot of homework done. I did a couple of years of college, mostly History and English (which I had an awkward talent for) but bailed after I realized I was never going to get a job whose sole requirement was reading books, and (probably the more honest reason) I discovered clubs, girls, parties, and drinking. And the rest (as they say, no pun intended) was history.

A certificate program for the chronically unemployed (the state's idea) and a hellish year of living at home with my dad as an adult (my family's idea), borrowing money all the while from my increasingly unsympathetic brothers and sisters got me a trade (clerking in accounting) and a one-way ticket (thanks, dad) to California to "wise up, grow a pair, and be a man."

So, do I seem real to you? If you saw me on the street, would you look twice? Or am I just another one of the soulless, faceless multitude, another body shuffling past you at the mall, on the street corner, in the supermarket parking lot? Am I someone else to ignore as you worry about potential personal crises, anticipate pleasures, relive and review recent painful social incidents. You sleepwalk through your own life, burning your present away, lost in fantasies of the past and future. And all around you are amazing beings, people like me, with stories, opinions, hopes, dreams, fears. Do they seem real to you, at all?

All right, all right, you've twisted my arm, I'll come clean. So to speak.

And yes, I was already planning to position myself in a breezy, well-ventilated place in Michael's apartment, so the rich, pervasive perfume of jail cells, sweat, beer, mildew and aluminum crutch that was turning into my own personal signature scent wouldn't prejudice any females of the species present at the aforesaid party against yours truly.

And yes, you are absolutely right, I had my work cut out for me. If I was going to come clean, clean in the physical sense, the sense I'm supposing you mean of being relatively dirt and odor-free, I certainly had a lot of cleaning up to do. But that's not the sense I was suggesting. I was aiming more at a metaphysical sense of clean.

The truth was I had not traveled down here to San Diego solely on a lark, although being my strangely attractive, rebellious, irresponsible self, I'd been known to do that at times. No, it wasn't pleasure that brought me to San Diego from Los Angeles, it was business. I was actually hiding out - badly, like an amateur hider, I give you that, but hiding out nonetheless. I was, to use my carefully collected Hollywood vocabulary garnered during the long collapse and ruin of my wasted youth, on the lam. I was running, and they were probably catching up. I needed to come up with a plan. I needed a point A, a point B, and a line.

At this point, you should probably know a little more about me. You do want to know more, don't you? More about humble moi? Of course you do. You're actively listening, anticipating my next phrase, hanging on my every word. Good. Good listener. I'd be patting you on your collective head, if it were within my reach at this moment. Pat. Pat. Pat. Good listener.

Yes.

So.

Uh, what was I about to say?

Completely forgot.

Oh well.

Let's see. What can we talk about? How about my looks? All right, then, my looks. Now, the one thing I have done consistently, even religiously, is go to the gym. Maybe not in the last 48 hours, but usually, believe me, it's something I feel compelled to do. By habit, yes, but mostly by decision. It's more, to me (and I could talk endlessly about this) along the lines of paying on a car insurance policy than it is doing something noble and health-giving – or maybe it's the same as paying into a savings account for your kid's college tuition (something I wouldn't know anything about, and neither would my dad). O.K., maybe my analogies are getting a tad weak and tired, not unlike myself, standing here at the gate of Michael's complex thinking about physical fitness. But what I mean to say is I don't do it to stay healthy, because it's the Right Thing To Do, I do it because it gets me girls and helps intimidate guys.

Yeah. I could talk the health game, talk it up with the best of them sure, but that was never the reason. I wasn't much of an athlete in high school, but one thing I did do was pump iron, an hour and a half a day, seven days a week, for years - and first impressions like a barrel chest, an 8-pack, watermelon arms and tree-trunk legs for some reason ignite certain DNA, hard-coded sequences in the human brain and get you things automatically - lots of things - things that you want that other guys aren't getting because they didn't take the time to think about igniting DNA.

I did think. I ignite. I am nothing if not practical. I do what works. I leave whatever else there is to do to someone else - and I let them do it. I am my father's son, I have to say that.

I could hear the apartment long before I could see it. Getting beeped through a gate and a door and hiking up three flights of narrow stairs is not the easiest activity when you're slightly buzzed, mostly soaked and totally on crutches. But I shouldered the responsibility manfully, and surprised Michael (I'm assuming it was Michael) at the door to a very small, very loud, and very crowded apartment ("Now, who are you, dude? Oh, right, Eddie's friend from L.A., yeah, what did you say? Oh hell, yeah, great party. Eddie? What? Oh, Eddie's already here, over in the back talking to the chick with the pink hair by the window. Pink Hair. Window. What? Come on in bud, come on in. No, not more girls, Eddie's friend - sorry dude someone just askin' me who was at the door. What? Beers in a keg under the counter or in bottles in the frig. Hey Jonesie, what the fuck? Give me five, man, give me five. Sorry, what did you say? The frig man, they're in the frig. And what the hell happened to your foot, man? Bummer."). Thus, I crutched my way in.

In this complicated process of greeting and entering, someone tripped on someone else, spilling a beer, resulting in louder laughter, resulting in someone turning up the music to drown out the laughter, which just served to make the laughter louder. A door with an irritated face opened up down the hallway as I slipped, hopping sideways, between Michael and another guy with spiky black hair and so I banged Michael's door shut with my shoulder as promptly and as firmly as is possible for a one-legged man to bang. I didn't want the police showing up (which looked to be more and more likely before the night was through). And if someone's fingers weren't already dialing the police somewhere in that apartment building, at the current rate of acceleration in decibels, I estimated the probability of it happening in the very near future to be good to excellent. I needed to get in and get out. I needed to speed-beer and bogey.

Having broad shoulders and an extra pair of aluminum legs isn't conducive to gliding effortlessly through a big party in a small place. It turned out Mr. Black Spiked Hair was having an argument with a decent-looking, big-chested girl with short brown hair and the only way to beer and blessed release was through the middle of it - so I pushed and apologized my way past, not unpleasantly pressing against more than a few female fronts and behinds in the long journey from door to beer, slipping on some puddles of spilled alcohol, racing a drag queen for the last Heineken (and losing). I positioned myself with some effort by the window, a Corona in each hand, and watched for flashing blue and red lights as I downed my first bottle as if it were a solo jello shot.

It was time to survey the environs, get the lay of the land, as I nursed Corona number two. Ms. Pink hair glanced my way, more than once, over Eddie's shoulder (even I could see trouble down that road), and Big Chest seemed consistently to have (angry) eyes only for Mr. Spiky, and as for the rest, well, surveying the room from my perch on the window sill, it looked like a party in full swing. Which was funny, because that's what it was. A night of possibilities. A land of opportunity for a guy like me, who had appetites and who had the skills to satisfy those appetites.

A few of the males there had definitely perked their ears up and sniffed the air when I stumbled my way to the kitchen, maybe even pressing a little too close as I squeezed by. I was getting a little play time. Well, to each his own. I'd always thought if I were gay, sex would be easier than falling off a bar stool. Well, at least as frequent, which was pretty frequent with me (both sex and the bar stool falling part, I mean).

Another girl with vinyl, stoplight-red pants had managed to catch my eye once or twice - now she blazed brightly in my head - a possibility and an opportunity - all wrapped up in one tight, primary-colored package. I was going to need a place to go and someone to go with tonight. She'd work.

I did my crooked smile, with the upraised eyebrow (about to look her way), inhaled, immediately regretted it, and opened the window up a little more to waft my stench street-wards rather than party-wards (maybe Michael had some deodorant I could borrow - do guys share deodorant? I'd asked to share a lot of things, girls included, but that's one I don't think I'd ever asked before). I glanced appreciatively at Red Pants, keeping it up until I was sure she caught it, and finished the last of the second beer as I pushed upwards and outwards, making my slow, wobbling way towards Michael and odorlessness. I managed to do a quick frontal press past Red Pants and Ms. Pink on my intersection course with Michael over by his people-strewn bed, and grab two more beers at the same time as I swung by the kitchen. At the rate I was going it was probably going to take another half hour to talk to Michael. No, scratch that, another hour. All of which was just fine. Hell, I had supplies enough to last at least that long.

I never made it. Two thirds of the way back over to Michael there was heavy banging on the door, and a gruff voice from the other side. Several people looked like they were throwing things out the window, exhaling repeatedly and waving their hands in front of their faces. Other people were laughing at the hand wavers, and helping them half-heartedly between fits of guffawing. The music turned off suddenly and in the distance, I could see Michael cracking the door open and talking to someone as they shouldered their way into the crowd. Two blue uniforms with San Diego City badges jimmied and jostled their ways into the crush, causing waves of compaction to ripple from the door across the room to the bed, kitchen, and window. I was squeezed the way you would a watermelon seed and spit through the mob and out up onto the bed where I plopped down, crutches, beers, stained black pants and all facing the wall. Beside me was the bathroom door, open, and the tiny bathroom, empty. I squished inside, sat on the toilet and let the door half-close.

As I finished my two beers I looked around. Amazingly, the medicine cabinet over my head was swung wide open, and on top of a three-quarter-used tube of well-squeezed toothpaste lay a roll-on bar of some professional-grade, nuclear-powered deodorant - the kind maybe an offshore drill worker would use between yanking-sessions, pulling pipe out of seabed. Shamelessly, over the sound of the party shutting down, I slathered the roll generously over various parts of my body. I probably wouldn't sweat again, anywhere, for a week. I finished and stood up just as a police flashlight prodded the door fully open.

Flushing (the toilet, not me), smiling weakly, and walking unsteadily (the last two weren't acting at this point), I managed to make my crippled way out with the stragglers from the party, was helped down the stairs by anonymous hands, and found myself tenderly deposited by the flow of party-goers onto the narrow sandy, cactus-filled strip of soil by (I looked up at the sign) 35th street, my shirt darkening again to blacker-than-black in the steady, by now all-too-familiar mist.

More than a little dizzy, I swayed in place on my crutches trying to get my bearings. The policeman were walking towards me. Just beyond them I could see Red Pants, smiling quizzically at me and waiting, hands on her hips. Then she arched one eyebrow, cracked a crooked smile and beamed it at me, rolling her eyes. I was in. But the solid wall of blue-uniformed pecs making their determined way towards me didn't look too hopeful, and I braced for a collision.

Quite the story, isn't it? You can hardly put it down, can you? You know I can't put it down. I love this shit. But then, I have a more personal interest in the story, because, well, it is, after all, my personal history. It's all about me. And on the street, at that moment, weaving on my crutches in the mist, I was all about me. Me. Me. Me. One hundred percent. Always. Me. But, you know, even though at that moment I couldn't imagine thinking otherwise, the truth is I'm not actually the center of the universe. I'm not the most interesting thing happening wherever I happen to be. I admit it. I'm not.

What do you think about all that? Have you ever had major life-changing thoughts after a night of being drunk and thrown out of parties by police? First I was - "it's all about me", then later (read: now) I'm "It's all about other people." Well, it feels and seems so clear now, but back then (at Michael's) it felt and seemed just as clear. Me or Them? How can they both be true? Life is strange. And it's always changing. Just when you get used to one thing, something else starts up. So much wasted time. So much wasted effort. And for what?

You're losing interest. O.K. All right. Enough with the whining and complaining. I should probably tell you why I'm in such trouble. I promise I'll keep the personal pathos down to a dull roar, although, speaking from past experience, I always find stories figuring myself as the protagonist riveting. Absolutely fascinating. As I'm sure you do also. Well, besides the fact I was acting like an idiot - drinking, wrecking, getting a record, running, hiding, impersonating a homeless person (an impersonation which was all too quickly turning into a fact), I was, in real life, an embezzler. And as it turned out, a stupid embezzler. Not because I had gotten caught (I had, but by accident, no fault of mine), but because of (and I found this out too late, much too late) whom I'd embezzled from. I'd inadvertently embezzled from the mob. The mob, as in organized crime, mafia, Murder Incorporated, winding-up-at-the-bottom-of-the-river-with-cement-nikes-on mob. I have a feeling they're not very happy with me at this point. To be truthful, I'm not too happy with me at this point either, but that's Life in the Big City.

My career goal didn't actually start out to become a corpse. I worked up to it. After trying out a few accounting positions I ended up being a lowly clerk for a big Engineering company that rebuilt freeways in almost all of the 50 states (I was doing my patriotic bit to re-invigorate 21st century America's infrastructure). I was one of the smallest of cogs in what turned out to be a very big wheel. As I was trained in, I noticed my small subsidiary seemed to have only one purpose - to perform elaborate enormous money transfers between thousands of bank accounts across the United States.

I would sit in my ratty, anonymous cube, get handwritten scraps of paper with Federal Reserve routing numbers, bank names, bank accounts, dollar amounts (never emails, never computer printouts) and move money eight hours a day, sometimes twelve hours a day at month end. Mostly they were humongous payroll transfers and government disbursements, but often they were miscellaneous, small, random dollar amount transfers - under $1000 - I'd do hundreds by the hour, going every which way, money furiously flying back and forth, hither and yon. Being inquisitive, and being the one doing the transfers with not a lot of oversight (something else that seemed odd), I had access to some of the account activity, and I formed some opinions - one would almost say the money was gradually losing its character, that it was being cleansed, perhaps, of its previous identity, possibly, one might argue, the money was even being washed, green as the day it first burst upon the financial world, fresh from one side of its natal journal entry in one of the vast, money-filled ledgers of the Federal Reserve At least that's how it seemed to me. And I thought to myself - Self? What if every so often some of that money came out of one of the thousands of accounts, but didn't go back in?

I kept it up for almost two years. I kept on promising myself I'd stop and quit my job, but I never did. I knew that once I left, the increasingly elaborate and delicate house of cards hiding my tracks that I'd built up through thousands of debits and credits, strewn across hundreds of virtual ledgers, would collapse in a boiling storm of un-reconcilable intercompany accounts within a week, two tops.

I didn't count on an executive submitting his expense report to the wrong department and getting lost in one of my "miscellaneous" transfers to my own bank account. I caught that on Tuesday. I saw the Internal Auditors sitting in the three-story glass-enclosed lobby as I went to work on Wednesday. I'd gone out bar-hopping with one of them (Kyle) before, not a whole lot of fun actually, we pre-discussed the relative advantages and disadvantages of each bar (to aid in a rational decision-making process, based upon our immediate objectives and the resources currently available to us) longer than the time we spent in each bar. Kyle was exceedingly thorough. Kyle was unimaginative. Kyle had little or no sense of humor. Kyle was really good at the details. I was fucked.

I knew the gig was up. I called in sick from the parking lot. I scrambled to get a cashier's check for $467,358.12 (closing out my money market account, saying it was for a house closing) and hid it in the lining of my suitcase, threw my suitcase in the trunk of my battered car, and tore out for Eddie's in San Diego. It wasn't until I was almost to Eddie's that I checked my voice mail and got the seven increasingly threatening and violent messages with suggestions about me, the money, my future, and if I had made out my will yet.

Man! Did they work quick or what? Their level of professionalism and sheer 21st century connectedness depressed the hell out of me. I was being chased at the speed of light.

Now I was standing in the rain, calmly observing San Diego's finest about to arrest my sorry ass. And, if you remember, I was car-less now - my car safely stored in some miscellaneous municipal impound lot someplace as a direct result of my DUI escapades the previous nights. An impound lot which was closed and locked by the time I got out of jail, but which hopefully might be un-padlocked and open on a Sunday morning. Tomorrow. If I was still free. If I had transportation to the lot. If I wasn't dead. A lot of ifs. It looked like my luck (such as it was) was running out. Or at the very minimum, was extremely strained. Things were certainly looking down a bit.

Then things looked up. The policemen pair rolled up, around, and past me, apparently intent on getting back to their cruiser, double-parked and flashing brilliantly in the wet night to one side of me. Red Pants did the bent, pointy-finger, come-hither motion and I felt myself pulled towards her as would the proverbial yo-yo bouncing back on its proverbial string. "Janice" she said, one of her arms on her hip, the other on my shoulder, when I crutched my way over and arrived in front of her.

I almost said "No it's not Janice, my name's Kevin" - but didn't. I get these strange impulse every now and then - like the embezzling thing - sometimes I act on them, sometimes I don't.

This time I didn't. Instead, I said "Of course you are" like James Bond said to Pussy Galore in Goldfinger, although in retrospect, it didn't make much sense to either of us. But I was smiling at her. And Janice smiled back at me. In any event, she put her arm in mine and she walked and I swung my way carefully down the soggy, uneven sidewalk away from the various knots of former Michael partiers, already on the prowl for the next bitching Saturday night party to crash. We disappeared, to all intents and purposes, into the night, And I forgot all about Eddie at first.

What can I say about Janice? She was comfortable in her body, willing to overlook a lot, very open to new people and to new situations. She was surfing the city and catching what waves there were, where and when she could. That night she caught me, and rode for a few hours. She was cautious about the large, smelly man she brought home from the party, but we took full advantage of each other, as I remember it, for the few hours I knew her. She seemed to know what she wanted, which was fine by me, I like girls who take the lead. And, luckily for me, what she wanted was exactly what I needed. So it worked, like I said, for the short while I knew her.

The first thing we did was get me into the shower back at her place, which required a great deal of help - due to excess plaster on my leg and excess alcohol in my bloodstream. Then there was a lot of cautious tumbling and unlikely gymnastic positions on the bed, the little I remember of them. Janice was a dancer, as in choreographer, not as in lap, so she was amazingly flexible. A good thing for an enthusiastic guy in a heavy cast. I did a lot of back-laying, side-laying, stomach-laying. And she kind of spun around me – a strangler fig vine in the jungle, slowly absorbing a huge tree that had fallen down and couldn't get up. I was that log. And a very happy log I was.

It was late night, early morning when I made my mistake. Janice's phone number safely stored in my cell, I ventured out into the night once again, slightly more sober than I was drunk, and made slow and steady progress towards Eddie's apartment, I don't know why. I don't know why I left for Eddie's. Maybe I was feeling lonely, again. Maybe I was just happy I'd met Janice and thought the world was a little less hostile of a place now. Maybe I was just drunk and stupid. Maybe all of the above. I don't know. I really don't know.

I didn't notice the van on the corner as I hobbled up Eddie's front steps to his door. It couldn't have been hard to miss, but I did. And I couldn't have been hard to miss, although, come to think of it, they probably weren't expecting an embezzler on crutches. Eddie wasn't answering his door buzzer, and I'd managed to lose the key sometime during the last day or so. I have to say they were pretty efficient. They bundled all six feet of me, cast and all, off the steps and into the van as if they did that sort of thing for a living (which of course, come to think of it, they probably did).

Anyways, in a few seconds we were driving down the block. I was hyperventilating and two guys were not so discreetly patting me down while pinning me to the van's gritty floor. It smelled like jasmine, jasmine and gardenias. In the gloom, in between kicks and tumbling and patting I looked around I saw why. This was some kind of florist's van. At least on the surface. And we were knocking into potted plants and flowers left and right, up and down. Things were getting broken. It didn't seem to bother anyone very much.

"Look, stop your struggling, hear?" said one of the larger guys (a guy I called Shaved Head) holding me down and flipping me around. His buddy, with red, greasy, stringy hair (and a forearm tattoo of a flaming skull gnawing on a human thigh bone, there was a heart with an arrow through it and "Mom" underneath that) started doing something with cords to my hands. He jerked my arm half out of its socket just to be sure I understood who was in charge at present. I was angry as hell, but my arms were tied up behind my back now, and I was sitting up resting against the side of the van, bouncing my head painfully against the ribbed metal sides, alternately swaying into the middle of the van, then smashing back into row upon row of potted jasmine, pressing my face into the flowers and turning pots over with my big old cast.

I rolled over on my side and our eyes met (Shaved's and mine) and he shook his head once. I felt that feeling you get when you're about to vomit, but what I really wanted to do was crack a couple of heads open while I threw up. Kill two birds with one stone, so to speak. I went to twist upwards and Shaved Head hit me hard, square in the jaw, while his buddy tightened the bungee cords or whatever it was they were using to tie me up, around my hands and around my feet and cast. My crutches were lying under my back, making a permanent dent in my spinal column. I wasn't happy.

I thought I ought to have seen my jaw ricocheting out of my

head against the back doors of the van after his fist so solidly connected with my head. I opened my mouth to see if it was still there and Shaved looked down at me again saying "Stop" and fastened a dirty gag in my mouth. One more nod, locking my eyes in his and he pulled an even dirtier burlap bag over my head. Everything between my ears ached and throbbed.

My jaw was sporting a few new loose teeth. The blood in my mouth made me retch. The bag didn't help - it reeked of wet, decaying potting soil and roots and mold. I threw up on myself in the bag, everyone, including me, agreed that was the wrong thing to do. I got a new bag and Shaved Head knocked three times on the wall of the van and we started out. Then apparently we all settled back for a serious session of rattling around in a fair imitation of bingo balls in the back of the van. We were driving all over the place - sprinting, slowing, stopping, turning our way through the night streets of the city, now practically the early dawn streets. Someone (Red Stringy Hair?) started humming to himself. Someone got punched and someone stopped humming.

I tried to figure out if we were on city streets, highway, country roads, whatever, then realized even if I could figure it all out I'd still be lost, lost, lost - I wouldn't know my way around San Diego enough to find the Pacific Ocean let alone puzzle out what part of the city I was travelling in. I was a well-wrapped, neatly-tied piece of ignorant human cargo. Eventually we went up, up, and over a long bridge or hill and we drove quietly and slowly down what seemed like suburban streets. We were pausing and jerking at a stop sign every block practically. Then we stopped completely, and the blindfold and gag came off (in that order) and Shaved Head and the guy with red, stringy hair pulled me upright, glaring at me glaring back at them.

I was scared shitless, sure, but I wasn't going to show them that. Big man, huh? I could be just as stupid as the next guy. Really, I had no cards in my hand, well one card actually (the check for almost half a million dollars), but not a lot of options left open for me. I hadn't thought things through. It was just like my dad always said. I didn't think, I didn't plan. I just did.

Although, on the subject of thinking, dad was never really big on that either. Doing, yes, and getting shit done. But the planning and thinking part, no. I don't know why I was suddenly thinking about that as the Shaved Head kicked the ribs of my side in and said "We'll do this once, where's the money?" Shaved was obviously a man of few words and little hair. When I didn't answer, he nodded and the Stringy Red Hair guy punched me in the gut, and right after that Shaved Head hit me in the face. I threw up again, but this time I didn't almost drown in it with a sack over my head. Shaved Head nodded again. Stringy Red pulled his hand back and someone pulled my head up by my hair, vertical and convenient, ready for the next set of face-fist encounters. And I thought - big realization - what am I doing this for? Who am I saving? - so I said "Wait."

He waited. Red waited. We all waited. They let go of my head. I looked up at them, my hair falling over my eyes, my face sweating and pale and black and blue, blood freely flowing now from my splintered jaw all over the black satin shirt, a shirt now liberally coated with noxious smelling beer vomit, and I decided I'd better do whatever it was they wanted me to do. So you see, towards the end I was rational. I thought. I planned. I tried. I did. I really did.

I guess I'm going to stop asking if you're following all this anymore. If you're not willing to be with me by now, you'll never be with me ever. If you haven't tried, you won't. If you can't feel what I've been going through, you never will.

I told them it was in a cashier's check made out to me, in some luggage, in my car, in a police impound lot, on a street somewhere called Imperial Avenue, honest to God that's what I knew. I mumbled a lot because my mouth wasn't working so well, swollen and broken like it was. I heard some muffled conversation with whoever was driving the van, back and forth for like thirty seconds, like maybe someone was googling San Diego Impound Lots on their IPhone, or calling 411, or some shit like that, and Shaved Head heard something, looked back at me, nodded his head, then did the knock three times, and like a rocket, we shot off again. Stopping and starting, stopping and starting our way through some residential neighborhood, and then it felt like we were going up, and up and up over some high bridge. My jaw bled. My face bled. The change in altitude wasn't doing my stomach any good. That's when it happened, that's when it all went down.

Remember, this time I could see, this time I could talk. They'd forgotten to blindfold me. I don't know if that was a good or bad thing for me and my immediate future. Maybe it didn't matter what I saw now. I don't know. Maybe there wasn't enough immediate future for me in my immediate future for them to care what I saw.

Anyways, the whole time we'd been back there, Red-And-Stringy had been complaining more and more about the smell, and even I would have said the same thing. My Corona vomit's not the most pleasant smell, having had to smell it more than a few times myself in the past. It was definitely getting pretty ripe back there. That's when I got my big break, that's when it happened.

We blew a tire - the rear left - bigtime, the same as if we'd hit a land mine, and bam! just like that we were throwing sparks out on the road and running on our rim. Everyone looked at Shaved Head. Shaved Head looked ahead, straight out the windshield for a second or two, probably cussing out some divinity who was supposed to be watching out for murderers and thieves but who was obviously fucking it up majorly, and said something in a harsh whisper to the driver. We rolled to a grinding, fireworks-filled stop. I kept on rolling, tumbling into endless rows of once-potted jasmines and finished looking as if I'd just come from a very festive, if somewhat violent Hawaiian luau.

Everyone froze and just went ape shit with the looking around at each other and tensing up and yelling and scrambling. Everyone except Shaved Head, that is. He stayed cool. Calm. He beat a few heads. He got some quiet. There was a half-minute or so of hushed conversation. Like I said, Shaved Head was a man of few words. People started patting their waists like they were carrying something down there, bustling around. They formed a line. They piled out of the van, pulling some kind of jack after them from under the passenger seat. I heard them disconnecting (a tire?) from under the van.

The strange thing was, the crazy thing was, we were on some kind of tilt. I remember thinking this must be some highway bridge because the whole van was tilting towards the driver side. Without any air coming in the windows, the stench was really too much, even for me, and finally Red had had enough.

Red pounded on the back of the van, and someone opened the door, and after another sixty seconds of intense whispering with some whining interspersed, Shaved Head's face appeared inside for a second, looking directly at me, and said "Don't even think about it" then disappeared and both doors opened wide.

Red jumped out, and vanished to one side of the van, retching sounds ensued for quite some time. I was trying to pick my face up out of the plants when I heard the sound of metal tearing in a loud scream and felt the van suddenly begin to tilt and it starting moving backwards and sideways. The motor was running. Lights were flashing on the dashboard, green, red, blue, it was Christmas up there. It revved some more, then the motor just took off. It sounded as if we were drag-racing on a Friday night. We must have been in Park, right?. But we bounced like a motherfucker. Up. Down. Sideways. Then we hit something and bounced one last time and stopped. The motor screamed. I looked up at the driver's seat. Then at the passenger seat. I couldn't see anybody. No one was in the truck. Except me.

All I could see was a streetlight shining into the two open back doors, wildly swinging open and shut, banging away, the whole truck at a crazy angle now, and in the background wisps of fog and mist were blowing across a section of railing and whooshing past a lamppost. I felt a cool breeze on my damaged face, and the low clouds overhead were lit up a garish pinkish-orange like they get in cities at night in Southern California with those crazy colored street lights they tend to use down here. I think it has something to do with the observatories and light pollution - I'm not totally ignorant - or as the Supreme Being said in Time Bandits - I'm not entirely dim. Anyways, that's what I saw. Although my mind, to be honest, was not contemplating the reasons for the different colors of the late night urban sky at that point. I just wanted to live. I mumbled for my life.

"Fuck! Guys! Get me outta here. Get me the hell outta here. Fuck! Guys! Guys!" the van felt as if it were starting to slide faster, downhill, wherever that was. Of course it was Shaved Head who reached in and pulled me out by my feet, as if I were a long roll of carpet he had to schlep, almost, but not quite, catching my head (hey, at least he tried) before it bumped on the back step, fender, and then onto the pavement. I was pretty dizzy. I rolled to my knees, but thought better of it, and lay back down again. I kept my eyes open, though, I made sure I did that, only because of what I was witnessing.

Witnessing, that is, along with the rest of them. A pink and purple colored Amy's Floral Designs truck with one wheel missing was practically floating in mid-air, half resting on the concrete divider between the lanes on the bridge. One of the guys was in the front seat of the van (it must have been some kind of front wheel van) gunning it forwards and backwards, manhandling the shift, trying to roll it back and forth away from the outer railing of the bridge, and it was edging away from me, slowly with a grinding sound. It was tilting at the same time, ominously.

I lay there, feeling the back of my head bleed onto the asphalt, and watched the truck shake and shimmy above me. I felt strangely peaceful. The mist on my face felt good.

It smelled like a refinery up there. Whoever was throttling it was going to town with it, the diesel smoke was as thick as fog. Three guys were yelling at each other, pulling on the bumper, trying to steady it, Red, Shaved, and a new guy with a baseball hat. There had to be a fourth guy trying to unjam the accelerator (maybe?-why was the truck racing forward like it had a mind of its own? I'll never know) – the door was open on the driver's side, so I couldn't see much of anything up in the front. But I could see the license plate now, upside down, over my head - California 9845BTRS - and I could see we were apparently on some high, curvy bridge thing which overlooked downtown maybe a mile or so away. I got up onto my one knee, off the pavement. I pushed myself onto one leg. I edged away. There wasn't another car or other person in sight. Just the yelling men, me hopping on one foot, and the possessed delivery vehicle.

You know, the odd thing was, the bridge curved up high, almost unnaturally, and in a circle, as if it were a boomerang propped up on stilts in the middle, ready to boomerang itself away from this crazy city and make its own way off into the starry unknown and a new, exciting, city-free life. Weird. And it sloped. Boy did it slope. It's a good thing San Diego didn't get much snow, huh? We were at the top.

The truck was doing a slow pirouette towards the water, a long, long, long ways down. I leaned my cast against the bridge railing, balancing against a light pole, just as one last jasmine petal inside the van must have shifted (that's my guess), and the entire van tilted and crashed over the concrete median strip in the middle, catching the front wheels on the side as it accelerated, rolled onto its top, crashed again, accelerated, rolled again, and with a horrible scrunching side, bit into the railing on the side of the bridge and hopped over, disappearing into a sudden silence, interrupted only by a smashing, splashing sound far away.

Suddenly it was very quiet on the bridge. All you could hear were the sounds of us four men breathing heavily (where was the guy who had been driver's seat now?), and maybe the faint sound of wind and the diesel exhaust whispering as it slipped around the lamp post I was leaning against.

For another minute or two everyone forgot about me. The silence and motionless ended. Then there was lots of yelling, screaming, wandering around in tight circles, looking up at the smoggy heavens and asking why – all that began. I started edging my way down the bridge towards the mainland (realistically, like a mile away, literally, yes, this was probably not the best plan, but it was the best I could come up with on the spur of the moment, with a concussion). I got maybe 15 feet. Shaved Head remembered there was something else missing up there on the bridge besides the drowned van and the driver and he started frowning. He looked to the right, then he looked to the left. That's when he saw me, hobbling with my cast, my legs still loosely tied together, my arms tied behind my back, edging along the railing towards the mainland and towards freedom.

I heard him yell something out at me. I thought I could see a car approaching from the other direction. It must have been like 4, maybe 5 AM or something on a Sunday morning, not a lot of traffic right about then, but it sure looked like headlights heading up that long, curving bridge in my direction.

Shaved Head spoke up, reasonable, unexcited. "I said wait, buddy" and stupidly, I turned around to see him and tripped and swung neatly out and over the edge of the bridge, resembling, I suppose, a human two by four being tossed over the side of the rooftop of a 20 story construction project headed for the trash pile, and just like that, I disappeared too, like the truck, like my future, into nothingness.

And that's the end of my exercise in empathy for today.

So, did you feel my life? Did any of it make any sense to you? I'm not sure how much of it made sense to me. Making sense wasn't what I was looking for. I think making sense is something I started learning a bit too late, something I wish I would have figured out a lot sooner.

Hey. Sorry. I'm babbling.

But I've got time, nothing but time now, so I guess I have the right to ramble and babble as much I want. What I mean, of course, what I'm talking about is the center of the universe thing.

175

So here it is. This is what I've learned. The center of everything is everywhere I'm not. The most interesting thing happening is everything but me. I always wanted something. Attention. Fame. Money. Power. I don't know. Something. And I never got as much as I thought I wanted. I was always left feeling as if I needed more. You know, it was never enough. Never. But maybe that's because I chased after the wrong thing.

So.

There you go.

That's it.

That's all.

Was it worth it? Did I waste your time?

Easy for me to say. My messy past is just that. Past. The muddling through is over for me.

But not for you. And if I could wish for you anything, I'd wish that you could see how incredibly and utterly mind-blowing each of you are, in reality, right now, right this very minute, the person reading this long tale about a lot of nothing – you in particular. I can see you. Each one of you. I see you, I see every bit of you. And you're beautiful.

Kevin's dad read and re-read the email. It was crazy long. It wasn't funny. Kev had gone too far this time. It had been sent at 4:47 AM California Standard Time, Sunday. It was now Monday afternoon. This was no way to start the week. He hadn't even turned on his phone yesterday, let alone looked at his email. And then this.

Retired guys shouldn't have to put up with this shit.

He looked up at the recipient list and saw, for the hundredth time, maybe 25 names - all Kev's brothers and sisters, himself, lots of other names he didn't recognize, but including ones that sounded suspiciously familiar, somehow, like EddieCAsd@hotmail and JaniceM91@gmail.

C'mon Kev. This sort of thing had to stop. It was a joke, right? Right?

He fumbled for his phone. Tried to call Kev on his cell, couldn't find Kev's number in his contacts even though he knew it was there, gave up, went to look it up in his old, ratty address book by the kitchen phone and that's when he noticed on his land line he'd gotten a new message this afternoon, from the San Diego Police Department. There were lots of other new messages on his land line's voice mail, from all his sons and daughters, all from Sunday and earlier today and suddenly he didn't want to know. He didn't want to call. He didn't want to listen.

But he did anyway. Just because it was hard, didn't mean you didn't do it. It just meant that it was hard.

He went to press play and for a moment couldn't find the button, what with a sudden tightness in his chest, and something or other in his eyes, so bad he couldn't see a damn thing. What he could see was the round-faced figure of blond-haired boy, standing in his bedroom, solemnly handing him his ribbons to pin on his uniform, one by one, outlined against bright sunlight flooding through the window and sweeping them both away. Together.

BUS STOP

"For crying out loud, goddamit all to hell"

Jim yelled upwards into the night, jumping forwards and away (too late), bashing his knee on his skateboard leaning on the glass wall beside him. He stared unbelievingly at a white pulsating mass attached to his hand, to his back pocket and to the brightly colored iron mesh bench he was sitting on. His cell chimed softly – the irritating doorbell sound he always forgot to reset – and shattered what used to be a meditative, expectant silence in this deserted bus stop. Well, yes, it would have been shattered and destroyed, if it already hadn't been completely demolished by Jim's hopping about and screaming at the sky and shaking his dirty hands at the empty streets in front of him. He examined his hand. He examined his cell. He shook his head. He yelled. It really didn't make him feel any better.

It also started to rain. Great. Just great.

Ding dong. Ding dong. He was getting an incoming text

apparently. He didn't even check to see who it was. This wasn't happening to him. Not on the way over to Melissa's. And whatever it was, looking at his hands it just didn't look right. What the fuck was this shit, anyways? Did a drooling camel with a head cold kneel here just a few seconds ago?

Ah shit, he knew, he knew. In the pink glow of the streetlight, smeared wetly all over the bench, malicious, malignant spots of pink bubblegum shone back up at him - with a strange absence of color, as if they were gum-sized, gooey holes in the universe – and they were everywhere. Smeared liberally all over the ass side of his best warm up pants and strung up in a nauseating web between his fingers, it was on his hands and his arm and there was some on the bus shelter wall and yes, Jim could feel it, there was even some on his face now. Shit.

Jim continued waving his hands around, smiling through his emotional pain (therapist-speak for helpless rage) in a gritting-through-your-teeth kind of way, scratching at himself, trying to get the slimy shit off of him, hating the feeling of touching things that had recently glopped around some stranger's tongue, teeth and other organs and was now sliding and sticking all over his own person. And all over his clothes. And, oh yes, look! – it was on his skateboard now, too.

None of it was coming free, none of it. What in the hell did you use to get this crap off anyways? Ice cubes? Kerosene? Soy Sauce? He couldn't remember exactly, his mom would've known, but she was gone, so, Jimmie, you are on your own on this one.

On your own, Jimmie.

That thought brought him to a total and complete stop. He saw her face again. No not her face, some stranger's face sleeping in his mom's coffin. The stranger was wearing his mom's favorite dress too. It made him sick to look at it. Jim grimaced, breathing heavily through his nose and closed his eyes. He rubbed the back of his hand against his forehead. He could feel gum rolling around on his head, probably getting into his hair, but he didn't care. No. Not again.

For the first few months after the funeral, he'd been numb, a frozen lump of bloodied ice and that had been worrying him, yeah it had, but now he felt he was on the verge of having a nervous breakdown his every waking second. The smallest thing set him off and he'd explode. His fuse was so short as to be non-existent. Ice or fire, which was worse? Didn't Jim get any other choices?

A quick, accustomed pain there somewhere in his chest found its way to his heart, gripped it, and squeezed tightly. He closed his eyes snugly shut this time, frowned, bit his lip, waited for the mind-jerking throb of loss to subside slowly - always an agonizing recovery, as if he'd hit his funny bone with an oversize croquet mallet. So much fun. He couldn't get enough of it. Really. Living large. This is the life. Loving it. Sign me up for more of this.

He felt his cheeks were wet. But he didn't want to do anything about it. All Jim could do was wait. Sometimes, with the pain, Jim was afraid he'd never be able to stop, that the feelings would flood-surge over his head and wash Jim entirely away, eroding him to nothing, leaving only a Jim-sized, empty hole and a fading Jim-colored stain behind.

When the pain was manageable again, he opened his eyes to find he was looking at his hands. Hands covered in saliva-filled fibrous goo. You know, sometimes – well, sometimes it was all too much - and what the hell did you do with this shit? All he could remember (no, do not think about the funeral again) about gum was that there was some trick to it.

His phone door-belled again at his waist. He looked helplessly at his hands. He couldn't even grab his phone to answer it. Not yet. And not only did the gum's color look alien somehow, Jim was sure he looked the fool here in this bus shelter late at night - a crazy homeless person off his meds, weeping and staring at his gummy butt and talking to himself on and on in public.

He glanced around, as carefully and as casually as he could do it, moving as little as possible, to see if anyone were watching - watching and laughing maybe, people could be so cruel, especially little kids - and caught a weird crunching rhythm at his feet, a strange sound he couldn't quite place, as if a herd of small gerbils were running away from him, munching on their nutty breakfast cereal, walking, gaining speed, trotting, then running faster and then faster still, now they were running for their lives. He looked quickly to his left and to his right.

Something was missing.

Shit! It was his board.

He launched himself towards the sound - chasing the echo of four expensive wheels rolling eagerly downhill trying to escape under parked cars, tiptoe across dark traffic lanes, lose themselves in the night. They were taking full advantage of this, their first, real chance at precious freedom, and they were going for broke.

Trailing strings of gum, Jim dove over the curb, kneeled on the street, and being thoroughly blinded by the unwelcome glare of bright city street lights above him, tried to triangulate by hearing alone, swinging his gummy earlobes left and right, fastening onto the gerbil-ly wheel sounds echoing all about him. An elderly bat would have had better luck trying to find four very quiet mosquitos here. No, it wasn't working. The gravel-crunching sounds were coming from everywhere and nowhere. The rain didn't help. Now he and his protective covering of gum were getting wetter and wetter.

He closed his eyes, trying to sharpen his pathetic hearing over the monotonous steady drizzle hissing around him, when he was surrounded by the wet sound of heavy tires and the low grunt and gasp of a diesel engine pulling itself heavily over the crest of the hill behind him. It was headed down Jim's street, towards Jim's bus stop, directly towards Jim himself – Jim being a bus patron who was currently crawling on all fours in the gutter, peering under a pickup truck in the misty rain. The bus would squash him as easily as a full can of soda and not even know it had done it. So Jim got up on his knees.

Suddenly and dramatically, Jim was silhouetted in an industrial-bright suite of headlights attached to this very large and very heavy approaching vehicle. Fuck. He couldn't see a thing. The whole world was all thermonuclear, radiant white and solid, matte black. No in betweens. No gray shapes. No nothing.

"Ah Shit! Come on! Give me a break." He turned, turned again, looked back over his shoulder at the bus growing larger and larger and looked forward again into the million places a rolling object could run off and hide away in. "That's my only board! That's my long board, my transportation man!"

He stood up quickly, trying to rub the gum and the gummy gravel off of his hands, his knees, his rear end and his arms, trying to look cool – he was just another dude, just another guy admiring the outside of a city bus stop shelter, and Jim kept a lookout, out of the side of his eyes, to see if he could spot a banana shaped patch of darkness somewhere under a car, in a gutter, rolling down the center lane, gamboling in the median, anything.

The bus was getting closer. He could see it wasn't his bus

anyway. It was brightly lit, but the sign said "999 Next Day" (whatever that was supposed to mean - probably it was just out of service), and there wasn't any passengers on it, and the driver was just a shadowy uniformed blob in the dark driving his rectangular block of blue-white light through these late-night/early morning city streets, on his or her way back to the garage at the end of their shift.

He (or she) must have thought Jim's pants-cleaning jumping and waving was bus-hailing, because the bus slowed down, moving towards the side of the road, and Jim started frantically making don't-notice-me motions wildly with both hands. This had the effect of attracting the driver's attention even more. The bus darted towards Jim, slid in alongside him, and with a hiss and a sigh, settled in front of him, the front doors flopped open directly in his face, and a nondescript man's voice bubbled up out of the darkness and said "well?"

Jim stood still, hands left dangling in the air above his head, squinting at the bus. Did he know the driver? He tried to peer in and see his face but it really was too dark.

"Well what?" said Jim, "What?"

Then he saw the driver was holding something - although all Jim could see was his hand sticking out at him, and that not very clearly. There was a hand and something being held in it. And the hand kept stretching out towards him, in an attention-getting kind of way, one that demanded action.

What the fuck? Was that a bus schedule? Or a list of city bus rules and regulations about not rolling around on the pavement into oncoming traffic in front of legally designated and signed bus stops? Still swiveling his head back and forth looking for his wayward board in the conveniently bright non-moving lights of the bus, Jim absentmindedly stepped forward and took a folded sheet of paper from a dimly back-lit hand.

With one eye now closed against the lights of the bus interior, he focused his skateboard-spying eyes on the street in front of him as the bus quickly swiveled its long length of mass-transit fluorescence back into the street and continued officiously and in a professional, business-like fashion to make its way down the rest of the rain-covered hill.

It rolled through the next three green stoplights until it slid under the viaduct at the crest of the next hill and glowingly disappeared from sight, although Jim could hear the distant echo of it making a soggy, sighing halt at a stop sign or a yield or something at some far-away block a few seconds later.

Now Jim was really alone. It was quiet. No rolling wheel sounds anymore, no cars and no people - no one in sight - and no background noise but the steady hiss of rain hitting sidewalks, automobiles, and once-dusty trees. His phone chimed again. He ignored it. It was probably Melissa. He was probably in trouble. Again. Come to think of it, it was probably too late to get a bus over to the west side of town anyways. He was in deep shit. And he was still covered in gum.

He sighed what he considered was a long, well-earned sigh, raised his hands up to the drizzle-filled heavens in a dramatic gesture of "why, universe, why?"

"Fuck me!" he yelled at the empty street. For some reason that felt good. Yes, the trees continued to drip down on him. Yes, his board was really gone. Yes, his girlfriend, well, one of them, was probably really gone too. All gone for good. And it was late. And he was walking. Then he realized he had something in his hand. A piece of paper. He opened the paper (which looked like it had been ripped out of a high school composition book, ruled with wide, clumsy-penmanship-forgiving blue lines) and strained to read the faint (but familiar) neat printing in ink.

He angled the rain-splattered page towards the street light, but it didn't help. All he managed to do was to step out farther into the rain. The note was getting pretty soggy.

It said "Don't Look Up" and something else was written underneath it in parentheses. So, of course, like anyone else, Jim looked up (hesitantly) just in time to get a direct hit in the eye by a passing (or, what was more likely, a wet and roosting) bird that had obviously recently eaten something that had given it the runs.

This time he didn't yell or jump. Although he wanted to very badly. He didn't want to give the universe the satisfaction of seeing him hopping around and swearing again.

So, Jim used the paper to wipe off his gummy hands, his shitty face, and the slimy shoulder of his shirt and some of his slimed-over hair. O.K. Great. Just great. First gluey saliva, now fresh shit. What was next? He looked himself over. You know, he really hadn't cleaned himself up at all. He did it all over again, the wiping, the scraping, but a little more diligently this time. Still not actually enough to do any cleaning. After about five more minutes of wasted effort and silent cursing, he held the almost illegible note up to his eyes again in the rain, closed one because the rain was dripping into it, and saw what the second sentence was. "If you had kept on reading, I would have warned you to step back, way back, all the way underneath the bus stop roof, fool. And get that gum and bird shit off before you ruin your uncle's upholstery."

Jim stared at the paper in disbelief. Now that he looked more closely, the paper looked like it had been used as a coaster more than once in its recent past. There were many yellowed bottle rings blotted all over the page. And the paper looked wrinkled. The rain fell and soaked him thoroughly, the streetlight above him shone down on his upraised hand, it shone down on the dripping, runny-ink note, and it shone down on his frozen one-eyed expression of irritation and blank astonishment. He stood still for quite some time.

This fucking took the fucking cake. Gum. Board. Bird. It was Jim 0, Universe 21 and the game was over. Jim shook his head and started walking his long wet walk home, shaking his head and muttering to himself. He'd probably get picked up and carted off to a mental institution. Then again, this was inner city San Diego, Jim probably fit in better tonight than he'd ever fit in before. Which wasn't the most encouraging thought. Shit. Melissa would never talk to him again. He missed her and the way she barely fit into her clothes. She really listened to Jim too, when he went off talking about the Chargers or his evil Pre-Calc Trig teacher, or how the road ate up cheap 78A wheels, just chomped on them for breakfast and spit them out, all kinds of stuff like that. Shit. It just wasn't fair. Shit.

With the dripping note balled up in one fist, he quietly let himself into his uncle's apartment where he was staying and pulled the blankets out from under the table by the sofa next to the front window and did the blanket-tossing, pillow-scrunching maneuvers he called "making my bed." It all took about 10 seconds. That included stripping off his wet, slimed, and gummed clothes. Jim could be quick, if he wanted to, and he wanted to. Jim had to be up early for school. He should've been asleep already. He threw himself into his blankets and wriggled into a warm position on his back. This left him staring up into the dark. He closed his eyes. He opened them. He closed them. He couldn't sleep.

The cell chimed accusingly again from some buried place under a cushion. He opened his eyes. Jim peered into the darkness of the living room finding and tracing a piercing sliver of the slightest pink light stealing in through a crack in the drapes from the street light out on the corner. He considered getting up and finding his cell. He looked at the slim beam of streetlight, and bit his lip again, and he sighed, and he thought, and he sighed again, and he closed his eyes. That accomplished nothing and quick. Yes, Jim thought too much, and too long and too often. He knew he did it. He just couldn't help it. That was the kind of guy he was. A thinker.

Sometimes it just all seemed too hard, and sometimes he just felt sorry for himself - sleeping on his uncle's sofa, taking the fucking bus to his girlfriend's, busting his ass working at a dry cleaners, hustling to get good grades in junior college so he could eventually transfer to the state university, being poor, pathetic and tragic and there was always the unspeakable weirdness of being an orphan and now there was this. This note shit. And no skateboard. That board hadn't been cheap. He'd saved for months for it. It just wasn't fair. Did other guys have it this hard?

He could hear his uncle snoring in the small bedroom on the other side of the wall. Jim sighed, loudly, into the darkness, rolled his shoulders to crack his neck and reached backwards over his head for the side table and his cell to hit the mute button, pushing a sofa cushion off the table first. He couldn't find his cell. Fuck it.

He rolled around, pulled his covers up to his chin and tried to sleep, but ended up listening to the rain and watching the ceiling some more. Really interesting stuff. He rolled to one side again, he just couldn't get comfortable.

And tonight. What the fuck was all this supposed to mean? What was he supposed to do with all of it? If this was one of Johnnie's jokes again, Jim would have had to say it was a good one. Johnnie'd really done it this time. How'd he get the bus driver to do that? He didn't even want to think about the bird. He rolled over yet again and realized he was feeling an uncomfortable wrinkle deep under his blanket that wouldn't go away, an obnoxious lump sandwiched between him and the couch. It was, of course, his pants. Pants that were now permanently glued via pink bubble gum to the aging tweed upholstery that covered his uncle's massive, ancient couch from the 80's. Great, just great.

Jim woke up late the next morning to a confusing chorus of

doorbells, and broken, vivid images of bus drivers, bird droppings, escaped skateboards, and prophetic scribblings. The doorbell seemed to be operating flawlessly without any perceptible interruption. Whoever was banging away at it was trying to be incredibly annoying. It had worked. Jim was incredibly annoyed.

He knocked a chair upside down and dragged half his blankets across the room trying to get over to the front door, opened the front door, realized he wasn't wearing anything (mostly because of the sensation of a crisp breeze in places where he usually didn't feel a breeze at all), slammed the front door, then realized no one had been outside hammering on the front doorbell, trying (successfully) to raise his blood pressure.

Yet the chiming continued. Pretty regularly. He stood, swaying in his uncle's Lilliputian living room, waiting to wake up, eyes squinty and kind of crusty in the corners still, knowing he needed to do something to stop the sound, but not knowing what it was exactly he needed to do. You know, he could still see wet pavement flushing green, then yellow, than red under the stoplights as he crawled on his knees through the midnight streets in that bizarre nightmare last night. His dreams were getting weirder and weirder. He wondered if something was wrong with him.

Ever since he'd left Greeley and Colorado after his mother died and ever since he'd come here to live with his uncle, an ex-priest, in his tiny bungalow in San Diego, Jim had felt off balance, just kind of wrong, permanently tilted sideways. Everything was different now, everything was either very uphill and difficult, or downhill and out of control. Nothing was just even anymore. It reminded Jim of the first year after his father had passed away when he was in elementary school. Lonely. Just a little kid. But guys in college weren't supposed to feel that way, were they? Well, no matter how he was supposed to feel, Jim felt shipwrecked. Washed up in this fuckin' cracked state of California, stuck in a sandy corner somewhere between Mexico and the Pacific, on his own private desert island hell.

Wouldn't that ringing ever stop? And as for his uncle, well Jim had never even seen a house this small before, let alone a purple, stucco bungalow with a bright red tile roof, in a little companionable circle of purple-stuccoed, red-tiled bungalow-ettes. It looked like a doll house from the outside. In a doll village. Every morning he set out for class, he expected to meet the Lollipop

League warming up in a small group (what other size group could it have been?) on the sidewalks rimming the tiny plaza in the middle of this miniature U-shaped complex.

He didn't say anything to his uncle Xavier or Uncle Hobby as he liked to be called, because he didn't want to be disrespectful, and really, he was grateful to have a place to crash. Uncle Hobby had offered repeatedly at the funeral to have Jim out here. Except he called Jim, Diego, which was officially his real name, but Jim only answered to Jim. Even his mom, towards the end, had given in and started calling him that. Fuck! That bell was going to drive him out of his mind. He started shaking his head and trying to zero in on the source.

That's when he saw his cell, not on mute like he'd thought, texting over and over, "ass" then "hole", "ass" then "hole" - it was Johnny of course. Jim smiled as he turned his phone off this time. He'd probably written a computer program or some shit like that to do that, Johnnie would know how, or else Johnnie was doing a helluva lot of typing. Jim hoped he was having to type all that crap. It would serve him right. Wait, fuck he was late to class.

Uncle Hobby was long gone, doing the responsible thing, off to work on his lawns and flowers and air conditioning ducts - he did landscape/maintenance work for a development down the block, responsible for all the buildings and plants. His nephew was doing the irresponsible thing apparently, but not for long. Then Jim saw his pants kind of glued to the sofa with some pink gluey stuff, and he felt a stab of panic as he looked at the side table where his phone lay. There was a crumpled piece of lined notebook paper next to it. He didn't look at the note. He didn't want to look at it. Then he started remembering.

He'd flaked out on Melissa last night. Great. Just fuckin' great. He didn't have a board anymore. This week was starting out in V.I.P. style. He threw a cushion over the gum on the sofa, threw on some clothes, grabbed his books, stuffed the mashed-up note into his front pocket, and tore out of his Uncle's tidy little cabana, spinning around to lock the door as he sprinted down the path and out onto the sidewalk, running for the bus stop. With any luck, he'd make it only 15 minutes late to his Intro to English Lit class.

Later, in a ratty coffee house near campus, Johnnie stared at the note, stared back at Jim, stared at the note again and said "You're shitting me, right? No way this is real. This is your own handwriting man. I should know, half the time I can't read your notes from class when you let me borrow 'em. When are you just going to give up the old stone and chisel and get a laptop to tap out notes like everyone else? Huh? Then I could just copy your files. Easy. Snap! And it'd be done. Just like that. Waddyasay, dude, huh? You could even put it up in the cloud, and then I wouldn't even have to ask you to copy them. I'd have them. In my capable hands. So, how about it? How about joining the 21st century with the rest of us?"

Johnnie ducked reflexively after that last sentence, as a half-eaten bagel sailed across the table on a collision course with his forehead, just like he'd thought it would. It hit him anyway.

"Fuck, man, that had cream cheese on it J - why'd you have to be that way?" Johnnie started winding up, sounding like he was going to complain in a more extensive, exhaustive way, but Jim just held his hand up in front of Johnnie's face, shaking his head.

"Sorry 'bout all that, but shit, dude, do you think you're kind of missing the point here?"

Jim exhaled loudly and significantly as he threw over a few extra napkins in Johnnie's direction across the well-used, scratched, rod-iron-and-plywood table they were sitting at.

"All right, all right" said Johnnie wiping his forehead and his eye and looking at Jim with a hesitant, tentative edge to his voice "so what are you going to do, J? I mean, What can you do about it?"

Jim kept on shaking his head, and wouldn't meet Johnnie's eyes directly, closing and unclosing his hand around the damp, creased and rumpled sheet of composition book paper lying on the table top. He opened his mouth to say something, then saw Johnnie's eyes go wide. He stopped, naturally. Johnnie winked at him. Johnnie raised his chin. Johnnie hit Jim's shoulder, probably a little harder than he needed to. He was still wiping cream cheese off his face.

"Don't look now, bud, but Melissa's walking our way and she doesn't exactly have the look of a happy coed. You know what? I think I'll be seeing you later. Text me about the note, that's way bizarre man."

Johnnie looked over again at the beeline Melissa was making for their table, as he spun up and out of his chair.

"Courage, dude, stiff upper lip, and you know, well, and all that."

That last part was due to their shared English Lit class. Johnnie punched Jim's shoulder again, not quite as hard, maybe more sympathetically this time, and then made a call me sign with his right hand as he dove backwards and ducked out the back door of the coffee shop. Jim braced for impact.

Afterwards, an hour or so later, Jim and Melissa were still rehashing last night, and he was walking Melissa to her bus stop. Jim was fingering the note in his pocket, and unconsciously surveying the surrounding streetscape for skate boards - although by now it'd be long ago picked up and claimed by some happy urban teenager - but you never could tell. They were starting uphill, getting close to the bus stop from last night - man! Just 12 or so hours ago. Hard to believe. It felt like years. Jim was trying to concentrate on listening to her. Really.

Melissa was talking to him. Barely. It was less of a conversation and more of a come-to-Jesus-meeting. She was a righteous avenging angel, he, a famously unrepentant sinner. Yeah, actually it was probably close to the truth.

Jim didn't know what he would do if he were dating himself. Probably dump himself in a New York minute (as Johnnie liked to say - he was from back East and wished every single day he was living back in New York City rather than in a little country town like San Diego). She was telling him how long she'd stayed up last night, waiting to get a text from him. She didn't know what to think about the note. She wanted to trust him, but could she?

Jim just hoped Deb or Maria didn't happen to run into the two of them anytime soon. Explaining multiple girlfriends to multiple girlfriends would have required more political skill than Jim thought he was capable of just now. Jim winced every time a bus went by. There was a lot of traffic out for noon on a Monday. Didn't anyone work anymore? As they turned the corner, Jim noticed it, the familiar bus stop, the bus stop from last night, and a bus just sitting there waiting at it at the top of the hill, a number 167, like the driver was on break or something. He forgot to breathe for a second. He didn't want to go near the thing. He slowed down. Melissa slowed down. He stopped. Melissa stopped.

Then Jim thought, hey! It's just a 167. So Jim started walking again. Melissa started walking too. Jim concentrated on Melissa's words again, but they were just sounds. They didn't make any sense. Jim was watching the bus, watching the bus driver and watching every patch of white that looked like it might be a skateboard shape. So, yes, he was missing a few words every sentence or so. And, yes, it was a dangerous situation to be in.

"And you know, Jim, I kept the phone next to me, on all night like I told you, so don't tell me you tried to call and I didn't answer, I know what I know and what I know is I was right there the whole time, the whole night, and I can't believe you've got me sitting next to a phone for hours waiting for you to call, next time I just go out and find some fun on my own, and let you break your promises with someone else, and now what's wrong? Why are you making that face, Jimmie? You're not still talking about that note are you? Cuz I can tell you, that's not gonna work. Not with me, not this time, Jimmie. We need to talk about this Jimmie. I'm serious. Look at me Jimmie."

Melissa paused and looked from Jimmie's face to the parked bus and then back to Jimmie again as they plowed forwards on their uphill hike. They had to walk carefully because of the wet leaves and the cracked sidewalk, pushed up at crazy angles by the muscular roots of all the immense eucalyptus trees that lined this avenue. Jimmie's hands were in his pockets. Guiltily. Melissa's were out, emphasizing her independence from Jimmie in broad, decisive hand gestures. The bus was just sitting there, as if it were waiting for the two of them.

As they got closer, Melissa started getting louder and angrier, at least it seemed that way to Jim. Jim wasn't catching more than one word out of ten now. They were walking slower and slower, each shoe-fall, every footstep requiring the movement of hundreds of pounds of weight, an enormous effort of willpower and patience and an exercise in unyeilding concentration. Just push one leg forward. Now the other one. That's right. Push. Push, Jim. One more. And another. And another…

"So, it's up to you, Jimmie, all up to you. If you want to see me you've got to show me some respect. You've got to treat me like I matter. Don't I matter to you? Are you listening to me, Jimmie? I don't just live and breathe to keep you happy. It's a two-way street, Jimmie, it goes both ways. Both ways, Jimmie, both ways. Are you listening? You hear me, Jimmie? Jimmie?"

Jim looked at the bus, as they shuffled painfully and inexorably uphill towards it, in horror not unmixed with frantic fascination.

He was one of those baby birds who couldn't fly yet in their nests watching a big black bull snake appear beside him, mouth wide open, and he, heart pounding wildly, eyes wide and staring, paralyzed, helpless to save himself. Jim. Look. Just look. The numbers on the bus had changed, now it said that 999 shit - had it always said that? Was he losing it? Then with a kind of shudder, with an acceptance of the inevitable, he forced himself to peer inside. He would ask the driver this time. He would find out who was messing with him. He closed both his eyes. He had rights, didn't he? He could take a joke like any other guy, but… He opened one of his eyes.

He saw (what a relief) the parked bus was empty. He closed his eyes again, sighed, thanked the universe, felt like laughing, tripped on a crack in the sidewalk. Yeah, big, bad Jim. What was he so afraid of? A little piece of paper?

He opened both eyes, so he wouldn't crack his head in two doing a header onto the broken concrete, and then he froze. There was something stuck in the door, a note, with his name on it, the way his mother used to write it "Diego Velazquez." As Melissa talked on (although a small voice deep inside himself said he'd regret turning his back on Melissa later) he deliberately, wordlessly, and mechanically stepped aside. He walked backwards and away from Melissa, ignoring her calling to him to come back, took the note, and inched back next to her again, trying to keep up with her quick, exasperated steps as they continued their walk in the weak winter sunlight. Except now Jim wasn't hearing anything Melissa was saying. Nothing. Not a word. He was fucked. As usual, it seemed. All he could think about was – yeah, the bus number had changed. Just like that. As he stuffed this latest, blue-lined, composition-book note into his satchel, he unfolded a corner of it. He read the first line.

It said "We have to talk."

Jim ducked into his uncle's place after leaving an increasingly and disturbingly quiet Melissa at a bus stop on Kansas street, waited for the 56 bus over on the corner of 25th street, and then he hoofed it home. The closer he got to the apartment the angrier he got. No female was going to leave him. If anybody was going to do any leaving it'd be Jim, not Melissa. Besides he always had Deb, and Maria was still friendly towards him, at least he thought she was. He couldn't remember exactly the last time he'd called her. It couldn't have been as long as last spring, could it? He was ripping leaves off bushes and shredding them as he stomped home, and he let the front door screen slam shut with a satisfying smash - potent aluminum pistons propelling the heavy metal security door punishingly into its splintered and old wood frame. The resulting explosion of metal on wood was a tad bit louder than he'd expected. Shit.

His uncle, unfortunately, was home and poked his head out of the kitchen, raising his eyebrows at the banging but saying nothing. Jim, a little chagrined, shut the red-painted, heavy oak front door much more gently behind him. His uncle continued to watch him standing by his chair by the refrigerator.

"Home early Dieguito? Good. You can help me with my books before dinner." Jim's uncle was always working, like three or four jobs, one of them was doing bookkeeping for some Latino shops down the avenue. He'd gotten Jim involved, and taught him how to record receipts. His uncle pushed his half-glasses further down his nose with his knuckles and Jim could see he'd been crying, but that didn't concern Jim overly much, since his hands were filled with half-chopped onions and a huge, vicious looking butcher's knife with a hole in the top which always reminded Jim of a villain's cartoon weapon, something Wile E. Coyote would own to chop and cook roadrunners with.

"You doing O.K., mijo? He caught Jim's squinched, angry eyes with his own watery ones from across the room and wouldn't let go of them, saying "What's going on?" He stopped and waited. Uncle could be very patient. Jim saw he wasn't going to get out of all this very easily.

What could he say? He was just irritated lately. The universe was fucking with him. And Melissa had made him worse. Why couldn't she be more understanding? Why couldn't she just trust him?

Taking a big breath and exhaling it slowly and quietly to himself, Jim abruptly didn't want to say anything.

Jim said "Nah, tio. Everything's fine. And, uh, sorry about the door. It's kind of windy out there right now." His uncle watched and waited.

"I've been fighting it all day" Jim added weakly, "the wind I mean" and started to mumble something else, then decided he'd better just keep his mouth shut, so he kind of cleared his throat to cover the strangled words. His uncle glanced at the window by the front door - at the unmoving bushes and the motionless trees visible through the wavy fifty-year-old window glass. "Uh huh. Well. I can see that." He bent his chin lower to get a better direct view of Jim, who started getting really interested in untying his shoes and unpacking his satchel and arranging everything by the sofa in a neat little pile.

"Uh huh" his uncle said, laying the onion down on the counter, still looking at Jim, then disappearing into the miniature kitchen again, where Jim could hear water running and feel the humidity in the air of something boiling. It had a smell too, rich and well, hot and homey in the apartment like they were having some kind of roast tonight. Almost like he was back in Greeley. Almost like he was back home.

But surprisingly the thought of Greeley didn't turn him inside out today. Jim felt himself starting to un-kink and un-wind and found himself spread as limp as improperly overcooked asparagus, over the sofa and over the ottoman and over part of a chair.

"Don't get too comfortable out there, we've got carrots to cut and two boxes of cash register rolls to enter before we eat." Jim smiled to himself and forgot to remember why Melissa was so unreasonable and life was so hard.

That night, Jim watched, mesmerized, as Johnnie in his stained sweat pants and an old t shirt, kicking way back, balanced unsteadily on the two hind legs of a wobbly, plastic dining room chair. There were in Johnnie's one room apartment. Johnnie was holding the latest note with one hand under a cone of light thrown out by an enormous black and white stucco floor lamp he'd picked up at a thrift store – for nothing man! – they paid me to take it out of the store! At the same time, he was reaching and groping randomly with his free hand for his beer. His beer bottle was resting, of course, six feet away from him on the card table he used as his all-purpose efficiency apartment horizontal work surface - when it wasn't being used as the impromptu trash can. Disaster was imminent. Jim listened to Johnnie read the note out loud for the third time.

Johnnie only had one dining room chair left - the others had fractured and exploded in the middle of just the kind of stunt Johnnie was pulling right now, right this very minute. And on at least one occasion in the past, an emergency room had figured into

Jim's visits to Johnnie and Johnnie's exploding dining room chairs. Johnnie frowned, made an unsuccessful, slightly inebriated lunge for his beer, and scowling, continued reading the note out loud.

"We have to talk. Buy a composition book and write in it. Keep the book safe, just that, keep it safe. You'll be hearing from me." Johnnie stopped and looked up at Jim crashing his chair down on all four legs to emphasize the last word "me."

"So, what do you think?" said Jim.

"I think Melissa's back on the market again, bro, that's what I think."

Jim stared at Johnnie, just stared, no expression. "Really, Johnnie? So that's what you think, huh?"

Johnnie took a swig from his beer, and said over the lip of the bottle

"Yup, that's my considered professional opinion. Your toast, dude, officially toast. Cut, buttered, and on the plate." Johnnie quickly added (as he saw Jim aiming what looked to be a painful, jabbing martial arts kick at his unprotected leg under the table) "but the note, J, the note now, that's interesting, very interesting."

Jim waited for more, but Johnnie just smiled at him. Finally Jim said "Interesting, Johnnie, because..."

Johnnie smiled some more, then seeing Jim was still waiting, took another long drink from his beer, sweeping his eyes lazily over the table, like he was looking for something to talk about. Then he looked at Jim with a pleading expression, then looked back a little more anxiously over the table, then looked at Jim. As Johnnie showed no sign of talking soon, Jim started to say "forget it" when Johnnie popped back to life, choking on his beer a little and said between coughs "because, my dear Watson, we could use this."

And he pulled out his almost entirely unused English Lit composition book (he usually photocopied Jim's notes, as he missed morning classes sometimes because of patently unfair changes in his shift schedule at the Sell-Lo Grocery store - they both hated his boss the meat and deli manager). Johnnie handed it over to Jim with a note of triumph in his eyes, and yes, it did look serviceable, even though someone had used it a lot as a kind of blotter for their beer bottles and coffee cups, that someone probably being Johnnie, but it was good of him to offer it. Jim appreciated having Johnnie as a friend. He could always count on Johnnie.

"So what are you going to write?" asked Johnnie importantly, tipping the bottle back once again to get the last few swallows out from under the remaining foam.

"Something simple" said Jim, and wrote in carefully printed block letters with one of Johnnie's black waterproof meat-marking pens from work "Who are you?" Jim admired his handiwork turning it this way and that, thinking "I hope they can read it" and "I've lost my motherfucking mind", his writing clearly appearing underneath a particularly black coffee ring stain on page one, which itself was under the beginning of some hastily scribbled, incoherent notes about Beowulf and alliteration and Anglo Saxon poetry.

Jim heard Johnnie chanting "something borrowed, something blue" and chuckling to himself from deep inside his tiny kitchen, Jim heard the refrigerator opening and heard Johnnie calling over the fan "You're fuckin' toast man. How's Deb doing, by the way? You want another cold one, J?"

Jim left Johnnie's late, and walked quickly in the humid cold (well, 60 degrees, but it felt cold for San Diego) and found himself walking down the hill again with the huge overhanging trees, the buckling sidewalks, and most importantly, the infamous bus stop. It was on the way to his uncle's place. Well, that wasn't entirely true. He could easily have skipped the big hills and gone directly home, but it was just as fast to go straight down the avenue, past the bus stop and take a right on 30th. Yeah, maybe it was even faster. Sure it was. Of course it was. This time the bus caught up to him even before he got to the bus shelter.

"Here" said a voice from the shadows of the front of the bus, and a folded object catapulted out of the darkened cab onto the ice plant by the side of the street at Jim's feet - seemingly, Jim wasn't even worth the added effort of a full stop this time around.

There was lots of traffic for some reason, and the bus had a hard time of it, squeezing laboriously back into the far left lane as it trundled off making its way down the hill, through the lights, over the next hill under the viaduct (amazingly without having to stop once) and dipping out of sight into who knows where. Probably the Twilight Zone.

Jim picked up what he took to be a note. It was paper folded in some complicated origami into the geometrically perfect shape of a soccer ball, or as his uncle would say a *futbol*. Jim wasn't even sure he wanted to see what, exactly, this white, blue-lined miniature piece of paper sports equipment contained. Fuck! He was tired of this. Immensely and unconditionally tired. But fascinated too. It was disturbing the kind of attraction and abhorrence he felt for it. He should just toss it away. Toss it in the trash as he walked home and keep on walking. This'd better not be some kind of bus portal to the land of the dead or some shit like that.

He held it up to the light. What if it was from his dad? Jim felt a warning stab of pain on the right side of his face and he felt like he couldn't catch his breath. Or what if it were from his mom? Jim squinched his eyes waiting for his breathing to slow down and for his chest to stop pounding. He felt a new, strange pain radiate from his right pec down his right arm. What the hell was that? I'm fucking having a coronary. A heart attack over some bored bus driver's ignorant idea of a practical joke. This isn't right. It just isn't right. Jim's hand was still shaking as he carefully unfolded the intricately creased paper and opened it out beneath a gentle fall of eerie pink-orange-sulphur light from a street lamp halfway up the hill.

Then he dropped it.

He dropped the much-folded paper - because he could see, could see right away that the paper had a (now faded) black coffee stain in the middle of the page, some (even more faded) notes about Beowulf on the top, and his own writing (black and clear) "Who are you?" towards the bottom of the page. A very familiar sheet of paper. Too familiar. Just then a burst of wind grabbed the much-folded note and Jim watched it plaster itself against the side of the bus stop, then float back down in its crumpled state onto the scraggly ice plant injudiciously struggling to grow straight out of the street pavement.

Jim sprang into action. He whipped out Johnnie's composition book, the book was there, along with a big black pen, right in his satchel where he'd left it and Jim turned to the first page, expecting to see the page ripped out and missing, stolen by someone in the last couple of hours and messengered over to this lunatic bus driver who had driven around the city all day at random, pursuing one Jim (also called Diego) Velasquez, so that said driver could play with his (Jim's) head and get his rocks off watching him (Jim) squirm every time a bus drove past him and potentially launch a new enigmatic paper missile at his black-haired, easily-targeted and oh-so-gullible head.

That's what Jim expected to find. But what he actually got was the page itself - whole, untorn, still firmly bound into the composition book - looking exactly the same as it had on Johnnie's card table in his apartment an hour ago - an hour ago when in front of Johnnie he had used the Del Rio Meat Packing pen to write his indelible question to the Universe-At-Large. Jim looked back down at the paper lying at his feet.

The note had turned over while it fell. On the back, between folds and crinkles, you could barely see the coffee stain as it had soaked through to the other side, and underneath that, in familiar block print, in a purpley-reddish kind of ink were the words "I am Diego Velasquez. I am you. I am Jim."

He had to stop for a second, his hand was shaking again. What kind of crap was this? It went on (of course it would, it couldn't be just mildly weird, no...) "I am you years and years from now, and I have a lot to tell you. I can save you a lot of time and a lot of grief and pain. I can make you a lot of money. Let's work together. I know you. I know you very well. I know you have too much of the pain and, yeah, too little of the money right now. And I can help. With both. Things can get better. Things will get better. Boy will they get better. Write back to me. Do it. Just write on the next page of the book. You'll be hearing my reply back soon. Do it Jim. Don't think about it, just do it. I guarantee you won't be sorry. Do it. Do it. DO IT."

Jim just wanted it all to go away. He wanted it to go away and leave him alone. Oh, and return his skateboard before it left.

Jim hightailed it back to Johnnie's, even though it was pretty late, convinced him to answer the intercom and open up, persuaded him to let him in and then immediately regretted it. Jim was in for a major grilling session. He could tell.

And Johnnie was a merciless, gifted, and untiring griller.

It also didn't help that Jim had woke him up and Johnnie was walking around costumed like some Jedi knight in a long blanket and a kind of towel hood wrapped around his neck. Johnnie took his Jedi-priest-advice-giving role seriously, very seriously. And Johnnie liked how Johnnie looked in a hood. But the main reason Johnnie was wrapped up in various, mysterious textiles was because Johnnie's apartment was the temperature of a meat freezer. Johnnie would know. Johnnie worked in one. Yeah, his apartment was always freezing, the landlord didn't turn on the heat often (this was

San Diego after all), and when begged she would reply - cold builds character. And since the utility bills for electric heaters were more outrageous than just going ahead and building fires out of dollar bills in Johnnie's ancient fireplace, you pretty much layered in Johnnie's apartment. And layered. And layered.

Yes, Johnnie called it "Character By Layering." Or C.B.L. It was their code phrase for all the shit you had to do when you were poor and young and under the thumb of lazy-ass, cheap "mature" adults. C.B.L. was their entire life as young, penny-pinching students. So Johnnie was not sympathetic to Jim. No. Johnnie was not a big fan of poverty, he hated do-it-yourself character building. It was not a voluntary glaciating occurring in Johnnie's apartment. Johnnie was involuntarily frosty. So, Johnnie was all for shortcuts. Shortcuts and heat. Shortcuts and heat and money.

And you know, Jim couldn't really blame him for that.

"This is your big chance, bro. What are you waiting for? What's there to think about? Girls, money, success, fame, fuck it - heat, warmth - it's all good man, all good." Johnnie focused one long Johnnie-glance at Jim and then shook his head in a pitying way.

But Jim wasn't so sure. Was he so weak and pathetic he couldn't make it on his own? Did he have to go and ask someone else to win the big game for him? Did everyone think Jim couldn't do it by himself? Jim looked up and saw Johnnie was waiting. Johnnie was waiting for Jim to say something, shaking his head slowly back and forth in the crisp apartment air. O.K. Jim would try and explain.

"Look, I just want to do it on my own, man, I just want…" and then he stumbled to a halt. Johnnie's head shaking became almost violent (the lack of heat was really getting Johnnie worked up) - he'd closed his eyes tight and was pulling up his blanket so he could efficiently pace the short eight feet of open apartment floor he had, pacing back and forth in front of Jim who was sitting on Johnnie's bed.

"No, No, you're just not getting it J." Then he whispered to himself "not getting it" and did a smart turn at his window and began pacing back towards the front door. "If you're eating well, who cares how much you paid for the food?" He turned and started back towards the window. "Does paying a fortune make it taste better? Or worse? Does paying nothing make it crap? Or vice versa? No, no and no. I repeat, no. It tastes the same, man - it tastes the same. It doesn't matter how you got it. It's just, you get to eat. You get to eat if you got the bucks. And now, bro, you got 'em. The bucks, I mean. You got the bucks, right? In that golden notebook of yours. Right? Am I right?"

"Well, I…" started Jim, but Johnnie was off and running again and wouldn't be stopped. In the end, Jim pulled out the notebook and wrote in careful block letters "What do you want me to do?" just to shut Johnnie up, and wrote underneath it in bigger letters "How does this all work anyways?" He asked the last question for himself. And with that he let himself out - walking briskly in the humid, cold streets back towards his uncle and warmth (his uncle at least got to control his own thermostat). The note got answered at another bus stop before he made it back to his uncle's apartment. It had been lying on a bench, glowing whitely, white as a bone in the pale moonlight.

He showed the note he got back to Johnnie at lunch the next day. His original note was on one side, the answer on the other and the paper looked like it had been ripped out of a bound book again - but the handwriting looked the same. It was brief. Well, as brief as Jim ever was, which actually when he thought about it, wasn't all that brief. People said he talked too much. He didn't think so. Did he think his older self talked too much? Jim wasn't sure what he thought about his older self yet exactly. If it was Jim, after all. It could be anybody. How would Jim ever know for sure? We're talking Composition Book Time Travel here. It was all too fuckin' weird for him.

He read out loud what the note said "There are things I'd like to change, you can do that. There are things I need to change, that need to happen if things are going to turn out the way they already have turned out - we just need to coordinate that stuff over the years. Keep this notebook. As long as you keep it, I'll have it years and years from now. And I'll be able to give you back the answers to your questions."

Not exactly the most encouraging letter. Older Jim sure didn't seem very interested in younger Jim's welfare. Jim wasn't sure about all that shit about "over the years" either - how long was he supposed to be working for this senior citizen here? Who did he think he was anyways? How much more of a total dick was he going to be to him? Jim, older Jim that is. Being a dick. To younger Jim. If that's who he was. Fuck. I am Jim. The word masochism drifted into his head. It drifted out again. Parts of this wasn't making sense, and parts of this were scaring him and parts refused to be anything at all. What kind of asshole, really truly an asshole, had he become? How had he gotten to be such a self-absorbed crank?

He lay down on the sofa that night, not comfortable, staring at the ceiling as usual (it was becoming a habit with him, this staring thing) and he heard his uncle getting up in the middle of the night to hit the bathroom. He must have shifted in his blanket, because his uncle called out in a low whisper which carried pretty well in the small space

"You still awake, Dieguito? Are you all right?"

Jim grunted a sleepy yes and turned over pinning his face against the wall of cushions on the back of the sofa. His uncle whispered "Good night, Dieguito" and Jim could hear him shuffling back in his slippers across the hardwood floors and the door creaking shut. Jim reached out by the side of his bed and pulled the ragged, stained book out of his satchel, thought of writing something - a question, a request - but put the book away as he searched for a pen in the dark. It was starting to be, what? - some kind of drug? - some kind of addiction? There was power being applied somewhere in this whole thing - someone was using someone else - but he couldn't tell who was the user and who was the one being used. He stared up at the ceiling for a long time, clutching the book to his chest with both hands. But he didn't write anything that night.

In fact, he didn't touch the book again for a week. He tried calling Maria, but got no answer. No response to emails, texts, voicemails, facebook scrawls, or even waving at her once in what he thought was a friendly, non-threatening manner when he saw her sitting at the back of a bus he was taking to work. Nada. And more nada. He guessed, yeah, it had probably been more than a few months since he'd last called her. Maybe he deserved the you-don't-exist-treatment.

Then, he actually got Deb to get together with him for coffee at a new place over on 30th, but ducked out through the back smoker's patio to the alley about 15 minutes into the date when he thought he saw Melissa sailing in the front door with some textbooks under her arm and a pad of paper. Deb hadn't appreciated that much - not much at all. He couldn't blame her. So he was flying solo for now.

Then, one day on the way to work, passing the bench, he saw another note with the name Jim in capital letters across the top. It was stuck awkwardly in a crack in the bench, whipping around in the small whirlwinds trailing every car and bus passing in front of it. This time Jim kept on walking. You know, it felt good. It felt dangerous too, somehow.

Coming home from the crazy long day at the Dry Cleaners and school, he took another street at random on purpose and with a sinking feeling saw two folded pieces of paper with his name on it at the bottom of a wire mesh trash can next to another bus stop, and another one ripped up on its seat and scattered over the grass.

The next day he saw three more in various locations, one with Diego Velazquez underlined and a couple of exclamation points after it in big red letters. It looked like there was some kind of warning written underneath it. He saw at least ten more just like it the first thing the next morning and the next day he saw at least a half dozen trash cans with notes to him piled in the bottom of bus shelters he passed, more on the grass and gravel, even some stuck in knotholes in fences and lying in the middle of someone's yard held down by a rock.

Notes were blowing up the street, flattened against fences in the wind, caught in bushes and lodged in trees. Notes were turning up everywhere, a couple were even laying in front of the plate glass doors at the front entrance to his job – the Dry Cleaners - one foggy morning. Luckily he'd gotten there first. But he obviously wasn't getting all of them, or even most of them.

Jim was surprised the police hadn't picked him up for some anti-social, notice-posting crime spree or aiding and abetting litterbugs, or even possibly unlawful dumping. Who knew where all this was heading? His name was everywhere. It was worrying him. Johnnie thought it was hilarious, and he'd picked a few of the notes up, well more than a few, and brought them back to his apartment, where they spent nights looking them over. They were all in the same handwriting, (Jim's) all on composition book paper, some had lotto numbers and dates on them, or stock quotes, or historical events, others had names of girls or boys or companies or friends or family and they included all kinds of details (Jim didn't read them once they got into particulars) which seemed to always have to do with betrayals and broken promises and vengeance and getting what you deserved - some were about that very day, some about next week, others described events and people decades in Jim's future. One even started to mention his skateboard and had an address nearby where it had found a new home. Jim had asked to keep that one and had folded it into a pocket on the side of his satchel, he didn't know why. What was he thinking he would do? Threaten somebody? Hurt somebody? Steal it back? It was crazy and just made him feel off and grungy and oddly unclean in an unpleasant kind of way. He didn't like it, that sticky, dirty feeling.

And what was strange was it sounded like they were being written by different people. Like different Jims of different ages in different lives were all trying to win him over, get him to do certain specific things, make certain choices and help them out. They were all sounding less and less friendly and more and more threatening. Like Jim owed them something. Like Jim was a loser without them. Like Jim was pathetic and lazy and whiny and complaining and young and clueless and a whole lot of other junk.

Jim had started automatically picking them up and throwing them away, but that had quickly turned into a full-time job so now he just let them roam the city free, blowing wherever they wanted, informing whatever casual passersby of the most intimate details of his life - present and future. He was getting so whenever he saw a stranger reading a piece of paper in public he freaked, ducked, and walked the other way.

One night a couple of weeks later, he was walking home from work, passing through campus, after a hard day of dry cleaning and trying to ignore all the stray pieces of trash blowing through the streets (you'd be surprised at the sheer number of odds and ends of white paper you could run into during a casual stroll through the city), when he ran into Melissa walking with a friend. They looked like they were catching the bus after class. Jim thought of running, but forced himself to continue walking forwards. He kind of smiled and waved from a distance and she stopped and looked at him and then amazingly said goodbye to her friend and began walking over towards him.

Jim hadn't expected that. He was unprepared, and yes, more than a little distracted note-wise of late (there was even one crammed in his back pocket he'd just found blowing across campus - he'd run it down between the library and the Social Sciences building). Jim didn't know why he'd done it. It was a reflex. It was panic. It made no difference. They were everywhere. Jim was numb.

He watched her approach. He tried to be casual and relaxed and then he froze, his smile fixed permanently in a kind of painful, compressed smirk you normally saw in a corpse after rigor mortis had begun to set in. It was becoming his usual facial expression. Melissa was carrying something. It looked familiar. Her fingers were holding just one corner of it, pinched between thumb and forefinger the way you would if you were carrying something contagious or poisonous or both. Her other hand and arm were clutching a pile of bulky books in a cloth bag from the student bookstore, and she had a determined look on her face. No scratch that. She had a frozen look and her eyes were red and puffy and she stared straight at him and she wasn't looking away. She obviously didn't know whether to talk to him first and strangle him later - or just strangle him now and save herself some time. Jim drew in a long breath between his grinning teeth, his pasted-on facial cramp (his smile) now permanently set and an inerasable feature of his face. He couldn't get rid of it if he tried. It was gradually morphing into a leer, or perhaps a snarl. Maybe he could start wearing a bag over his head.

"Hey, Melissa. How's it going?" he managed to hiss out of his locked jaws. Jim, the lisping, friendly, neighborhood zombie.

"You look great, babe" he added just to emphasize the casualness, the ordinariness of it all. Maybe he could deflect the conversation into something flirty - a hopeless proposition he knew - or at the very least, maybe he could start an argument. But Melissa was on to him. She was on to him so quick his grinning head spun on his young, clenched shoulders.

"Have you seen this?" With a commanding look in her red-rimmed eyes, Melissa demanded he answer her, handing over a note (of course) with a great deal of small, carefully written handwriting. It was some long series of adventures, crazy deceptions, wild arguments, and passionate reconciliations involving Jim, Melissa, Deb, Maria, and a few other girls he'd never even heard of before. "Do you think this is funny, Jim? Do you really think this is funny? Do you know where I found this?

This," and she grabbed back the sheet of paper, ripping it in two in the process "this thing was blowing on the plaza by the traffic circle next to the transportation hub, right by the ticket kiosk. By the kiosk! In the middle of campus. This and like a dozen others like it. Just blowing across the plaza. In front of everybody." Jim didn't know what to say. "I'm sorry" he sort of whispered, but she didn't hear him.

"Jim, who is Maria? Who is Jennifer?" She looked like she was going to cry. "What's going on? What kind of a freak are you?" She moved closer. That surprised him. He flinched, expecting a punch. But, no, now she was crying and just standing there. He felt as if he were the one who ought to feel mad and misused, misunderstood, unjustly accused. Maybe because he was, huh? And he thought that he'd feel angry, when he heard her start talking, when he saw what she was holding, when he saw how upset she was, and how angry she was with him, and how unfair she was acting. But he didn't. All he thought was - she's in a lot of pain - and she's in pain because she knows me. She's in pain because I put her there. And he didn't feel virtuous or unselfish or magnanimous saying that. He didn't feel he was doing the right thing. He just felt like shit.

"Why are you doing this, Jim?" This time she started to raise her fists up, weakly, to hit him, dropped her book bag and then just collapsed into his chest, pinning her arms against him, and all he could hear was her sobbing and all he could feel was the uneven, bumping collisions of her slim body against his as she feebly beat at his shoulders with her fists and tried to draw in some shuddering breaths.

"Who are you, Jim?" She stopped to take a breath, and continued in almost a whisper, "Who do you think I am?" He held her, and felt something inside of himself, something that was cruel and proud break into small pieces. What was left didn't have a name. It wasn't very pleasant. He wouldn't recommend it as a fun way to spend a school night. But it was real. And it was his. And it was right.

Two days later, he stayed up late with Johnnie and wrote and re-wrote and re-wrote again a note in the 4th page of the composition book. What he wanted to say was that what was important wasn't the past, it wasn't the future, it was the present. No. That wasn't it. What he wanted to say was that all those future Jims had gotten it back-asswards. He wanted to tell them that stuff like losing your family and being poor and working hard weren't problems, they just were. Yeah. That was closer. He wanted to say that the truth was you only had each individual second of the present to live your life in - that was what needed their attention. Not winning the game, getting all the girls, having all the money, living like a rock start, getting all you wanted, the envy of all the guys around you. Yeah, even better. You had to want to live in the now. In the right now. And pay attention to what and who was right in front of you. But he didn't know how to say it. Not in any way that future Jim would believe. Jim thought future Jim was truly a piece of work. Future Jim had a hard head and a convenient cynicism and a lot of time to make Jim's life miserable. What an idiot. So... Jim and Johnnie kept writing it up on Johnnie's Mac – Johnnie typing and rubbing his hands to keep warm, and editing and rubbing and re-editing and re-wording it - Jim dictating and Johnnie typing and both kibitzing freely in between. Finally, it was two or three paragraphs long. Jim read it over one last time. Johnnie read it out loud and nodded his head. Jim read it and suddenly he couldn't take it anymore.

This thing was taking over his whole life. This was just crap. He grabbed a big felt tip pen and wrote in huge, terrorist-kidnapper style letters "Fuck off Dipshit. Get the Fuck Out of My Life."

"Well, that's one way to say it" commented Johnnie, looking over Jim's shoulder as Jim scrawled savagely into the book as if he were writing on a toilet wall with a crayon. "Short, honest, and to the point. Why do you even bother asking for my opinion?"

Jim finished the last violent slashing letter (the "e") with a flourish, and looked up at Johnnie, wrapped in two blankets and wearing two pair of socks. Johnnie was smiling. Smiling and nodding. Jim handed the felt tip pen, which now that he looked at it, looked a little bloody, like it had spent a few days in the Meat Department marking freshly slaughtered and quartered steers. It was a violent pen, with a violent past. Jim liked it.

Jim didn't get back to his uncle's that night before he started getting responses. Not the responses he'd wanted or expected, however. In fact, he was getting more than a little concerned, which was concerning Jim in and of itself. This thing was consuming him. It seemed to be escalating. Yes, it was definitely getting worse. Not better. The page with his felt tip pen message started appearing on benches and by trees all the way home. The same page, and the responses were basically variants of one outraged thought - "You'll be sorry."

So. How do you go to the police to tell them that you, yourself, in a future year, were threatening your past self with violence - by means of messages written on ripped-out pages from a high school composition book? How do you get a restraining order for that?

But you know what? Strangely, Jim was not stressing over all this. He was instead experiencing an odd sense of calm and flashes of peace. It was unexpected. A sense of centeredness, yeah, maybe what a stone feels as it's pitched over the side of an ocean liner in mid-Atlantic and finds itself in freefall, tumbling three miles to a muddy, sandy sea bottom, to sink and disappear into the ocean floor, forever, and never be heard from again. Finality. Hopelessness. Way beyond saving.

Which he supposed was what being saved felt like - being beyond the struggle, being beyond the fight. Or maybe, maybe it felt like something else entirely, something new. He didn't know. Sometimes it felt good to make a stand. Sometimes it felt good to accept the inevitable. Accepting what you couldn't evade. That almost sounded adult and sensible. God help him if he was growing up. He'd have to ask Johnnie. Was Jim getting old?

All he knew was that sometimes it was better just to face it and get it all over with rather than run and duck for cover. At least that's what he was telling himself. He wanted it to be better. But really, it was better, he was better. And he still didn't know why.

Melissa was walking beside him as they made their way to class the next day. She'd called and asked about hitting the bus together and he'd said O.K. So here they were. Jim was a little nervous. He didn't exactly know what he was feeling about Melissa, and he didn't quite trust himself, especially seeing what kind of a shithead he could be in the future if things didn't always go his way. He wanted to tell her to move on and find someone else, someone who wasn't so messed up, someone more stable. He wasn't even sure he was going to finish Junior College, stay in San Diego, live with his uncle. Sometimes it felt like he was 12 years old, sometimes it felt like he was 75. Did that make any sense at all? Did it ever get any easier?

He wondered what she was thinking. There were pieces of suspiciously composition-book-like paper blowing hither and yon across the plaza by the traffic circle, more were piled in trash cans on the walks on campus between buildings. Jim wasn't looking at any of them. Melissa was quiet beside him. Then, he felt his free hand, his right hand being nudged, and uncurling his fist, felt another slim hand slip into his. Well. Hmmmm. That felt good. It was a start, he supposed.

That night, Johnnie suggested it first. Jim thought about it, then said fine. Johnnie said "You know, there's no guarantee this will stop anything, in fact bro, we might just be making it worse." Jim shrugged his shoulders in a sort of helpless gesture of and-what-else-can-I-do kind of way and Johnnie raised and bobbed his eyebrows back at him, nodding with his quick, birdlike nods in agreement, like he always did when he definitely, absolutely, and unreservedly agreed with Jim - not something that happened all that often, actually.

It wasn't much. Yes, it could make it worse. But it was all they could do. They left for Jim's uncle's house, and finding his uncle not at home, they went into the miniscule dining room where his uncle did his bookkeeping. There by the side of the fold-out dining room table was a big-ass machine, a professional-grade shredder, which his uncle used to destroy a client's personal info when it needed to cease to exist, when it was serving no one any purpose, when it was just taking up space and was in the way. It was good at that. But it would work just as well at consuming, say, a composition book, one page at a time, munching enthusiastically with its voracious, pointy-toothed, aluminum mouth until every last shred of coffee-stained paper was reduced to a well-masticated pulp. It could do that too.

It took all of two minutes. They ended up of course, with coffee stained confetti. Johnnie was the one who started stuffing the shredded evidence of time travel down Jim's shirt first. Jim naturally returned the favor. Then as this went on they both took turns ripping the cover to shreds with pinking shears they found at the bottom of a drawer in the old, tiny built-in china cabinet by the back door. It wouldn't have been so strange except for Jim's smiling all the time, he couldn't help it, watching Johnnie cut up the covers into the shapes of pork chops, rib-eye steaks, and piles of confetti he called cardboard hamburger. Once a meat-packer always a meat packer. Jim's phone chimed; a text from Melissa. He flipped his phone open to type back, fitfully batting away another shredded paper assault by Johnnie on the backside of his pants.

They were just finishing up, with a cardboard deli display on the counter by the sink, and their shirts and pants overflowing with long crinkled strips of white, blue-lined paper when his uncle came in suddenly (through the back door) carrying an empty garbage pail and muddy gloves and a much used garden trowel. He stopped, one foot over the sill, one foot still on the back step listening and observing what had the look and sound of mayhem, joyous mayhem, yes, but mayhem nonetheless in his formerly spotless kitchen.

He looked at Jim. He looked at Johnnie. Then he looked at the two of them, and after moment of hesitation, he smiled. "I'm not going to ask, I probably wouldn't believe it if I did." He announced that and shouldered his way past his kitchen-full of shoving, laughing college students and hit the back of his front closet, to drop of the tools of the trade he followed up north here in the wild and woolly U. S. of A. and get a new garbage sack for the empty (and liner-less) trash can he carried in his hand.

THE NOSTRIL OF THE ARCHANGEL

What you are about to hear is a story – which is just a bunch of words strung together - a this happened, and then this happened, and then this happened. Stories are as necessary and normal to us as the flora and fauna of our intestinal tracts – they infect us, we humans pick them up as easily as touching our finger to our eye, and we need them in order to live.

This one is about two men and one angel. Well, an archangel to be precise.

And just like the rest of us, not one of the three of them knew at their respective beginnings why and where their stories were taking them. They were chained to the disinterested, demanding arrow of time, chained as you and I are also, carried against their will into their own futures, and there was nothing they could really do about it.

And I suppose that their endings, like most endings, turned out to be somewhat of a surprise. But change is what life is all about, and surprise is nothing but rapid change, rapidly felt. Which is to say, life, rapidly felt. So change is life is surprise, I guess.

As to the angel, well, suffice it to say that he was a crusading angel - the kind that led armies of perfect, numberless soldiers equipped with the standard six wings and forty eyes into enormous conflicts of cosmic proportions - that kind of an angel - and his name was Michael.

And as to the two men, one was fond of angels, and the other didn't have much use for them - not that an angel would care much if you or I are fond of him or not. But all that will come later, you'll see.

Some might say that in the greater scheme of things their experiences were so inconsequential as to be utterly forgettable. But with respect, I disagree. And since I am the teller, and you the hearer, I have the honor and the responsibility to decide what's important to remember and what is not.

So... here they are, presented for your attention and inspection - the unimportant incidents in the histories of random entities, taking place during a few rainy days one autumn in a couple of far-away places (far-away, that is, for the people involved at least).

All utter insignificance, yes, of course. But to the three of them, all of this meant a great deal. It was their lives, after all.

John Michael bravely drifted off to sleep, although he was thrown occasionally from one side to the other, his hands barely saving the book he had been reading from being ejected from his lap on some unplanned flight into the back seat or out the window. The car bounced, shuddered, coughed self consciously to itself. It was German. It couldn't help it. It didn't like making a fuss, drawing attention to itself, apparently. The air blowing on John Michael's face smelled of green things drying to brown. He was worn out. The seat felt warm. The sun was out. For a change. It would be nice not to think for a moment. Just be.

He had just closed his eyes when he felt them opening again

and a kind of wheel within a wheel, with a brassy, triumphant, supremely self-confident voice hovered above him - or was it a towering fire, with a voice like the oceans pouring and pounding down on top of him? He really couldn't tell for sure. At any rate, it seemed to be speaking loudly, and in a deliberate bantering tone: *Don't talk to me about mankind. I know all about Man. Man is so short-lived - born, barely unburdened of childhood, and he is felled in his strength by disease or age, collapsing into dust again - all in the blinking of an eye. Just when you get to know them, they're gone. After a while, it gets to be too much. Millions, rising and falling, waves of them dazzling the mind, it's hardly possible to keep track of it all.*

There was silence afterwards. John Michael wondered what he was supposed to do with this information. Then abruptly the voice started up once more, a little less confident, a little less matter-of-fact, with a lot more of a bellyaching in it.

What? The richness and abundance of life? It is overly rich and overflowingly abundant and has become to me a great burden. I am heartily sick of it. Yes, I say it out loud. Heartily sick. Just watching and waiting, watching and waiting - I'm no good at it. Now, leading and fighting, those make sense to me.

Silence again. Obviously just another pause, and then more complaining. *No. Yes. Yes, obviously, but I'm not as clear anymore about what I'm fighting against, who it is I'm fighting for, and why I started fighting at all in the first place.*

No, that doesn't leave much left.

Then there was a mega-pause, almost as if a lengthy rebuttal were being attended to impatiently. He could feel a frantic, searching pressure pumping off and out of the fiery wheel thing that was both floating in front of him and not floating in front of him. The energy was flowing towards him in great waves. He could feel them on his face. It was heat. But it wasn't heat. It was heat that had been sent skidding sideways somehow.

Was he supposed to be saying something, participating somehow? What in the heck would he have to say? Why was he here, listening, anyways? While he was asking himself these things, the voice broke loudly into the uneasy silence without any warning, shocking John Michael, who jumped off his seat as if he'd touched a live electrical socket. He must be a tad on the nervous side at the moment. And who wouldn't be nervous, standing (well, sitting) in front of a talking fire that seemed to be having a very public crisis of faith?

The only way to make sense of it is to talk about it. Talk and talk and talk and try to work as much of it out as you're able. Lately the talking is the only thing that gives me any hope of having a sense of purpose. I need to talk so I can understand what I'm feeling - I need to tell someone else so I can hear myself understanding. I didn't used to be this way. Does any of this make sense?

Definitely a question then. He'd kind of enjoyed the sound of its voice, the sound of the words, the rolling, rumbling sentences, at least when it wasn't sounding so anguished, so torn, so loud. The pain in the voice was almost another color, a new color without a name, rolling off the spinning wheel along with the yellow tongues of fire and the blue waves of ocean water and sparks of molten metal of some kind or another.

And what a strange speech he was hearing. He wasn't sure if he were eavesdropping though. It certainly sounded like he was. He probably shouldn't be. Especially to holy wheels. Probably not the best idea. It was as annoying, confusing, and embarrassing as hearing one half of a cell-phone conversation. One you were starting to get interested in. One you had no business listening in on. He felt he had to do something. Say hello, let them know he was there, comment on the fire – he had to do something, he didn't know what, really.

Or how.

The pause was long this time and kept on getting longer, in fact if it kept up the way it was going, it would turn into a complete stop. So he took a deep breath, looked upward at the wheel, and answered quietly into the silence, without moving his lips much.

"Yes, the talking part made sense. The short-lived part was kind of depressing though."

The voice answered with a suddenness and authority that made John Michael instantly regret his ever having made a sound - and he squirmed, feeling some immense attention turning solely and ruthlessly down upon him, and him alone.

Who is that?

And thereupon, it promptly disappeared.

John Michael pitched violently forward as Bill braked suddenly. Bill, thinking they were missing a turn again brought the car to a skidding halt on the narrow, grassy shoulder, and John Michael woke up with a disconcerting suddenness - the seat belt drawing a life-choking grip over his chest and his chin, intent on saving his body from what it apparently calculated would be a certain and painful dismemberment.

Bill was muttering to himself, more and more coherently, as John Michael struggled upwards back to consciousness, pulling the seat belt free so he could breathe again. John Michael yawned and stretched, glad not to be mangled in a corner of the windshield. He looked but his less-fortunate book was nowhere to be found. The car turned around and accelerated once again back down the road, leaving ugly tire marks in the grass. John Michael realized Bill hadn't even noticed he'd been asleep. Bill's aggravated voice repeatedly rose above the cool, measured hum of the engine and the late summer/early fall air whooshing in through the open windows.

"Well, John Michael, why don't you say something? Anything?"

"Don't you have any opinions?"

"Any thoughts?"

"Any at all?"

"Is there anything going on up there? Anything I might be interested in? "

Bill broke off and scowled because while he'd been eliciting comments (well, if he were honest, free-style ranting really), the severe, control-oriented woman who was the voice of their GPS navigator had warned them of a fork in the road. The fork was approaching. The fork had manifested. The fork had come and gone. Bill hadn't heard her properly. Maybe he hadn't been listening. Maybe he hadn't been wanting to listen. Maybe it didn't fucking matter. Now the voice seemed more austere and even more caustic (in a self-righteous, Teutonic kind of tone) and was counseling an emergency U-turn, repeatedly, fervently, and indefatigably. This German bitch never let up.

John Michael leaned forward, gripping his python-like seat belt, and perched in this way, nervously awake, surveyed the road from the passenger's side of the car. He was keeping quiet, gnawing on his lip, and staring disconsolately and blankly forward, out over the hood of their rented Mercedes (an A Class - Bill called it their tightly German-engineered roller skate). The asphalt continued disappearing regularly and steadily under the sleek lines of this highly reflective, self-consciously aerodynamic, white car Bill had picked out personally in the rental lot.

They barreled forward. Down a little-used coastal road in western France, across a French salt meadow, scaring French coastal birds in the process. Bill wanted noise. He wanted motion. He wanted consequences. To Bill, the determined quiet to his right (that is: John Michael) was unwarranted and unhelpful. No, not just unhelpful, it was aggressive. It was a pouring of gasoline on a brush fire in a high wind, and John Michael knew it. He knew how Bill felt. He knew what silence did to Bill lately. And if he didn't, then he damn well ought to have.

Bill wanted to fight. John Michael didn't. Bill knew it. And yes, John Michael (resignedly and painfully) knew it. There was a lot of uncomfortably shaped knowledge rolling about in their car, right now.

"We could be fumbling our way along highway 1 in California, driving into L.A. through Malibu for all the interest you're showing in France."

John Michael stared straight ahead.

"Why did we even fucking come here, John Michael? Why? Why did we spend fucking umpteen thousand dollars to go on a trip you didn't want to make?"

John Michael peered at the hood, squinting his eyes and waited. There would be more. There was always more.

"Why, John Michael? Why?"

John Michael breathed in an out, in and out, but softly so Bill couldn't hear it. Sometimes, if he just waited…

Bill could feel himself cheerfully edging down into a ferocious fit of self-destruction. It felt good. Tearing at John Michael with choice, sharp-edged and pointed words designed to draw the maximum of blood and pain – yes, he was doing it, but no, he couldn't help himself, he wouldn't help himself, he didn't want to help himself.

"John Michael?"

Bill didn't want help, actually. He wanted to hurt, he wanted, actually to be hurt. He wanted a lot of hurting to go on, in his near vicinity. He wanted it. Now. He wanted to feel. Now. He wanted to feel something, anything, feel alive, feel as if he were taking up space and as if he weren't imaginary. Bill was still here. He was still alive, goddamit. He wanted a painful give and take. You know, it was all very simple. Not civilized simple. Just simple. Bloodlust was simple. Bloodlust was real. Bill was real. It was simple.

He was pretty sure his life now wasn't. Real, that is. Or simple. But he could try to make it real, couldn't he? Shouldn't he? Why shouldn't he? This was not the final melancholy limp through the last months of his (Bill's) sad life. It wasn't. Bill refused to turn into a cliché, you know, something you saw in old B-movies from the 40's - the doomed man with only a few months to live, his last poignant hurrah, the lesson-filled tragedy of the terminally diseased, all that shit. That was not going to be Bill's last taste of life and living. No. Not Bill.

All right. He was all that, he knew it (again, yes, if he were honest with himself, he understood all this shit, but really who needs so much honesty?). And yes, thanks to a malignant tumor buried deeply and safely (from the tumor's perspective) in the gray matter of Bill's brain and yes, thanks to Bill's superstitious reluctance (he wouldn't call it a fear, not by a long shot) to see any doctor on a regular basis, here they were. He and John Michael. Touring in France. On this narrow road. In very early autumn. Going 80 miles (excuse me, 130 kilometers) per hour. And Bill yelling his fool head off.

Not bad for a dead man, huh?

Night falling. French byway. At the start of an expensive, spur-of-the-moment trip to Europe which they really couldn't afford. Back home, John Michael had seemed more than suspicious when Bill had announced their leaving that weekend. Bill hadn't told John Michael yet about the test results. He wasn't sure when he was going to do it. If ever. A voice in his head said that somehow if Bill didn't say it out loud, the cancer wouldn't be there, the test results wouldn't be final and it wouldn't be true. Ever.

Childish, well, yes. But sometimes the wisdom of children made adults look silly. Right? Right. So, there it was. No need for John Michael to know about it. Not yet.

Of course, it occurred to Bill that John Michael might have already puzzled the situation out for himself. But he didn't really believe it. No. John Michael knew nothing. John Michael wasn't the puzzling sort. He didn't puzzle. He felt. He felt his way through life, quietly, without a fuss, which, actually, was infuriating at times and really unnecessary and... and... and...

"John Michael."

"John Michael?"

"John Michael!"

This triple, verbal explosion, which was met with an adamantine and thin-lipped silence, forced Bill to lapse, finally, into fierce non-communication. His foot ground the gas pedal to the floor. He viciously torpedoed the car forward through the flat French coastal marshes, pointing it directly at a dark mass of rock plopped into the middle of a vast blue-gray sea of tiny angry waves. He glanced over at the now, equally non-communicative John Michael from time to time with varying expressions on his face. Emotions washed over Bill's features which would have been hard to disentangle, even if John Michael had been trying. Which he wasn't.

John Michael ignored Bill and watched a mountainous, craggy island gradually rise on the horizon. Observing the mountain was a more peaceful short-term solution, at present, to the long-term problem called Bill than anything else John Michael could think of, jetting along in this rented missile. And John Michael knew Bill needed a little peace right now. Even if he didn't know it himself. So he gave it to him.

The mountain was huge. It felt as if it were a person. The mountain ascended fully into view - some vast protruding body-part of a gargantuan sierra-range-sized man - a colossal someone whose feet would easily be tickled by snow storms in the Ukraine while his eyes smarted in the salt spray foaming off the North Sea. A being a thousand miles long. A large man. A significant man. John Michael thought to himself - we're talking someone powerful and immeasurable, someone you should be careful of and approach with extreme caution (as the signs next to dangerous things always say, trying to warn you, often too late).

And they were clearly heading right towards him. Or it. This piece of a continental-sized body. Consciously, rapidly and blithely. They were headed directly at him. And, yes, it was big. John Michael felt himself pushing deeper and deeper into his cushy German leather seat, trying to give it more room.

And the closer they got, the more clearly John Michael could see that he and Bill were small things. Tiny living creatures. Smaller than gnats. Smaller than the smallest parasites. They were one-celled animals bumbling their way through their ten seconds of vacation during their intense seven-hour-lives. They travelled, in their one-celled way over the well-oiled planet-sized terrain of what? who? - maybe a god, a sunbathing real estate agent god

216

getting a tan on a crowded celestial Mediterranean beach. He, the god-sunbather, could turn over at any time and crush them, the little microbes, it could happen at any moment. And then where would they be? By the time the god-sunbather went to sleep tonight, the two of them, he and Bill, the microbes, would be long dead. Who knows if anyone would remember them? Who knows if anybody even would have noticed if they'd existed? Probably no one would. Certainly not the god-sunbathers. Certainly no one else on the celestial beach. No one. No. They were too small. Way too small.

John Michael shivered. He closed the window he'd had half-open on his side. It was getting chilly, but that's not why he'd closed it. He felt exposed.

He looked over at Bill, who was looking intently at the road ahead of them. John Michael felt disjointed, sort of dislocated and misplaced. He hated it when he got this way - all maudlin and sad - and he didn't want to ruin their trip. But he couldn't help feeling what he was feeling. He just wouldn't let on to Bill, that's one thing he could do for Bill. Don't make it harder for him than it already was. That was best. Considering the circumstances.

The car tumbled through salt grass and wildly meandering sea marshes. The pavement on the highway beamed back at them, crisply black and the stripes white and proud against a wet, blue, wind-blown autumn sky.

He watched Bill. Bill had stopped yelling. Bill was driving faster today than yesterday. Bill was talking under his breath now and again, like he was alone, like John Michael wasn't there right beside him, like he had to do everything all by himself, like he had no help. But that was normal. Nowadays. He did that sometimes. He didn't used to. But he did now. And he did yell a lot, but the yelling, well, it was becoming more bearable, more predictable, more repetitive. And John Michael didn't mind. Not really. He was getting used to it and all things Bill. John Michael had better be getting used to Bill, after seven years of marriage with him. Yes, Bill was Bill. John Michael liked watching Bill. He liked sitting next to him and watching Bill drive too fast. Well, maybe not this fast.

With John Michael watching him, Bill turned on the headlights with a savage jab to the dash and a another punch to the accelerator. Bill could tell John Michael was peering his way. He was probably smiling like he usually did. What could he be thinking, grinning like that? Bill wouldn't look over at him, though. The afternoon began to fail and the light got all watery and weak. Bill couldn't tell if there was a rain falling, it was misting, or fog was rolling over them. The tires hissed with new moisture on the road. Sometimes it felt as if they'd lifted off the road entirely and were tunneling through solid, turquoise-colored air in their white bullet. It felt good. It felt real.

Yes, John Michael thought they might be going a little too fast, but he didn't say anything. Not yet. Bill looked more peaceful, even though he was smacking and kicking at the car. John Michael looked off to the left, through a whitish film of salt and dust on the windshield as the island (yes it was an island-mountain), incredibly, continued to get larger and larger. John Michael pulled his sweatshirt around his body tightly and hugged himself with his elbows willing himself not to shiver. It didn't work. Bill punched it again, and they picked up a little more speed. Now they were definitely going too fast. The light got dimmer. The island got larger as it faded away. He was trying to figure out what shape the island reminded him of. It was on the tip of his tongue, but he couldn't pin it down. They took a curve, levitated gracefully off the roadway and sent a spray of gravel arcing out over the salt marsh.

"Bill?"

"What?"

"Bill?"

"What?"

"Bill?"

"Oh all right. You win."

They slowed down.

Fog was rolling in to their right. But directly in front of them, the sun came out from behind the clouds just before it set in the westering sea, and a brilliant, solid-looking beam of light, maybe a celestial two-by-four, miles not feet long, fell upon the top of the rocky island, bursting into splinters of fiery radiation. It spread over the cathedral on top of the rock, firing some golden, sliver-sharp statue on the top of the cathedral, which in turn, promptly burst into a blazing, straw-colored nimbus of fire, a minuscule second sun floating and bobbing in the muddy agate-blue sky.

John Michael held his breath. He was afraid that even a miniature blast of air out of his lungs would disturb some chain of air molecules and cause the fog to rise and wrap the statue again in a blanket of wind and opaque, corrosive sea mist. He wanted, he needed to see what was going to happen next up there. Up in the brilliance.

Bill was cursing under his breath. They were late to their reservations at the hotel. Bill didn't think they'd hold the room for them. No, he was positive they wouldn't hold the room for them. He grunted and moaned. And across the waters, over the gold green grass, rising over the walled city and battlement-crusted rock of Mont-Saint-Michel, Michael, the Archangel, leader of the Heavenly Host Militant continued flashing in the setting sun at the highest point on the steeple. Flashing and spitting sparks at the night. Leading the hosts of light, and beaming back a message of hope to a small, speeding rented car, crawling forward in the deepening twilight, across the marshes and through the fields, towards a darkening, quiet harbor town.

Bill didn't hear the message. He didn't see it. He didn't see any of that. Which was probably good. Bill needed to be concentrating on the road.

But John Michael saw it. And he liked it. He liked it being that way. He felt it. As if it were happening to him too, hanging high above Mont-Saint-Michel. And he didn't try to explain these feelings to Bill. Bill wasn't poetic enough, he wasn't built that way. He was a realist, a pragmatist, a how-does-it-work kind of man. Bill was more concerned with gas mileage, less concerned about sunsets. John Michael knew all these things. Bill probably didn't even see the church. Bill certainly didn't see the statue. Or know who the statue was. But John Michael knew. He definitely knew who that was. The Archangel Michael was an old friend of his.

Now, John Michael's real name was Juan Miguel (Juan Miguel Xavier Velazquez de Tamay if you wanted his full name, which only his mother ever called him, and only when he'd done something he was really, really going to regret). And Bill's was Guillermo, usually 'Memo for short, their conversations were all in Spanish, and really they weren't talking about Los Angeles and highway 1, but were talking about el D.F. (the Federal District, that

219

is - Mexico City, where they lived), and the highway 95 they used to drive south on to go up to Cuernavaca and get out of the heat and smog of the City's colonias.

Oh, and the voice John Michael heard in his dream also wasn't English, which may or may not have been obvious - but it wasn't Spanish exactly either. It was a Siglo de Oro, 17th century, De Vega and Cervantes, biblical Spanish, studded with many vosotros that sounded to John Michael's ears the way a gilded four-story altar and silver reredos and cupid-encrusted cathedral doors looked to John Michael's eyes. Gorgeous. Classical. Rich. And courteous and ancient and official and decadent and affected. Definitely not no-nonsense, plebian, citizen-like, every-day, hardworking Mexican.

You'll probably want to know more about these guys, more about their stories. John Michael had originally been born in Argentina, but a bad economy and deaths in the family had forced him to start all over, early in life, first in Uruguay, then in Columbia, finally growing up in southern Mexico with one of his many uncles. Later, more misfortune forced him to start over once again in the U.S. with another uncle, this time his favorite uncle (nicknamed Hobby), a former priest (also from Argentina), named Xavier - the Xavier that John Michael was named after. He lived for a few years with his uncle Hobby, went to college up north there in San Diego, and met Bill (Guillermo) one memorable moment in a bar while Bill was up doing business in the U.S. and felt the need for companionship on a cold (well, 52 degree), San Diegan January night.

John Michael had moved out of his uncle's by then, living with some friends in a kind of free-for-all living arrangement in a house in the near suburbs behind a small mountain range. There were up to eight guys living there on and off at any one time. John Michael kind of hated it and kind of loved it. It was the same as living with a big family, the same as being at home, in a home, in these lonely cities of North America. But he felt something was missing in his life.

In a word.

Love.

Things progressed. Bill and John Michael got hitched six months later when it became evident that they were wasting rent payments on John Michael's room in the crowded house – besides he was never there - he spent all his time with Bill and loved the feeling of being owner and owned - they belonged to each other. So he'd packed everything he possessed, thrown it in Bill's car and driven south, crossing the border at Tijuana, starting over once again, and he'd never looked back.

John Michael had never told Bill, but just before he'd met him, he'd been on the point of joining a Benedictine monastery on a peak in Oregon, one named for his patron saint, the Archangel Michael. He was sure Bill would not have understand. Bill would have thought it was a kind of cowardice. A running away from life. An escape. But that wasn't true. John Michael hadn't and didn't want to escape from life. John Michael wanted to fight for it.

They were similar, the archangel Michael and the human John Michael. John Michael had always wanted to be a soldier, like the archangel. And John Michael had always liked mountains and caves like the archangel. John Michael saw the two of them – the human and the archangel - he saw it as a true friendship based on shared interests. He was one of two Michaels. Through all the many drastic changes in his life, his relationship with the other Michael, the one who had been named to protect him when he was just a tiny baby, that had been the one constant in his life.

Bill, on the other hand had led a very different life.

But more of that later.

Bill carried the two larger luggage bags into the room, John Michael had offered to carry them, but Bill had been stubborn (as usual). He'd do it. By himself. John Michael followed through darkly wooded passages, low ceilings, warped floors, everything waxed, painted, polished - their room had a bay window that looked out over a courtyard, the mullions filled with a criss-cross pattern of small panes of glass, rippled with age. It was much nicer than the one they'd had last night, which they'd stumbled upon almost by accident in what looked like a farmer's field.

That hotel last night must have been for truckers. It looked like it had been built a few years ago, in three hours, from factory-made components, and screwed together haphazardly from poorly labelled parts. Push tab B in slot A and you were done. Bill loved it for its engineering. The key was dispensed (cleverly, John Michael had to admit) by a machine outside the front door, and the room was built to be indestructible – which was good because it was well-used, as if a soccer team had stayed there and practiced kicking goals for a few days inside, to escape the rain. But it had been cheap, and there were no other rooms to be had that late near Chartres, and Bill had been tired and angry. But what else was new?

Bill had demanded loudly and long that they make up some time since they'd gotten into some problems with the car rental at the airport in Frankfurt and were impossibly late. The sun went down on them on the autobahn, as they tore out of Frankfurt at 125 miles per hour. They'd driven into the Deutsch night, crossed the border and managed to get lost a couple of times in the rural French early morning when they hit poorly marked detours. And that had been their first day and the beginning of their first night here in Europe.

Bill had not been happy.

And of course, Bill not being happy had made John Michael not happy. But more than that, it also made him worried.

John Michael remembered, or rather tried not to remember, all that unhappiness – What was the point in remembering it? Bill had taken all his frustrations and anxieties out on him. Yes, but why should Bill be happy? He was a wounded animal right now. John Michael could see that. Anyone could see that. John Michael wanted to hold Bill somewhere, somehow, get him calm, get him to look John Michael in the eye and see - Bill was not alone. But John Michael didn't know where to hold him. Or how. He'd have to be patient, he guessed. Yes, not the first time, he needed a great deal of patience to be with Bill.

But that did not prevent John Michael from being miserable while he was being patient. While he was waiting. He was miserable with Bill's misery. Yes, yes, for better or worse, yes. No doubt about that. None at all. But, really, it wasn't all that bad. He loved Bill, consciously and helplessly - and there wasn't much anyone could do, even Bill, to forestall John Michael's love.

John Michael kept a fire burning for the two of them in his heart. It was there whenever Bill wanted it. It was there for John Michael, too, of course. John Michael just fed it and kept it burning quietly in a protected place. In a place where he could always see it. See it and remember it. John Michael smiled to himself. He was mangling a guidebook about Normandy in his hands, remembering. But he liked sitting and thinking about the two of them. He probably should get into the shower soon. Or maybe Bill would want to go first.

Bill glanced over at John Michael, sitting on the edge of the bed, rolling and unrolling a Michelin, waiting on Bill.

Bill saw it was going to be a long night. His head had started hurting again, but he'd always been way too tense, and headaches had come and gone all the time, his whole life. It was stress. Stress was tension. Tension was pain sometimes. It was definitely not one of "those" headaches. But if he were truthful, he expected the headaches to start and never stop one of these days. That hadn't happened yet, obviously, but... It would. Yes. It was just a matter of time. It picked and poked at him. This strange throbbing starting in the back of his head - sometimes medication helped. Most times it didn't. He didn't want something that put him out completely - why be alive? To lie there and drool? Jeez. It hurt. It really hurt. Right over his left ear. In the back. He needed to talk about all this with his Johnny. Really. Yes. Do it, Bill. You should. Do it. Now. Now. Do it. Tell him. Now.

No. Not now. Not yet, not just yet. Tomorrow. Or the next day. This was Europe. This was Bill and John Michael in Europe. Finally. There was time. Surely there was still plenty of time.

Time. Time. Time. That's all he thought about anymore. No one else had to think about time. Not the way he did.

Bill glanced down, saw that his cell had registered three calls at some point in the hellish last hours of this limp, sodden excuse of a holiday. Had John Michael called him? John Michael? Man! It felt as if parts of his skull were falling off the back of his head. He looked over at John Michael who was looking at the bathroom for some reason. What was he looking at? The shower? Why was John Michael looking at the shower? Why shouldn't he be? Bill was sounding confused even to Bill himself. He remembered he had something in his hand. His cell. Someone had called him. Not John Michael. It couldn't have been John Michael.

Who then? It couldn't be his job. No. Who? Who could it be? All right. Yes. He would check. He'll open his phone and check his voice mail. Now. Right now. Here he goes.

Instead Bill stayed sitting on the bed. He felt sick. He felt weary. And he felt filthy, as if he'd been throwing up all over himself, spewing ugly chunks of anger and frustration all afternoon, covering himself and what was more important, John Michael, in a pile of misery. Misery loves... What was it again that misery loved? Appreciation? No. It scared him now when he couldn't remember things. He used to forget things before, but now it all screamed at him - death, death, death. And so he screamed back, at whomever was closest by and easiest to scream at.

Why did John Michael stay with him? He wasn't sure what he would do if the roles were reversed. O.K. Yes, he was scared. Scared of the past, scared of the present, scared of the future (that pretty much covered everything, didn't it?) Yes, Bill was scared. There, he'd said it. Was everyone satisfied?

The future seemed a particularly pointless and blank wall. With hands. And a mouth. A very near nothingness approaching with a slap-happy grin and a five fingers extended towards him, waiting to meet the famous Bill. An annihilating wall-ish nothingness that had heard so much about Bill and wanted to squash him flat it loved him so much.

The inside of the whole of the back of his head was on fire. What if it doesn't stop this time? What if it never stops? What?

Bill shook his head a little from side to side to see if it hurt more when he moved it. It did. That wasn't the smartest thing he'd ever done.

His cell went off again, he noticed it only because it was vibrating the suitcase he was sitting next to. Why hadn't he ever thought of death seriously before? No one lives forever.

Bill wasn't sure when he would tell John Michael he'd left his job at Pemex too. That part of his life was over. How strange to say it – even to yourself. He didn't work anymore. He was done.

Too many secrets, too many. A few more secrets and he'd be so far away from John Michael, so hidden by lies and fantasies and what-might-have-beens that John Michael wouldn't be able to see him at all. Bill would fade. Fade to black. Behind mysteries and lies.

Then Bill would be alone. Really alone. But no, he was already alone. Loneliness was one of his best friends now, he felt alone, all the time, no matter who was with him, or where he happened to be, or what he was doing. Even in Europe, loneliness had followed him, his faithful companion.

He'd stayed too long at this party - life - he should've left a long time ago when everyone was still laughing with him. When he was still laughing. When he was…

His phone started, again, to beep that it had a message. He stood up, paced for a second, then sat down again by John Michael and felt his hand being enclosed by his. But Bill pulled away. John Michael didn't say anything. He thought he might have heard a sigh. But maybe he didn't. Bill wasn't sure. Bill couldn't tell what was real and what wasn't anymore. Or maybe he could. Maybe he just didn't want to try and figure it out.

Bill was being one pig-headed motherfucker. He grabbed his cell when out of the corner of his eye he recognized numbers - the hospital and finally his oncologist had called him back – Bill had been trying to get the oncologist to talk to him for at least a couple of days.

Bill moved off into the bathroom to listen. His head was hurting so much he couldn't think. He didn't close the door this time, like he usually did. He didn't know why he didn't. He just didn't. That was the first time he'd ever done that. Listening to his oncologist in front of John Michael. It was the same as stepping off a cliff. He was in mid-air. Nothing was familiar. But the covering up, it was too much work now, he didn't have the strength to play that game anymore. Right? Or maybe he just forgot. This one time. It was just one time. That was what he told himself.

John Michael looked over at him as he listened in, his face expectant and concerned and tormented. So this is how Bill was going to tell him. The messages were short. At first they were just a kind of one-sided phone tag, then they were an attempt to arrange some kind of time when they'd be able to get him in person. That time had just passed. That had been the last call. Bill didn't listen to the next one. Bill took a deep breath, looked back into John Michael's eyes, said "it's the doctor" and walked back into the room while he played back this last message, putting the phone on speaker this time so John Michael could hear it all, clearly and accurately, the same time Bill heard it.

It was the head nurse under Doctor Montoya. She was apologizing. She sounded so sad. The lab or the x-ray technician, or someone, she wasn't sure who, had made some kind of mistake. They didn't think it was malignant. It wasn't a good thing to have, this lump of his, but it wasn't going to kill him.

John Michael sat and watched Bill. But only for a second.

Bill didn't remember much after that, John Miguel's arms were around his shoulders and he was crying and laughing and John Michael was crying and laughing with him. There was a lot of joking around, Bill kept calling him "kid", his pet name for him, since John Michael was a few years younger than Bill. They collapsed, the two of them, back on their tall, stylish featherbed with just a sheet and a comforter beneath their elaborate plasterwork ceiling and the woodwork-covered walls and looked out through the drapes of their small balcony to see just the top of Mont Saint Michel peering over the roof of the inn, lit in a wettish, whitish light in the rainy evening, a grey-gold silhouette of a lumpy old pyramid against a wall of blackest fog.

They stayed that way for quite a while.

That night, curled one against the other, for the first time in a long time, both fell asleep, famously, dramatically, extravagantly. John Michael threw himself at sleep as would a spring avalanche lobbing itself over a steep, forested slope, flying and plunging to envelop a distant valley floor it never thought it could've reached. Well, he almost did that. Almost. That was the plan at least. As soon as he settled into it, immediately his eyes popped open again to the same sounds and sights of all-devouring flames, irascible wheels, drowning oceans and small voices echoing loudly around him from a great distance away.

Don't talk to me at all then. Please, let's not speak of it. I've already said, there's no point. No point at all.

The old voice from before. But before what? And when and where? John Michael remembered it from, well, from… what? A dream? Someone he knew? A movie? He couldn't place where he'd heard the voice before, just that it was a familiar one. And it was pained. It was in pain, and it was irritated and filled up to overflowing with hopelessness.

You continue to ask. Very well. Let us be honest and clear. We both know striving is as useless as waiting - it all comes to the same thing in the end.

John Michael held his breath.

He felt very small and unwelcome. Wait, no, not unwelcome exactly, more like unnoticed, but not in a hurtful way - he was unnoticed in an entirely friendly and insignificant way. Which was a little uncomfortable, to tell the truth. Why was he hearing all this? Someone was in a great deal of trouble, and that someone didn't see a way out of it, and John Michael felt, well, he felt he ought to help. But invisible people can't help out very much can they?

No, victory only sets up the conditions for the next defeat. Defeat is just a stopping place on the way to victory. Don't you see it? First, one, then the other, then the other. The wheel turns. I've done it all before, so many, many times. Yes. As have you, I know, we both...

He exhaled, and the tiny sound caused the voice abruptly to cut off.

Silence. And then more silence. And then more. He was alone. For what seemed a long time. The voice had been unpleasantly rumbling – the sounds of cracking crystal boulders grinding themselves down to bits at the bottom of a flash flood of splintered glass – but the silence, it was much worse.

He waited.

It wasn't making a great deal of sense to John Michael.

He waited some more. But he was tired. He needed to get some sleep. Surely there was nothing wrong with that?

He wanted to leave. He wanted to be let go. Let this thing find its way to some kind of peace on its own. It was a desolation – it was a hail of poison gas – it was a bed of razor blades. The voice seemed contrived and twisted, the argument itself was becoming too heavy to continue, there was no reason for all this suffering. John Michael could tell it wanted to stop. Stop once and for all. John Michael wanted it to stop too. Everyone wanted it to stop. So just do it. Stop.

Thundering billowed outwards, towards him, in a rush.

No. That's not the point. There is no point. No point at all.

All right. Good. At that, John Michael felt he had to say something.

He surprised himself at the depths of passion he felt. He had some opinions about pointlessness, some experience with out-matched battles and lost causes. Other people hurt. Other people lost things that were precious to them. Other people lost their way.

He waited for something else from the voice, and when there was nothing, and more nothing and more of it, John Michael spoke up into the great void that seemed to stretch upwards on all sides around his ears.

"No point? There are plenty of points. There's caring. That's one point. There's giving. That's another"

John Michael projected his small squeaking voice in the general direction of up and to the left, which is where he imagined the heaving, booming voice to be coming from.

Silence was the loud result all around him. Not hearing anything to the contrary, John Michael stubbornly kept on. He was many things, and stubborn was one of them.

"There's all different kinds of fighting. The hardest is sometimes the kind that doesn't look like fighting, but looks like something else. Like waiting. Like listening. Like caring and giving"

John Michael said all this looking off to his right this time, just in case he'd gotten the direction wrong before.

Unbidden, and unexpected, the image of a point gleaming on the tip of a spear gleaming on a steeple gleaming on a tower came into his head. A kind of archangelic gleaming. The silence became less strained now, it seemed less driven, less hysterical.

Who is that?

John Michael continued. Doggedly. What use was his advice? He was just a mosquito buzzing into the ear of a giant.

"Perhaps the fight is pointless, but the fight is not the point. The person I was named after, both people I was named after know that fighting or not fighting, that's not important. The most important thing to remember is to love. Love doesn't have a point, and it can't be pointless, it just simply is."

He stopped for a second.

"At least that's the way I see it"

John Miguel said that a little more softly.

Almost immediately he heard a grumbling roar.

Love?

"If I had any that would help you" said John Miguel even more softly, "it is yours to take. Take it. Use it. I give it freely."

He felt a kind of spinning release and a gentling of the darkness around him, and felt, rather than heard floodwaters receding and wildfires dying, and storms shredding themselves into untamed, impossibly blue skies.

And deep down – John Michael felt a quiet, inaction, a kind of peace floating him upwards and spinning him in circles, pushing him up and around and lightly depositing him in a heavy, abundant sleep from which he didn't wake until Bill jostled him by accident early the next morning. Bill had been awake for an hour already, bustling busily, but tentatively, with preparations for their adventures for that day.

As he stretched and rubbed at his eyes, John Michael watched Bill. Bill made John Michael smile, watching Bill's shy happiness that morning. It felt as if Bill had come back after being gone for a long, long time on a long, long journey. It felt something like home.

Bill, on the other hand, was feeling his way carefully through this new morning, as would a blind man feeling his way through a strange apartment filled with objects that tripped and bruised. Yes, he was a new man. Yes, he felt shaky and weak with the terrible news that hope was possible again. Having a future felt odd to him, it was having an extra arm attached to his torso. How do you move about with three arms? Everything was more complicated than it had been just a few hours before. Everything had to be re-learned. It was going to be work. It was all going to take time. It was going to take some getting used to.

They'd gotten up before dawn. All the way over to the Mont-Saint-Michel that morning, Bill had talked constantly to John Michael. John Michael had smiled. And watched. And listened. And smiled.

They drove slowly. They circled carefully through the traffic circles, they slid easily and quietly past acres of harvested fields of corn. They aimed, always, for the causeway to the mountain-island. Bill wanted to see the sun rise and the new day blast the island with first light. Bill wanted to taste the air. Bill wanted to push his feet into tidal pools and run his hand against the solid walls of an archangel's city. Bill wanted to walk across the sands that were drowned twice a day.

John Michael wasn't so sure about all that. Especially the sand-walking. But he continued listening. And he continued smiling. They stopped for a breakfast and some espresso at a tiny place for fishermen by the ramp down to the sand where they were going to park, except that it wasn't open yet. Oh well. Somehow it didn't make much difference.

Bill was Bill. He was happy like he used to be. John Michael felt something that had been tight and knotted inside him come undone. He was being unfurled. Into the morning. The sky was still gray and dark and chilly and it was more than a little windy. John Michael shivered, whether from cold or something else he couldn't tell. That's when Bill saw his phone flashing at him again.

After he heard the message, without expression on his face, without explanation, Bill handed the phone to John Michael and walked towards the back of the car, wandering, shuffling, the way an old, old man would, leaving John Michael to fend for himself and listen for himself.

It was Doctor Montoya calling this time, sounding angry and apologetic and frustrated, all at once.

He was saying that there had been some mix up. Bill shouldn't have gotten a call from his nurse at all, more tests had come back, yes, but it looked unclear at best. He apologized again and said they needed to take some more pictures of his head with a different device of some name John Michael had never heard of before - something that sounded new and expensive, something you wouldn't use if you could get a better answer any other way.

John Michael started looking around for Bill, the phone jammed against his ear. He looked to the left and the right and in back of him. Where was Bill? Dr. Montoya halted momentarily, took a deep breath, and ploughed on in a business-like manner. Bill was supposed to call him as soon as the plane hit the runway back home. They'd take him right in. John Michael didn't listen to the rest, tossing the phone on the Mercedes front driver's seat as the small voice continued to explain Bill's situation to an empty car. He was looking for Bill everywhere now, holding his hand over his eyes in the blinding early morning light coming over the fields. The horizon was a bright copper strip, glowing red and pink and streaked in yellow. It was a great bruise. It hurt to see it.

Bill wasn't by the car. Bill wasn't in the parking area. He was nowhere in sight.

John Michael panicked. He'd read that the incoming tide here flowed in and out at the speed of a running horse. He didn't even want to think how someone would've found that out. Where was he? What was he doing? Was he going for a last walk? Bill couldn't swim. But, then again, neither could John Michael. What could he do?

John Michael looked out over the sands, low and level and strung with dark threads of water and long blurry drifts of muddy gray, a river flowed off to his right towards the sea, away from the uncertain post-dawn sky in the east, the causeway was to his left, the island was only a quarter mile away. He looked and looked. But there was no one was out on the sands. No one was by the few cars parked there this early. He was by himself. Alone. He started walking. He carefully placed his feet on the rolling sands, creeping over the shadows and the rocks towards the river to see if Bill had fallen, or was hiding from John Michael's view, or...

Where did he go? Why? Why was he doing this?

Well, if it was a last walk, Bill wanted, Bill wouldn't be doing it alone. They were doing it together. They were going to do all of it together. Everything. Every single bit of their lives. Together. Starting this morning. Starting right now. Starting here. Even if it was only for the next thirty minutes. They'd be together.

John Michael started running. Faster and faster. Running across the sand, as weightless as a kite in the dawn wind. He ran away from the light. He ran towards the invisible sea. He thought he could see footsteps ahead of him, they went towards the enormous rock of Mont St. Michel thrust up straight out of the bottom of the seafloor itself. Yes. There they were. Where is he? Where did he go? He wasn't getting away this time. He was never getting away again.

"Hey where are you going, kid?" said a familiar voice from way back behind the car. "So quickly, and without me."

John Michael tripped on some bottom-of-the-sea rock or hole or something, turned around as he fell, and managed to twist his ankle in the process. He got up and tried to limp back to the car and to Bill, but Bill put a quick stop to that, draping one John-Michael-arm over his shoulder, and leading him back, three-legged, over the salty smelling sand and the mud flats.

The sun had started to rise. Off beyond the salt marshes and the meadows, the town was coming to life, cars were moving, people were walking. China was long up, Russia had been up for a while, It was France's turn, now.

"What were you thinking? You'll never get rid of me that easily" said Bill in what sounded like typical Bill sarcasm, but was coming out more as if he were pleading.

"Don't you know there's quicksand out there? And sea monsters? And eagle-eyed spouses who will never let a handsome thing like you out of their sight for more than a couple of seconds?"

John Michael looked out of the side of his eyes at the man supporting him as they got the car doors open, and Bill carefully placed John Michael in the passenger's seat, kneeling down to look at his swelling, reddish ankle in the dim morning light - light that was pouring liberally out of the sky and bouncing softly off the tawny walls and towers of Mont Saint Michel behind them.

John Michael watched Bill poking softly at his ankle and thought he could see the island smiling in the open air above Bill's head. Or maybe it was just someone at the top of the steeple who was smiling. Smiling an angelic, no, archangelic smile. You know, sometimes you just had to smile. Smile at the mess the world was in. If you were going to hang around, smiling was better than any number of alternatives.

"I don't know if we're going to get to see Mont-Saint-Michel today" said Bill "And I know how much you wanted to."

"But what about you, old man, didn't you say you needed to get up there?" said John Michael, wincing every so often as Bill felt his way along his ankle, "Feel the wind on your face? Watch the sun rise over Europe under the sword of Michael? Wasn't that you who said you needed all those things? That's why we came here, right?"

"I have everything I need right here" said Bill, and looking down, John Michael could see Bill was not looking at John Michael, but was peering out over the sand flats in the new dawn light, sitting with his back against the side of the car. He was holding on to John Michael, however, while he watched. He was holding onto him firmly, and with both hands.

"Everything," Bill said again "everything's right here."

So there it is. Nothing spectacular. Nothing worlds-shattering. Just endings and beginnings - just small occurrences in certain lives that were again were far more interesting to the persons involved than they are probably to you or to me. But I thought... well, by now you probably know more than you wanted or wished to know about what I think and how I do it.

Miracles – sometimes you have to really look to see them, and sometimes they hit you on the head, knock you out cold, maybe twist your ankle and put you in an emergency room.

And what of angels? Consider this: if the merest ghost of an exhalation from an angel's nostril might successfully brush a sub-atomic quark - a thing we cannot directly see, and if in brushing, bumped the infinitesimal quark's fractional mass in a colorful way (the adverb successfully, of course meaning with a probability of movement of anywhere from zero to one exclusive), and moreover, if it did all this in a space of time so short as to be immeasurable by us - well, how would you approach such an incredibly tiny, quick creature? What common language could you possibly use to communicate with something that could do that with a breath from its nostril? What would you say to it if you could?

And again: if with another slight respiration, the same nostril, larger than a cluster of galaxies, nudged a thousand, young, burning stars through a rich interstellar dust cloud over a period of billions of years, over and over again, a time span longer than oceans have existed, longer than continents have been cycling up from muddy sea floors into mountains and falling back down again into oceanic trenches - well, how would you communicate with such a being of such size in time and space? How would you even sense its existence?

What's more to the point, how would it begin to notice you? And why would it notice you?

Yes, I know, I know – morals aren't fashionable nowadays. Irony and understated, or un-stated epiphanies are what 21st century readers want in their stories. But bear with me…

Maybe we are all made of the same stuff, men and angels together. Maybe we're all fumbling through our own existences, reaching for some things, being pushed by others, wondering what all the fuss is about, waiting for some clarity, needing help, and sometimes even asking for it. Maybe we're made of the same stuff and maybe the stuff we're made of is love.

That would make a lot of things simpler.

If that were true.

And maybe what we're reaching towards ultimately is love also.

And maybe the way we're doing it is by loving.

So… let's see - that would make us all love, reaching out for love, with love.

Not bad, as a working hypothesis.

And all the rest of life, well, I would suppose it would be flotsam and jetsam - miscellaneous details that float into life, collide painfully, and sometimes require thoughtful extraction. Junk in other words. It floats and jets into everybody, forcing its way even into the existences of angels and men. But it's nice to know that love is out there too - often in the form of friends, sometimes in the form of unlikely friends, but friends nonetheless.

And we all, even angels, get by with a little help from our friends.

SNOW ON SAGEBRUSH

"Hey no need to eat so fast, bro" said Baillo "it's not gonna jump up and run away. Take your time."

Eddie smiled, not trusting himself to say anything, shy and angry for being shy, wondering why he was making such a pig of himself, and what was he was really doing there with Baillo in this trailer, eating dinner with a guy he'd just met? What did Baillo really think of him? Why was he letting Eddie stay over? Eddie was positive his scraggly beard made him look even younger than he was – and what was he? - boy-hobo, scruffy runaway, a societal leftover? He was laughable. He was naïve. He and his peach-fuzzed baby-face knew nothing about the ways of the world - whatever those were. Usually he was invisible. And invisible meant safe. So, Eddie, what are you doing here, showing up all over the place?

Some people thought he was slow. Eddie played along. It just made things easier. It made it easier for Eddie to get through all the endless, confusing verbal and physical dances called social interaction. He loathed social interaction. It was painful. Life was confusing. And people were live landmines in an unmapped battlefield smothered by a heavy fog.

A guy never knew what was going to explode in his face, or when, or why, or how. But the fact that there was going to be an explosion – yes, those happened all the time.

Talking embarrassed Eddie. A lot of things embarrassed Eddie. What in the heck did "the ways of the world" mean most of the time, anyways. What could it mean except "I'm better than you" and "I'm a winner, you're a loser?" Stuff like that. But it seemed to Eddie that other 19 year-olds knew exactly what the ways of the world were and how to work them with gusto, with confidence. Eddie just didn't get it, couldn't get it, wouldn't get it. Explosions. That's all that happened to him. Craters and shrapnel. That was home to Eddie.

Eddie felt he let people down, mainly. He was a disaster, a runaway, he should be back home this summer working. What kind of person just got on a bike and rode away from his family straight into the mountains for months on end? Flunked out of their first year of college? Joined strict fundamentalist churches and then ran away from them? Guys that couldn't follow through on anything. Irresponsible, selfish, strange guys. Guys like Eddie.

Eating here with Baillo tonight, he was sure his movements were awkward and ungainly, more like a robot than a man. Surely he was sitting too straight, moving and rotating his limbs at strict right angles, talking about obvious things, smiling at the odd times. He was a Martian, no a Martian artifact, an orphaned machine, dropped to earth and left to fend for itself.

Sometimes he wasn't even sure he existed.

He'd had this crazy idea that somehow by following highways up and down mountain passes, pedaling his cheap 10 speed, he'd have to eventually run into himself somewhere along the way - find out who Eddie was and why he was here and what he should be doing with his life, and what the next step should be, and why nothing made sense. So far none of that had happened. It had been a big blank. Well mostly.

Baillo was observing him, a crooked smile on his face.

"Sure", said Eddie, "slower", realizing he'd taken way too long to answer. Putting down one of the two tortillas he was shoveling beans with, he looked over at Baillo skillfully and efficiently pushing crushed-up fritos across his plate into a ragged, half-eaten piece of folded tortilla he'd just ripped off from the steaming pile in front of them. That had been the first time Eddie had eaten home-made tortillas, and the first time he'd used tortillas as a substitute for a fork, the first time he'd eaten in a mobile home, the first time he'd made a friend in a new state, in New Mexico. The number of firsts was a little overwhelming. And that was a first too. And there was one more thing. But more of that later. So, so far, it was all O.K. It was new. He liked it, which surprised him. But he still waited for the random explosions to start. He still braced for the scorn and pain to begin. He wasn't going to be fooled by a lot of new. Not tonight. He wasn't stupid.

But in the meantime, they'd been a revelation, an epiphany, those tortillas. At least for a white suburban boy from the city. So that's what they were supposed to taste like. Almost like dessert. Eddie looked across the low table at Baillo and opened his mouth to speak, closed it, opened it again, then closed it again, coughing elaborately to cover up his odd fish-gulping-the-air behavior. He wanted to talk, really. But his mind was blank, quiet, unmoving, scared.

Well, not quiet. It was spinning as usual. He wanted to tell Baillo about the tortillas and maybe some of what he was feeling, but where to begin? How? It was always like this, he could never connect with people. Never. He tried again, met Baillo's eyes briefly, then looked away, blinking and annoyed at his persistent cowardice. Baillo stopped eating for a second and looked at him.

"Hey, hey, I was just kidding, man. Plenty more where that came from, really. Eat up, 'mano. Mira, bro, we're out of beans, no problem, just hold up here and I'll go and get us some more."

Baillo smiled over at Eddie with what looked like a normal smile as he stood up with the empty bowl and padded his way back into his small kitchen.

Eddie's heart fluttered and skipped.

He knew he was blushing, he knew it. "Man alive! this wasn't happening to him. Not again, not now." Trying to stop it just made Eddie blush all the more. Think about something else, Eddie. Anything else. Think about icebergs. Think about hotel ice machines filled to bursting with frosty cubes. Think about... He could feel his face burning brighter and brighter. It actually hurt, feeling it frying his skin from the inside out. Baillo was banging some pan with a spoon behind his refrigerator. Eddie blinked and breathed. Think. Think. Think.

All right. Let's see... what did he do today? He met Baillo in church that afternoon, and they bummed around Santa Fe, bumping up and down dusty streets, rolling past lines of pinky-beige colored adobe walls, all studded with the ends of logs sticking out their tops. After doing the Rocky Mountains for weeks, it was strange not to be riding, not to have a hundred miles of highway to push behind him every day before sunset.

The long bike trip through the Rockies (he'd started the month before in May, way up north in Colorado) quickly turned out to be less of a continuous, rapturous National Geographic nature special, and more of a simple daily endurance test - more mental than physical. Maybe that's the way everything was in the end, more mental than physical. Maybe it's always in your head, all of it. There. He was learning something from this trip.

Anyways, it wasn't what he'd expected. Lots of silence. Lots of thinking. Rashes on your rear end from riding. Worrying about where you'd camp the next night, or which way the wind was blowing, or if the road was starting to slant more uphill than downhill now and how long the uphill would continue.

Uphill - the answer to that last question was sometimes thirty miles or more. But he was in the Rockies. He'd never thought he'd ever do that much uphill climbing, day after day. Not Eddie. Not sedentary Eddie. He was no biker, no athlete, no fitness fanatic. He'd gotten to know where all his thigh muscles were, really well. And his calf muscles. And the skin of his crotch. And the hard edges of his unsatisfactorily padded bicycle seat. He should've gotten a leather one and broken the seat in first. Instead his bike had broken in Eddie's crotch first.

But that had all sorted itself out at the beginning of the Great Bike Hike, months ago.

"You, O.K., guy? Feeling all right?" said Baillo as he got back, laying the hot, bean-drip-stained bowl with the bent spoon back on the short-legged coffee table they were sitting, more like, crouching in front of. "You look a little red man. Maybe too much salsa, it can be a little hot, if you're not used to it."

Eddie ducked his head down, smiling and thinking ferociously. He was not going to act strange. He was not.

"Nah, I'm fine, maybe sunburned some, I don't know."

He blinked his eyes, to cover his confusion, and grabbed some more beans to cover his bashfulness. Baillo was back to eating anyways. Sunburned? Eddie beat at himself mentally. What a lame answer! Baillo probably didn't know what to say to an answer like that. So here they were. Baillo eating and Eddie blushing. Again. What a great guest Eddie was.

Baillo pushed the bowl back over to Eddie after pouring out a river of beans on his plate for himself, and topping it all off with an unstable mesa of partially crushed fritos balanced precariously off to one one side. Eddie couldn't tell if Baillo wanted him to say something or if Baillo just wanted some peace and quiet. Baillo was probably wondering if he should let Eddie stay over after all. Eddie was thinking he probably wouldn't want Eddie around if he were Baillo - he'd tell him it wasn't working out, he'd tell him he should probably find someplace else to stay – sorry guy. Eddie started wondering how far he would get and where he would pitch his tent when he had to leave after all. He'd have to get over to the mountains behind the city. There'd be open campgrounds there, right? But he'd need to do it while there was still light. Eddie started frowning into his beans. Let's see...

School was confusing, church was confusing, and this bike trip was confusing. And now Baillo was confusing. Did it ever get any easier? He hoped it'd be better when he hit his twenties. Didn't you get it all figured out by the time you were older and more grown up and like twenty-one? Or twenty-five tops. He hoped it would happen soon. It sure wasn't happening now.

But back to the other thing. The other reason Eddie was blushing. Eddie felt attracted to Baillo. And that was confusing too.

He'd begun to realize his uncomplicated, but lonely days were numbered when he started noticing men around him – that had been two or so years or ago - they were giving off audible radar blips of pure, unadulterated maleness that had a tendency to bounce as lightly off his head as would well-aimed tennis balls served by a circuit pro.

Confusion. Men staggered and stunned him, he never expected it when it hit him. And when it did hit, he felt as if he were being pulled into quicksand, sucked under the surface of a bubbling pot of lust with both heels digging (uselessly) in. Generally on his part, there was a lot of sweating, blushing, a rapid pulse rate coupled with increased difficulty in breathing, and of course, confusion. It couldn't be healthy. He was sure of that. It surely was the equivalent of a heart-attack.

He'd never acted on it. He'd tried to forget it when it wasn't happening. He felt the need to avoid it. It wasn't guilt exactly. Maybe it was shame. No, it wasn't that. All he knew was that it just felt inconvenient and uncomfortable and confusing. Maybe if he ever gave into this very fleshly, body-centered urge, it would just prove he was human like everyone else. Subject to the same ungovernable feelings as any other member of the species. No Martian. So, maybe he was normal. Maybe he wasn't a freak. Just a shy guy. Who liked other guys.

But when he'd seen Baillo in fellowship after church from across the Fellowship Hall, he'd felt sure his tennis shoes had left a long, dual set of meandering skid marks across the church linoleum floors, starting from his corner by the front door and continuing diagonally all the way over to the other corner by the stage - the place where Baillo happened to be standing. It was as if he'd been magnetized or something. Screech. For fifty feet. He was sucked over to him. It felt that way, but no, he'd just walked right over, one foot after the other. His face blazing a three-alarm fire. He'd surprised himself. It was another first. The first of many. The first of the many firsts of this trip of many things.

After dinner, there'd been more red faces (on Eddie's part), too-short responses to longish questions, and a lot of Eddie listening to Baillo (which was actually fine with Eddie).

Eddie had felt tense. Eddie vibrated. Eddie levitated with the awareness that he and Baillo were alone and in close proximity in Baillo's trailer. And what about Baillo? Baillo apparently hadn't been aware of a thing. Eddie was just Eddie. A church-bike friend, a new church-bike friend, if there were such things. So Eddie was disappointed and Eddie was grateful. Both at the same time. But then it got to be later. And later. And then it was 10 or so. Baillo started yawning.

"You know, Eddie, if you want to get up late, that's O.K., just be sure and lock up behind you, bro. I have to get up and get myself over to my auntie's first thing Monday morning to help out with her oven. It's that new *horno* I was telling you about. Me and my cousins are building her a new one closer to her back door and to her porch, the one off the backyard. Gotta use some bricks and stones from the old one too, so we gotta knock that one down."

Baillo turned around suddenly with a puzzled expression on his face, and Eddie tensed, expecting, well, he didn't know what he expected, but he was sure it wouldn't be good.

"Hey, you know what, Eduardo? You could come if you wanted to. Really, it's not hard work, man, not hard at all, just a lot of carrying and stacking. My brothers are doing the adobe and the bricks. And of course there's gonna be beer and auntie Chi's enchiladas and tortillas and homemade tamales. I'd carry auntie all the way to Taos and back just for a chance at some of her homemade tamales."

Baillo chose that moment to slap Eddie just below his right shoulder. Eddie felt the impression of Baillo's hand on his shoulder long after Baillo had drawn his hand back, needing to use it for other purposes. It would have been nice of Baillo just to have left it there, resting for a while. The hand print burned. It was a kind of throbbing, insistent itch on his skin. He didn't want to scratch it exactly. Yeah, he wanted to leave it there, let it sink in, deep, leave a mark. Eddie felt his face, and knew he was blushing again. He was losing his mind. He didn't want it to stop, though.

"Bro" said Baillo, "I tell you, those tamales are excellent! My auntie, she lives over by Abiqui. We all do, I mean did. I mean that's my family's land from way back, you know, out north there. "

Baillo smiled and slapped/punched Eddie, this time on the arm, just a little harder. Eddie wasn't complaining. Baillo waited a second to see if Eddie was going to say yes, but Eddie just shrugged, smiling and looking at the carpet. He didn't trust himself to speak, it was hard enough just looking at Baillo.

Baillo broke the silence. "But if you gotta go, you gotta go, can't stop a man from doing what a man's gotta do."

A final punch, a smile, and after that Baillo didn't say much, just showed Eddie the bathroom, demonstrated how to get the shower to work with the pliers on the ledge by the window, and located where the toilet plunger was for Eddie (just in case, because the pipes usually weren't all that cooperative sometimes). Then Baillo headed over to the small dining room six feet away from Eddie which turned out to have a bench that folded out into the official Baillo bed. Baillo was unconscious and snoring in no time. Eddie broke out his sleeping bag and curled up in a corner next to the bathroom door.

So, a pretty uneventful night. Especially after all the build-up in Eddie's mind. But he was always doing that to himself, getting himself all stretched out of shape. And always for nothing.

It was confusing. Eddie was so tired of confusing.

Actually Eddie was plain tired. Eddie sank into a pile of plastic and disappeared. Eaten alive by his bright blue sleeping bag and digested all night long until he was regurgitated the next morning. Pretty much a daily occurrence on this trip. It got very quiet. Except for the rumbling coming from Baillo's corner of the trailer. Soon matched by equally raucous thundering from within the pile of blue plastic.

There was a reason his sleeping bag was called a mummy bag. Once a week or so it tried to smother him in his sleep. The next morning, blind and twisted in a strange and somewhat painful position against the bathroom door, which by the way was also rubbing a fair-sized hole into his shoulder, Eddie crawled and clambered his way back up into wakefulness. He came to, blinking and gasping, sweating like a Norwegian in a midwinter sauna and realizing the bag was pulled completely over his head, rotated and closed secure and tight – tight as a twist tie over a bagged loaf of bread. He was hermetically sealed. His head was throbbing. He felt dizzy. He was lucky to be alive, huh?

He slept naked, so his sweaty skin was slipping and sliding Eddie's body up and down in the airless, clammy bag every time he breathed. It was irritating as all get out, probably dangerous, and finally got him motivated enough to decide to unzip and unknot himself. But how? How to get out? He began to try in a vague and sleepy way to come up with a plan. As he squirmed to get his arms above his head, Eddie woke up more quickly than he'd wanted when someone walked into and onto his bag, tripping over him and collapsing on top of him, landing with a dull thud. The thud shot Eddie to the side of his bag the same way a fist slamming into a half-used tube of toothpaste shoots toothpaste all over your bathroom. Except this toothpaste tube had its cap on tight. And the toothpaste was human and more than a little worried. Eddie started moving his shoulders and pushing towards the top of the bag trying to escape. It wasn't working. He started to panic.

Someone was laughing. That someone, who Eddie quickly figured out was Baillo, was in his underwear and appeared to be about as alert and wide-awake as Eddie had been just a few minutes before. Which is to say, Baillo was practically sleepwalking.

Eddie continued to scramble, but without much success. He

gave up going out the top, and settled for squeezing out of his bag by unzipping the side and twisting out, only to find himself rolling his face right into Baillo's, and smacking his sweaty self in a bodyslam into Baillo's warm body at the same time.

Eddie remembered laughing, the both of them shaking their heads and crying they were laughing so hard when all of a sudden Eddie realized Baillo wasn't laughing anymore, but was just looking at him, a funny look in his eyes, inches away from his. For a solid five minutes Baillo stared at Eddie and Eddie forgot to breathe, although he could feel Baillo's hot breath puffing in and out of Baillo's nostrils and into Eddie's. Various body parts were active that morning, as they usually were in the morning, but Eddie wasn't shy about it, and Baillo didn't seem to be either. They were barely touching. It was cool in the trailer, and the gray light of dawn submerged the two of them in a kind of hazy gray-purple glow.

Baillo continued his look into Eddie's eyes, breathing in and out, slowly but deeply. Eddie allowed himself to start breathing and they settled into a rhythm, one breathing in while the other exhaled. Eddie could have done it forever. Then Baillo took a long shuddering breath, got a kind of a broken smile, raised his eyebrows and pushed himself effortlessly to his feet, twisting the doorknob as he jumped over Eddie, and sliding into the bathroom before Eddie even knew what had happened. One minute Baillo was there, the next minute he wasn't. Eddie wondered if it had really happened.

"Eddie, man, sorry 'bout that. Hey, go back to sleep. Promise I'll step over you next time" came drifting out to Eddie's ears from behind the closed door. Then he heard the sound of a pair of pliers working on a handle, and the loud splattering of a shower starting. Eddie closed his eyes again. He should feel cold, lying out there sweat-covered and bare, but the truth was he didn't even feel his body. He was vibrating with a surging, singing kind of vibration – a happily high-strung, high-tension power line hum, a power line humming in a hurricane. It wasn't a bad feeling.

He lay in the living room, by the bathroom door, the dawn just lighting the skies beyond the trailer windows and stared at the ancient mobile home ceiling curving above him. It was just becoming visible in the pinkish light. The carpet on the floor underneath his bare back was shag, orange shag, but had some gravel or dirt on it. He was picking up dust and pebbles on his wet skin – a teenage Eddie sponge. The air got warmer. He started to dry off. He lay and thought and lay and thought as the room got brighter and the day got closer.

When he heard Baillo fumbling with the bathroom door, he flipped over, lying on his chest, underneath the sleeping bag, pulling it over his head again and pretended to sleep.

Baillo disappeared for ten minutes, making small noises on the far side of the trailer, then quietly let himself out the front door (well, the only working door), and Eddie heard him writing and leaving a note or something on the table just as he left. When he heard his pickup truck pull away and everything had gotten quiet again, Eddie peeled back the bag, packed, showered, and grabbed the note - just a few words reminding him to lock up.

He felt disappointed. Typical. He was still invisible. And confused. All of which was starting to become a habit with him this trip, when he turned the paper over. On the back was Baillo's phone number and address and a note with a happy face saying he should come back and visit him again, soon, and he'd always have a place to stay if he wanted to come back here to Santa Fe, maybe he'd even have a place to crash at and get settled in if he decided to move down here and stay awhile. Baillo told him to think about it.

Well. Well. Well. Maybe not so invisible. Maybe not so confused. Maybe not the same old same old anymore.

Maybe.

And now he was back on the road and heading south, and still shaking like a leaf. Did he have a cold or something? Yeah, right. But, yeah it felt good. Maybe he'd catch this cold and stay sick for the rest of his life. And that's when he saw it.

He'd unchained his bike, packed it, and been wheeling his bicycle down the dirt path away from Baillo's place, back onto the highway. The highway that had refused to go west for Eddie and had kept on curving him back towards the south away from where he wanted to go - Arizona - but this was the Rio Grande valley and all canyons and streams ultimately led south to Mexico, not east, not west, but south.

Eddie grabbed his handlebars, threw a foot into the toe-clip of one pedal and swung his body and other leg over the top, successfully missing seat, luggage, and his fluorescent orange don't-run-me-over biker's flag, balancing his machine in the soft red dirt, shifting his weight, bent-kneed and rolling backwards and forwards, swaying left and right in the crisp Santa Fe morning cool. Unconsciously, he was enjoying the now familiar smell of sagebrush rising in clouds about and beside him and the sharp smell of manure angling in from some horse barn down the road and blinking in the bright light. Mostly he was thinking about Baillo.

Just as he pushed off and got the second foot safely toe-clip-ensconced he happened to glance briefly across a cracked and obviously well-used stretch of rutted asphalt at the open fields opposite Baillo's place. In clear relief against a relentlessly Renaissance blue sky the outlines of a fantastic melted cathedral rose in front of him.

Eddie stopped. He dropped his feet into the gray spiky grass and mesquite clustered about Baillo's mailbox, leaned his heavily-laden bike (he didn't have a kick stand) gracelessly on one of the taller mesquite which promptly crunched and sagged backwards with a weary, wooden sigh. He carefully inched towards an opening in the barbed wire fence on the other side of the road, half-afraid the cathedral would evaporate in the low-lying sunlight before he got to it.

Another rutted track crossed the ditch by the road's shoulder and ended in a wide clearing next to an ancient red pickup truck with a tiny trailer on it, covered with a tarp of canvas tied down with rope and staked down on three sides. In back of it was a miniature baroque church. It had been going up for years and years, you could tell. Wooden scaffolding to one side of Eddie looked weathered to an almost transparent white-gray, and excavations for additional walls and towers lay crisscrossed in front of him looking random and haphazard, like someone had changed their mind - a lot. All of it was covered in weeds. And there were more mysterious shallow dimples and mounds - so many sad, dry ponds and miscellaneous humps crowding everywhere - as if hundreds of pitcher's mounds for hundreds of ball parks had been started and stopped and relocated and started again – a maze of them lay exposed, all in the same red desert dirt, all eroded almost to the point of being erased.

Eddie could see his breath as he walked towards the church. His early morning shadow stretched crazily in front of him, sprinting ahead of Eddie to run its hands over the fantastic walls, poke through the door-less doorways, lean against the half-built towers. The sun rolled around on the jagged horizon behind him - an orangey-red marble - keeping the mountains in purple morning shadow at his back. The church was there just for him. Eddie could imagine himself working on it, laying brick, pushing columns upright. He wanted to be in it, a part of it, he wanted to breathe in the flat sour smell of cement dust and scrape his arms moving two-by-fours and feel the sweat dripping down his dust-covered forehead. He wanted to put himself inside the stones and the walls.

Beyond a wheelbarrow lying on its side, behind a lumpy gray cement mixer and a tumble-down row of cement blocks and steel rods, Eddie could make out fat columns, oversized garland-strewn vases, gables, cherubs, and pediments resting here and there and leaning against each other in odd piles. Mesquite was taking over, poking up between them, patiently, arching over them spikily, reclaiming this desert clearing for itself.

One tower was mostly finished. A large cross sagged underneath it. And behind that, beyond that, gleaming through open doors and unfinished windows, the high desert in spring glittered with its unnatural greens and carpets of fast-blooming orange and yellow and blue flowers.

It was soft and quiet and it was like a kind of benediction. He could see hills, and hills beyond that, and mesas way off in the distance, and far-away the San Juan mountains, and farther still the empty sky. Dew covered everything. His socks and shoes were soaked. Birds were singing someplace, but mostly it was deathly still, all ruins, unfinished courtyard, pieces and bits of church everywhere.

Lifting, sawing, nailing, cementing, Eddie could easily see himself constructing the cathedral, he could see himself being constructed, being the cathedral, walls going up, a tight roof to keep the rain out, decorations that meant something. This morning, in dawn light, it felt like Eddie was the beginning of something. This morning it felt like Eddie was also the end of something. All of it, all at the same time, all of it Eddie. Beginning. Ending. Beginning. Ending.

Eddie walked forward. He held his breath, afraid he was dreaming wide awake.

Rubbing his hands together and putting them under his armpits to get them warmer, he stepped over the sagging barbed wire fence. He heard something, a whispering, a rubbing echo from between the roofless colonnades in shadow in front of him. From somewhere behind the facade of the church, behind the huge, tumbledown three-story front with welcoming baroque curves turning in and out and in again, from behind the skeletons of the two stumpy towers there was a sound. Sand. Scuffing. Footsteps. Footsteps crunched towards him. Eddie stopped and bent down on one knee (thoroughly soaking his jean cutoffs in the process), putting his hand to his forehead to try and force his eyes to see something in the gloom and the decay.

A still voice seeped up, dripping out from somewhere, way in the back, it had a bluntness and an awkwardness to it, but also a sort of upside-down melody in it, as if English were not its first language. Or Spanish.

"You're trespassing."

Eddie stayed down, in mid-kneel. He froze. He strained his ears to hear whatever would come next. An odd clicking sound got his immediate attention. Eddie really didn't know, but he thought, maybe, what he was hearing was the sound of a rifle being cocked. Did they really make that sound? In real life?

An unfrowning, unsmiling face appeared in the shadows and repeated in its flat, unaccented, singing voice "You're trespassing." Eddie opened his mouth to ask, or comment, or thank the face, but thought better of it. It didn't speak again.

He straightened up deliberately and carefully, slowly turned himself around, and made an exaggerated, obvious and dignified withdrawal, when he must have accidentally kicked over a shovel or something and an explosion burst over him.

Suddenly Eddie was face-down in the red dirt and wet spiky grass. It took a few seconds of closed eyes and a wildly beating heart to realize that nothing chemical had combusted, no landmine had burst underneath him, that in fact it had been an explosion of wings, bodies, feathers flying around him. He saw a torrent of brilliant white and gray flashes erupt over him in the thin morning light. White doves - pigeons really, now that he thought about it - an avian version of a grenade - shot out in a fluffy white chevron, and disappeared west through a half-finished (rose?) window into the wet, cold morning and the bright, bright light falling out of the sky.

Eddie was laughing. Laughing and crying at the same time. He'd started doing that lately. Maybe God was trying to tell him something. Yes. Maybe Eddie was not quite so invisible after all. Birds saw him. So did cathedral builders. And so did hunky New Mexicans.

Congratulations.

Yes.

Eddie was now visible.

You may now see Eddie.

All right. One at a time. No need to crowd him. There's enough Eddie to go around. Yup. Here he is. Eddie. In 3-D.

He jumped over the ditch to Baillo's place, still smiling wide and big – a crazy person - threw his body on his bike, and caught sight of a darkened church doorway with a barely discernible shadow observing his retreat, and Eddie jerked into a familiar motion – pedals, calves, thighs, back and arms working together furiously. He spun out of the gravel on the shoulder and he hit the highway, and of course, it was very much uphill. He pressed onwards and upwards, doggedly, climbing as he headed south in a long curve on the road out of town - out once more into desert and into broken canyon-lands, out once more to find a road that would lead him west, through mountains, and over rivers, and hopefully all the way out towards Arizona and beyond.

Out to places he could test out this new first.

Out to test out his new-found visibility.

Ed was tired. Ed was lonely. Ed was less sure each day why he even bothered. Why? Why did he go to the trouble of forcing himself (painfully – yeah it hurt – he wasn't going to lie about it) up and out of bed, getting himself dressed, brushing his teeth, you know, the whole bit - only to stumble into his empty, silent living room, so he could make another heroic attempt at squeezing some small drips and drops of enjoyment out of another long, solitary Ed day? Why? Why do it? That was his mornings. Every morning. That was Ed's life. And what a life it was.

And it got better.

When the sun went down, he had to do it all over again, but in reverse: brush his teeth, undress, try to get comfortable in bed - although he never could find a position which didn't throw some part of him painfully out of joint anymore, and breathing at all on your back was always fun too – try it some time with oxygen tubes stuffed in your nose – and yeah, trying to think about nothing, trying to get your mind to relax for once and settle and quiet and allow a guy some sleep so he could get some strength back, so, presumably, he could get up the next day, so that he could, well, what? – of course, so he could start the whole process all over. Again. And again. And again. And again.

Now is that a life? Is it? Is it?

Each day blended into the next in a blur of pain, weakness, weariness, and always the numbing sameness. Why? Why do it? Why continue? No one ever answered him (who would? He was alone) and Ed was beginning to run out of reasons of his own, if he hadn't already. Maybe it was just habit that was keeping him going now. Pitiful, isn't it? Whatever had happened to Ed? Ed didn't know sometimes. Ed didn't know who Ed was anymore.

When Marie had been around, he hadn't had this problem with reasons. But it was useless thinking about what you couldn't have. He wished desperately sometimes, late in the silence of a companionless night, that she were still alive and bustling about and nagging him from the other room to do some fool thing or other. Sometimes he still thought he could hear her, washing up, doing dishes, getting dinner ready, or just lying there breathing softly next to him, keeping him company, through the long nights.

Reading to him..

Sitting beside him.

Holding his hand.

God, he missed her.

Although, truth to tell, he hadn't been the best person to be keeping company with, while she was still alive. He'd acted like he'd wanted her gone more often than not. He'd gotten so he'd yell and grumble almost every day, even talked about divorce. He'd done a lot of fool things, hurtful things. To everyone. Especially to his Marie. His head hurt thinking about it now. Being sick all the time had made him ornery. That's what he used to tell himself. Well, he'd been difficult and contrary even before that. He'd been that way even when Timmy was still alive.

Timmy. Alive. Now how many years ago was that? How many years since he'd gotten that telephone call? Let's see…they called him at work, he remembered that like it was yesterday. No it wasn't work. It was a Saturday. How could he have been at work? Wait, yes, Ed had to have been working. They were doing that big project, working overtime, that elementary school, or was it the new shopping mall? – no, Timmie was in High School when they built the mall, he worked in the movie theaters there, so, it had to have been, what? the new exit on the I-35 spur? – must have been, that's right, Ed was working on the paperwork, in the crummy site trailer with a broken heater, they'd poured concrete that morning and had to wait, make sure it cooled down and settled O.K. and the phone rang and Ed just reached over and picked up the phone and they told him the news that his son Timmy wasn't alive anymore, that Timmie was dead and Ed would never talk to him again, like they were talking about the weather or politics. In a quiet voice. Casually. Ed asked them to repeat it. But their words didn't make any sense. What did they say again? They said, well, they told him, they told him... Timmy missing, a pilot error, a mid-air crash, wreckage, the mountains, or was it... ah, he didn't want to remember any more of it now. He was tired of remembering. And how long had it been, Ed? How long? Too long. The truth was that Ed had lived too long. He'd over-lived himself, in fact. His past due date had come and gone. Years ago. Too many years. Too many memories. Too many everythings. Ed was tired.

You know, Ed thought he could remember loving the mountains and the mountain valleys. Not anymore. Maybe he'd never loved them. No, he'd loved the mountains. He had. He remembered that much. Colorado, New Mexico. There weren't any real mountains here in San Diego, just desert. Not like Denver. Not like Santa Fe. And there had been Baillo. The mountains, the mountainous passions of his mountainous youth. Up and down and a lot of effort and a lot of fear.

Baillo. He hadn't thought of him in years.

And if he were honest, he been half in love with Baillo. Or in lust. He'd been so young. Too young to even know there was a difference. If there was.

God. He hadn't thought about that in years. Baillo. Timmy. Ed felt himself getting choked up and was glad he was alone where no one could see. How could he not have thought about Timmy? He should think about Timmy every day. He missed his Tim-boy. He missed his Marie.

Ed had trouble seeing again, felt his eyes puffing up again with tears. Goddamit! How could a man be in his sixties and still be such a fool? Not to know what you have when you have it? Not to know to let go of what you can't have? Not to give up trying to get back what you can never have again? When did you actually grow up and become a grown-up? When, Ed, when? When did it become any easier?

Not now. That's for sure.

Then as fast as the storm of tears and sorrow broke, it washed through him and out of him, leaving him breathless and empty. Well at least he could still feel. That part was still working. My feelers fine. Got to count your blessings.

"Staring at the floor remembering and blubbering all morning long, Ed, isn't going to get breakfast made any faster."

Ed talked out loud, but there was no one there to listen anymore. He did that a lot nowadays. Didn't hurt anyone. It was good to hear a human voice.

Ed took a deep breath, wiped his eyes with the slightly cleaner but still ragged end of one of his bathrobe sleeves and shuffled himself and his slippers with the holes in them into the kitchen. He smelled the shoulder of his robe. He needed to wash this fool thing. That was something to do today. He walked slowly as always, pulling his oxygen canister across the hardwood floors behind him, the canister making the gratifying sound of a heavy artillery brigade rolling across a wooden bridge in his World War II movies. Those movies – they were loud and they were predictable. Ed liked that. So few things are.

Now, let's see. Making breakfast - that's something Marie would've suggested. Always practical, his Marie was. Well, most of the time, leastways. No. That wasn't true. Always. She always made sense. Marie liked breakfast. She was good at it. Breakfast made sense with Marie. Marie made sense.

"O.K. All right, Marie, all right, you win" he said to his empty home, and feeling slightly comforted by a firm decision and a clear goal, Ed moved decisively in the quiet of the morning towards the coffee maker and the toaster by the stove.

Santa Fe. And a spring almost fifty years gone. So much time. So much time lost. He'd been a different Ed back then. Obviously.

Ed had never been able to find that church, that cathedral in Santa Fe again, no matter how many times he'd looked, no matter how carefully he re-traced his travels, on all the trips he and Marie had made back to Santa Fe over the years. Ed and Marie had scoured the area. Ed hadn't really told Marie exactly what they were scouring for. But they did it anyways. Marie liked scouring. She liked finding things that were lost. But did they find anything? No. Nothing. No trace. Zero. And Ed remembered there'd been quite a few trips. More than six, maybe seven or eight.

Ed wrinkled his nose, the air hose for his oxygen tank always made his nose itch the when he got up and started walking around every morning. And afterwards too. And later. To be truthful, it always itched. He didn't like being tethered - as if he were a Thanksgiving Day parade balloon - to this ridiculous heavy iron cart with its heavy oxygen tank on it. But he really didn't have a choice now, did he? Sometimes he'd drift off to sleep, wake up frightened or angry about some crazy thing he'd been dreaming about, and jump up not thinking and nearly yank his head off.

Ed went to the refrigerator to get some butter, some bread, some bacon and a jar of strawberry jam and shook his head a little bit - an irritated old water buffalo - to get the tube loosened a little and give him some relief. It didn't help much. He turned on the electric burner, and put a frying pan on it, dropped a dollop of butter in, smearing it around with Marie's wooden spoon in little, quick figure-eights like Marie used to do, and laid out some bacon on a plate next to the stove. He thought about it a moment, dropped a little more butter on the frying pan, then carefully laid six of the strips of bacon, in neat parallel rows, diagonally, across the cold, black, iron pan. Ed tried to be neat and tidy when he cooked. He'd learned that from Marie too. He swirled and puttered with the butter some more. The pan started to heat up. He'd fry some bread next. Toast it first. He liked bacon and fried toast.

Yeah, he didn't do it often, but Ed liked bacon some mornings. Sometimes he did it in the microwave. Sometimes he didn't. Sometimes he yearned for the smell of it, the butter and the frying bacon, the toast, all of it. It smelled like home. It smelled like Marie. Marie and Timmy. Marie and Timmy and Ed. He stopped in a mid-swirl and just smiled. He guessed today was one of those days. He dropped the spoon on the plate by the bacon slices he wasn't cooking and turned away, backing the oxygen cart in and out like he was parallel parking a car, and walked to the other side of the kitchen. He scowled down at the cart as he pulled. He left his food sitting there. Suddenly he wasn't hungry.

You'd think he'd be used to it by now. The oxygen hissed away in a business-like manner at his knee. The coffee maker started gasping and plopping, making his daily three-cup pot, and the smell of it welcomed him (in an evil way) to the new day – as if this were a home of health, as if he were a healthy man with a wife and a son, as if he had things to do and promises to keep and miles to go.

And miles to go, well... The trip was over for Ed, and there weren't many miles left for him. Not for him. Just the sleep ahead. He was alone. He was sick. He had nothing to occupy him the whole day long. Nothing and a whole lot more of nothing.

Yeah, thinking like that was just going to get him more upset than he already was.

He stopped to use his sleeve to wipe his eyes, and the top of his head. He sniffed at it. Gotta wash this fool thing.

He wondered about what had ever happened to Baillo. Life had seemed like one enormous possibility back then. Open doors everywhere. He'd always meant to go back and see Baillo. He never had. And now he couldn't. Now it was all bricked up windows and nailed-over entrances. Enormous impossibilities. All that was left for Ed was the big celestial Exit Sign flashing at him every day, all day long.

What had Baillo done with all his time, all these last fifty odd years? Probably a lot. Baillo had seemed to know what he was doing. He hoped Baillo had made better choices than Ed had. No, no that wasn't true. He wouldn't trade Marie and Timmy for the world. He wouldn't.

"I wouldn't" he said to the coffeemaker and the oxygen tank. They agreed with him by keeping their silence. His hands hurt again. It was hard sometimes to get them around the canister handle so he could pull it along behind him. Didn't want to work.

Oh well.

Ed found himself walking through the living room, on a long, looping trajectory towards the hall and the bedroom. He liked to walk while he thought. Marie used to call it "pacing the floors." Marie said Ed did it just to get her nervous. But really, Ed just liked to walk. He liked to keep moving, like that trip that summer through New Mexico. That's why he hadn't stayed with Baillo. He'd wanted to keep on moving. Maybe it had been a mistake. Who knows? Who knows what might have been? Ed kept on walking in lazy circles around the living room, the oxygen cart bumping irately across the wooden floor behind him.

He thought of putting the T.V. on like always, for the noise of it, for the movement and the life of it, but the prospect of a constant dribbling of meaningless chatter into his ears for the next ten hours made him more than slightly nauseous this morning. Guess not.

He sighed.

Great.

This was going to be a bad day anyway. He wasn't feeling good and it was the six month anniversary of Marie's death. And there were those new pills he was taking. What were they for? He didn't feel good. Marie would've known why. She would've known what to do to make it better. Marie made it all make sense.

She was always good at taking care of him. She'd done it well enough for the last forty-one years. Until last summer. It had always been Ed and Marie. Now it was just Ed. And, you know, it didn't seem like Ed all by himself was nearly enough. He wrinkled his nose. He thought he could smell something burning. Ed stopped and tried to get a bigger whiff, but the oxygen tank kept on thinning out whatever the heck it was that Ed was smelling. Ed figured he'd just burned the toast again. Give it time. It'd dissipate. Maybe he should open a window. In the back.

He found his way back to the back bedroom. Sunlight crept over the sill of the window and spilled out over the floor of their (not theirs, now just his) condo. It was a nice place. Big windows. Safe. Second story. No it was the third story. Wasn't it? Anyways. Plenty of room. Balcony.

He had to stand guard, looking out over the alley sometimes from this bedroom window. He had the big rocker set up right by the heater duct so he could be warm and watchful all at the same time. You never knew what fool would be trying something down there - drugs, robbery, sex, murder - Ed didn't know what they thought they could get away with down there, thinking no one was watching. But Ed was watching, and those fool teenagers messing around had found out the hard way. Yes they had. More than once.

Marie used to kid him about it, but Ed knew better. He had eyes and a telephone and wasn't shy about using either of them. Ed was on the job - well, not all the time. Really, just sometimes, and less since he'd been getting sicker, and with Marie gone and all the rest of the junk life had been throwing at him, less and less, if he were honest. In fact, he couldn't remember the last time he'd sat in that big rocker. Last week?

But it always paid to keep 'em guessing. Ed found himself looking thoughtfully out that very bedroom window. Maybe he'd stay here a minute or three. The rocker was just sitting there. He could smell the coffee ready in the other room. He wondered how Marie was getting on with the toast. Where was she? He was getting hungry. "Marie?" he yelled over into the kitchen, watching a young guy skateboard up the alley underneath him. That was suspicious. "Marie?" Where'd he put the phone? Marie always moved it on him. "Marie?"

He always remembered one beat too late. It always hurt. Always. He was waiting for it to hurt less, but it hadn't started happening yet. He still wasn't used to her being gone. How did someone get used to something like that?

The way the light fell on the arch by the back entrance in the alley reminded Ed of the shadows in the broken-down, half-wrecked cathedral he'd seen in Sante Fe that morning. He watched the skateboarder slink away and slide from sight around a corner at the end of the building.

Ed hadn't thought of Baillo in almost forty-five years. He could still see him in his mind's eye - a stringy, muscly teenager with a big grin, but the truth was, Baillo was an old man just like Ed now. At least he would be if he were still alive. Ed shook his head. All the things that had happened to Ed since he last saw Baillo - sometimes it seemed like an eternity and well, sometimes, well a lot of the time now really, it seemed to Ed like it was just a day ago, like it was just yesterday. The past - that summer biking in the mountains for example - was more real, more saturated, more alive and important to Ed than what he done yesterday or even what he had done this very morning. Yeah. Well. It was a whole life, that's what had happened to Ed since then, or most of one anyways. And the same had happened to Baillo. A whole life, lived.

What would have happened if he had stopped that day? Stopped and stayed with Baillo? Had Baillo felt the same way that Ed felt? Well, like he'd said, who knows? Ed had been scared and lonely back then too. Just like now. Ed shook his head and coughed. It was too much. All the lives that might have been. He hadn't thought about all this in years. He could definitely smell something burning now. Where was Marie? What was she doing in the kitchen anyways? She'd have the fire alarm going off in a second, he just knew it. She never thought of that stuff until it was too late. He'd have to get the stepladder to reach the alarm. She didn't think about that, when she burned toast. Then he caught himself again.

Damn. It was just as painful.

His chest hurt.

He was still standing up. He should sit down in the rocker.

Think of something else.

Something else.

Baillo.

Let's see, that had been the middle of the trip, the Sunday in Santa Fe, right? Yeah. What had he done before that? How had he gotten to Santa Fe? Wait, wait a second, just before that he'd ridden through the mountains. Yeah, the slow way to Santa Fe through the mountains east and south of Taos. The back road. The endless ups and downs, crossing mountains and rivers and meadows, passing through sleepy Saturday afternoon towns, riding over the tops of ridges under great leaning Ponderosa pines. You could smell the pine sap in the heat. Blue sky. Green trees. Red dirt. Pedaling the road less taken. Pedaling the back way. Pedaling the hard way. Ed always did things the hard way, didn't he?

He swayed on his feet and squinted his eyes trying to remember.

The sun was getting low in the sky as Eddie pulled late into Santa Fe. As usual, he'd miscalculated his day's ride - how long it would take for him to get from Taos into the capital city. It was nothing but uphill and downhill all the way from Taos through Las Truchas, at least five mountain passes, maybe more. Unexpectedly, he'd come upon the dramatic drop on the spines of mesas through a kind of moonscape, and coasted all the way down into Espanola. Then the long uphill past the stone camel. Then more uphill past the opera house, and finally the last crest where you could see all of Santa Fe spread out before you as if it were a movie set - ribbons of bright red hillside and too-bright, green polka dot cedars and fake, decorative sand-colored adobes. Except it was all real. Dusk hit. It started to get hard to see. It was kind of late to be arriving in a strange town.

Eddie pointed his bike uphill again and started pushing his way towards the big mountain behind town as he passed through the plaza. The road got steeper, thinner, and less well maintained and Eddie started to worry a little as it followed a smallish creek up into the foothills. He was feeling it now. Ed was pumping his pedals up and down about three to a breath. If it got any steeper, he'd be down to one to a breath. And that was going to happen soon. He hoped he wasn't lost. He hoped he wasn't on the high road to Amarillo, Texas.

He clicked down to his lowest mountain gear and slowed his breathing, and ratcheted his brain down into don't-think-about-it-just-make-it-happen mode. It was getting dark, darker every minute. Cars (with their lights on now) nearly sideswiped him on narrow curves. The edges of the pavement were crumbling, disappearing, and then, it was official, this street was shoulder-less. A tiny road. A toy highway. The strip of asphalt continued resolutely twining its way up through huge old cottonwoods and jumped the dry creek bed it was following, over and back and over again, using tiny wooden bridges with absolutely no shoulder room at all. Exciting? Maybe. No, not really. Not exactly the safest place. But he needed a campground soon - any campground, any at all. It was supposed to be here.

Still no sign of it. Where the heck was it? Had he already passed it in the twilight? Was he riding to the top of a mountain in the middle of the night? Coming down off this pass would be even more fun in total darkness. All right. Don't panic. You've done this many times before. Not a problem. Just keep going. Up and up and up.

He crossed two more bridges. He dodged six more cars. He didn't have a light on his bike. He'd have to make a decision soon.

The highway pulled out of its follow-the-creek-bed-gulch strategy and struck out for the open mountain-side. It was beginning to climb up a series of switchbacks onto the steep side of the mountain that hung over Santa Fe's back. The last flickering light-giving rays of the sun had already faded. The little illumination left was rapidly being lost amongst the mesas and canyons of the Rio Grande valley far, far off to the west. In between cars and bouts of heavy breathing, rounding each curve Eddie could see for a hundred miles straight out towards California. Valleys upon canyons upon mountains upon more mountains. To his back, oranges, yellows, purples, and deep blues. Ahead of him, an unforgiving pitch black.

One last horseshoe bend, and he saw a steeply sloping gravel road angle off to the left. He pulled on his brakes (pretty much unnecessary, he wasn't exactly flying uphill) and glided across the highway, down a short slope, slotted himself into the first open campsite he saw - off to itself by a stand of cottonwoods by another small stream - and skidded his heavily-loaded 10 speed to a halt. It took ten minutes or so for his calf muscles to figure out they weren't still pedaling him upwards into thin Santa Fe air and trying to push him over a pass. He made his camp as the last of the light disappeared and a full moon rose through pinon pine trees on a steep ridge behind him.

There had to be a dozen or more teenagers right next to him, laughing, talking in an easy, conspiratorial way, half in Spanish, half in English, everyone sprawled around a raging campfire Eddie could see it blazing away through the trees. He was just finishing heating up his second can of stew and thinking about putting out his tiny sterno can flame, which was almost gone anyways (or maybe opening another sterno and firing up a third can of whatever this other stuff was – what was menudo anyways?) when he heard something. Someone was clomping noisily over through the piles of brush and old leaves lying under immense cylinders of shadow (that he'd realized were cottonwood trees) all around him.

Eddie tensed – resembling a human hammer on a cocked gun.

High school had not been (surprise, surprise) the best of times for Eddie, and groups of teenagers usually meant some elaborate and vicious torture session for him. Eddie had always been a kind of loner. He didn't want and didn't need people. That much probably seems obvious by now. And he hadn't ridden hundreds of miles, pedaling up over purpled mountains and down along fruited plains, seeking the standard Colorado John Denver Rocky Mountain epiphany only to end up getting beaten up by a gang drunken seniors from Santa Fe High School, had he? Guess the answer to that was a big – maybe yes.

But what could you do about it? What could he ever have done about it?

The sound of footsteps approached nearer. Eddie exhaled and

forced himself to inhale and exhale again. Breathe. Breathe. He crossed his arms across his chest, uncrossed them, crossed them again, lay down, got up, mostly he just waited. Probably he should finish his dinner first. He picked up his spoon. Then he thought Eddie - you should probably get your stuff put away before they get over to you – be easier if you had to make a quick exit. He started to grab his stuff.

"Hey man, how's it hangin'?" said a voice much closer to Eddie than he'd expected it to be, catching him sitting on a stone, one hand holding an unopened can of the menudo stuff, the other holding a can opener. "We heard you over here, you from Santa Fe bro?"

Eddie thought he could hear at least three guys nearby, maybe more. He exhaled again, forgot to inhale, got dizzy, shook his head to say no (since he didn't trust his voice), and realized they probably couldn't see his head or face any more than he could see theirs. Great. He announced in as clear a voice as he could with almost no breath in his lungs "Nah, I'm just passing through. I'm from Colorado. On a bike hike. For the summer." Eddie thought he could hear appreciative murmurs. At least they sounded appreciative. He wasn't sure how they murmured down here in New Mexico.

"Cool. Cool man. Hey you smoke?" There were some easygoing laughs and another voice broke out from far away, over by the fire, rising over the sound of the talking teenagers next door. "Joey means weed, man, do you smoke weed is what he's asking." There was some more laughter as someone gave someone else a punch, and someone else punched back.

Eddie said "No" and then quickly added "Thanks, though. Really." No one had ever asked him that before, asked him join them. He felt oddly as if he were an Eddie-door that had been nailed shut and was in the process of being pried open unexpectedly. Or maybe the door had already been open. Maybe he'd only thought it had been closed. It was confusing.

"Well, come on over anyway, we're all graduating next week from Central and we're up here partying. Partying all night. Maybe you'll change your mind. Come on over bro."

Eddie remembered gliding in on his bike, spying a group of fifteen or twenty guys and girls draped and clumped around a blazing pile of sweet-smelling logs. Well, the smoke around the campfire had been sweet anyways. Whether it was sweet logs or sweet something else, didn't really matter, not to Eddie. Breathe. Just breathe.

Let it go. Let them go. Be safe.

But open doors weren't safe, were they? You couldn't leave them that way. You had to walk through them, right? No choice.

Or close them.

Had he really biked over mountain passes just to close doors? Had he?

It took a try or three to get his voice working properly.

"Uh, hey, uh, yeah. Great. Wait up."

"Cool, bro."

He shuffled over through the leaves to their fire. He stayed quiet. He stayed scared. But he stayed. That had been another first.

And in the morning he'd met Baillo. He'd walked over and met him. Just like any normal guy would.

Ed could definitely smell something burning, he could even see a kind of hazy veil of bluish cloud beginning to condense in the air up by the ceiling fan out in the hallway, leading back towards the living room and the kitchen. At least he thought he could. He didn't have his glasses on after all. It wasn't a pleasant smell. But it couldn't be serious if the smoke alarm wasn't going off, could it? No, it couldn't. Unless Marie had taken the batteries out again. But no, that wasn't possible. She hadn't done that since they'd moved to California. The ceilings were too high. No. No, it must be a neighbor. Yeah, a neighbor. What in the heck were they doing? Do they still burn trash here in San Diego? That's what it smelled like. Trash and metal. He must've left a window open up front.

It did - it smelled just like the smell of burning garbage Ed remembered from backyard garbage fires when he was a little kid. You know if it kept up, he'd better open this bedroom window up in the back, he'd better open it if that smell got worse. He coughed, coughed again, then really hacked and whooped and the oxygen tube shot out of his nose and across the room. He left the tube strung up over the cart, where he could find it again easily, and turned his oxygen off for now. Some people. Crazy neighbors. Just no consideration for others.

Still, he was nervous. He sat down in the rocker. He kept on coughing, it came in streaks, more than a couple of times. He'd stop, and then he'd start up again. He itched to do something about it. He found himself idly opening and closing the sock drawer of the dresser he was sitting next to. It was unnerving. Something was rolling around in the sock drawer. He ought to… then he caught a flicker of motion out of the side of his eye, and saw the skateboarder returning down the alley, jumping up and down off curbs as he rolled noisily towards Ed and Ed's window perch, the perch that overlooked Ed's entire back alley world.

Ed decided to watch him just in case he made a break for the enticing waist-high walls of raised flower beds, apparently built perfectly for bank turns. The flower beds were the ones Marie liked so much, the ones in the plaza between the three condo buildings. The bald skaters, covered in tattoos, did their little jumps on and off of them, all the damn time, even when you yelled at them, and then they did it even more loudly, talking louder and louder, like they didn't care who heard them or who saw them or what people thought of them. Ed knew how to take care of that problem. He had the San Diego police on speed dial on his phone. All he had to press was number 7 and bam! no more skaters.

Hah! Let 'em try. Ed stood up. He picked up the phone and put it close to his good eye. There was the seven. He put his finger on it. Lay the phone down on the dresser. And he waited.

But this skater (who had a lot of hair, a pigtail of it, in fact, and a beard, and only a few tattoos) didn't stop. He rolled by, unaware of his close call with Ed-danger, ignorant of any possible meetings with policemen he'd just narrowly avoided. Ed watched him as he flowed on down past Ed's window, accelerating and rumbling over the concrete apron of the alley, skidding on to the sidewalk sideways and propelling himself expertly out of Ed's view, unmolested, this time.

Damn kids.

Ed waited a minute to make sure he wasn't coming back, then reached for his rocker, sat back in it, and heaved a sigh. Guarding too a lot of work. It took a lot of energy getting up. It took more sitting down. He was having trouble breathing. He squinched his nose again and shook his head to get the nostril hose thingies more comfortable. Didn't help. But that was probably because his nostril thingies were gone. The hose was gone. Where? What? Then he remembered his hose was sitting on the cart right next to him. Something was still bothering his damn nose. And his eyes were bothering him. He started coughing, again. This time the coughing wouldn't stop.

What had he been thinking about before that shaved head noise-maker had interrupted him? He couldn't remember. Something. And something else. Something a few minutes ago had reminded him of something, but it was something completely different. It was important. It had seemed important. Ah, no use thinking about it. If it was so urgent, it'd come back to him, Ed was sure of it.

He was fiddling with his dresser drawer again, found he was shaking some junk he'd grabbed onto in the sock drawer in his hand. They were batteries. They felt good to toss around a little bit as he watched out the window, making a satisfying clacking sound whenever he rolled them together. Clack. Clack. He tried to clear his throat and ended up hacking for a while, hurting his chest. He told himself he needed to try and cough more softly. No need to hurt yourself just clearing your throat.

He thought and thought for a long while. Of Baillo, Marie, of his son and summers long past, of lonely apartments and angry Christmases, of betrayals and of losses, of hopes relied upon and of promises kept. And even though he'd complained about it all, often and loudly and to whomever would listen to it, Ed was glad he'd been here to do it. If anyone cared about what Ed thought about life in general, well, Ed was for it in the end. It was worth it. He'd tell anyone that.

He picked up more of the brightly colored batteries out of the drawer and looked them over. They looked new. They seemed familiar. They meant something. What? What in the heck would a battery mean?

Something was on the tip of his tongue, he could feel it, but all Ed was doing was sitting here and wool-gathering in front of the alley window. What a waste of the morning. But typical. He guessed that's what old men do. No, he knew that's what old men do. He smiled and coughed to himself. Breathing was getting a little harder. Harder than what he was used to. Where was his oxygen? What was he trying to remember?

No idea.

Well.

He'd let whatever it was that needed thinking about, yeah, he'd let it stew a little longer. It felt good just sitting here and remembering sometimes. The coughing was annoying, though. Where was his oxygen? Thinking and remembering. You know he really didn't do it all that often. He didn't waste that much time. Not really.

He coughed. This was getting ridiculous. Where was his oxygen? It got harder to breathe. He gasped. Then he couldn't stop coughing and gulping air.

He bent his legs open with an effort and put his face down between them because he'd coughed so much that he'd coughed himself into feeling faint and lightheaded. If he was going to panic, it would get even harder. No sense in that.

Panic never helped. That's what Marie said. She made sense. She always did.

Marie made him put his head down when he got faint sometimes.

You know, it helped.

Maybe he'd stay like this for a moment or two. Just to get his head clear.

You need to distract yourself. You need to think of something else. You need to think about the trip again.

Snow.

There was something about snow that trip, he knew it. Somewhere along the line he'd gotten mixed up with snow. Ed breathed in deep, all bent over like he was, it wasn't easy but he did it, and seeing the world upside-down helped him somewhat, but the air tasted funny and felt thick somehow, and he was holding these damn batteries in his hand. Why? Great. His lungs were filling up with phlegm. He wanted to clear them out, but he was afraid if he started coughing again he wouldn't be able to stop coughing.

Best to be calm. Calm. Think of snow.

Snow. He tried to breathe in slowly and deeply. Snow. Calm. And think about snow. Snow. Think about deep, mountain snow. Yeah. The snow. The snow he'd seen before he'd gotten to Santa Fe. The snow he'd seen before he'd gotten to New Mexico even.

It had started out cloudy, and in the 50's in the Colorado high country that morning, at least in the valleys, and since it was all uphill out of Poncha Springs, up and over Poncha Pass, Eddie and his 70 pounds of packed stuff had started out responsibly in the early morning, leaving plenty of time to get up and completely over the top and down the other side into the San Luis valley by late afternoon. That way he'd avoid mountain storms. But he'd somehow gotten sidetracked by something or other (he couldn't remember exactly what) and had ended up starting over the pass after 1 P.M. Not the best time. Eddie had known better. But he'd gone anyways. Eddie was young. Young and strong and of course, immortal.

The sun shone, cutting through wispy, foggy clouds around him like a ghost of the sun - it was all bright patches of blue and gold alternating with this dim, indistinct silvery light - a light which thickened and thinned around him in a witchy kind of way, as the day wore on and as Eddie gained altitude. It was as if he were riding into a fairy tale. One of those fairy tales where no matter what you do, you lose. He was trespassing, he was doing something wrong, something was going to punish him, there was no escaping it.

The pass, by Colorado standards was hardly a pass - more like a long slide uphill between a pair of pine-spotted, rock-covered foothills, a long ribbon of road shadowing a shallow creek bed. It was a gentle monster. Poncha Pass wasn't man-eating beast like Wolf Creek or Independence, climbing way above tree line. It was more human, more forgiving. Eddie wasn't worried.

The mountains were alive to Eddie. They just made him happy. They flung their heads high into the Colorado sky and dared rain, snow, sky, clouds, and wind to do their worst. The tops of the peaks were solid masses of rock - all of them. They showed weathered faces of grey and orange cliffs in the summer, tucked into blankets of pines and aspen at their feet - miles-wide swaths of forest draped over every lower foothill in sight.

They were uncomplicated, uncompromising, and demanded respect just because of what they were and what they were capable of. They could kill you and not even notice it. He felt hugely small next to them, pedaling quietly and insolently over their muscle-bound bulks. He felt small, but intensely free. He loved being in the middle of them. They were big lumbering creatures that allowed you, from time to time, to share their long geological walks with them.

This was a good day - one of the best days, he decided, and congratulated himself (nice one Ed!) on his decision to go over the pass today and not wait till tomorrow, even though he was going too late in the day. He forgot to notice, between hard breaths taken every second downstroke, that a steady massing of clouds was piling up, layer after layer, in heavy winter cloud-quilts behind him. They moved slowly, heavy with snow and cold and were thrown down cloud upon cloud onto the pass, efficiently closing the sky up behind him into a solid wall of grayish white. He should have been paying attention. But he hadn't been.

As he rounded a bend, nearing the top around 9,000 feet, Eddie unexpectedly sprinted forward with a vengeance - the wind was picking up behind his back - which was good, as it made the pedaling easier, but was actually a little uncomfortable as it was also an icy cold, wet-smelling wind. He stopped to unpack a sweat shirt, started to get back on his bike as he pulled it on, thought better of it, got out his rain poncho too, the one with the big hood that made him into an eerie, floating, amorphous balloon of gray plastic when he rode his bike while wearing it. Then he started back onto his bike, but stopped before he got both legs over the crossbar.

In front of him, a peak of snow and rock rose high in a deep almost purple-blue sky. A stray ray of sunlight was catching the top and setting the snow ablaze with light, almost as if it was lit from within - from some kind of supernatural, mineral bonfire spreading across the top of its rocky summit. The mountain's enormous cap of snow, which was blowing off an impossibly large and improbably cantilevered drift, spread into the May air over the pass in a plume that extended a couple of miles further downwind. It made a haze of all the sky to the south of him, and was spreading across much of the county behind him.

And then, he noticed the snow, one leg still half-striding his pannier-laden bike, wind whipping at his rain poncho and his bare legs under his biker's shorts.

Snowflakes the size of his fist had started to drift down around

Eddie. The wind that had caused him to stop and bundle up disappeared as if it had never been. It was absolutely still. The peak was lost to sight. Snowfall settled all around him. The top of the mountain he was on, the pass ahead of him, the pines surrounding the circular meadow just sprouting their new sprigs of grass, the miniscule spring wildflowers on the highway shoulder in front of him and the ditch beside him filled with gray-green sagebrush, all of it, everything, stood quiet in a an expectant hush.

It was waiting for Eddie. Waiting for Eddie to say something.

He gawked, one arm in his poncho, the other still poncho-less and hanging out in a curtain of crystal feathers falling to his left and to his right. The snowflakes were falling in endless succession, in countless layers from as far as he could see ahead and behind him and upwards in a white, white on white, fluff-engorged sky. Eddie looked up into millions of rotating, floating, descending columns of slow-drifting snowflakes, and Eddie felt himself falling - falling up and up, higher and higher, faster and faster, falling off the planet and cartwheeling helplessly heavenwards through the bright, wide sky above him into higher and higher parts, into blue-black emptiness.

He heard himself laughing. It was a crazy feeling. It was a feeling he liked. He felt alive. He felt happy. He felt he was exactly where he needed to be.

For the first few minutes the snowflakes didn't melt at all when they hit pavement, pine trees, sagebrush, grass. They landed and balanced, delicately, on whatever they'd happen to fall upon – a congregation of bright white butterflies resting from a long flight down from the ethereal blue. Eddie expected any moment for the entire snowstorm to get up and fly away, flocking off to a new mountain, leaving him and his pass dry and empty, just like it had been only a few minutes ago.

He stood. And watched. And waited.

Flakes were melting on his cheeks and his forehead, his legs and his arms. He inhaled, athletically, over and over again, pulling the air deep inside - the smells filling him up - of snow falling and its sharp iron tang, of sodden and sweet and bitter sagebrush, of wet, bright pine sap drifting in off the forests at the edge of his little clearing, of the rock and metal smell of clean, black highway running through the clearing's middle, of dirty oil and lubricant from his derailleurs.

He didn't know how long he stood there, watching the meadow fill with snow, accumulating flakes on his eyeglasses and his unprotected arm. The road had disappeared. Meadow and highway had become one continuous surface of white. The only thing left with any color was Ed and his bike and his pack. Hanging. In a white void.

He didn't ever want to move again.

The wind picked up. He noticed he was starting to get cold. Really soaked and really chilled. A spasm of difficult breathing and adrenalin kicked in, and his biking body reflexes took over. What was he doing there? Standing still, frozen in a snowstorm, at the top of a mountain pass? Ed knew better.

He shook his head, slapped his hands and stamped his feet to get the blood flowing again. He inched his bike back onto the slippery pavement, carefully mounted it, almost losing his bike underneath him, and sliding off into a ditch, and started very slowly, over the top. The next four hours were some of the most harrowing hours of Eddie's young life - dodging cars and trucks, pedaling carefully and following what he hoped was the edge of the snow-covered shoulder of the highway, kicking his feet against the pedals to keep them from freezing, kicking to get the accumulation of snow and slush off his bike, hoping against hope to make it some place, any place before night fell, before the light failed and before the temperature sank below freezing.

He'd been lucky. He ended up finding the only laundromat in a sixty mile radius, in a tiny town, and it was still open. The incredulous owner allowed the snow-covered bicyclist to camp overnight inside the laundromat, and Eddie pulled everything - bike, panniers, luggage, sleeping bag, cans of stew, everything - into a small, narrow room, already filled with ancient washers and dryers, to warm up, eat, and begin to dry out his sopping, frozen clothes and his sopping, frozen self.

The laundromat was great. It was warm and clean and dry and safe, and his little nest of a sleeping bag between the rows of dryers felt like a sort of home, under the buzzing of the hanging fluorescent lights, listening to the thump thump thump of the dryer working on his tennis shoes. Later, he watched the snow continue to fall outside the floor-to-ceiling glass of the storefront window. It put him to sleep.

Ed was coughing all the time now. But he didn't notice it all that much. He knew he should be looking for his oxygen. It would take him time to find it. He should call out to Marie to get it for him. That's what he would do. In a moment. After he took a little nap. He just wanted to sleep. So tired. Marie would take care of it. She always did. Marie. Sensible. Take care of it.

He rolled off his chair. He lay down on the floor. That was better. He even coughed less down here. You could hardly smell that smoke anymore down here.

He could see the snow from 50 years ago in front of him. It was drifting up against the window. The back of the dryer he was leaning against was warm. He was safe.

Snow. Safe. Something had happened to him up there. Up among the growing dollops of snow, snow piling up all around him in that silent little field of sagebrush, all by himself, just Ed and his bike, falling upwards at the top of the world. The snow. It was trying to tell him something. But what? He didn't know what.

Maybe that there are no endings, only beginnings. That one thing blended into another so quickly and easily, you hardly felt it when it happened.

Or… what? Who knows what? Change is hope? Which is a hopeful thing. Hopeful, since you can't ever stop things from changing, even if you wanted them to stop.

Or… maybe it meant something entirely different. Snow. Snow. Ed didn't know. Not for sure.

Who could know what snow would want to tell a person?

He could feel the hardwood floor pressing into his face. At least he thought he could. He was coughing too much. Actually his head was bouncing against the wood, not leaning against it. He tried to suck air in, in between bounces, but not much was getting inside. And he was cold. He should be panicking. But he wasn't. There was snow falling. Snow falling all over the condo. It was trying to tell him something. He was listening. Go ahead.

Yes, he had heard it. He was sure of that. He'd heard the snow. And he would remember. Remember it for a time when he was older when hope might be hidden a little more deeply, for a time when hope might be a little harder to find, for a time when change would be hammering him into a new shape before he was really ready. Maybe. Maybe for then. Maybe for a time like that. Maybe for a time like now.

The snow picked him up, and he was falling upwards, up and up and up, and once again, Ed didn't want to stop, and this time he didn't.

TWO MEADOWS

It all started innocently enough, one long, lazy, luxurious Vermont day in my favorite month, June of course, in the middle of my second favorite grassy clearing, resting against a stalk of something that smelled exactly the way a summer should smell. I can remember it all, just like it was yesterday.

Aislann was doing that irritating backflip thing she does when she wants everyone to admire her. I hate it when she does that. And then, what's worse, as she rolled right-side up again, she tweaked the mouse-ear hawksweed she'd been sitting on, just with the very tops of the toes of her feet, just enough, so it swayed crazily back and forth, up and down. She did it on purpose, I know she did. She curtseyed in mid-air as it bowed towards her, and she grabbed it as it bobbed away. She hugged and kissed it with loud smacking noises as if to say "look at me, look at me." I could hear

Eithne and Iphria giggling under a nearby stand of celandine. It was childish and aggravating and I pretended not to notice. Then Aislann bit her lip, smiling in delight at her own cleverness, peering this way and that around her rocking and rumpled hawksweed lover (studiously ignoring me, sitting right in front of her, having to witness her shameless shenanigans) and drifted off nonchalantly across the field, floating on her back, doing a languid, exaggerated backstroke, with her eyes firmly closed.

I did not watch. I breathed a little easier. The farther away she got, the more I felt I might actually be able to enjoy the rest of my day in peace and quiet, at least partially free from her infantile antics and her endless prancing and preening. But, as you probably already guessed, I was wrong.

Aislann made sure I could still see her - now weaving and dodging through stalks of switchgrass and bluestem, now bounding over vetch and toadflax, all on her back, sometimes doing the occasional flying handstand on an unsuspecting clover just to show us she could. Yes, it was annoying. It was so typical of her. Then with a sly, unreadable glance backwards, she slowed to a stop. I looked up, despite myself. She darted a quick glance directly at my cinquefoils - the ones I had specifically chosen and was resting so carefully and peacefully against, my soothing, beautiful yellow flowers (Aislann knows I like yellow best – its presence calms me – unlike Aislann's). I was trying to soak in a few moments of well-earned, sun-filled silence – and she pushed her head down, pointed her nose forward and raced recklessly through the foliage in a beeline straight towards me.

"Come, sister, come Etain" she called into the air, her wings beating faster and faster, until they were only a misty blur of sparking, iridescent purple. As if she were the only one who could fly so quickly and so prettily. As if she hadn't learned everything she knew from me. You'd think she'd treat me with more respect. I was the eldest after all. But that didn't matter to Aislann, no, not in the least, not to her. She tore past me, blowing my hair every which way, a bolt of pink lightning, and she zipped on into the summery distance. She kept throwing knowing looks back at me with an irritating, superior kind of simper spread over every inch of her face as she made her way towards the children. Again. She knew better than that. She might be seen. Children were dangerous.

Well. I wasn't falling for it this time. She knew it and I knew it.

Not this time.

But the day *was* perfect, thick humid air, awash with heavy scents of meadow and forest and everything in between, buzzing with the activity of millions of lives working themselves out under the hot rays of a summer sun at noon. Oh, all right. Yes. Yes, it would be glorious to skimmer over the bowing heads of the grass and race her to the forest's edge. And if we happened to fly towards the children, well, then fly we would. I wasn't made of stone.

Aislann wasn't the only one that knew how to swoop and soar, dart and dash. She'd feel the buzz of my wings in her face as I disappeared in front of her before our race was through. I could hear Eithne and Iphria and, this time, Oillel and Yvalbane whispering and giggling at the two of us as I shot over the knotted and nodding heads of the hay-grass in hot pursuit of Aislann. It was an extraordinary morning. The beginnings of a beautiful afternoon. And this time Aislann would lose. I was sure of it.

Lizbeth felt an ache in her stomach. It felt big and icy and heavy.

"Ruthie! Where are you? I can't see you! Ruthie! Come back!" Lizbeth tried to talk out loud, but the sounds didn't want to come. They never came anymore. Lizbeth looked and looked and looked but she couldn't see anyone. She couldn't see anyone anywhere. She saw the woods. She saw the field she was in. She saw her Grandpa's barn at the bottom of the field. But she couldn't see Ruthie. With her little brow creased with lines of worry, Lizbeth kneeled in the grass and carefully gathered together the pile of dandelions she'd picked into a small mound, once again.

She looked up every so often. She listened hard. She worked hard too. She made it so all the blossoms were at one end of the pile, pointing in the same direction. She looked up again. She patted the pile down, smoothed it, and then she frowned. "Ruthie! Ruthie!" She was breathing hard. But that was the only sound she was making. Her voice didn't want to work. She looked down at the pile and waited. No one came. Lizbeth didn't like this.

She needed to see Ruthie nearby, she needed to make sure Ruthie wouldn't just go away and leave Lizbeth all by herself in the meadow. Ruthie should be here. Right now. The warm air blew in soft gasps over her bare arms. She looked at her arms. They used to be white, a few weeks ago, back when they lived in the city. Now, living at the farm, they were turning brown as nuts. That's what her grandma said "brown as nuts." Lizbeth like saying it to herself too. She liked being a nut. Nuts were hard to hurt. Nuts were safe.

The sun was making a dark puddle of shadow right underneath her when she leaned over. She patted her hands in its inky blackness. Where was Ruthie?

She looked up at the sun, shading her eyes from the bright light, but it hurt, so she looked down at her bent knees and the grass she was sitting on again, blue and green circles dancing and fading in front of her, every which way she looked. She sat still and listened. She felt the sun shining straight down, like an arrow of light, pouring heat and light straight down onto the top of her head. A whirring sound in back of her caught her attention and Lizbeth watched a pink dragonfly buzz up to her and fly past her.

When she got up to follow it, she jumped backwards into the grass behind her when a grasshopper jumped onto her shoulder with his stickly feet and refused to leave. He stayed stuck to her day dress for long time while she shook her shoulder trying to get him off. In the end, she touched his back and he finally jumped off as quickly as he'd jumped on, pushing down on her shoulder with his strong legs and bounding into the grass – a green gold spring - where he could hide in the shadows.

Lizbeth was proud she hadn't gotten scared. Not the whole time the grasshopper was sitting on her. Not once. She wished Ruthie could have seen the grasshopper. Where was Ruthie? "Ruthie!" she said as loudly as she could, but no noise came out. Nothing. The heaviness in Lizbeth ate up all the words before they could get out of Lizbeth and get into the world.

Lizbeth looked down and saw she had kicked away some of the dandelions - they were sticking out at funny angles now. "Make it nice and neat" she said deep inside herself, and nodding her head and pointing her finger like her momma always did, she re-arranged them again, methodically this time, putting the long- stemmed ones on the bottom first and the shorter-stemmed ones on the top after that. Long. Long. Short. Short. There. That was good. That looked pretty. She wanted to show Ruthie her pile. The dragonfly came back and whirred past her like a rocket. Another one sped by a second later. It was yellow.

Lizbeth wasn't liking this. She wasn't liking being left alone. "Ruthie! I need you! Where are you, Ruthie?" She yelled wordlessly into the bright daylight. She looked up again to see if she could see Ruthie anywhere. She gave out an exaggerated, loud sigh, and collapsed backwards into the grass. A couple of grasshoppers felt her coming and exploded into action, jumping this way and that. She wasn't sure she liked being in such tall grass. She wondered if the grasshoppers were going to jump on her again. Now, laying in the tall grass all she could see was a big, blue, empty bowl of sky. The sky was a little scary, because it seemed to have no use for something as small as Lizbeth, or even her older sister Ruthie. Now she wasn't liking the sky, either. She felt her chest tighten in an uncomfortable way and thought she was going to cry. Her eyes started to feel itchy.

She didn't like this. She strained her ears, but all she could hear was a loud humming noise. Her mommy had said it was grasshoppers rubbing their legs together. She'd tried rubbing her legs together, but all she did was wrinkle her stockings and she never made any noise at all. She'd wanted to ask her mommy why she couldn't make a noise, but everyone had told her she couldn't. Couldn't ask her mommy that is. Her mommy was gone. Her papa was far away trying to find a new home for them, they'd see him in the fall. But not her mommy. Her mommy was in heaven.

She felt afraid. She started to cry again, but she didn't try yelling out for Ruthie this time. No one could hear her inside-talk anyways. Besides, Ruthie wouldn't come. Ruthie was gone. Her mommy was gone. Her papa was gone. Lizbeth was alone now. All alone. The tears were flowing and she couldn't stop them now, even if she tried. But she didn't want to try. She was alone. The dragonflies flew back, and although she couldn't see them, or even hear them, she could feel them watching her, just a little ways away, off to the right and a few inches above her head.

The dragonflies liked her. They flew around her all the time. Somehow she felt less scared and less unprotected with the dragonflies watching over her. She didn't feel so alone. Maybe she wasn't. Her chest loosened, she stopped crying and she let the grass fold above her and support her as she relaxed into it. She didn't even worry about grasshoppers. She was being brave.

She felt peaceful. She felt quiet all of a sudden. Even her tummy hurt less. She remembered what Ruthie had taught her, to look for shapes in the clouds in the sky and they had looked and looked all morning already and seen all kinds of things. Lions and castles and horses and sailing ships. All kinds of things.

Lizbeth carefully brushed the dirt from her palms and fingers, rubbed her eyes with the back of her hands and squinted through the stalks of grass to see the sky. There. A few fluffy clouds like lambs were trotting across the top of the sky, sneaking past the sun and making for the mountains in the distance. The lambs were going home. They were going to be safe. Lizbeth started counting them out loud, well, on the inside at least.

"One. Two. Three…"

Ruthie touched Lizbeth lightly on the top of her head with the tips of the two fingers of her right hand, using the index finger of her left hand across her mouth to tell Lizbeth to be very, very quiet and very, very still. Lizbeth gasped and squirmed, then seeing Ruthie's warning expression, stopped moving and lay motionless, her eyes getting very wide, as she watched to see what Ruthie would do next.

Ruthie was moving her left hand in a small kind of pointing motion. Was it bees? Was it bears? Were they in trouble with Grandpa? What was it? Lizbeth started to get up, and Ruthie shook her head, keeping her hand on Lizbeth and continuing to point. Ruthie was telling Lizbeth to look over her shoulder. Lizbeth nodded twice to show she understood, put her teeth on her lower lip to concentrate, and then held her breath as she courageously rolled slowly onto her right side and even more slowly looked up.

Under torrents of dazzling sunlight, two slim women, about two inches or so high, pink and purple and blue and gold and copper-colored floated gracefully in the breeze on long, rapidly-beating wings a few feet away from them, hovering over some yellow and orange flowers. Lizbeth couldn't be sure, but it sounded like they were talking to them.

Lizbeth thought they should introduce themselves and so she said in her inside talk "Excuse me, my name is E-liz-a-beth Kate (she always stumbled over her long first name) and this is my sister Ruthie Anne." She didn't notice until after the fairies had been sniggering at her for a few moments (which seemed a little impolite, her grandma wouldn't have let Lizbeth do that to them), that not only had the fairies been staring, but her Ruthie had been staring and looking at Lizbeth with a strange, broken grin.

Lizbeth realized the words had come out loud this time and not just in her head. She was talking again. Outside. Lizbeth felt something hard and cold inside of her chest begin to melt into nothing. It had started doing that a little while ago, and had finally, just a second before, broken up into little, tiny pieces.

Lizbeth started saying whatever she wanted, whatever the word was she thought of, and it just ran off her tongue like water, and she couldn't stop talking. It was easy. It was a little scary. But she did it. She explained and commented and questioned on and on, all afternoon long. The fairies couldn't stop laughing at her. Ruthie just smiled. So did Lizbeth.

So that was how we left the Long Meadows for the Short ones. And we haven't been able to get back since (Aislann is saying to me now "Etain, don't forget to mention Kate." I won't. Now she's writing it in the air all around me in golden, glowing dust, Kate's name in English over and over again. I'm wearing a large, misshapen, and tilting "K" on my head like an odd, flat-topped hat with wings. Will she ever stop? Aislann says no).

I'd always known there was another world, another place filled with lumbering, earth-anchored people who lived and died and were stuck in time like ants in honey, but I'd never visited there. They were glued in place, never touching, tasting, smelling, seeing the Long Meadows - never seeing real colors, glowing pulsing luminosity, never seeing rippling currents of lights and webs of life rolling, washing, and knitting everything around you into one raucous, joyous whole. They never really got to see. They were stuck, you understand. Stuck in time.

And now, well, I'm stuck too. At least somewhat. Time still seems very unreal to me. I'm not very good at it yet. But I'm trying, I'm here. I'm here with Aislann. It's almost as if it's a punishment. I wrack my brains to discover what I did to deserve this. I think, I consider, I ponder, but all in vain. I was always sweet, kind, and gentle, soft-spoken, slow to anger, quick to forgive - the whole bit. It was Aislann who was pure trouble. Aislann. She's laughing and shaking her finger at me. But she knows, she knows.

I'm trying to write all this down, but Aislann keeps distracting me, running through the pollen-ink, dancing on the leaves as I write on them mingling her footprints with my words, hiding the packets of stitched leaves that are completed and taunting me to find them. Maybe this living-in-time is easy for her, but it's certainly not for me. If I'd known helping out that little girl would pull us into this world the way a rock drops through ice into a frozen pond, well, I might not have worked even the slightest glimmer or glamour for her and there I'd be, still happily sitting under a leaf or a yellow flower, dreaming in the summer sunshine.

But that's not entirely true. Elizabeth needed our help - she was the one who was a sinking stone disappearing into a frozen pond. Although I'd seen thousands, no millions of mortals in much worse shape before and not helped them, for some reason this time when I felt the itch, I gave in and scratched. Elizabeth got better. I (we) got worse.

To be truthful, I didn't help Elizabeth on my own. Aislann helped also. And, I guess I could say that it was Aislann's daring me to do something for Elizabeth that probably pushed me over the edge that summery noon and got me to help her, and got us both into this mess. Possibly. Probably. Who can tell?

I'm actually surprised Aislann hasn't begged me already to write down her whole story, all about Aislann and her life and her adventures on these leaves. Usually she'd be all over me, as pestering as a cloud of mayflies, begging me nonstop to "write it down, write it down. Tell them all about me." Now she's strangely quiet. Well. A nice change. We'll see how long it lasts.

It's also odd, I've been getting thinner and thinner, at least it feels that way. So thin, it seems, neither Elizabeth or Ruth notice us at all anymore, if ever. It's very disconcerting. I look again and again at my hands and arms to see if I've become invisible. As if I, Etain, am written in disappearing ink. I seem to be fading, as colors in human sunlight do (instead of getting brighter in sunlight as they should) in this crazy mirror-image world all these people live in.

I have a theory, though. Time is burning through us – it's a fire, and we're firewood and we have to hoard as much energy as possible - all our thought and strength - in order to survive on this side, in the Short Meadows. Aislann, of course, disagrees. Does she have a better idea? Who knows? She's not saying. She probably

Anders Flagstad

hasn't. Aislann is a reflexive disagree-er. She's been notorious for it. Now she's walking on my writing again. Stop it Aislann! Really. Younger sisters. I don't know how Ruth put up with it.

So, back to this time stuff, where one thing happens, then another happens, then another in boring lockstep on and on and on as far as the eye can see. I'm sick of it. So... Elizabeth grew up, there was something called a Great Depression which ended, a World War which started, and then stopped, and then Elizabeth met a man, got married and moved to a place called Arizona. We had to follow.

Aislann says that's a lot of time passing. But how would she know about time?

Apparently we were tied to Elizabeth in some way. Maybe we couldn't get back to the Long Meadows on our own. Maybe she had to release us. Maybe. But we were here, and we felt drawn to her. We felt safer, somehow. So we stayed close. And we followed.

Aislann! I don't know if you can see it but Aislann's written Kate all over this page in her wriggly, worm-squiggle writing. No, it's fading now. I don't know sometimes, I just don't know. How much can one older sibling endure? I guess I'm finding out the hard way, firsthand, here in the Short Meadows with Aislann. If there were any justice in the world, Aislann would have a little sister. Someone to test her, torment her, torture her every waking... All right, All right then, Aislann. I said All right.

Kate. We'll talk about Kate for a while. Kate it is. Anything to make you stop. Kate. Kate. Kate. Kate. Kate. There. Are you happy?

I should mention before I go on, that it is my great passion now, my only mission in life to get the both of us back to the Long Meadows in one piece. Or at least with some color in us, before we go entirely transparent and wink out of existence - two dancing candle flames pinched between time's thumb and forefinger. How did we ever get ourselves into this mess? It was Aislann's fault. Well, mostly. It was... If I don't start talking about Kate I will have no peace, no peace at all, I'm seeing that very clearly now. Stop it! Enough Aislann! I said enough! Oh! Oh, now, come Aislann. Please. Come back Aislann. I'm sorry, I'm sorry. I didn't mean to yell. Come back. I'll write about Kate. About Kate and Elizabeth. Here, look, I'm writing already. Here.

Elizabeth's little daughter is Kate. She's nearly four years old.

Kate is scared and sad and getting sadder. Kate doesn't understand why her mother is crying so much all the time. It makes her want to help her mother, but she doesn't know how. She thinks she has done something wrong, and if she would only fix it, her mother would be happy again. Oh, and Elizabeth has just learned that she is going to have another child. Aislann has already told me, she will name it John. I didn't ask her how she knew. Sometimes Aislann just knows things.

Aislann wanders around the house a lot, she tells me these things, although I have eyes, I can see them for myself. But Aislann talks about them all the time, now, more and more, it's getting to be an obsession with her.

All right, Aislann! I have ears. I hear you. Back to Kate.

When Kate sees her mother with tears on her face, she sits quietly beside her. She talks to herself, whispering "Bad Kate, why do you do bad things Kate?" Sometimes she says to her mother "I'll be good, now, mama. Look at me, I'm being good." Then, sometimes, Elizabeth smiles after that. And then again, sometimes she doesn't.

But Aislann wants me to say that she can tell that Kate is scared. And that Elizabeth is getting worse. Sometimes sisters are so infuriating. Especially younger sisters. Aislann doesn't have to point out the obvious to me. Even a blind mole could tell where this home is heading. Things are not going well here. And, yes, I admit it Aislann, it is troubling here. It is distressing, and things don't look good. I can see it. Yes, I can see it too. You aren't the only one.

Aislann tells me also, that in the last week, Elizabeth has stopped crying almost entirely - she doesn't cry at all anymore. But I don't think that's so good. I think that's not good at all. And little Kate. I bet her dry-eyed mother has her even more scared than her weeping mother had her before.

Aislann is frowning now. She doesn't like me talking about Kate getting more frightened. Now I don't know - I don't know for sure, but I have a theory. Aislann says I'm always having theories. She's bouncing around me now singing "theories, theories, theories." Well, I do. I do have them, Aislann. I can't help it. I theorize spontaneously. It's my nature. Like yours is to terrorize spontaneously (the chanting hasn't stopped. She will drive me to madness. She will. I know it.)

I think children, human children, are very perceptive. Or receptive. They are flesh-colored sponges, so to speak. They absorb. More than is healthy for them sometimes. They don't have as many defenses and walls and so sometimes see things in the stark, menacing way they really are, rather than seeing things the way they would wish them to be. At least that's been my experience with human children.

And Elizabeth? Well, crying sounds to me as if she is someone who is lost and is hoping and trying to be found again. Rescue is still a hope. And hope is still possible.

But silence. Silence is different. Silence is what hopelessness sounds like. Silence is accepting being lost forever. Elizabeth lost, with Kate and the little baby Anne, and the unborn John, and Aislann, and myself. All lost. All of us lost.

Aislann badgers me constantly to do something about it. But we are thin and fading. Weak and getting weaker every month. We don't have the strength to spare to help others. We don't, Aislann, I'm telling you we don't. We don't have strength enough anymore, Aislann, even to help ourselves. Aislann has flown off now, to wander outside like she always does when she doesn't want to face something ugly.

She never faces things. She leaves all the hopelessness to me. She refuses to worry and fret about anything, let alone something as grand and important as our fate. This could very well be the end. But Aislann doesn't want to see any of it. None of the sadness, none of the weakness, nothing forlorn or lost or impossible. She doesn't want to think about our poor future. She certainly doesn't want to talk about it. Not at all. Aislann sees only Kate and Elizabeth. All she talks about is Kate and Elizabeth. And meanwhile things only get worse and worse. For all of us.

I can see it. We're in trouble. They're in trouble. Elizabeth is scared and confused too – I can feel a gap in her, deep and wide, that I haven't felt in years. Elizabeth lost herself, cut herself off from life and her old friends in this flimsy construction of brick and sticks she lives in - this newly-built, split-level ranch home, in an isolated sea of ranch homes, in a beige world filled with short, three-foot-high crazy people – she's surrounded now by blasting things called televisions and radios, and needy, screaming, and helpless persons needing her attention constantly. So much. All at once. At least that's what I think she's feeling. That's what it feels like she's feeling.

She doesn't know how long she can do it. She doesn't know how long she can keep it up. She's afraid she's losing her grip, letting go. It's too much. She felt untethered before. When she was very little and her mother left them. Now she feels as if she's spinning away, wild and out of control. And there's no one there to hold her. No one to hug her. No one to grasp her hand and pull her back up the cliff. No one. Not anymore. Even though I wouldn't tell Aislann, sometimes even I want to help. But I can't. We can't. We can barely hold on ourselves.

In the last year it's only gotten worse. Her soldier-husband is missing in action someplace on the other side of the world – a mortal war being fought in snow-covered mountains over an imaginary line - typical of mortals, Aislann tells me about it, I don't pretend to understand it - and Elizabeth's just found out for certain that she's pregnant again today, this very day - and on top of it all Ruth and Elizabeth haven't talked in years - some silly fight about moving west - and Elizabeth feels as if she's falling, falling into an emotional whirlpool inside. She's falling in, and she's falling apart. Crumbling into unrelated pieces. All over again. She's done it before, she's doing it again.

Or maybe she's freezing up. Her heart and her feelings and her thoughts are getting slower and colder and more and more quiet and soon she'll be stuck fast - a frozen block of Elizabeth ice - without any feelings and without any love to give to Kate or her younger sister Anne or to the new baby that's on its way (which she doesn't know is a boy yet, and certainly doesn't know it's going to be clowning, sly, quick-witted John – all of this from Aislann, of course).

Elizabeth is deathly afraid that she will disappear again into helplessness, although I don't think she remembers clearly what happened to her when her mother died. But she knows in her heart, something large and arctic, a sierra-sized mountain of an iceberg is paddling towards her, and rolling on top of her and pinning her down and sealing her off from everyone around her and she won't be able to get it off again.

That's what she's feeling. That's what Kate is watching. That's actually what we two are watching too.

Aislann is back. Back from, well, wherever she says she goes when she goes outside and leaves me alone to worry my worrisome thoughts all by myself. She can't stop talking. She never can. She says the moon is full and rising sweetly in the south and east as night approaches. That the evening star and her companions smile and wink at her as she rides the cooling gusts that come with sunset. That in the mountains the air is clear and clean and the horizon is streaked with blue and violet, the exact color of spiderwort and chicory back home. Oh, and the dark color at the highest point of the sky, apparently, is a bottomless blue-black, the deep color that you get from the stillest water in the deepest part of the deepest well, and that she's sure I've never seen this color before, so very high up, pinned to the very top of the topmost part of the sky.

She likes to call this place, this frowning land we're exiled in, the Orange Meadows. She says, and I quote "Yes, Etain, it's dry and stark, which being so similar to your own personality, one would think you would take to it - a duck to water" (Do you see what I have to put up with?)

Aislann is adamant. "But it *is* a meadow, Etain, no matter what you say, as living and busy and filled with cares and stories and adventures and turmoils as much as any meadow is back home. Maybe more so. How would you know? You never move an inch, you wrinkled june-bug. I hope I don't get as sour as you when I grow old."

I do my best to ignore here when she's in this kind of mood.

Yes, Aislann is back and so my peace is ended. She tortures me like this. Frequently. She begs me to accompany her on her pointless excursions. I refuse to go. I had never heard of an Arizona before we were kidnapped and I don't intend to learn about an Arizona now. We may be forced to inhabit this water-less prison of lifeless stones, but I will not make the best of it, as Aislann says, and explore it and observe it and enjoy it.

What is there to enjoy? What is there to explore? If you've seen one rock piled upon the other you've seen them all. I won't do it, Aislann, I won't. She's telling me about the frogs and the tiny wasps and the plants with leaves that could be pines with pine needles, but they only have a few needles, here and there, and they're very sharp. Who wants to see a bald pine tree? Now she's telling me about the fish that live and die in a day. I don't believe it. I don't believe her. Oh, she says that, no that's not right. She's saying they live a week. Or two.

I still don't believe her.

It's been a day or a week or a month or a year or so since I last wrote (or something, I'm so bad at time – it couldn't really have been a year could it? Aislann would know, but Aislann can't speak right now). I'm absolutely beside myself today. I'm so angry. I'm so furious with Aislann. I can hardly write. I told her to conserve her strength. I told her, how many times did I tell her? Numberless times. Over and over. Yet, still she went and helped Elizabeth. As soon as I saw the glimmer around Elizabeth's head I knew what had happened. And the result? As I warned her, just as I warned her. She's dying. And for what? I can barely see her. She's thinner than a piece of straw, straying and blowing in the autumn wind. She has no voice.

Oh, Aislann! Why? Why did you do it? It's difficult even to hold her hand, she's fading so. She keeps on pointing to an object in this white-walled cube Elizabeth lives in. Really, it's exactly the same as living in a pat of butter. Colorless and scentless. Well, except for the diapers. But she keeps on motioning with her eyes at a (typically) colorless, lumpy thing on a small table of light blond (of course) wood. At least I think she's motioning with her eyes. It's very difficult to tell. What does she want? Oh, Aislann! Why did you do it? Why?

It was earlier today. She did a dusting, a small glamour, hovering about Elizabeth, over the handkerchief tied over Elizabeth's unruly hair and I heard Elizabeth begin to tell Kate a story. Her eyes were soft and almost smiling as she remembered the story, she looked very different from the way she's been for the longest time. A story about tiny fairies that appeared to her in a summer's field a long, long time ago, and how beautiful the field was and how pretty the fairies and how love, like the plants in winter are really always there, though sometimes you have to remember them hard and know they'll come back, when all the world is buried in winter snow.

Kate asked her mother what snow was again, and she explained (and I could tell Elizabeth was enjoying the explanation – miraculous! Where was that coming from?) I was distracted by Aislann's flitting and frisking about me, pestering and pushing, getting me closer and closer to that unfortunate pale table.

It was the oddest thing. Even though we were in this Arizona wasteland, I could distinctly smell a musky odor of seasons-deep carpets of long pine needles and many-pointed maple leaves, hear the sound of beetles and worms digging through loam, and ants scuttling across it. I could see fat, sap-filled sycamores and spicy-sweet meadow sage and tall, ribbed, tasseled grasses. We were back home. Or they were. Aislann prodded and yelled and I couldn't understand what she was getting at. It sounded like "Ruth". She was almost gone. I could barely make out her face, let alone try and read her lips.

Ah well. I didn't really want to stay shackled to this tiny house in this dry and rocky excuse for a meadow for very long all by myself. If Aislann could make this last effort, her older sister could do no less. I pushed what remaining (little) sparkle and glimmer I had over the lump and immediately could no longer see my arms in front of my face. I could see Aislann in front of me, though. She was smiling. She was holding out her long, slim hands towards mine and beckoning me saying "Come sister, come Etain" like she always did. She was so faint, I saw only an outline, floating above the floor - a bit of spider's web in the shape of my sister. I supposed I was no better at this point. I smiled. There was Aislann. There was my sister.

The object, which had an odd decoration of a transparent circle incised with smaller circles, gave off the sound of a thousand tinkling bells and it startled me so much I bounced up and off the ceiling. Twice. Elizabeth picked the object apart and brought one part up to her ear.

"Ruth?" she said "What's wrong?" Then, "Nothing? But why did you call? Me? I didn't call you. I didn't. Ruth, why would I call you?" Elizabeth stopped and was chewing on her lower lip now. "Ruth, you haven't asked about me in years. You don't care. Why would you start caring now?"

If I squinted my eyes I could just see Aislann over by the window. She was flying out. The glass was hardly a barrier to her now. She was mostly not there. Mostly gone.

"Ruth..." Elizabeth said, then she stopped, listening to something, then said in a different voice "Oh, Ruthie, I just don't know. Oh Ruthie..." and she started to cry, but it sounded less as if it were the last drops of water pouring from an emptied bucket and more as if it were a mountain stream letting loose after a long winter of lonely, icy immobility.

Kate sat on her knee. She was pointing at the window. And laughing. Could she see Aislann? Admittedly Aislann was flopping around out there, comically, doing a great deal of nearly transparent somersaults and backflips. She could never stop. Never. But Kate shouldn't be able to see her. It just wasn't possible. Even I could barely see Aislann now.

Little Kate looked up, suddenly, twisting her head around and lifting her arm up towards the top of the room. Was she pointing at me now? I was so distracted I bounced off the ceiling repeatedly and came to a temporary rest sitting precariously, upside down on the ledge on the top of the window. Kate laughed even louder. Elizabeth through her tears was looking out of the side of her eyes at Kate, crying and talking at the same time to Ruth. Was that the start of a smile on Elizabeth's face?

Sometimes to see the shafts of sunlight connecting earth and sky, there has to be bitter smoke or cold fog blowing through them to make them visible. That's what Aislann says sometimes. She calls it - the smoke in the sunlight. When the sadness outlines the joy. When you finally see what had been there the whole time. The sunlight. It's always there. It was always there.

Well, I guess Aislann has her points.

Sometimes.

So, what was I to do? What would you have done? I made a decision, lying upside-down on the top of the window, and with my last bit of will and strength I pushed my way through the air and out of that house and smack into one of those hairless plants that grow in this "Orange Meadow" of Aislann's. The last thing I remembered before I disappeared entirely was Aislann winking at me and smirking again, nodding her head with her arms crossed over her chest.

She'd got me to come outside after all. She'd done it again. How did she always get me to do these things? Always.

Kate wondered if she needed a new prescription for her contact lenses. She kept on seeing colors streaking here and there out of the side of her eyes. Although maybe she was just tired. She blinked a couple of times. Having four kids would definitely do it.

Kate looked around for her eleven-year-old daughter Elly and wondered for the umpteenth time that day "How long does it take a young girl to get ready to go out to the airport?" The answer was elastic. Whatever time you gave her, she'd stretch it into twice its size. Kate yelled up the stairs.

"Elly! Elly! Get down here on the double. Your sister Margaret somehow made it down to the car in less than an hour. Your grandmother's here and has been sitting in the car for ten minutes already. Elly! Elly! Are you listening to me?" (that actually was a stupid question, Kate mentally hit herself – sometimes she found herself sounding exactly like her mom, it irritated her, but mostly she was proud of it).

"Elizabeth!" (She was named after her grandmother – but Elly hated the old-fashioned, formal name, so naturally Kate used it on special occasions – special occasions of rabid hardheadedness like this). Elizabeth! I'm not calling for my health. Come down. Now. We have to leave."

There was a profound silence from upstairs. If it had been the middle of the night, all you would have heard would have been crickets and frogs. Kate felt herself starting to lose her composure and her calm, what little she had left.

"Elizabeth Sara O'Donnell. I mean you, and I mean now, young lady! Now!"

When had Kate started talking in continuous exclamation points? What year?

"Don't make me come up there!"

What was worse, it was getting harder and harder to remember a time when she didn't. "All right. Have it your way. I'm coming up" she said in a more normal conversational yell. Everyone knew, in the McDonnell household, the politer the sound of the mom threat, the graver the mom consequences.

An explosion of activity and a flurry of syllables exploded from upstairs. Kate hollered from behind her door. "O.K. All right. I'm coming down, mom. I'm coming. Really. Here I am." Kate listened, but still no Elly-sounds. Shaking her head and rolling her eyes, she started towards the staircase. Even as she did it, Kate wondered for whose benefit she performed all these dramatic rituals of exasperation? Rolling? Shaking? No one was watching

Kate. No one could see her. Kate had to admit, however, it just felt good. It appealed to a contrariness she'd rejoiced in and battled against her whole life. She had to admit, reluctantly, that she and her daughter were alike in more ways than one.

Kate clomped loudly on the first couple of steps starting the promised walk upstairs - hitting the creak on the third step particularly hard - that usually brought results - although how Elly picked up on a distant piece of wood crying out with music and cell phone conversations and texting and emails and videos running on her tablet and who knows what else, Kate had no idea - but Elly usually did.

Before Kate could take another step, she heard a door unlock, briefly witnessed a crescendo of bass and guitar, and then the sound of an MP3 player being de-streamed and turned off with an amplified, wireless thunk in her daughter's bedroom. The expected loud sound of adolescent sighing got louder and louder. Elly made her way, moaning and gasping, slowly, into the upstairs hall, made her way towards the top of the stairs, organized her bag, brushed her hair, pulled on her shoes, tied up her hair and hopped step by step down the staircase pulling on her socks, all the way down and out the front door. She was talking on her cell the whole time. Kate gritted her teeth and closed her eyes. Well, she kept one eye open, so she could catch Elly, and prevent an emergency room detour on their trip today. Elly was sliding her hand across her phone and grimacing at Kate as she sailed by.

"I still don't know why I have to go to the airport with everyone. It's not as if we don't already have enough people going. Val and Maria are going to Fashion Valley Mall this afternoon and I'm going to be missing everything. Everything. And Val never tells me what happens. Never. And..." Kate, satisfied that her oldest was well on her way towards the van looked out to make sure the twins were still doing O.K. Both were sleeping peacefully beside Granma, in the back seat, strapped, tied down, and practically attached to the seat – as safe as two cases of thin-shelled eggs.

So far so good.

There was a rainbow trying to gain ocular control of Kate. Up and down, left and right, tiny flashes of multi-colored light splashed around her. There they were again. And now, there they weren't. Kate blinked five times, slowly. She felt in her purse for some rewetting drops for her eyes. She wondered if she should make a note on her phone to make an appointment with the optometrist. But she forgot all about it, when she couldn't find any drops, and one of the twins started crying in the car. That, of course, started the other one too.

Her husband Matt was gone on a business trip until next Friday. They'd just moved to San Diego a month before, and Granma Hobbs, Elizabeth, Kate's mother had flown in to help them get settled in and do some babysitting and generally be a support. Kate was more than grateful. She was impressed. Kate tended to watch out for her mother a little, tried to smooth her way, be a support to her. She saw her mother as fragile. She saw her as weak, but too proud to admit it. Her mom always seemed to be a little too melancholy and serious. Kate just wanted her to be happy.

It was a good thing, Kate thought to herself, that her mother hadn't been saddled with a hell-raiser like Elly. What would she have done with Elly? Kate sometimes tried to picture her mom trying to sort out Elly's opinionated life. Kate remembered herself as being pretty easy to raise as a teenager. Her mother would just get quiet and smile with her thin-lipped, polite, but just-oh-so-slightly-sarcastic smile whenever Kate brought it up. Well, her mom had the right to remember Kate's youth any way she wanted to at this point.

Kate looked over at her mom, sitting by the twins, tucking them in now, giggling and gurgling, the crying over and forgotten, and Kate listened to her mom talk to John (Kate's little brother, not so little anymore, huh?) as John pretended to be a rap singer, drumming away on the dashboard and the steering wheel and making splooshing noises with his lips in some complicated rhythm. John was a musician and a song writer. And he was very poor. God, Kate loved him. And she loved her mom. More than she could say. That didn't mean they might not be at each other's throats in half an hour. But as would a beleaguered herd of musk oxen in the arctic, when threatened by dangers and disasters, the Hobbs family circled up and defended itself admirably when called upon. Somewhere along the line they'd learned to stick together.

And Elly. Elly was stubborn and headstrong as a, well, as a what? A combination ox, brick wall, immoveable object, and unstoppable force. But she was a Hobbs through and through, all the Hobbs were like that. It'd get her into trouble someday. She'd learn. Like Kate had had to learn. Learn the hard way. It's a good thing they all had thick foreheads.

And then there was John. He was the easygoing one of the family. Most times he was the calm glue that mended many a disagreement. This move of the McDonnells was turning into a family reunion. Aunt Ruth might even show up from back East. If her hip wasn't acting up. You never knew. But John was here. And that was fine with Kate too. He was the chauffeur for the day. The San Diego International Airport Express. Her other sister Anne was flying in from San Francisco in 87 minutes. Kate sighed. They'd never make it.

It was turning into the typical Hobbs family circus. The Hobbs clan never missed a chance to party, if they could. They were a dangerous combination – all of them together. Kate knew that sometimes she and Anne took things a little too far. But they just liked being close. They were sisters for Chrissake.

What was wrong with a little love, followed by confusion, argument, enmity, World War, retaliation, chagrin, shame, and heartfelt forgiveness, bringing you all back to love? Sometimes it took smoke for you to see sunbeams. Kate could never remember where she'd heard that first. She'd said it since she was just a little girl. Her mother had said it wasn't her who told it to Kate. Well, then, it had to be somebody. Some other person in their family. Sometimes mom could be so mysterious. But the saying just made sense. And Kate was all about making sense. And making sunbeams. And the smoke too. If that's what it took to get the sunbeams.

Later that week, after dinner, while they were washing the dishes, Kate's little daughter Margaret asked to hear about the fairies again – she called it the "little women story" – and Elly rolled her eyes, and Kate and Anne looked at each other, and then both of them looked at Granma Hobbs and at Aunt Ruth (Aunt Ruth had flown back after all from Vermont exhausting her air miles account completely but happily). Aunt Ruth and Granma just looked secretive, but with the merest of smiles lighting up their faces.

Granma Hobbs said "I think we can manage that." John had left earlier to hear a band in the Gaslamp District, and the twins were in bed already, in the spare bedroom with the broken door that was permanently swung wide open just down the hall. Before they all settled down on pillows and cushions, John called (barely audible above a loud Zydeco beat) and unsuccessfully tried to convince at least one sister or aunt to come down and hit the clubs with him and there ensued a half hour of constant, simultaneous conversation that only a Hobbs could follow.

Then Granma Hobbs settled back into the couch, stirring the tea she'd just made and pushed the sugar bowl with Kate's baby spoon sticking out of it across the coffee table (a table which was actually just a big piece of driftwood - really a shellacked log) and when it was in reaching distance, Elizabeth pounced on it, but thought better of the calories and pushed it on towards Ruth and Kate. Soon four women were blowing on their tea and sipping it to see if it needed lemon. Margy had a small glass of milk, which she'd already managed to spill once. But the second one was mostly gone. Kate was ready anyway with a now-moist-and-used napkin by her side.

"Now, where to begin?" said Granma Hobbs glancing over at Margy with a puzzled, questioning glance.

"The meadow, the meadow, start with the meadow, Ganma" said Margy in an excited, piping voice, and placing her hands properly down on in her lap in anticipation. Looking upwards, with a serious adult frown on her face, she stopped talking and waited in her best correct story-listening pose.

"All right, then, the meadow" said Granma Hobbs "Listen carefully - this is our story, the Hobbs story. And you too, Elly so you can tell your daughters or your nieces someday" Kate gave Elizabeth and Margaret a warning look not to gasp or sigh or make a face, but she could see for once both of them were appropriately rapt and paying close attention. Well, their eyes were pointing towards their Granma, and neither of them had earbuds in their ears, which was about the same thing.

Granma Hobbs told the story of the meadow behind the barn when she was a little girl, and the two, bright, tiny women, she called them Etty and Aisy, and how she'd got to talk with them for a whole day, how she could feel them zipping around her the whole time, and what color their hair was, and what they asked her, and what their voices sounded like and what their dresses were like and on and on. Margy's eyes got big. And surprisingly, Elly's were thoughtful. Aunt Ruth was nodding and saying it was all just that way. Kate picked up the story about the two miniature, pale women who flew around their home in Arizona. Granma Hobbs was nodding this time. Margy's eyes got even bigger. But she was yawning too. Kate could see they needed to stop, it was getting late. Elly didn't say much. She seemed to be fighting some battle within herself. Whatever it was, silence won. They all went to bed.

The next morning, Elly pulled her mother Kate aside and whispered to her in the hall, while she was waiting to use the bathroom after Aunt Ruth. "Do you really believe all that stuff about fairies, mom?" she spoke out of the side of her mouth, like she was watching out for someone, looking down the hallway out of the side of her eyes. Kate looked down the hallway but couldn't see anything, nothing, that is except the now familiar flashes of color. They reminded her of something, somehow, somewhere.

"Well, honey" Kate said, but Elizabeth interrupted her, speaking even more softly "I mean everything you and Granma and Aunt Ruth were talking about. Did it really happen? Really?" and then she said, abruptly. with exceptionally clear enunciation that sounded to Kate like the electronic voice of her GPS navigator "Could we go to the beach today, mom, if it's sunny out?" Elly's eyebrows went up, and she made motions with her eyes down at the floor.

That stopped Kate for a second, but she could feel a small body squeezing past her from the back, Margy, making her way busily out to the living room. Elly didn't start talking again until after Margy rounded the corner, and they both heard the kitchen screen door slam.

"I mean, mom, I think I've seen them too. And they live here with us. Here in San Diego now. I mean Etty and Aisy."

For some reason, that didn't faze Kate at all. Rainbow flashes. Hmm.

"And, mom, I think they need our help."

Who would have thought it? That I would have lived in time for so long. That I can even use the words "time" and "long" in a sentence now. It's been a long, long time. Did I say how long it's been? Very, very long.

Things are complicated, confused. How could I have known that helping Kate was what we needed to do, that not-helping was making us disappear? None of it makes sense to me. Aislann here is saying it all makes sense to her. Well good for you Aislann. I'm sure we're all very happy for you.

And the fading problem? Well, I have so much color now I almost scare myself. I drip color. I weep chromatically. I laugh the same way. I fly and colors whip off of me the way fields of dandelion seeds spread in clouds in a strong wind. I reek of color. It's embarrassing, actually (Aislann says that yes, she is embarrassed for me. Thank you, Aislann). And the more color you give out, the more you have to give. Who knew? Who would have thought of all that? (Do I even have to say that Aislann says she knew it all along? No, I don't).

But I still have to find a way to get Aislann and myself home. Now Aislann is silent. Could it be that Aislann doesn't already know how to do *that*. Apparently not. Well, that's a first.

It's been over 8 years since the family reunion when Kate and Matt moved out to San Diego. Just last year, Kate and Matt moved back to Vermont, in a town near where Ruth lives. I know these things by myself now, I don't have to ask Aislann. That in itself is sad to me. I refuse to get comfortable in these Short Meadows. I refuse to make my home here. I won't.

Elly calls herself Elizabeth now, and lives in an apartment with a couple of girlfriends and goes to SDSU (San Diego State University – I even know what an abbreviation is – shocking, just shocking – I'll be mortal soon). She just broke up with one boyfriend, David, a pretty rough and rocky relationship, and doesn't know it, but she's going to fall for his former roommate Michael any day now. Aislann has glimmered and glamoured a little for Elly, but, really, it's all Elly now. Elly's all grown up.

Her mom is visiting her right this minute (minute! Who'd have thought I'd ever use such language), and her roommates are away for the weekend, and so we don't have to stay as much out of sight. We're streaking up a storm. It's very odd. I think of Elly as my daughter. But I also think of Kate as my daughter. And Granma Hobbs, or Elizabeth, she's my daughter too. All three. Very dear. Love brings you to strange new places if you give it half a chance. I'll be the first to admit it.

The two of them (Kate and Elly) have been huddled in Elly's bedroom now for an hour. Aislann told me we can't go in. I can't imagine why. She's shaking her head at me and darting back and forth so fast about the door she's blurring into a fairy force-field. I can't believe I'm using Sci Fi references. I can't believe I even know what Sci Fi means. Help me someone! Please! Get me out of here before it's too late. Never mind. I think it already is too late.

Now Aislann is smiling and the doorknob is turning and Kate and Elizabeth are walking out hand in hand. They're holding something. It's a flower. And its stuck in a letter – a letter from Granma Hobbs, our young Elizabeth from so long ago. But it's obviously old, very old. It's dry, flat, and pressed in what looks like waxy paper. Aislann is smiling so hard her face will break. It's a dandelion. What's so special about a dandelion? Especially such a poor specimen. There's hardly anything left of it. Just a little very faded green and a small, flattened mop of crinkly yellow. Aislann is motioning and I look down, flying in for a closer look. Aislann is peering over my shoulder and giggling.

My moon and stars! Aislann is right. It's a dandelion from our field. One of THE dandelion's from that first summer noon when we met this mortal family. I can still see some of Aislann's old glamour sparking around it. Amazing! And the two of them are placing it carefully down on the hardwood floor in front us. Kate looks like she's going to cry. Aislann lands on one side. She beckons me to land on the other. Kate and Elly step back.

The two mortal women seem to be casting a glimmering glamour of their own, I feel swept up in a cloud of golden sparks coming off of both of them and the dandelion in floods, (how do they know how to do that?) Aislann's hand's around my waist and we are both enveloped in thankfulness and a sincere wish for our own happiness and then the hallway gets brighter and brighter and soon all we can see is their two faces, and then their eyes, and then all the brilliance condenses into one eye which turns out to be the sun, and Aislann and I are sitting under a swaying tassel of goldenrod, listening to the wind whisper through the tall grass and the sun above is shining his summer-brightest, just for us. And Oillel and Yvalbane and Eithne and Iphria are coming out from behind a fuzzy bearberry, pirouetting and pulling the pink-white flower-bowls over their heads into floppy hats, pretending to be a pair of farm girls, pouting their lips and batting their eyelids at everyone in sight and laughing at themselves and laughing at us.

We're home.

"Where did you go?" said Yvalbane, "We waited, by the

cinquefoil and counted and counted thinking you were hiding and you wanted us to follow. But we didn't even get to count to a hundred before you got back. Why were you so quick? Why did you return? What did you see? What did you do? Where are the children? Tell us everything. Why are you laughing at us? Why aren't you talking? Oh, you sisters."

NEW MOON

If you've talked with any of my friends, then you already know, I'm a pretty level-headed guy. Stable. I don't get excited, I take things easy.

I look the world straight in the eye, I accept life for what it is, get what I can out of it, and I go. No big buildups, no drawn-out endings. Drama to a minimum. That's me.

But that night, for some reason it was different.

I remember it being dark, very dark. O.K., it was night. It had a reason to be dark.

But it was also very familiar. Too familiar. And, you know what? I didn't want to do it again. Not again. Who would? A moonless night. Black mountains of water pushing, jostling, wrestling, pounding and crashing their way towards me. Black wave after black wave. Rearing and throwing their weight at me. Deafening thunder. Tons of water collapsing. I knew where I was. I knew this exact place. I was sure I'd been here before.

I remember I was in the shallows. Each rising wave picked itself up and efficiently expanded its black self upwards to the height of an office building. All shining from within, lit with a dim spirit-glow, green-white on black-blue, iridescent spots of light running along their black foaming crests. The last enormous wave broke viciously, right on top of my head, dragging me under, filling my nostrils, filling my mouth with stinging salt water, foam and liquid and bits of floating junk, leaving me flattened, panting, and twitching, limp in a cold, retreating surf. Backwash sucked at my body, pulling me into deeper water, whistling past my ears. Heavy strands of kelp twisted and wound tighter across my face and chest.

I found I couldn't breathe. I tried, believe me, I tried. But I couldn't get any air in my lungs this time. I felt, rather than heard, another wave approaching. I was floating. Sort of. I could no longer move my own muscles to push air in and out of my lungs. I couldn't move my arms and legs. I couldn't move my head. I heard the bellowing rush of a wave beginning to break and saw a strange green light hanging in the water over my head rising higher and higher and higher.

I woke up, clawing at Jamie's shoulder stretched across my chest, trying desperately to roll his arm off my torso, get the heaviness off, get some air in my body. Anything. I was a little berserk. The rolling and rumbling of the monster wave continued to echo louder and louder in Jamie's bedroom, and when I'd poked him and punched him sufficiently awake to respond to my questions he looked confused, then ashamed, then slyly secretive with a broken smile, mumbling unhelpfully as he turned over "'S' always like this."

Soon I started to hear the more familiar rhythmic pounding of Jamie's snoring, but I wasn't done.

So I poked him again and got "You mus'b' dreaming, jus' go to sleep, always stops, always."

Guess I was done after all.

Since I had work tomorrow, early, Jamie had come up with the sensible solution as usual. That's Jamie, practical and rational. And the rumbling wet blackness did stop. Eventually. And I forgot about the whole thing. Even Jamie's uncharacteristic smile. Until later.

What about Jamie? Well, he's my current fling. My other half Darrell was out of town on an audit (he's with an international CPA firm) and I had five weeks of boredom ahead of me and I never let myself stay undistracted for that long. So I started sniffing around once the coast was clear and Darrell was safely on another continent, making sure my cell phone was un-suspiciously easy for Darrell to reach day or night, and Jamie just popped up. Really. Out of nowhere.

I think I may have been his first guy, I don't know. I keep meaning to ask, but then I forget. What I do remember is the struggle to land him. Clearly. Lots of memories there. It was fun. Same as hooking a well-muscled marlin. It took a few weeks of reeling him in, giving him slack and generally wearing him down until one night I attacked him on his stained couch and we ended up giving the couch and his carpet some newer and more interesting stains.

He kept on saying he just wanted to be friends. But that's not what I wanted. Not from the beginning. I mean, I only have five weeks, hey, c'mon! – not that I'd ever tell Jamie that. I'm not stupid. The punch line is I think I'm starting to fall for him. I mean really fall for him. Which is a problem. A big hairy, messy, and yes, a stupidly unforeseen complication. I don't like complications. I must be slipping. I'm too smart to be doing this, man, way too smart.

I first met Jamie at a used bookstore, one gray, rain-ruined afternoon. He stood with his back to me. His whole body blocked my light, outlined against the dim, streaky glow that passed for sunlight leaking steadily in through the smudged and taped-over front windows of the shop. He held something large and heavy in his arms, and leaned against a V-shaped alcove of high, tottering bookshelves, any one of which looked like they might collapse if his broad-muscled shoulders stopped propping them up for even a second. He didn't see me.

In the humid, winter air that year in San Diego, that particular corner of the shop reeked more than usual of moldering pulp and decaying bindings. A sharp citrus smell hung over it all, which was probably the remnants of an ineffectual disinfecting foray in the near past involving a nearly-empty can of Lysol by the shop's owner, Mr. Bradley Cooke – a man not given to frequent bursts of hygienic frenzy – this last burst, unhappily, hadn't lasted very long. In other words, the place stunk.

Lee (as Mr Cooke likes to be called), an old man at 29, was half-dozing at a counter at the front of the shop, nearly hidden behind various stacks of paperbacks sorted by subject matter lined up in front of him. The height of the piles changed from week to week, but the stacks had been there for years.

Lee had an open copy of a beautiful hardback edition of *The Education of Henry Adams* balanced on one knee and a very thick English translation of a manga involving attenuated aliens in (probably) Paris balanced on the other. Well, the manga could've been in Las Vegas or Tokyo - the lurid front cover had an anime picture of a colorful melting Eiffel Tower and a naked, soulful-eyed girl clothed in a boa - the reptile kind not the feathers kind, and lots of shiny rockets flying hither and yon. I didn't like manga, so I wouldn't know what the fuck was up with that cover, would I? No. Not a clue. All I knew is you read 'em backwards. Mangas that is. Lee loved 'em. He loved to read generally. When he wasn't napping.

I think he thought reading books backwards was kinky. He sure did a lot of it. I didn't have an opinion on the matter. Whatever floats your boat is my motto.

Anyways, both books lay in imminent danger of falling and disappearing into the anonymity of the book-covered floor. As usual, the cashier stand had experienced the constant and reliable ventilation of Lee's restful snores and heavy breathing in and out, in and out, all afternoon long. What can I say? Lee's Collectible and Used Bookstore Emporium was a restful place. Lee was sensitive to restful places. So he rested.

I'd known Lee for years at this point. We were friends now from way back. At least five years, which in gay years is a lifetime. Well, it is when you're in your twenties, which I am, and I'm proud of it. In the distant past, we'd starting going out, long before Darrell, spending the occasional long evening together, waiting for the romantic spark to ignite (an ignition which failed), and we ended up laughing in bed more often than we ended up sweating and grunting in it. At some point the balance tipped, and we were more like brothers than lovers. Thus, we were best friends. Sisters even. I could count on him. And he could count on me. I knew he'd cover for me with Darrell if I asked him to. He had in the past. No reason he wouldn't continue doing so in the future.

Some people I know give me a hard time saying I sleep with all my friends. But they have it backwards. The thing is, usually, with a few notable exceptions, I become good friends with people I sleep with. The sleeping, friends shtick got a little more complicated once I had a spouse. Just a little. But so far things have worked out, knock on wood. And there are worse things, let me tell you, than being friendly and decent with people you sleep with. Even if you're being a bit of a schmuck by doing it. But I digress. I have a tendency to do that at times, which I'm sure you'll notice after a while.

Back to Jamie. We left him standing in watery light in Lee's bookstore. Jamie had turned around and backed up closer to the light of the front window. I'd ducked behind a bookcase and snuck beside him, standing next to the window, pretending to search for a mystery novel. I began cataloguing his physical traits using only my peripheral vision – a cruising talent I've cultivated successfully for years and am now an expert at.

He was of medium height but stocky, strong chest and shoulders like a bull. Blond, spiky hair. Green eyes. He looked like he could crack walnuts with his buttocks. He had a kind of an edgy nervousness in the nonchalant, but exact way he positioned and re-positioned himself precisely against the shelves. I decided I liked him. He was holding a massive, cordovan-leather covered, gilt-edged volume of Sherlock Holmes stories, with his arms extended. I could see his biceps bulging and twitching even from ten feet away. That sucker must have been heavy. And he was reading it upside down. He was also humming to himself, sort of tunelessly, but it sounded oddly like "How much is that doggie in the window?" I even thought I could make out some singing woof, woofs every so often.

I think it was the woof woofs that pushed me over the edge. Jamie was just the cutest thing I'd seen in I don't know how long. Just my type. And he didn't know it yet, but we two, Jamie and I, were going to get much better acquainted, in the very near future, if I had anything to do with it. And I did.

I didn't realize until much later I was apparently standing in his light. He muttered to himself a couple of times, angling the page he was trying to read this way and that, tilting it and moving it to capture the maximum number of photons he could, deep in the gloom of that musty canyon of books. I assumed he was trying to read a really small-print footnote or something. Footnotes must be hard to read upside down.

I don't know if I've mentioned it before, but I love books and I love used bookstores. And, as it turns out, I love Jamie. There, I've said it. I've said it out loud. But we should go back to Jamie again. I love going back to Jamie.

He finally looked up with an irritated expression on his face, trying to work out the cause of his reading-light denigration, and glancing unexpectedly over his shoulder discovered me looking at him, watching him looking at me. I stopped. I didn't look away. I had the good manners to blush. He, on the other hand, burst into a full-blown scowl. But he remained silent.

I finally quipped casually in his direction "Don't you think it would be easier to read right-side up, bud?", while I fingered a dilapidated mystery novel that shed not only its blood-red graphic cover as I pulled it out, but also along with it, a couple of chapters worth of yellowed and curling paper. Basically it exploded in my hand.

Jamie's scowl deepened (whoops), as the pages floated down about our feet, spreading in a thick patchwork quilt of six-decades-old, mass-paperback confetti on Lee's much-abused linoleum floor. Jamie looked at me, looked at his heavy book, then turned it over to look at its cover, sighed, rolled his eyes, then mutely showed me the front, back and then the text. The cover was printed upside down, and backwards. Well, well, well. Maybe that's why the book had found its way to Lee's odoriferous Land of Misfit Literature. Kinky Holmes. And does upside-down covers qualify as collectible? It must. There was an interested, irritated, and inquisitive look in Jamie's eyes now. I guessed it was my move. Or that's the way I intended to see it, anyway.

And thus - as they say in the motion picture industry - it began. Then I met Joe.

I met Joe by accident one evening, coming early to meet Jamie at his place. It's strange when you look back at someone you come to know so well, someone you despise and loath at one point, Joe I mean, how quickly and reasonably it can all start, and how rapidly everything goes to hell after that.

I should mention at first that Jamie lives in a kind of strange apartment building. It's a converted bowling alley, that's now condos and apartments, and it's done up to look like a cross between a Disney version of a Spanish cathedral and an anonymous cement city block of government-built housing projects for the down and out. In other words, a typical new development in Southern California – extravagant stage-design architecture and flimsy stucco construction. Did I mention I wanted to be an architect at one point in my life? Sometimes I'm boggled at all the things I could have been, and all the people I could have been them with. So many, and so little time. But I'm losing my train of thought again. You've got to help me keep myself on topic. Where were we?

Yeah. So, someone else had buzzed me into Jamie's apartment complex. A neighbor. Somebody. I don't remember. I heard Jamie talking to a mystery person around the corner as I got off the elevator on Jamie's floor, sushi takeout in one hand (a coup on my part, Jamie hated trying new food) and a bunch of loose DVD's in the other. One of the DVD's I was lugging over to Jamie's happened to be one of my all-time favorites - an old copy of the movie *The Ritz* (Warner Brothers, 1976, starring the incomparable Rita Moreno, which shockingly Jamie had never heard of before – Rita or The Ritz). I was content. No, I was happy. I was anticipating a night of good food, interesting cinema, and significant huffing and groaning later on in Jamie's bedroom. Life was good. Or so it seemed. You be the judge.

Darrell (my husband) called as I sauntered through the lobby. It must be the middle of the night where he was. Or tomorrow morning. Why was he calling? By the time I'd freed my hands enough to get to my cell, it had started to roll over to voice mail. Oh well. I could still catch it. But no. I just let things roll. Like I usually do. That's how I roll – I roll. I picked up my stuff again, hit the elevators, waited forever, and climbed in when they graciously opened and allowed me to enter. The getting in part wasn't easy, let me tell you.

The elevator doors creaked and groaned their way open on my smiling face. It was a circus act. They kept on closing and opening, closing and opening, as if the building was defending itself from me. I noted the rhythm of the gnashing doors, propelled myself in during a lull, and I punched buttons madly. I balanced and re-balanced food and movies in either hand for more than a couple of seconds. Almost successfully. We lurched upwards. Reluctantly, it seemed to me. I finally made it up to Jamie's floor. After more struggling I finally made it out of the elevator. The doors opened and closed a lot, trying to grab at my shirt apparently, before they remained closed. They succeeded in getting one of my shoes. Then they shut. The elevator rumbled and moaned at me from behind the doors (digesting the shoe?) for at least a minute. What a joke this building was.

I was punching at the down button, over and over, trying to get the friggin' doors to open again, when I heard Jamie's voice. Was he on the phone? In the hall? Why? I started walking, lopsidedly, with one shoe, towards the sound. The elevators are in a kind of long "L" shaped part of Jamie's floor, and I'd have only a few seconds of eavesdropping, since I'm a quick walker, even partially shod, before I'd get to the corner and surprise him, so I slowed down slightly to see what was up. But the more I heard, the harder I listened and the slower I walked, until finally I was at a dead stop, six inches from the corner, listening with all my might. I couldn't believe it. I felt like someone had hit me in the stomach. How could I have been so wrong about Jamie? He was two-timing me! What a bastard!

"Look, he can't see you here" Jamie was whispering loudly "we can meet later. He wouldn't understand."

Someone else was answering in a hoarse guttural hissing sound that I couldn't really make out, but Jamie interrupted him "No, not now, I'm telling you he's coming over and he's coming right now." Then more insistent deep-throated hissing. "O.K. All right, all right, keep it down. All right. You win. I'll try and get rid of him as soon as I can." Hiss, hiss, hiss. "I promise. I promise. Later. Later tonight. Just an hour or two. Be patient. You can wait an hour or two."

At this point I didn't know what to think. Or feel. Or do.

I ended up making a loud couple of bumping sounds (hoping it sounded like a pair of malevolent, dilapidated elevator doors closing) and stamped out some comical footstep-clumping on the bruised, blond, hardwood floors they have in these narrow hallways of Jamie's building. I've always thought it makes the halls look like one-laned bowling alleys - I always find myself looking for the ball-return at the beginning of the hallway when I get off the elevator, that and some cheap plastic seats and a few forgotten beers and scorecards. Anywho, the talking, of course, stopped immediately. I felt sick. I couldn't think. I took a deep breath. I rounded the corner.

As Jamie swung into view, I caught an odd hurt and worried expression on the side of his face as he watched the door to the stairs at the end of the hallway close, and an even odder expression of exasperation as he turned around to face me. I took another deep breath. I plodded manfully forward. I knew my face was beaming out a bright red - a demonic lighthouse set at a million watts of power. I pasted on a fair copy of a boyfriend's smile (yes, I was his boyfriend, I was – kind of). I tried to remember that I had to exhale at some point. No one said a word.

I know. I know. I realize I was in no position here to be jealous. Or hurt. Or even scared. Jamie had never heard of Darrell, and never would, at least not from me, and to be fair, neither of us had brought up the topic of exclusive dating. I mean, how could I? What would I say? But then why did I feel like someone had just rabbit-punched me with a radioactive pile of poison oak? Well, you make up an appropriate metaphor. Just make sure it's a non-trivial, and supernaturally painful one, because brother was I hurting! Not the most pleasant feeling. Not when you're carrying some DVDs, sushi, and relishing the memories of events that haven't happened yet of a long night of hard physical labor on top of a mattress.

I bent forward to kiss Jamie as both my arms were full of raw fish and I couldn't exactly give him a hug. I missed, because he jerked to one side at the last minute and I ended up giving him a sort of neck and shoulder hug with the pointy part of my chin instead. I juggled to keep hold of the sack of sushi, but missed the DVD's. They clattered to the floor. One or two opened. I scurried to pick them up. Jamie didn't move a muscle.

Huh! Man! I wasn't doing the in-out thing with oxygen. No breathing was occurring. My chest felt as if someone had punctured it with an industrial air hose and was inflating it to the size of one of those tires they use on mining dump trucks that are like 30 feet tall, in those big strip mines, up in Montana (Jamie liked to force both of us to watch Science Channel reruns - one reason I had purposefully brought over Rita with me tonight – a brain can only take so much force-fed, factual information). Yes, my lungs were inflated to their maximum. I was going to explode. Something had to give.

I didn't trust myself to speak yet. I kind of moaned a greeting. Jamie looked great in his tank top and his athletic shorts. He always dressed like that at home. Jamie's eyebrows went up and he looked quizzically at me, but didn't say anything and led me to his door, which was already open. I went inside, with the distinct emotions of someone going to an execution. My own. The door closed. I swear I could hear footsteps in the hall walk down, stop, and stay there outside the door, motionless, waiting, listening, scheming. I was a mess. On the point of blacking out, I finally did it. I figured out how to work my lungs again. I let out a long, shuddering breath.

Jamie was just beginning to ask me what I had brought, eyeing the DVD pile with considerable skepticism and the bags of sushi with even more, when I jumped up in mid-sentence and left his living room. As silently and quickly as I could, I padded to Jamie's tiny entrance tile area, remembering at the last minute to drop off the food and movies I still had in each hand, and pounced on the front door, flipping all the various locks open successively with both hands as would a world-class typist punching his way through the Olympic trials for competitive keyboarding.

I triumphantly flung the door open with a kind of startling yell – having the brilliant idea that this would maximize the element of surprise, and peered out. The yawningly vacant hallway was filled with the slightest sound of buzzing from a faulty fluorescent light just outside and to the right of Jamie's door. Other than that, Jamie's floor was empty and quiet as a tomb. Not even the stair door was closing this time.

When I closed and re-locked the twenty locks the front door had and turned to go back inside Jamie's apartment, Jamie was saying something, probably uncomplimentary, and probably appropriate and cutting, but I couldn't hear it. I couldn't hear a thing. The rumbling had started again, the rumbling that was always going on in his apartment. Jamie said is was the A.C. I suddenly realized precisely what that was the sound of. It was the sound of something heavy, a heavy thing, repeatedly rolling. It was a heavy thing moving across and down a long, wooden floor. Yeah, maybe like a wooden lane. Yeah, maybe, like a heavy bowling ball. Exactly like an angry, uncoordinated bowler throwing the odd ball over and over again down a lane to work off steam.

And it was loud.

And it just went on and on and on.

The evening went downhill from there, if that were possible.

Early the next morning I was weakly nursing my second double-espresso. Lee had made it for me. I was whining and whimpering in his book shop. I hadn't slept a wink last night. Jamie threw me out about a half hour after I'd arrived. I'd stayed up all night thinking. This wasn't like me. What was happening to me? I didn't know if Jamie was ever going to see me again. I didn't know what I was going to do. What's worse, I'd completely forgotten Rita when I left. And I'd left my California State San Diego hoody there too. How would I ever get her, my sweatshirt and Jamie back, all at the same time? Why did these things always have to happen to me? Why to me? Always to me? Why? Why?

Oh, and I'd forgotten to call Darrell.

Lee had to tell me his name. I couldn't remember it.

What the fuck was happening to my life?

"I don't know what I'm going to do if I can't see Jamie again" I whispered to Lee, sipping and blowing on my tiny, boiling-hot thimble of coffee. "It feels as if he's stolen a piece of my soul, run off with my very essence, and I want it back. What I need is a good plan." I liked the soul and essence shit. It made it all sound deep and spiritual somehow.

"I wonder what Darrell would suggest?" Lee's voice floated back over one of the walls of neatly mounded books in front of me. I pushed and pushed the nearest mound with the side of my very-hot cup until I watched it collapse in a satisfying cloud of paper and bindings onto the floor on the other side of the cashier stand beside Lee. I heard a sigh.

"Just go and see this Jamie guy. Go and get it over with." I could hear Lee pushing the fallen books into a new floor pile with his feet and stool as he talked to me. "If you don't think about it too much, you'll just take care of it." I could hear him moving something heavy onto the counter behind him. "You'll fix it. You'll do it. You'll see. You always do." Lee starting searching for something, loudly, bumping his chair against the wall, against the books, cursing expansively when he caught his hand between the counter and his stool. Lee just didn't understand. Lee couldn't understand. Lee wasn't in love.

Peeking through the new fissure in the book pile barrier in front of me, I could just see, barely, if I poked my head through the gap, (which I did) that Lee had started sorting his way through a new box of books he'd just purchased ten minutes before from that thin, argumentative girl in cowboy boots who'd so effectively interrupted and ruined my first thimble-ful of espresso.

I wiggled my eyebrows at him. Made a sad puppy face.

Sometimes Lee let me help him do the sorting, although he always reserved for himself the last word on categorization – he had the executive veto to my legislative proposal.

He looked over at me. Looked at the box. Sighed. Looked at the ceiling for a second. Then I saw him shrug.

He flashed a book on saddles at me and my sleep-deprived face and I said "Sexual Aids and Adult Toys." He didn't blink. He didn't bat an eyelash. The book moved to some obscure pile, in a long line of piles, to the back and left of him.

He flashed a self-help, self-acupuncture book at me and motioned with his eyes – should it go in the overflowing health/medical stack or should he place it in the anemic philosophy stack instead? "Put it in Sports" I said, looking forlornly out the plate glass window hoping to see Jamie walk by. Guys walked past, but none were my Jamie. I was uninterested. I was hopeless.

"You know, some people wouldn't call that helping" said Lee.

"You're right, you're not" I said.

I heard him call out to me as I pushed open the double front doors of Lee's shop and hit the sidewalk "Hey, I'm just trying to get your mind off of it, man, there's no talking to you when you get in these moods, you know, I only..."

But I didn't hear the rest. The doors closed. The windows were double glazed. I could see his lips moving, but that was all. I stumbled down the cracked sidewalk. I walked for an hour or two. I found myself walking towards Jamie's place.

It was a Saturday, he might be there. I went and buzzed his apartment. I swear over the loudspeaker I heard "How much is that doggie in the window" playing distorted in the background. At any rate, the buzzer sounded and I was too impatient to wait for the elevator so I hoofed it up to the top floor and went to open the door (the door from the stairwell to the hallway) and almost toppled backwards.

The door opened up in my face and a stocky guy wearing a kind of retro outfit with brightly-colored shoes and "Joe" embroidered over his left pec was staring me down. He had wavy black hair, with a little too much gel for my taste, and a rugged chin and brown eyes that weren't smiling at me. In fact, I mentally prepared my face to be punched in. Sometime in the very near future.

"You spending time with Jamie?" he said, still pushing on the stairs door, and still standing in my way. There was a turquoise and red anvil-shaped bag on the floor beside him. I definitely could hear Doris Day singing in a tinny voice in the background, over a bad set of loudspeakers. And the rumbling was deafening today. Was that cheering going on? The light looked dimmer somehow and faint. A kind of unconvincing twilight. Even I could tell something wasn't right.

"Where's Jamie?" I said, ducking under his substantial arm to see the hallway behind him. He moved, blocking me so I couldn't see. I dodged the other way around and he moved just as quickly. He was fast on his feet, nimble as a cat.

"Jamie don't want to see you", said Joe. "Can't you unnerstan' that? Go home. Go." I went for the hinge-side of the door and when Joe shifted his bulk to one side again to stop me, I rolled over his feet, propelling myself against the door jamb on the other side and painfully bouncing out onto the hallway floor, successfully bludgeoning my head on the wood flooring and skidding backwards to a stop.

Only it wasn't wood flooring. Not anymore, it was garish yellow and green linoleum squares. Joe had turned around and now I was staring at those bright leather shoes, only in close-up this time.

"That was a mistake, mister." Joe said and started to move towards me, cautiously, balancing a little on the balls of his feet. I pushed backwards, did a back somersault (did I mention I lettered in gymnastics?) and ran. Straight into the bowling alley.

Over the sound of pins cracking and balls careening and random laughter I somehow managed to hear heavy footfalls following close behind me. The bowling alley was small, and it ended in a blank, concrete wall with some kind of space-age angular design pressed into the cement. It looked like it was going to take off. It said Turquoise Twilight Room in pink cursive neon writing and there was a blue neon spaceship and a huge white neon moon with craters hanging over a circular door which looked as if it opened into a bar. At least I could see a lot of red leather (or red leatherette) inside, and cold, blue-back lighting. Yeah, and over the bar there were a few porthole windows near the ceiling which showed only a flat black beyond their glass. Really flat. Really empty. Really black. And some raindrops dripping down onto the glass. But I didn't see any outside doors.

I skidded to a stop - nothing lay in front of me except another glass wall opening onto pitch black outside, with water spitting up on the windows from time to time. It looked like a storm. Or it could have been waves. Maybe ocean waves. How can you tell when there's no light? You can't. You can't tell.

But the more I looked, the more it didn't seem like rain. The drops were spraying up, man, fucking up. That was ocean outside there. It was foaming and clawing at the windows. It wanted to get inside. It was looking for something. Or someone.

Great.

At any rate I had nowhere to go. A dead end. I pivoted on my right foot to twist and reverse direction, and Joe was on me in a second. I looked everywhere, but the only thing that had the look of an exterior window or exit or door of any kind in this place was the door I'd come in at. The stairs door. The one I could barely see with the (yes! Salvation at last) beckoning exit sign gleaming redly - far, far away - in its shadowy, distant corner.

Then suddenly I could see it better. I could see everything better. And I found out why. Quickly.

Joe had picked me up by the scruff of my shirt as if I were a stray alley cat - one he wanted to drown. I was hanging now two feet off the floor. "Hey, what's the idea?" said Joe pushing me against the wall with the rocket spouting its blue electric flame above my head and the moon going through its same four white electric phases off to my right. Over and over and over again. I felt dizzy watching it.

I tried to find something else to look at. Joe's face pretty much took up the center of my range of vision. He was looking at me almost thoughtfully. "You're not wanted, you hear?" he hissed into my face, but he sounded less and less convinced. "Not wanted", he repeated flat without intonation.

I had to get out of there. I tried to catch someone's eyes. I looked for help. But no one else in the bowling alley had even noticed me or Joe arriving, let alone observed our racing or our wrestling or our intense conversations. Families, and dates, teams and couples, looking for all the world as if they were extras on a set for "Happy Days", talked loudly over the cheerful cannonade of diligent bowling bombarding them from every side. Everyone was having a great time. Everyone but me. I'm not much of a bowler, I guess. I wasn't having a great time. I had a headache. I couldn't hear myself think. I was suspended a couple of feet off of the floor from my shirt.

A familiar torso and a way of holding his head at an angle while he lined up his ball-throwing hand to the pins, they caught my eye. There was something odd about the guy bowling at the far end of the alley. Joe shook me a little and said "You listening to me, kid?" But I kept watching that guy. I'd seen him before. When the mystery bowler jogged his three quick steps prior to his throw, it came to me. That was a well-known set of shoulders. And a well-known butt. That was Jamie.

And just then, Jamie looked over his shoulder at me, but I could tell it wasn't my eyes he was searching for, not my attention he wanted. He wanted Joe's.

Something snapped. I let it. I let Jamie go (right! - as if I had had a choice - but I pretended it was my choice). All of a sudden Jamie wasn't so urgent to me. Seeing Joe and Jamie together, well, it changed things. I can be so fickle, I know. Joe, on the other hand interested me more and more. Why was Jamie so fascinated with him? What made Joe so much more interesting than me? Maybe I wanted to know. Maybe I would know. I stopped looking over at Jamie. I started smiling down at Joe. Joe looked back, an undecipherable expression on his broad face.

Joe shook me some more, but I could tell he was losing interest. Maybe it was my sudden friendliness, my unsatisfying, limp, un-fighting body, maybe my puzzling grinning, but Joe suddenly let me go. "Get" he said, but he didn't sound like he meant it. Was he peering at me? Was that the rudiments of a smile starting up on his face? The more time I spent today around Joe's longshoreman's physique, the less I wanted to run away from his manhandling. Joe obviously had his points. Like I said, I'm hopeless. Joe patted me on the back, more gently than I expected, and he pushed me, unmistakably, in the direction of the stairwell door.

A week and a half later, no moon out tonight, dark, Lee's shop was unlit, empty, and shuttered as I wandered past. It was a Thursday night. Maybe, what? 11 PM? maybe earlier, maybe later. I don't really know. People were starting their weekends early. Lee and I had been texting for days about getting together, maybe having a beer, but I'd always been late arriving, although always full of excuses. This time I was determined. This time I'd do it. And here I was again, too late. Hours too late.

"So, you and lover-boy are taking a break now, huh?" echoed a voice from a dim, overhung niche at the end of the Lee's building.

It housed a bar, such as it was, packed with guys, with a small outdoor patio in front, and a large-ish dance floor in the back. I knew the voice. I knew the bar.

"And you think you have some time to waste, so, naturally you think of your long-suffering friends." I sidled over towards the sarcastic shadow, and hopped the railing. Nobody said anything. The bouncers didn't notice. The voice continued "Yeah, get your sorry ass over here and buy me a Heineken, starry eyes. I'm thirsty."

I did as I was told.

"You're what?", said Lee grimacing, setting his bottle back on a ledge in the bar's railing and yelling a little to be heard over the steady thump, thump of club music playing over about a dozen speakers placed every two feet in every direction. The music was strange, foreign to me. Lately, if it hadn't been a hit during the Eisenhower administration, I hadn't been listening to it. Joe liked the golden oldies. He really liked them. I mean, really. He got mad if... Lee bawled something at me. I shook my head at him. He tried again.

"Who's this Joe guy?"

I leaned my ear into his mouth and made signs for him to repeat himself. This was going to be a long conversation. But that was O.K. as long as it wasn't too long. I'm finding I want to spend less and less time away from Joe, the more I go back to the Twilight Turquoise room. And I go back pretty often. I'm probably there more than I'm not there. I must have been daydreaming again, because Lee was yelling into my ear.

"What's happening to you, guy? Where's your head at?"

He was frowning at me when I pulled back to see what his face looked like, it was all wrinkled up in worried, unhappy lines, it really wasn't very becoming for Lee. I started to tell him that. It made him look old – like a guy in his thirties – if he didn't watch out...

Lee interrupted me. "I am worried about you. Are you listening to me? I. Am. Worried. About. You."

He was probably worried about how thin I was getting. It was true. I was thin. I would even admit that I was maybe a tad too thin, maybe beyond svelte at this point. But I'd needed to lose a few pounds. The thing of it is, I just kept forgetting to eat. It was just so hard to remember sometimes. Besides, Joe said I looked great. What a guy, that Joe! What a find! My luck was finally starting to change!

Lee's face blurred back into view and I realized he was waiting for something. He was looking at me with that concerned look he gets when he's really, well, concerned would be the word for it. Lee was waiting. For me. I couldn't remember the question exactly. Had there been a question? To me? What were we talking about?

So. Probably a nod would be in order. So I nodded. He nodded back, raising his eyebrows at me. I nodded a little more slowly that I understood, or at least that I thought I understood. Man! It was just a lot easier talking to Joe. He knew what I was going to say even before I got the chance to say it out loud. In fact, we really didn't talk all that much. Yeah, we really didn't talk at all. Not like at the beginning. But that's what I liked about him. Joe was easy to be with. Real easy.

Lee was scouring my face still, as if he were trying to find signs of some reaction to what he was saying to me, and starting to look desperate. But he didn't need to worry. Really. I was fine. I was great. I was better than fine.

Lee motioned rapidly with his fingers to show he wanted to go back to yelling in my ear "When was the last time you were home?" He leaned back, watched my face with a kind of sick hopelessness and I'm sure I shrugged. I'm sure of it. Why was he getting so emotional? I was listening. I was reacting, right? A shrug is a reaction.

We got up. We slunk and squeezed through laughing men, trying to keep our beers vertical. Lee tried to talk to me, I'm pretty sure. And I tried to listen. Lots of words were expressed. But dance bars require a lot of bobbing and weaving, and there's the alcohol, and you never know if the person you're talking to is understanding what you're trying to say. Basically you're left with non-verbal communications – wandering hands, lingering glances, pressing your thigh against theirs, you know, the whole bit. It's hard to mistake that. Words are a different story. They're plentiful, cheap, and easily forgotten. Besides, when does anybody really understand anybody else? How could they? When does anybody really listen? Talking is overrated. I mean, look at me and Joe.

But Lee wouldn't let up. I let him talk at me. It made him feel good.

"...and I think you should let this thing that you and Joe have going, well, let it rest for a while, man. Give it a break, O.K?"

Lee was still talking about something, and still doing his searching, looking thing, only he stopped, and pulled back and there it was – I could see all of his anxiety and all of his sincerity – it was sweating plainly out of every pore of his face. I could see he'd stopped even pretending to drink his beer a long time ago. He was working up to something. I could tell. Well, I didn't need to leave right away. I had a minute or so to spare. I could wait. I could listen.

"Come over and spend the night with me, huh? Like the good old days. What do you say?"

He was serious. It was touching. But, of course, it was impossible. Joe was expecting me in just a few minutes, we had an appointment. In fact, you know, actually, I was probably already late. If appointment and late meant anything where I was going. I smiled at Lee in response and he was baffled. Oh well. I melted backwards into the bar crowd, disappeared into the bouncing, gyrating boys around me and that was the last time I saw Lee.

I used to hear Darrell or Lee's voice over the music and the sound of bowling balls being thrown about. Sometimes. It was distant - they were calling out my name. At least I thought I did. But you never know for sure. It hasn't happened for a long, long time now, and I don't really hear them anymore. I also think I may have glimpsed Jamie once or twice bowling and looking my way on one of the lanes close to the exit sign. It's possible. Maybe. But that was just at the very beginning. That was when Joe and I were just getting to know each other. That doesn't happen anymore either. I took care of that. Jamie had a little accident in the stairwell. After he got back from the hospital, well, Jamie moved away. Now no one comes in the stairwell. Now it's just me and Joe. Joe and me. A two-man team. Bowling our fool heads off. Having the times of our lives. Just the two of us.

No one comes between us. No one.

No one.

You hear me? Wise guy?

Yeah, I thought you did.

So, who are you exactly?

And why do you need to use the stairs?

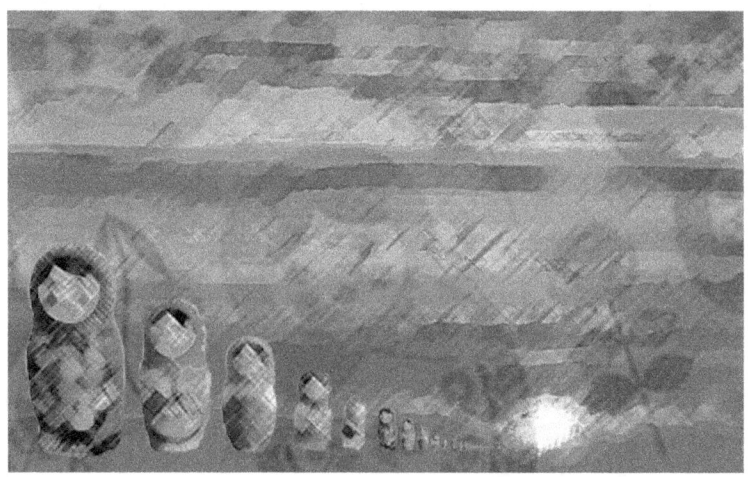

BABUSHKAS

Mia first noticed it on Monday morning. Early. Too early, in fact.

She'd been leaning backwards on her elbows, casually balancing on a balustrade on a balcony (that was odd, that was something Mia never did, Mia hated heights, not to mention balconies), she'd been laughing at something Ruffi had said. It looked like it was maybe the covered walkway leading up to the front door of her condo way up on the third floor, but then again, it might not have been, it looked changed somehow, tilted, twisted, the wrong colors and the wrong textures, too long, or too short, just wrong.

Ruffi had just started to ask Mia a question, when she interrupted herself and pointed over Mia's shoulder "Look at them. What fools. What idiots." Mia turned her neck and glanced sideways out of the sides of her eyes over her shoulder and squinted into the dimly-lit distance following Ruffi's finger.

The horizon was a patchwork of clouds, gangrenous oranges and greens, shot through with vivid infectious reds, the sun lost from sight except as a vaguely brighter blur of scabby tangerine, hanging low, very low in the sky. The ground was a rusty red color, in fact it was the color of dried blood, and was broken into a series of jagged termite mounds pointing obscenely up at the oozing sky, alternating with suspicious round depressions filled with rocky sand. The strangest thing was the soldiers.

A block of them, five rows wide, three deep, with one in front and one in back marched forward, guns at their shoulders, pointed in every direction outwards. The one in front kept pushing the butt of his gun into the soil. He'd push, wait, then motion the mass forward and then order them to a stop, then he'd poke some more. Mia was terrified. Something horrible was going to happen. She looked over at Ruffi's face and saw her turn away with a shake of her head and a sigh of disgust. That's when she noticed Ruffi's head was bleeding.

There was the loud sound of a bell and the men stopped and then it happened. A sudden, vicious clacking sound came out of nowhere. The ground burst open at the soldiers' feet and clouds of white, pudgy cylinders boiled upwards, stripping the men to bones, then consuming even those and stopping their screams almost before they'd started. In a moment, even the uniforms were gone, and it was quiet again. Many men still stood. Of the others, all that was left were sticky, red stains and pools, littering the ground here and there. And new shallow depressions.

Mia froze, tried to scream but no sound came out, reached for Ruffi's hand, but no hand was there. She stumbled backwards and finally ran into her. Ruffi was standing with her back to her, arms crossed in front of her, shaking her head and muttering "Stupid, just stupid. It's their own fault". Mia heard the bell sound again and looked back over the railing. The remaining men had fallen into a group of four rows by three with only one man in front, just at the point of pushing his rifle into the ground with one hand up signaling them to stop. Again, the white mass surging upwards, through the rich, red mud, and now there were three rows by three with two in front. Mia grabbed hold of the back of both of Ruffi's shoulders, shaking her and babbling "Make them stop, Ruffi. Do something. Ruffi, Stop them."

Ruffi was whispering to the wall in front of her, holding her hand up to her head to stop the bleeding, although it wasn't working very well "They brought it on themselves. They're on their own now" and Mia heard the bell ringing again and wouldn't look.

And then it rang again. And again. And again. And again. It seemed like it would never stop. The same almost-screams, the same almost-clicking, almost-whooshing sound. The same sickening, liquid sounds of moist things falling off onto dry ground. And then it was quiet. She took her hands off of Ruffi's shoulder and shaking, waited some more. Then she looked back.

She was holding a rifle. Her uniform was covered in streaks of red and mud. She was standing on wet, red sand. The sun came out from behind the clouds. It was as red as a puncture in a blood vessel, and a flood of white light hit her directly in her face, blinding her. When her eyes worked again, Mia could clearly see that only one man was standing next to her, only one man was left, only one man looked back at her, and he was motioning with his eyes, desperately wanting her to poke her gun down into the black-red dust and desperately wanting the two of them to move forward, when she heard the ringing again, and he was gone, and then the ringing and she felt the ground begin to open up under her feet as excited, smug clicking sounds filled her ears and she saw her legs begin to evaporate in a red mist as she fell to the ground, spinning, collapsing, falling, always falling, always falling.

The phone was ringing. With a groan, she rolled over onto her side, kicking the afghan twisted around her legs away from her feet, stretching and rolling her ankles around, clockwise, then counter-clockwise to get some feeling back into them and generally wriggled about this way and that. Her legs were swelling up again. Well, what else was new? In the process, she heard her knees creaking in a familiar but sore-and-stinging kind of way – today would not be a day for a lot of walking and bending, she could tell that already - and opened one eye painfully and deliberately onto her corner window.

The phone stopped ringing. The silence was irritating. Mia was irritated. She felt expectant, not in a good way, she was waiting and expecting for something to happen. Waiting for a sound to start up. What sound? An abrasive echo, or an infuriating clicking sound, someone snapping their fingers, someone clucking their tongue - why was she stuck on that? She felt edgy and nervous, but she hadn't drank too many cups of coffee today, Mia hadn't drank anything at all today. How could she? She'd just woken up.

What a day she was going to have, if this is how she started her morning the moment her eyes opened.

She was in the living room. She'd fallen asleep on the couch again, She did it sometimes because it helped her lower back when she slept sitting up, but the funny squinching necessary to get comfortable played hell with rest of her lower body. It was always something. If not one thing, then another. But that's not what had awakened her so suddenly out of her not-so-dreamless sleep.

What? What had she been thinking about? Dreaming about? The light in here was crazy, psychedelic, intense. She quickly closed her one open eye again and squeezed it shut. There. That was better, wasn't it? Yes, better. Then she cautiously re-opened it.

Square in front of her was a solid wall of militantly joyous illumination, a window of sunlight of biblical intensity, as loudly attention-grabbing as three-foot woofers experienced from the front row of a rock concert and maybe even more relentless.

Sun? What was sun doing in her living room? She never had sun in her living room. She never had sun, period. That's what curtains were for. She always closed her house up tight, clean, sealed, quiet, and safe. She would never open it up. Never. Besides this was beyond sun. This was having a supernova for an alarm clock. Mia was not pleased. The sometimes boring, but always predictable and steady rhythm of her life was being interrupted, invaded even. It felt as if it were an intervention. It probably was. Mia was not pleased at all.

The phone started ringing again, Mia jumped. She closed her eyes tighter. Both of them this time. Who was calling? Why were they bothering her?

She groaned extravagantly. Only the four walls surrounding her witnessed it. She was alone, yes. She was lonely, she was afraid, yes and yes again. The fear was an old companion to her now. And lonely and alone often weren't always the same thing, but in her case they usually were. She would admit to that. She wasn't about to start lying to herself, not at this point in the game.

But she liked things the way they were. It was all hers – her loneliness, her aloneness, her fear. She could make whatever life she wanted and whatever sounds she wanted too. No one could tell her to please stop it Mia just stop for God's sake, for once. No one did that. No one. She made an experimental moaning noise again, loud and long, and listened to the broad silence above her envelop and extinguish it afterwards. Then there was only quiet. Peace and quiet. No one here. Just us Mias.

The groaning experiment made her uneasy though and a little queasy. She could feel something at the back of her head, something vague - bloody and yelling. Where was that coming from? It felt like a new kind of headache. What dust-clogged, age-begrimed basement in her subconscious had overflowed and let that out? Clicking? Clacking? Clucking? She didn't want to think about any of it. No more thinking, no more groaning, not this morning.

The phone started ringing again.

She noticed uneasily that her breathing was rapid and shallow. Five minutes awake and she was panicking. She needed to relax and forget. But now she wasn't sure she wanted to go back to sleep either. Now something was waiting for her, just on the other side of sleep, something patient, and not particularly nice. That's it. That's what it felt like. When would the damn phone ever stop ringing?

The phone stopped ringing.

Huh! Guess that serve went to Mia.

But still, way too early to wake up and way too late to sleep. Mia was trapped. Mia was irritated. She was trapped, irritated and confused. It wasn't a good feeling. She started to rattle off the value of Pi in her head, trying to clear out all this angst with something crystalline and familiar and tidy – if an irrational number could be called tidy – and her breathing calmed down as she got twenty or so digits in. Better. She ticked off twenty more in her head. Better and better. That usually helped. That usually did the trick. Well, maybe she could sleep now.

She gripped the unraveling corners of her afghan, pulled and stretched and yanked it over her head with stiff, uncooperative fingers and lay perfectly still. However, this tactic pulled the covers completely off her legs. Unconsciously, she pushed her stiff knees straight outwards a couple of times in a movement she recognized as a swimmer's kick – a behavior left over from her youth, when her tendons had been elastic and her joints supple and her immune system actually defended her instead of doing what it did now – attack her and eat her alive – as if her whole body were a disease.

Mia was making the ancient, barely-remembered motion to push her way back down and under the surface of the water, and in this case, back down and under the layer of covers and deep under the surface of a mindless sleep – but, as in other areas of her life,

Mia was finding reflexive behaviors weren't always the best of solutions. Reflexes were not her friend. Not anymore.

In sum - it wasn't doing much good, to tell the truth.

Mia needed something else.

Her uncovered feet started to get cold. She obstinately continued to stay still, willing herself by brute psychic force into an aimless drift towards drowsiness. Sleep, Mia, sleep, you're floating, nothing's happening, you can't concentrate, it's all going hazy, everything's blurred, sleep, sleep, sleep, sleep, sleep.

Sleep.

The afghan was making her nose itch again.

Sleep.

She remembered the making of this afghan, just this last year.

Or was it two years ago now? Could it be three? That long? Well, in any case it had taken her months to do it, since it had been her first time crocheting. Getting and keeping the various stitches tight and even, making sure that... well, let's just say it was much harder than it looked. And it took time. Lots of time. But she'd persevered. She'd learned to crochet. All by herself. But she'd been a different person then. A whole person, not just a piece of a person. She'd been the old Mia Esposito. The Mia without a raging case of Lupus. The Mia who's body wasn't attacking itself, who wasn't constantly teetering on the edge of general poor health about to tip over into haphazard degeneration ending in a nasty freefall of random organ failures.

The phone started to ring, then stopped, abruptly, as if someone had pulled the cord right out of the wall. Mia contemplated peeking out and seeing if someone had destroyed her land line, but reminded herself she was trying to nod off. Sleep, Mia, just sleep. This wasn't coming very easy.

Crocheting. She'd been surprised. She'd thought of crocheting as a hobby. Busywork. That was something to keep your hands busy. Her mother had done it, crocheting. She'd seen her grandmother doing it too. It was something you did in the odd free moment during a kid-and-husband-filled day. She, of course, had had another reason for doing it. A serious purpose. A special Mia purpose. She winced remembering her former life teaching mathematics to the bored and coerced at Community College. How energetic she'd been! How purposeful and optimistic!

Now look at her. And to think she'd originally taken it up to try

318

and crochet abstract geometrical solids like hyperbolic pseudospheres. She'd been wildly enthusiastic. Soft, indestructible teaching aids. She wondered now how anyone had put up with her. If Mia today had met old Mia, she wouldn't even have given her the time of day. What a waste – thinking that teaching mattered so much, thinking that people mattered at all. It was better being alone. She'd yelled at all her friends until they stopped coming and seeing about her. It had taken a while, but she'd managed it. They'd stopped. Even Ruffi. She was safe. Safe and alone. And her house was closed and sealed. Her life was as simple as she could make it. She needed simple like other people needed oxygen. And she'd gotten it. Mia usually got what she wanted.

She remembered when people had asked what she was creating she'd said "a lovely seven syllable phrase softly expressed in brightly colored yarn." Well. What could you say to someone who talked like that? Nothing. Hopeless. How could a person like that cope with the situation she was in now? The answer was, of course, that she wouldn't. She wouldn't and she couldn't. That person had had to die. A hard choice, but well, life was hard, wasn't it? Hard and unfair. She'd been a different person back then. Very different.

Well, maybe not so different. But weaker definitely. And pathetically needy. And still relying on people. And not relying on herself. But now she was better. She was stronger. She was wiser. Wasn't she? Sometimes she didn't know. Honestly, sometimes she just didn't know anymore.

Geometric solids, huh? She smiled to herself under her covers. She was funny that way. She liked being unexpected. She liked being unpredictable. She was a little proud of it. It made her confident when she saw she had the power to surprise others. That was the past, though. That was long ago. No more surprises from Mia anymore. No more energy for surprises.

Her best friend, well, her ex-best friend, on the other hand, had said Mia was trying to knit a pseudo-refrigerator. Then she'd laugh. What could a person do with that? What could you say? It was just like Ruffi not to know the difference between knitting and crocheting, let alone anything about pseudospheres, or geometry even.

Ruffi hadn't ever seriously interested herself in what Mia was doing, what Mia was about, not really. And then to say that. Well, Mia hadn't dignified that comment with a response. Of course that was back when she and Ruffi were still talking to each other. They'd talked almost every day. No more. And Mia had never told Ruffi that the abstract solid had ended up after months of effort turning into a lumpy blanket. No, Mia hadn't ever mentioned crocheting again. Ruffi would have had a field day with that one. Boy would she ever.

The phone started ringing again. Mia wished she could turn the phone into a lump of puddled, steaming plastic by thought alone. She tried beaming the necessary mental energy out from under the afghan over to the phone stand and at the chrome and black and white device yodeling its pseudo-ring so loudly into her morning. She beamed and beamed. It rang and rang. This was obviously not one of her talents. She'd never make it as a psychic headliner in a show on the Vegas strip.

You know, if Mia concentrated, right this minute, she could clearly identify what part of the afghan's pattern was pressing against her forehead and what part of it was laying against her forearm by the touch of the stitches alone. The half-born pseudosphere was still clear and present in her mind. She was lying in it. Mia stopped herself, inhaled deeply, exhaled, and tried to clear her head. She heard a scrunching sound, like a rifle butt twisting and grinding down into gravelly dust, and the sound of many feet moving restlessly and uneasily. She didn't like that sound.

The yarn was scratching her upper lip and her nose. All the time now. She was going to sneeze. This was not dozing. She wasn't even slightly drowsy now. She could do square roots in her head at this point and not even break a sweat. What was the square root of 1,577,851? Lets' see... No. Stop it. This was not sleep. This was awake. Wide awake. Face it, Mia, it just wasn't working.

She opened one eye again. All she'd managed to do with her couch acrobatics was knock her living room around a bit. Bills, magazines, tea-stained notes with phone numbers and names scrawled at odd angles, unopened correspondence from banks and credit cards, and torn notices still stuck in their ominously impersonal envelopes from the State Employment Development Department (notifying her of the exhaustion of her State Disability Insurance benefits) had morphed from a somewhat untidy pile on the table next to the T.V. remote to a demonstrably very untidy explosion of paper on her mostly clean living room carpet.

She couldn't deal with this. The phone. The Disability. Up went the afghan again over her head. Mia sighed to herself, from deep inside her warm, yarny cocoon. No, no matter what she did, the morning wasn't going to go away. She poked her head further outside and took in a deep breath.

The phone stopped ringing again, but gracefully this time, and she could see across the room that she had a couple of messages blinking their exasperated Morse code across the room straight into her afghan – "listen to me, listen to me" – Mia looked away.

Why were the blinds up? That was something she never, ever allowed to happen, her house was hermetically sealed at night – in this her house resembled the leftovers she wrapped in foil and cellophane and dated and set safely in orderly rows in her freezer to be available for her future use and comfort. Everything was wrapped up tight. She was responsible. Or she had been. She made good decisions. Mostly that is, as much as anyone, really. She made sure she got things done right. Yes, that she did almost always.

And letting people see her sleep was not one of them.

The thing of it was, Mia was a private person. And a self-contained one, everyone knew that, or they ought to by now. She kept to herself. And she watched out for herself. She looked out for number one. No one else was going to do it for her - she'd learned that the hard way, and once Mia learned something she learned it for good, you'd better be sure of that. The thing was, you had to love yourself first. Take care of yourself first. Mia did that. She also didn't bother other people. And she didn't expect to be bothered by others. Couldn't people just leave each other and Mia alone and watch out for themselves, really was it so much to ask?

Whatever happened to respect? Whatever happened to privacy? What?

Blah, blah, blah, blah, blah. Mia's internal tirade – which was an old one for her, of such ancient pedigree she almost didn't hear herself thinking it anymore - it just ran on and on in the background of her mind, all day long, looping on a track set and forgotten, stuck on continuous play. Blah, blah, blah, blah, blah.

Well, this time, the tirade gradually wound down, eroded away by wave upon wave of morning sunshine beating down through her irises onto her retinas. It was enervating. It was embarrassing. It was dangerous. She felt transfixed and unusually helpless, a delicate butterfly pierced on sharp beams of light pouring through that naked window, a butterfly pinned and ready for the chloroform.

This was not normal sunlight.

For one, it would not let her alone.

And two, it was green.

It was as bright a light as if someone had set an emerald on fire, no, as if a pile of emeralds were blazing away merrily, and the man with the flame thrower was still enthusiastically ladling it on, thickly and generously, over everything in sight. Outside the window, layers on layers of phosphorescing stem, leaf, branch and twig piled deeply one upon the other. She squinted her eyes at it. But she couldn't make out what she was looking at exactly. There had to be a pattern. But it just wouldn't come, she just couldn't see it. And she couldn't turn away, either. It drew her out. But she didn't want to come out. She didn't want to go anywhere. How had she not ever noticed this before? This neon vegetable circus? Right outside her window?

The different shades of green were what astounded Mia, the dazzling variations, the well-thought out combinations. It made her nose itch and her ears twitch with the smells of loamy under-soil and crisp sap-filled leaves, with the remembered reflections of water twinkling black-green and green-white on the underside of bushes and of sunlight half-seen through translucent stalks of greenish-blue. She could taste the light, it was that heavy, that sodden.

She expected the utter greenness of it all to drip and glop, puddling a chlorophyll stream right onto the worn fabric of her beige carpet. It would stain the blunt steel heads of the carpet nails showing through under the corner window. And it would soak downwards, thoroughly, to color in a permanent green, the old waxed and rutted floorboards hiding underneath every room in Mia's off-white apartment. Floorboards which had been concealed, of course, and decently concealed, for years under frayed matting and a ridiculously expensive white Berber rayon.

Yes, Mia had carpet. Ruffi had been astounded. Ruffi distrusted rugs you couldn't beat or wash. But Mia had been resolute, immovable, unbendable. Mia had finally decided to go wall to wall and hang up her waxing mop forever, and had never regretted it, not once. No matter what Ruffi hinted at or intimated. She was proud of her carpet decision.

Goodness, that was a long time back, a long, long time ago.

Other people had lived and argued in this apartment then.

Another Mia. Another Ruffi.

Sleep. Just try and sleep.

The light, though, the light was insistent. It was incandescent. It wouldn't let her alone, wouldn't let her think. She wondered if it kept up this way, all the way through till nightfall, how she'd ever sleep again, how could anyone ever get to sleep with so much light? So much? She blinked and her eyes started to water. It was so bright.

She realized her eyes were gummy and a little irritated (from sleep? - what sleep?) so she pulled her hands out of the warmth of her blanket and did a thorough rub-down of each eye with her slim hands balled up into poor simulacrums of fists, knuckles swollen and irritated, yes, but still perfectly capable of serving satisfactorily as eye-cleaners, as long as Mia was careful. She felt she was a little girl again, waking up in her bedroom at home, listening for the sound of her mommy making breakfast downstairs, hearing her mom's clear soprano voice calling up for little Mia to hurry and get herself dressed. But Mia wasn't back home, was she?. She was here. In the condo. And it was still bright, very bright, and green, even through her fingers.

And then it wasn't. Then it was just her living room window and just her view of, what? A window that looked out onto the open air, three stories above a patio, onto a bottomless, cloudless and anonymous Southern Californian sky. There were a few distant palm trees. Other than that, it was just another normal Mia morning of another normal Mia day. The jungle was gone.

Mia cautiously pushed herself up and made her limping way to the bathroom, half expecting, for some reason, troops of flying monkeys to drop out of the kitchen ceiling or squads of sad, doomed marines to overtake her down her long walk down the back hallway on the way to the shower. Her imagination hadn't been running away with her like this for years.

She didn't realize until later that day, that she'd forgotten to draw the curtains back across that corner window again. And even then, after she had thought the whole window situation over very thoroughly, she didn't go over and close it up tight like it had been before, like it had been for years. She let it be. She left it wide open. Mia realized with surprise that she didn't want to close her condo up again, and lock it down. Or at least not all of it.

What was happening to her? She was slipping. Her discipline

was breaking down. This was how it started. She was sliding off the edge. Off the edge and into that long fall that wouldn't end with her being healthy and happy, but end with her living in a nursing home and then being six feet under.

No. People in her situation couldn't lose their discipline. No. They couldn't get careless. No. They always had to be on their guard - watching, adjusting, compensating, attacking, strategically retreating, planning, adjusting, retreating, adjusting.

A life of Lupus was a life of battle

If you wanted to win, you had to be disciplined. Without fail. Without a break. Mia wanted to win.

And those that didn't want to win, well, they disappeared.

No. This would not be happening to Mia. She would not disappear. She needed to get a hold of herself. Who knows what would happen next, what else she would stop doing? Stop taking her pills? Stop bathing? Stop eating? No.

She tried to get upset, but for some reason it just wouldn't happen this time, she just couldn't take it seriously, she couldn't work herself up into a flustered mess and go and close those damned corner window blinds. She was crying. But she wouldn't do it.

O.K. All right. Calm down. Calm. Think. One window open to the light, really, what was the worst that could happen, Mia? How bad could it get?

If you haven't figured it out by now, you will soon - Mia had a longstanding love-affair with numbers. She liked them a lot. After her mother had passed away when she was still in elementary school, after she'd been sent to Aunt Edie's to live, they'd become her certain friends in an uncertain world. That and poetry. And music. And, well, lots of things, really. But it was the patterns and the rhythms, it was the waves and the cycles, that's what had gotten to her, that's what had burrowed under her skin. Touching mathematics, you felt alive and you felt you belonged. You felt you were a citizen of something much bigger than just your young self and your young friends, at least for a little while, you were a citizen of infinity. And it was a good feeling.

But numbers, well, you could always count on numbers (pun intended) and they never let you down. Mia liked the changing and shifting of them – that was algebra and calculus, and the layers of secrets you could find in imaginary numbers, and impossible numerical places you could travel to like infinitessimals and negative infinity. She even had favorites, ones that made her feel protected somehow.

What kind of numbers did she like? Well, there were all kinds. Mia liked prime numbers, special numbers (like 3 to the 3rd power, 27) and the named ones, the constants like Avogadro's number, Planck's constant, the speed of light, and of course, Pi. There was always something pure and clean about numbers. Something proud and independent. They were strong, they needed no one and nothing. They didn't get sick, they didn't die. They just were. And they didn't need anyone's permission to be that way.

But Mia could never talk about all this with anyone – no one understood, it was a secret she kept to herself and for herself alone. Back in college, Ruffi would look politely interested, stare at her face, nod at the right time, stare some more, and then ask her about a movie or school or a rock band or a boy, and the first break she got in one of Mia's breathless speeches about mathematics, she'd put on a tape of the Rolling Stones and drift away from the conversation swaying to the beat, smiling at Mia.

That had been Ruffi. Ruffi and Mia and math.

It was afternoon. Mia made a grab for the phone, thinking she ought to call Ruffi and ask her if the sun had seemed especially bright that morning, and had been on the point of dialing when she remembered that she and Ruffi weren't exactly on speaking terms anymore. Mia had refused to talk to Ruffi, well, it had been years now, years and years. Did that telephone number even work anymore?

Mia was doing that more lately. The forgetting part, that is, not the calling part. That worried Mia. She blamed it on the painkillers she had to take, and realistically, (that actually was a favorite word of Ruffi's – the word "realistically" – and Mia had gotten used to hearing it crop up a hundred times a day, often in surprisingly inappropriate situations – but Ruffi had always been a big one on realism and its many virtues and its uses), well, realistically anyways, Mia was thinking, realistically, that her forgetting was probably the drugs. It wasn't because she was getting worse, that she was progressing. No. It wasn't that the end was approaching. No. That wasn't the reason. Mia wouldn't accept that. You couldn't' make her accept that.

She didn't think it likely it was dementia or the big A-word (Alzheimers), but then again, you never could tell, could you? You never really knew. Not until it was too late. And realistically (God, Mia was missing Ruffi all of a sudden), Mia would welcome the A-word at this point. Well, not really. Knock on wood. But she wasn't having a very good month, or even a very good year this year, in fact this last decade hadn't been all that hot either.

Mia didn't want to think about all that. No, she didn't, she wouldn't. But she did. If she set her mind to it, she could worry herself into a quivering mass of hysterical Mia-jello, staring at the ceiling, going over and over the list of all the things gone or about to go wrong in her life. She could do that (and had), but no, she didn't want to. These fits of unrestrained negativity may have felt good at first, but they had a way of leaving her breathless, weak, and nauseous for a long time after. A very long time. Not the best thing. Not for Mia. Not now. Not ever, realistically.

She wanted to forget about it. About everything. But then the world has a way of piling trouble on misery (another Ruffi phrase) and Mia guessed it was just her turn to be dumped on. But she didn't have to wallow around in it, did she? No she didn't.

Her money was running out, she didn't know what she was going to do. And now this. She was losing her mind.

O.K. Mia had ended up punching some buttons anyway, and Mia's answering machine had sprung to life. She was listening to a voicemail message from the complex manager telling her to look at her front door. There were a bunch of other calls without messages on her phone, all from a single phone number. She'd never seen that number before. But then again, she usually never looked at her phone. For that matter, she never looked at her front door, either. She always talked to the grocery delivery guy through the side door, the one by the kitchen. She crossed the living room, hesitantly, quietly, cautiously.

Shaking, Mia opened the front door. She found a sloppily taped, yellowed, water-stained piece of paper with angry red capital letters emblazoned across the top affixed at an angle at eye-level on her fire-proof steel barrier to the outside world. It had a black border and an official seal on it, just so Mia wouldn't mistake it for a love note. Foreclosure Notice. What was it? Was that what she thought it was? Well, Mia, the title is pretty self-explanatory. I'd say Mia, it was a Foreclosure Notice myself.

Mia wanted to smile, she felt like she needed to smile, but smiles lately were so far away and so lost and hidden she didn't even know where to begin to look for them. She felt hollow. Gutted, a perch, waiting for the frying pan. That was Mia. She was someone else's dinner. What was happening to her? How had she ever gotten to this point? But what was more important, what had she ever done to get so much bad luck, so close together, and all at a time when she was barely feeling well enough to fall out of bed each day and hobble herself painfully towards the bathroom? What? What had she done? She'd ask anybody, the Universe even. What precisely had Mia Esposito done to deserve all this?

She didn't know if it was legal or not, but the ripping and tearing sound the paper made as it got pulled off her front door and balled up in her fist were as loud and deeply satisfying to Mia as they were short. It only lasted a moment. But what a moment! Hah! She stood by her open front door, tossing the ball of tape and dirty yellow paper back and forth from one hand to the other, breathing heavily. She couldn't catch her breath. It wouldn't come. It felt as if her lungs had shrunk to one-tenth their original size in the space of a minute. She tossed one more time, and the ball of Foreclosure Notice flew out of her hand, bounced off the walkway, over the balcony, and into the open air three stories above the courtyard her front door opened out onto. She thought she heard a splash far below. Her empty hands hung in the air, palms upward, sticking out from under her afghan she had draped around her thin shoulders.

That stopped her, but just for a moment.

She breathed in and out, in and out. In the distance she heard a siren, a fire truck or a police car start up suddenly, then get closer and closer. Were they coming for her? How fast did foreclosures happen? How old was that notice? Her heart was beating is if it wanted to jump out and find a new chest to live in, one that was more law-abiding. She should never have ripped those papers up. She should never have tossed them away. How could they know so soon that she'd broken the law? What was going to happen to her?

Calm. Calm yourself, Mia. Breathe. Calm. No, of course they weren't after you. No of course, you haven't done anything wrong. Inhale. Exhale. Mia, it's O.K.

But somehow the Foreclosure Notice made her feel unclean - she was set apart from everyone else, all the other law-abiding tenants in the condo building now. It was as if she carried some communicable failure disease that she was consciously spreading to everyone she came into contact with, causing lifelong dreams to quiver, fade and disappear, in a matter of seconds, by the hundreds, by the thousands even. She was a menace. She heard footsteps and inhaled one of her slow breaths, but forgot to exhale. They got closer, closer, closer, then distant, more distant, and even more distant. It was strange, but they sounded military, as if they were made by army boots, many army boots marching in soft gravel. Or sand. Or mud, even, red mud.

This was ridiculous. She was ridiculous. She still hadn't breathed, not properly, so she loudly forced the air out of her chest and sucked another lungful in. There. She could respirate. With the best of them. She knew how.

Only another fourteen thousand more to go today. Easy. She looked down the outside walkway of her condo building up and down to see if anyone had seen her willfully and gleefully destroying government notices in plain sight, and then huffing and puffing noisily about the walkway afterwards. No one was around. No one saw. No one ever saw Mia anymore. No one noticed her standing there. And soon she wouldn't even be standing there to be noticed. She'd be gone. She'd be foreclosed.

She scowled and bit her lip. Well, she'd wanted privacy. Now she had it. Permanent privacy. If homelessness was privacy. She felt her eyes beginning to tear up and shook her head to stop it. They weren't worth it, these evictors. Scraps of ripped and torn paper flapped by her, piteously, in a stray breeze, held by various pieces of hastily placed packing tape on her door. Guess she hadn't gotten all of it. She stared down at the end of the walkway but really wasn't seeing anything.

They must have come and gone in seconds, these evictor

persons. At three in the morning. Didn't want anyone to see them doing it. Probably snuck in the back gate like criminals. Or over the courtyard walls from the alley. Who would want a job like that? Tearing people's lives apart? Suddenly Mia felt violated, frightened, then murderously angry. All at once. It wasn't good for her. But what could she do about it? Those murderers. They killed people. They had no right. No right at all. They were animals, doing something like this to someone in the middle of the night. They were beasts.

She swung her head around toward the left and towards the right. Her eyes were filling up and overflowing and filling up again, she probably looked as if she were searching for something, but what Mia was searching for would never be found in that walkway.

She wanted a way back. Mia was searching for a way back to a life with people and purpose and hope. "Stupid" she said to herself over and over. "Stupid to want what you can't have."

She kept on looking at the cement walkway in front of her, a crazy light in her eyes, not even bothering to wipe the tears away. Let 'em look. Let 'em see what they've accomplished.

Mia didn't know what she would've done if she'd caught them at it, the evictors, the foreclosers. Another thing she didn't want to know. She stood there for quite a while, thinking, breathing, balling her thin fingers into hard almost-fists, blinking away her tears away until she felt calmer. It took a while. She pulled the afghan closer around her. She came to herself. She found she was staring at shreds of Foreclosure Notice still waving at her under the pathetic fluorescent light in the walkway over her door. The front door light stayed on even though it was full daylight. One more thing she should ask the manager about, one more thing to get fixed, but she knew she wouldn't. She should clean her door off, but she didn't have the energy to do all that scraping, not just now. She just didn't. That was just how it was. More things she couldn't do.

She closed one eye and stared out the end of the balcony walkway, out at the blue sky and the palm trees swaying in clear California air. The morning light was streaming in from the side, as loud as a windstorm, casting long black streamers of shadows. Otherwise, it was quiet. No birds, no traffic sounds. Then, her phone started ringing again. And something small and nimble breezed past her feet and scurried into the house before she could even look down.

Mia closed the door before anything else, paper or animal could make its way into her morning. No, it was afternoon, Mia. No, it's not, it's morning. Well, whichever it was, Mia wasn't going to answer the phone. Her day had been quite full enough for Mia as it was. Quite full, thank you.

She looked and looked, in the entry way, in the living room, in the kitchen, for whatever it was that had scampered over her bare feet with its own tiny feet, but Mia couldn't find anything. She must have been imagining things, she must have fallen asleep, standing up. That must be it. On one pass through the living room, down the hallway she noticed a cracked plastic grille hanging by her front door, swinging back and forth. It was fastened to the wall now by only two screws. And that started her pondering. And worrying. And wondering.

So she got to work on her intercom, got it functioning again, somewhat, so that she could buzz people into her condo complex from the front and the back gates once more. That took all the rest of her morning and a good part of her afternoon. She didn't want to do it, but she figured, well, she had to. She wanted to hear if anyone was trying to sneak in again, trying to spy on her, trying to get her to notice them, or trying to evict her. Her breathing got all short and gaspy again. It was the eviction thing that really got her going. That's why she was doing all these repairs. That was the reason. She was being forced. And she didn't like it.

She wanted to know ahead of time, this time. She wanted to know. It had been a long time since she'd felt this strongly about something. And, forewarned was forearmed. That was another Ruffi saying. Or was it hers? She couldn't remember now who had said it first. Ruffi would claim it for herself, of course, but… Well, let it be both of theirs. It could be community property, they'd hold it jointly. She was humming to herself as she worked, murmuring words out loud at random (Chelsea! Drugstore! Mr. Jimmy! Cherry! Red!), warbling in a singsong, cracking voice she hadn't heard herself use in years, and sucking on her fingers when she missed the screw head and jabbed herself with the screwdriver.

In any event, it had been years since she'd heard that buzzer go off. Years. Had to be. That in itself was not surprising, it would have been a little difficult to hear it, since, after all, she herself had cut the wires. She wasn't sure she'd even recognize the sound of it any more. Maybe that was the ghost-clicking sound she'd been hearing all day in the back of her head. A broken intercom trying to make a broken sound in a broken house for a broken person.

You know, she really hadn't missed it after she'd killed it. She hadn't needed it. Mia never had visitors. Not anymore. Ever. The grocery people always got buzzed in by the maintenance shed people or by the manager. The quiet gardener from Argentina who did their grounds had a key to her mailbox and left Mia's mail for her by Mia's back door. He put it under the groceries if there were groceries, stuck them in the screen door if there weren't. He was a kind man, actually. Mia felt lucky, Mia felt grateful, although she didn't speak to him, hardly at all. No buzzers, no talking. It had left Mia satisfied and self-contained, no one needing her, and her needing no one.

Until now. Now the buzzer was there and she was being forced to open herself to the desires of any random person who might walk by the condo, see her condo door, and choose to buzz her condo buzzer, for whatever reason, at any time of the day or night. It wasn't fair. It made her exposed. But what else could Mia have done? Nothing. She had to know.

Mia had laboriously worked her way through her small, very late lunch. Well, it wasn't really a lunch, it was more of a dinner. What do you call lunch-dinner? Dinch? Lunner? She'd been so preoccupied, she'd burnt her toast three times. The fourth set was still black, but it was edible if she didn't look at it too closely. Or not at all. It was so bright in here now. It was hard not to see things. You had to really work at it. She was eating her can of soup cold. She didn't feel like dirtying a dish or a bowl or a sauce pan to heat it up. She scooped it out of the can with her favorite solid silver soup spoon she'd inherited from her mother. She'd just rediscovered it. It had fallen behind the sink, by her toolbox. You know, everyone ate gazpacho cold. It was soup. Green pea and ham wasn't that much different than gazpacho. Right? Right. Soup is soup is soup. Is soup. Is soup. It sounded like a song.

There was a noise down the hall that had been bothering her for hours. Her house was always quiet. No music. No T.V. No activity. And now, suddenly this afternoon, there was something else besides Mia moving around in here. It was that front door thing. The thing that had run in. Had to be. Except it sounded like a person. People didn't squeeze between your legs unnoticed. O.K. Not a person. But what was it? All Mia knew was that she didn't like it, all the same. Of all days. Why now? Why her? What was next? What?

If she kept quiet and still, Mia could hear someone talking, someone breathing their words out shrilly, in yes, a tuneful kind of way, but in such a loud stage whisper any fool could hear it, even through a closed oak door. Like the second bedroom's door. The door to the bedroom she never used.

O.K.

She crept down her hall. She tiptoed. She realized she'd been hearing this all afternoon. And now she had them. Finally. She bent down, steadying herself cautiously with her right hand against the door jamb, balancing carefully, creaking forward on the balls of her feet. Her afghan fell off one shoulder. She pulled it tight again, around her neck. She tensed. She pushed with her aching back muscles, and summoned all her willpower so as not to collapse into a pile of rheumatoid-ridden joints against her purple-flowered, peeling, velvet-flocked wallpaper - paper she had put up herself, many long years ago, which covered both walls of the long hallway back to her main bedroom. If she went down, she'd probably tear down the whole wall of it with her this time. Parts had torn off before when she'd collided with it. Oh well.

So, Mia just don't fall. Don't. You can do it.

Mia pressed her lips firmly together, framed her eyes into narrow slits of righteous determination, and shaking a little bit from the effort, carefully positioned her ear firmly on the crack where the door didn't quite meet the wall. She waited patiently. And waited. She felt her knees beginning to go.

Muffled mumbling. More mumbling. She couldn't hear a thing. Not a thing. This was ridiculous. In her own house, even. Well, she'd see about that. She could take care of herself. No one made a laughingstock of her. She could feel her face getting red, she was so upset.

With even more effort, she pushed herself upright, straightening her back against its constant complaints, and let go with a ringing, indignant cry of "Get back Rover, Get back. Down, Rover, down" which she hoped they could hear, hit the wall hard, repeatedly, to make the sounds of a large, ferocious, protective animal being reluctantly restrained in a small condo hallway, and made a grab for the doorknob. Swiftly and silently, she was as quiet as a bird of prey she thought, as a hawk, she yanked the door open in one swift movement – a performance expressly designed to bewilder and befuddle whomever was plotting and scheming this mischief for her in an unused room. She'd catch them. Mia would do it. In mid-plot. She'd get them red-handed.

It took her two tries to get the squeaky door all the way open. Yes, it must have reduced the element of surprise, but when she finally surveyed the space in front of her, looking from ceiling to floor, from corner to corner, she found the extra bedroom empty. Or nearly empty. A startled bird gripped the window sill on the far side of the room with its tiny clawed feet, hopping back and forth in front and in back of the billowing drapes, its beak opening and closing but no song coming out. In fact, it made no noise. None at all.

He didn't seem to know if he wanted to leave or wanted to stay. That's how Mia first bumped into Milt the sparrow (named after Milton the poet, and sometimes Mia called him John when he was being recalcitrant – the him part was always a puzzle, Mia thought Milt was a him, but really, how could you tell?). At any rate, that's how they first met. It was a little disconcerting sharing her simple and well-ordered life with something or someone so free. She ended up taking the screen off, leaving the spare bedroom window wide open, that day, and the days that followed. Milt generally stayed there. He slept with her in her bedroom. She spread newspapers underneath him, there in his room, and there in hers.

That made two windows, an intercom and a door now, four things that were completely open and helpless to the outside.

Where was this all headed? What was Mia plunging towards? Mia wanted to know.

It wasn't until much, much later that afternoon, you really had to call it evening by then, that Mia found out who was sliding swift as a white spirit in the spaces between the furniture, padding softly down hallways when Mia wasn't looking, breathing quietly in corners in close places Mia hadn't dusted in for years, making the occasional odd, unexpected noise. Once, around 7 P.M. she saw a pink nose sticking out behind a sofa cushion, another time around 8, she saw a delicate footprint impressed on the high, fuzzy pile of the old rug in front of her vanity, the one with the tub and shower, when she went to wash her hands. She was staring incredulously and a little malevolently at it when a soft silkiness enveloped her bare feet in a kind of podiatric epiphany. She looked down.

A white cat with improbably innocent blue eyes looked back up at her. There was, of course, a loud purring sound, and Pope (that's what Mia ended up calling him, after yet another poet, although his name changed to Alexander when he was naughty) squeezed his eyes shut as he did a fair imitation of an infinite loop, a furry Moebius Strip, circling her ankles in tight figure-eights, curving around one of Mia's legs while he almost met his own tail still uncurling around Mia's other leg.

It was later, as the sun was setting, painting the sturdy beige walls of her living room lurid shades of flame and inflammation, that Mia heard the sound of sand shifting. Distantly. Faintly. But deliberately. Where was it? What was it? She was surrounded by a steady slinking and sliding of streams of sand as if something or someone were crawling on their belly purposefully, carefully, hopelessly, inescapably, and very close by. Her breathing became erratic. She gnawed on her lip with her incisors, closed one eye and cocked her head to hear the slithering better, more accurately. Yes.

There. There it was. Outside. She quickly drew her breath in and held it. She could hear it now. She could hear it clearly.

She'd been napping on her couch, keeping her calves and feet elevated to get the swelling down some (it never really worked out all that well, but she had to try at least) and had been thinking about maybe heating up some leftover pasta for a late dinner she had in the freezer from last week, and worrying about what she had in the way of food for her new responsibilities – the bird and the cat – Milt and Pope - to live on until the next grocery delivery hit her back door, and planning on how she was going to attack her bedroom tomorrow with the vacuum cleaner and a good dust rag, and oh, a few other things, repairs, duties. It was unnerving to have things to do. It should have worn her out. But it made Mia feel strangely energetic.

Then she heard it. Again. It made a louder sound. It was coming towards her. Closer and closer. She was sure it was just outside her front door. Sand? Crawling? It? They? Where had she heard it before? She hobbled to her feet and shuffled to the window by the door – it was closed - and pulled the drapes back just a half an inch to let her peer out with one eye.

The gold and crimson light blinded her. It hurt. She couldn't see a thing. She cautiously backed up and pulled back the deadbolts and twisted the front door's doorknob slowly so that the sound of tumblers turning was barely discernible over the sand-scraping sound outside. She could be careful when she had to. She opened the door and fell into an orange-striped yellow world of pain.

She stumbled onto the balustrade on the walk in front of her door. Looking down three floors she could see red, glistening ground, termite mounds, formations of soldiers pushing their feet through clotted sand. Ringing and a clicking sounds started up, and Mia pitched forward, even more, her hands covering her ears, and she felt herself tilting over the top of the railing, and saw the land, swarming with fat, white, pudgy, hungry insects rushing up towards her, to meet her as she fell downwards, headfirst, her day dress flapping in the hot wind, the sun hot on her face and arms, the bubbling red and white ground growing closer and closer, hotter and hotter.

She was falling.

Finally.

It was over.

Then a shape fitted itself between her legs and the balustrade, white and friendly, a furry shape, and she was tumbling sideways instead of straight down into the gnashing screaming mass beneath her. She felt a tug at the back of her dress like a beak hooking into her neck hem and she was flying, soaring over her condo complex, soaring above the fields of blood and sun and something cool was on her forehead and something soft was stroking her cheek. She closed her eyes to feel it more deeply. She wanted it. Deeper and deeper. She heard her name being called. Over and over. Calling and calling.

She opened her eyes.

She thought she heard a familiar song somewhere. A tune she remembered. A melody that moved in easy ways that made you feel good. And words, comfortable words rolling through her head, flipping and stumbling, tumbling over each other in their excitement to be free, foaming up and spilling over, soaking everything in sight as she blinked and coughed, trying to get her breath back, trying to see.

"You can't always get what you want. But sometimes…"

Yes, she knew this part.

"You might find…"

What would you find?

"You get what you need."

Yes, someone was singing.

Who was that in front of her? She put her hand on her forehead so that she could see through all this bright light.

Ruffi stood in front of her. One hand was on Mia's shoulder, her other hand was on Mia's cheek, a wet washcloth was on her head. Mia was lying down. The front door was open. The sun was just setting. Mia felt she had just been thinking about something, or looking at something, or seeing something that was very important to her, but she couldn't for the life of her remember what it was.

"Mia! Mia! What were you thinking? Walking around outside at sundown in your flimsy dress? In your condition? And I've been calling you all day. What were those messages about? The ones you left me. It sounded as if you were dragging empty trash cans around on a gravel parking lot. And the clicking? What were you thinking?"

Ruffi took a breath and stopped, but Mia didn't say anything. Ruffi looked down, shaking her head. It looked like Ruffi had been crying some. And she had the faintest of bittersweet smiles. Mia felt patient and calm. Mia could wait.

"And Mia, honey, what are you doing with all your windows wide open? And the front door? Realistically, have you gone and lost what little sense you had, woman?"

Ruffi's words were angry, but her voice was calm and slow, the way, maybe, you'd talk to a frightened child. Well, Mia was frightened. That made sense. Or she used to be frightened.

Ruffi was smiling at her, waiting on her. Yes, Mia was relaxed, yes, she was surprisingly calm. Mia still didn't say anything, she just looked up at Ruffi's face. It was new. It was old. It was fresh. It was restoring. It was Ruffi. It was drinking a cold cup of water on a hot summer's day. She could drink Ruffi up forever.

CIRCLES AND WHEELS

Nikolai realized he'd just read the last sentence "How do you ride your last wave" five times and still had no idea what it meant.

Quite abruptly he'd had enough. Enough of this apartment and enough of this bed, and definitely enough of this useless book and if anyone was listening, enough of everything that looks good but gets you nowhere fast, and enough with love and enough with desire and enough with Alexei. He was done. He was through. He punched the book off the bed. He wanted to be caught. He wanted to get it over with. He wanted his old life back.

Narrowly missing Alexei's head which was buried under well-worn blankets, the book flew off after a manner, a new species of bird, pages flapping, bindings pumping the air, arcing away from their bed and away from Nikolai and Alexei and out into open space. Nikolai tried, dispassionately, as a University student should, to predict where it would land. It should have been easy for him, it was a practical vector force problem in his Physics class - but the book jerked and flipped - it was a wild thing – it didn't want to be the object of anybody's predicting – and it moved with a primitive and dangerous will of its own, flying and twitching and making noises as if it were trying to raise an alarm. Then the book hit the bare floor, satisfyingly thumping and spinning. Its worn, green felt cover gathered even more scratches, and its embossed figure of a silver snake swallowing its own head spiraled in infinite regression in front of Nikolai, endlessly, round and round and round. Nikolai stared at it, caught in fascination, waiting for something terrible, some violence to happen.

It was a polar-cold winter's night. The concrete walls, which were painted a faded green, glowed white in the sputtering blue illumination in the flat. The light's source, the television, fizzing and hissing, leaked its dirty blue-white static into their drafty room, over their bed, intermittently onto the still-gyrating book, and also over the naked, but mostly bedspread-covered bodies of Nikolai and Alexei.

Alexei, whom Nikolai had started calling by his nickname Lyosha only hours before hadn't noticed any of this. That was because Alexei's nose was stuck insistently and less and less gently in the thoughtful and thorough nuzzling of Nikolai's bare, unprotected belly button. Nikolai had been liking it, in fact, he'd been liking it a lot just a few minutes ago. Now he wasn't so sure.

Nikolai struggled to push the blankets on the bed down and off, the better to grab Alexei's head and hold him still, so that he could tell Alexei that he, Nikolai, had to leave, tell him it was all a mistake, tell him it was over. Unfortunately, this action also allowed rafts of frigid air to float in, invade, and settle down into the warm cocoon of heat they'd made – a nest of blankets that buffered the two of them from the startling drafts blowing about Alexei's apartment. The cold was almost a third person in the room with the two of them. It stuck its nose alertly into all their private business, if they let it.

"Hey" said Alexei's muffled voice, as he talked directly into Nikolai's stomach "You're killing me with frostbite down here. Stop." Nikolai was irritated with Alexei for no reason he could remember. "Lyosha!" Nikolai whispered hoarsely down at his waist, "Enough. No, you stop. Stop already." Alexei pulled the blankets back over his head, and moved lower down Nikolai's torso and ignored him. Alexei's hot breath was on his waist, then his thigh. Then it was…

"Stop it Lyosha!" Nikolai kicked under the many layers of insulating textiles and felt another body go rigid, stay still for few moments, and then go limp as Alexei crawled upwards and stuck his head out over the top of the covers. "It's like ice out here, Kolya" said Alexei, hugging him with a questioning tone in his voice that sounded like a whine to Nikolai and was something Nikolai could have gotten at home, any night of the week lately, with his wife, Sonya. Nikolai felt something unpleasant and bitter stir inside of him. Lately it came and went, appeared and disappeared. What did Alexei think Nikolai was doing here? What, in fact, was Nikolai thinking Nikolai was doing here?

It was quiet and still in the flat. It was very late, that was true. The neighbors were all asleep, you couldn't hear a thing from neighboring flats, above, below, left or right. Outside it was quiet, except for the occasional gear-complaining truck or car on some important but mysterious midnight errand. There was no wind outside.

Muffling snow drifted down evenly in all directions, as far as you could see out the window, which admittedly was only a short distance - you could see only as far as the rust-decorated wall of the next grey, tall apartment block. It was maybe not as cold as it had been, the last couple of nights, when it had been clear and the stars had shone sharp and emotionless as minerals, as cut diamonds tacked onto black, indifferent obsidian skies. Frost fell freely on them then and on all of the city those nights, unprotected and open to the bottomless, absolute cold of outer space. But here inside, with Alexei, under the covers and away from the frigid concrete walls Nikolai had been warm. Last night. The night before that. Nikolai was warm tonight too.

He should be home with his Sonya. He shouldn't be here. Not here. Not with Alexei. For an uncomfortable moment, he felt sickened by the touch of Alexei, awash with sloppy currents of shame and guilt and fear of the future, then, he felt breathless with a giddy euphoria, this was the only place he needed to be, the reason he'd been born, to be in Alexei's arms.

"It's cold" repeated Alexei, "It's cold and you're so quiet."

The Metro in Saint Petersburg wasn't the best place, or even a common place to meet men, but that hadn't stopped Alexei. Or Nikolai. For three months, as a fall turned into a winter, Nikolai noticed someone noticing him, getting on the 2 at Nevsky Prospect and getting off five stops later, shuffling past the old Soviet building at Moskavaya square, bundling his jacket tighter against the wind blowing down the wide boulevards. At first he hardly gave it a thought. But gradually, Nikolai became skillful at identifying a familiar figure, bundled into a nearly shapeless ball - as are all the winter citizens of St. Petersburg - and Nikolai had pretended not to notice a red-cheeked face turning casually his way and a pair of wide-set gold-green eyes occasionally and accidentally following his quick walk down partially shoveled, snow-banked streets.

Then it happened more often. Sometimes Nikolai saw Alexei on the train as he travelled on the Metro to and from University each day. Sometimes he saw him as he ran up the Metro stairs. Or while he was stamping his feet and clapping his hands for warmth when he made the long walks across the exposed, breeze-scoured squares. Or waiting for the bus. Or standing at an intersection waiting to cross. Or just standing and waiting, hardly daring to breathe, hoping to see green eyes and red cheeks approach, pass, and disappear into the distance. If you'd asked Nikolai why he was waiting around for no reason, he would have been surprised at the question. He couldn't have told you. He didn't know himself. It was a question he'd somehow made sure never to ask himself.

Finally, last week, Alexei had stopped next to him, as Nikolai fumbled his cold fingers, trying, with gloves on, to tie his shoelaces in the frigid wind blowing off the Gulf of Finland. Nikolai had been pretending to perform this simple task for the last twenty minutes, over and over again. He'd been getting quite frozen, all the way through. But he'd had to wait. He'd had to see.

It happened at the center of the square, in front of the undeniably emphatic and resolute statue of Lenin, who stood there day and night pointing the way for invisible multitudes to follow, encouraging them with a brave smile to march towards a destination no one wanted to go to anymore. There Nikolai was, bent over, a pair of shoes suddenly appearing in his line of sight on the ice-covered concrete before him, and Nikolai was looking up, helplessly following the shoes up to a pair of long legs, then a coat, then two crossed arms, then, with a sharp pang of surprise which was almost physically painful, a well-known set of cheeks and two familiar eyes. Nikolai suddenly found he was without the capacity for speech.

He didn't remember what he said afterwards, but it wasn't much, obviously, and he did remember smiling. And he remembered Alexei's smile. You could have lit the whole of the Leningrad District with Alexei's smile. With both their smiles. And Nikolai had felt transmuted. As if from one element to another element. As if from the common, to the noble. Changed. In an instant. Into something else. Into something whole.

Nikolai had walked straight west with Alexei that night, out of the square, to Alexei's uncle's flat, instead of turning right and going home in the bus. Alexei's uncle was a long-distance truck driver, currently on a run to Marseilles to pick up some containers, or that's what Alexei had thought at the time. Whatever the reason, it meant Alexei had the flat for himself. Privacy was a gift as precious as, well, you just didn't turn it down when it came your way, not in St. Petersburg, not in the winter, not if you were a student and young and acting foolishly and weren't asking yourself questions. So Nikolai followed Alexei.

And you know, Nikolai didn't even remember making a choice. The choice had been patiently waiting for him all along, for years as it turned out, under Lenin's outstretched finger. It had been there the whole time. Nikolai just hadn't noticed it before.

And now here he was, staring into those same mischievous eyes, after a week's worth of nights with Alexei. He didn't know what he was doing. He decided he didn't want to know, not yet, not now. He pulled Alexei's face towards his own, gently, quietly, proprietarily, saying softly in his ear "My Lyosha, my Lyosha."

When the front door locks started clicking, unbarring themselves one by one, and the heavy door rotated awkwardly open on squealing hinges, neither of them had a chance to do much more than pull on a pair of jeans. A tired and inebriated and angry voice called out Alexei's name as heavy boots stomped outside in the hallway. The boots knocked whatever snow and dirty ice remained on them, and then two swift thumps reverberated against the wall, as they were kicked off onto the salt-covered mat covering most of the floor in the hallway by the front door.

Tired footsteps of a large person made their way slowly with the carefulness of someone who is trying to keep and maintain a hard-won balance, down the hall, around the corner, and into the living room that Alexei was using as a bedroom, and both of them heard them, the footsteps, as they came to a sudden and disbelieving stop in the open doorway. Nikolai, scrambling, just in the act of pulling a sweater over his head, and Alexei, with a blanket around his shoulders apparently turning casually to look out a window, they...

"With a blanket around his shoulders" and something about a window - the words in the book swam in and out of focus for Jack, which was a bother, but that was nothing new to him, not today.

"With a blanket..." Jack blinked, he blinked hard. "With a..." His eyes were tired, they were actually sore from reading, the light was unnaturally bright, but he needed to be doing something while he sat there waiting, something that would keep his admittedly active intelligence, his agile mind occupied. He looked around the empty cab of the truck in a desultory search. Nothing. Just like the last ten times, no hundred times he'd looked. Only this green book. A book about homosexuals, drug dealers, and sad adolescent girls. An odd mix to say the least. Obviously, one of her books - a Sarah book. Not something he would choose to read, not that he read all that much, but still. A bit plebeian. Not up to his standards. Actually, not his type of reading material at all.

It was hot. No, it was bloody hot. A tight knot of anxiety started to pull at his chest muscles, stretching them snug across his ribs, prompting his lungs, in turn, to become uncooperative and breathing was suddenly incredibly and surprisingly difficult. Bother. He scrambled blindly for the inhaler in his right pocket. This involved a great deal of tugging and pulling, and in all this heat more stinging sweat rolled down his forehead and directly into his eyes, of course.

Now he couldn't see or breathe. Normally, he would have wanted to have used his hanky on his forehead, but it had, unfortunately, fallen out of his hands the night before and buried itself somewhere at his feet and was apparently unreachable - as he couldn't bend over, stretch, retrieve or even touch anything below his knees over his ample frame no matter how loudly he grunted and strained. So he used his shirt collar. The cast on his foot wasn't making things any easier, as usual.

He carefully re-inserted the inhaler in his right front pocket, this time.

He glanced down at the book. He could barely see the words. A phrase, and then another, rolled around and around in his head, over and over again, syllables without meaning, the sound of an empty soup can tumbling along a windy highway no one was walking down.

Where was she? What could Sarah have been doing all this time?

Silence lay heavily in Jack's truck, as the sun set about happily roasting him in it alive. Jack felt he had to reply to it, the unconvinced silence of the desert all around him - "It's this sun and the bloody flies and the..." and then, smashing his fist repeatedly onto the dashboard he repeated what he'd been saying for the last 36 hours "where" (pound) "the blazes" (pound, pound) " is she?" (pound, pound, pound).

He could feel a vein pulsing in his forehead. Somewhere underneath it all, underneath the sweat and sunburn, somewhere buried inside was the old Jack. The bespoke-besuited, soft-spoken Jack. The gorgeously confident *homme d'affaires*, with only a slightly receding hairline Jack. The Jack whose brilliant accent and soft vowels held more than a merely casual acquaintance with the Queen's English, hinting at broader horizons and subtler understandings and Very Important Connections. The Jack people paid attention to, who commanded attention, who demanded it. The Jack whose jokes brought laughter, sometimes applause (yes, it had happened), and who inevitably caused jumping when he chose to do some calling. In other words, the Jack who was the very satisfied and very satisfactory partner in a well-known firm (well-known in Western Australia, Perth's own Smith, Smith, Smythe and Taylor) – a well-known, substantial and well-respected firm of Chartered Accountants. Not, despite present appearances, Chartered Stockmen, for heaven's sake.

Yes. That Jack. Where was he? Why right here, of course. Silly. He wasn't going anywhere. He hadn't changed.

A lizard which had been moving in and out of the shadow inside the truck by the rear-view mirror just to Jack's right, alternately jumping in and out of the sun all morning, suddenly decided to shoot down under Jack's feet. It scampered, claws making tiny scratching sounds on the cab carpeting, fled past his tepid plastic gallon jug half-full of water, dodged between his crutches splayed down the middle of the cab over the clutch, and dove into calmer pastures in the back seat, far from the dangerous calisthenics involved in Jack-hysterics. Other than that, that brief interlude of movement and life, there was silence, something he had a great quantity of. Of which his future supply boded to be inexhaustible.

Jack sat very still for quite some time, breathing heavily and ponderously, brooding darkly on Sarah's unpunctuality, and scowling at the orange-red desert in which he was starting to feel more and more immobilized - a Jack-fly caught in outback-amber.

Eventually, the lizard cautiously moved once again into view, or maybe it was a second lizard, at any rate it eyed him from the back of the driver's seat, just out of Jack's reach. Jack cast a large baleful eye in its direction. His unformed plans regarding said lizard were forestalled by more annoying sweat, more inefficient wiping, and a buzzing in his head that wouldn't stop, as if a cloud of locusts were swarming in under his sunburnt forehead. And to top it all off, under his cast, his foot felt like as if he'd stepped on an anthill – it itched ferociously, demanding, not asking his immediate attention. He beat at the plaster on his leg, his eyes tearing up again. This is futile, Jack, get a grip on yourself. He stopped his hand from its compulsive clawing at the cast by gripping it with his other hand, but soon it started again of its own accord. Focus. He needed to focus. On something other than his foot.

He heard something move outside the truck. It sounded large. What could he do?

He banged his cast against the side of the cab in helpless angst. It didn't actually make much noise. He looked out. Oh. A piece of canvas had come undone. It was flapping against the side of the vehicle. The lizard moved onto the seat next to him. It seemed less and less afraid of him. Actually, he really couldn't move his leg all that much. It was getting stiff, just sitting there all day long. Stiff and swollen and itchy in the hot cab of the truck. The lizard moved closer. He shushed at the lizard. It ignored him. He rammed his feet repeatedly into the passenger door now, over and over. He wasn't sure he could stop. He pounded rhythmically away, happy to be doing something. The lizard sat in the shade and closed its eyes.

Oh, and now he needed to use the bathroom.

Fantastic.

Opening the door, leaning out, un-belting, unzipping,

reconfiguring – it all took a great deal more time than Jack thought it should have, or could have. His pants were only a little wet afterwards. For about 30 seconds, Then the heat took care of the stains for him.

The lizard scooted for cover again, this time on over to the driver's seat, by the speedometer on the dash. It waited in the shade by the fuel gauge, observing Jack's slow movements, examining him impassively from top to bottom in easy patience, lifting first one foot then the other in the noonday heat, and doing little push-ups in between. It closed its eyes again.

It had seemed so easy. The last three years, under his careful direction, of course, he'd had Sarah moving money around in, out, and through customer's accounts as would water in the plumbing of a fountain. Sucked in here, squirted out there. Sarah had managed it all. Short term investments of excess working capital, long term investments in growth funds, always in a different currency than Australian dollars. Jack was of course the mastermind. And it was his signature that authorized it all. They always held over a small amount as a kind of under-the-table commission in the conversion rates, a little Jack-Sarah extra. It had been tidy and neat. But it had been slow, as Sarah ceaselessly and abundantly made clear. It would have taken decades to make any decent money. So Sarah had just taken it all.

Jack had of course been flabbergasted at first, but since she had managed to convert it into three suitcases bursting with currency of many denominations (obviously Sarah was a girl who moved in certain social circles, the existence of which Jack had never before contemplated except as the stuff of cheap pulp novels and unlikely Hollywood action fluff – but then, Jack's had been a sheltered existence, far removed from the skills necessary for such gross conversions as changing financial investments into baggage trunks filled with – hopefully unmarked - paper money). He'd argued with her for all of ten minutes. Then he'd chivalrously offered to carry the heavy suitcases out to his car, all on his own.

So, with the truck packed, and his career with Smith et al. essentially at an end, Jack had cheerfully, as he saw it, given in to the inevitable – optimistic surrender to one's fate being the decision any rational man would have come to under the same or similar circumstances. And... the game was afoot.

They had shot out of Perth in the middle of the night, motoring on back roads vaguely north and west, apparently (in retrospect) making for Kalgoorlie, but it all looked the same to Jack. Flat. Trees. Sand. Sarah had driven, sunglasses on and a beige scarf tying up her hair, which smelled significantly of hair dye. Jack had slept. He'd been exhausted by the whole experience. Simply worn out. So he wasn't quite sure where they'd ended up exactly.

Oh. He'd been dozing. The lizard was on his hand. He shook it off. The sun was almost directly overhead, the red dust of the road radiated a wan, sickly pink into the air above it, the hood of the Holden, (or was it the engine?) was clicking and pinging in the heat. Low stands of eucalyptus and regular dots of hummock grass were clearly outlined and weirdly without shadow. Later, just before night, the shadows would appear and cover the truck, like they had last night and the night before. And then it would be cold. A bit brisk. He'd want some heat then. But Jack wasn't going to be here another night, was he? With any luck he wouldn't be here another hour, would he? Where the devil was she?

The week before, as he was getting into Sarah's car, after leaving a motel in Jondalup during one of their afternoon, "planning retreats" (which, yes, usually did involve disrobing at some point), Sarah had accidentally tripped Jack coming down the back stairs (they hadn't used the lobby stairs, Jack had a reputation, after all, to consider) as Jack tried to re-robe, hastily, en route. They'd been late. He'd been tucking in his shirt, pulling up his pants, adjusting his belt, and negotiating a steep staircase, all at the same time, when suddenly he'd noticed a red high-heel jutting out in front of his Elden Dress Oxfords, and it was all pretty much a jumble after that. Jack had laughed it off, as he was a few gin and tonics past feeling the minor pain of a broken bone in his ankle, but, as they both found out later that afternoon, it wasn't a laughing matter. In fact, Jack couldn't walk. He hobbled. Sometimes he crawled. He spent the night in hospital. One ankle broken. The other sprained.

Because of his injuries, and his crutches, when they'd arrived here to hide the money, it had been Sarah who had dragged the bulky suitcases, sweating and grunting in the late afternoon sun, and Jack who had stayed behind resting in the passenger's seat, gathering his strength for their run for Sydney. Sarah had come up with the idea of hiding it – the money that is - in an old mine Sarah knew about – how she knew such things, Jack had no idea. Old mines? Jack was beginning to understand he really didn't know very

347

much about Sarah at all. She constantly surprised him. She had strong opinions. She argued strenuously. She didn't brook disagreement. She was adamant about hiding their ill-gotten gains. And adamant about hiding it in the mine. Well, Jack could be as magnanimous as the next man, he could lose an argument gracefully. So hide it they did.

They had a couple of years to lay low. Then they'd come back for the money. Sarah had explained it all carefully in the two days of driving they'd done. Too carefully, in fact. As if Jack hadn't come up with the entire plan in the first place (with the minor exception of the mineralogical nature of the place of hiding). But, still, Sarah had seemed to want to be thorough, businesslike even in this. Details again. So, Jack had humored her. It seemed the best idea at the time. He was, as he'd mentioned, a gentleman. He deferred. So they'd parked. She'd tramped off, dragging the money. He'd graciously held down the fort here in the Holden. And he was still holding it, with only a little less grace, almost a day, no two days later.

There had been only one scare, so far, and that wasn't really much of a scare, not to an old veteran like Jack. Just at the beginning, an hour or so after Sarah had left him to wait, a newer model truck drove by, speeding madly past him. Jack's truck lay safely hidden, parked beyond the ditch on the side of the highway (well, not a highway, really just the suggestion of a track over this waste of gray-green stone and red sand), and Jack had started to wave frantically at the newcomer (Sarah? – had she forgotten where they'd parked?) bearing down on him. It trailed great massy clouds of red dust, as would one of the four horsemen of the Apocalypse, and accelerated the closer it got to him and Jack threw both arms out of the passenger side window and yelled himself hoarse. Then, at the last minute, Jack threw himself back in the truck, ducked down, and attempted to be quiet as the proverbial church mouse. He was proud of himself (later) for thinking quickly (now that he was a wanted fugitive, laying low so to speak – both figuratively and literally, to use the vernacular), and Jack had only stolen the merest glance (peeking over the top of the dashboard) at the back of the driver's head - a shock of red hair, probably a man, though it could have been a woman, there wasn't much to see, there was a lot of hyperventilating occurring at that point - before collapsing over the clutch shift breathing shakily into the cracked upholstery of the Holden and counting to a thousand.

He hadn't straightened up for fifteen minutes. A nice bit of undercover work, that. He'd been silent and invisible, in the end. Although he had maneuvered about here and there to get at his inhaler. But that was only natural. He was asthmatic. Anyone with asthma would have moved about. He'd been as quiet as was humanly possible. That's when he'd found the book, jammed under the driver's seat, its bent cover with the peeling silver snake, the binding broken and the whole thing encrusted with grit and mud.

And looking up, he'd noticed the steering column, the naked steering column, and he'd discovered (after a frantic 2 hour search) that Sarah had inadvertently taken the keys to the truck with her.

Bother.

There hadn't been any more cars/trucks/apocalyptic horsemen since then, luckily.

One large mottled arm had been sitting in the sun for an hour or more already, he could feel himself crisping in the UV rays as a leg of bacon would over an outback campfire. Oh. He'd been dozing again. He shuffled and shifted in the passenger seat towards the center of the truck to remove his arm from danger. A breath of air, which would not have elicited the slightest surprise in a steel foundry, puffed through his open window and out the open one on the empty driver's side. It was going to be an absolute scorcher again today.

The lizard seemed to be dancing about in the shade. It was running over his legs. He was too tired to swat at it. Oh. There it was on his hand. Yes, it definitely seemed to be unafraid of him. Curiouser and curiouser.

Thinking it over, he doubted anyone could even see his Holden from the road, unless you knew where to look. He was under a tree. In a gully. His vehicle was covered in red dust. He was definitely off the grid, as Sarah would say. He didn't even have a cell. Sarah had the cell. Actually, he could sit here for years, and no one would be able to find him. Years. He was safe.

Not that he'd be here that long.

Surely.

Sarah would be here.

Any moment now.

Damn her.

Where was she?

Jack noticed the lizard was now sitting quite near him. Actually it was on his shoulder. It hadn't even bothered to move when he'd shifted himself out of the sun. Had he shifted? Had he moved? He couldn't remember quite. For a moment the lizard watched Jack quite closely, then lost interest. It scuttled slightly to the right, then a bit to the left to get back out of the direct sun and into a shadowy recess under his earlobe, then it seemed to close its eyes and rest. It lay still. As if it were waiting for something.

"Then it seemed to close its eyes and rest. It lay still. As if it were waiting for something. The End" Maria read out loud, pronouncing the harsh consonants of English and its limping, stumbling word-endings as exactly as she could. "The End" part, though, was in Spanish. Jose didn't say anything.

The sound of the airplane's propellers filled the cabin with a constant buzzing which sounded to Maria as if it were the beating of a billion bee's wings. Since she was deathly allergic to bee stings, it wasn't the most comforting image or sound, but she smiled bravely over at Jose anyway, as he clutched the steering handles with white knuckles and stared ahead into the gathering dusk. The storm lay to one side of them.

The book dropped between the seat and the side-door of the plane. She let it. She wasn't sure she was feeling up to reading anymore out loud. She felt a little ill. And a lot more scared.

Maria unconsciously felt her belly when the plane bucked and jerked. She worried the still-flat skin over her abdomen with her hand. It had been only 9 weeks. It couldn't hurt her yet, could it? She was expecting, but just barely. She wished her mother were here. She wished her family and sisters were here. But everyone was back north in Montevideo, safe on the ground, and here she was suspended between the heavens and the earth with an angelically colossal black wall of sullen misery and irritation aiming its slow-moving anger lazily in their direction – that's how the thunderstorm appeared, at least to her, she couldn't help thinking of it that way.

No, she didn't want her family up here with her. She didn't

want Jose up here with her. But here they were. And there was the storm. Innocent butterflies seeing the windshield of a truck approaching them probably felt the same way. These dark things, these clouds would crush them. And not even know it. She should have told Jose about the baby before they left. She should have told him.

Sheets of rain began to pelt the plane, long liquid fingers trying to drag them wetly back down to Uruguay, or into the ocean, or just fling them off into space to be lost forever flying round and round among the stars. Night was falling. Or was it just the storm darkening the whole world with its own sick fear, its need to make everyone feel small, its strong desire to hurt the helpless? Maria could feel her eyes beginning to fill with tears. She wouldn't bring her hands up to wipe them though. She wouldn't give the storm that satisfaction.

She was Anna Maria Cristina Morazo Rojas de Rodriguez, wife of a Rojas, Jose Rodrigo Teodato Rojas de Gonzalez, a very handsome man, a very popular man in many barrios of Montevideo. She was lucky. Everyone said this. She'd met Jose at a dance, in the plaza, in front of the church. He'd bowed to her parents, asked permission, it had all been proper, that had been their first dance. He'd been very respectful. The green, blue, and yellow paper lanterns had glowed like small multicolored moons rising over the cobblestones and over her and over him.

They'd danced all evening. Even if he was a narco-trafico, even if he had been, all the drugs, all the mysterious tasks, all that was over. He'd said so. Over and done with. Jose had said (and she'd believed him) that they were starting over. And here they were – starting. The plane tossed and jumped like a horse trying to get free of its riders. Maria felt her cheeks growing wet with long streaks of warmth. She could taste a saltiness in the back of her nose and throat.

Jose was silent, wrestling with the plane and the storm. Maria watched him, but he didn't look at her. The laughing eyes, the expressive eyebrows, always moving, always joking, they were gone, replaced by the blankness of a face of a stranger. Sitting next to her was a man she didn't know, someone she'd never met, someone she didn't know if she'd ever want to meet. Cold, calculating eyes, a determined mouth – who knows what a face like that was capable of? Who knows if he really loved her at all? How could she tell?

"Maria stop!" she whispered to herself under her breath. "Enough. You're no child. Those days are gone. You are a mother and a wife now. Enough." It didn't help much. She could hear it - the voice of her mother inside of her. That was her mother's words. It didn't make her brave and strong like her mother. Why was that? Still, she wouldn't panic, she wouldn't doubt. She didn't have that luxury anymore. Maybe that's what her mother's bravery was – the necessity of feeling but not acting. It was a hard thing to do. Very hard.

The small plane started weaving and bobbing, bouncing through invisible air pockets, ricocheting off unseen air walls, laboriously rising and then, almost in repentance, abruptly and shamefully dropping again, lower than it had been before. It was making more book reading unlikely. But Maria knew Jose liked to hear her voice. He'd liked the last two stories.

Sometimes the English was difficult, and hard to understand. But it helped her to practice. And he liked it. He'd been smiling. Why didn't he say anything, though? Below them, the blue green bumps of the Atlantic stretched out to darkness, far off, to the right, she could feel it, unseen the sun had begun to set behind the unimaginably distant Andes.

Lights started winking on beneath their feet. Bits of light showing purpose and thought, care and love. Trails of spots strung out along roads mimicking diagrams of the nervous system, individual houses were nerve endings, clustered nerve ganglia were settlements, and far away, far off to the south ahead of them, a monstrous glow - Buenos Aires, below the horizon - that then must be the brain. Maria was studying to be a nurse. So if all that busy humanity below them was a nervous system, what was Maria? What was Jose? They must be thoughts. Ephemeral, insubstantial, notions that flickered along the network briefly then disappeared, as quickly as they'd arisen. The world was thinking and it did its thinking through the living of Jose and Maria.

She could settle for that. For being a thought. They were the living thoughts of God.

Maria didn't want to say anything, but the bumps were getting worse. The storm was more and more in front of them, and all around them, and not just to one side anymore. It was racing them to the city.

She needed something to take her mind off of all this. She pried the book out from beside the seat, but didn't open it. How could she read? She started playing with the pages of the book with the ends of her fingers, running her fingernails over the peeling green felt on the cover.

The storm got worse. One gust nearly knocked them end over end and it took Jose a few minutes to get their little craft steady again. It wasn't fair, Maria thought furiously, it was unjust. They were trying to start over, trying to do the right thing. Why were they being punished for trying?

Jose briefly touched her hand, which startled her, she hadn't seen him reaching out, but he couldn't look over at her, even for just the smallest of moments and catch her eyes. His hand quickly returned to the plane's controls. It felt now, as if the small, feverish machine were trying to jump out of its own skin. She was glad now he wasn't trying to get a glimpse of her face. "A few drops of rain, what is it to us, my love?" He spoke loudly, and peered ahead, forcing his gaze through sheer willpower through the storm and out of it, seeing the clear skies ahead, laughing at the water pouring over the plane as if they were flying through a river.

Seeing his eyes, she remembered cobblestones and green and yellow lanterns. And the dancing. And he was her Jose. He was always her Jose. He yelled to be heard over the propellers and the wind, "We have the arms of each other. We are as strong together as angels. And what do angels worry about wind and rain? Ouah! That's what they think of wind and rain. Nothing. Nothing at all."

She stopped biting her lip and forced herself to stare ahead with a slight smile on her face as if all of this were an amusement they were diverting themselves with. And she believed him.

"And she believed him." The clumsy, melted together words in English skipped across her mind in a jumble. Not at all like Japanese. She had received awards for her English. More than once. She was good at it. Everyone said so. But today, it was different for her. Today, the words were bulky and awkward in her mind and couldn't be moved without an effort. They were stones. No, that wasn't exactly right. She was the stone.

Flat and round, and useful for throwing and skipping across

water, but heavy and earth-bound, they inevitably sank when they hit a wave too big for them to leap over. They sank and disappeared from sight, as if they had never flown. Everyone knows that stones can't fly. Everyone but her father. Her father had taught her that they could. And he'd been right. Sometimes stones did fly. She'd seen them. And she had flown too, at least for a while. But that was the past. There was no use thinking about the past. The book still rested, open, beckoning her, on her lap.

She tried, for a moment, to think in English, like her sensei in Lower School had taught her, and attacked the English words with a concentrated energy. And, yes, at first it worked. But as Netsuko forced sentence after sentence through her eyeballs into her foggy head, she found herself more and more looking out the window of the bullet train, watching for low mountains hiding and jumping out from under gray mist and fog. They winked on and off in the distance, reappearing less and less often the farther north they travelled. Is that how Hokkaido would be? She tried imagining what it would feel like to live in the middle of mountains, to walk on clouds.

She finally gave up, and quietly put the book away in her electric pink and powder blue backpack. The low wall by the side of the rails rose higher as they banked to the left. They were flying through a town now. Electrical lines swung by, singing in the cold humidity, concrete apartment blocks flashed in front of her eyes, each window a life, each life, like hers filled with hopes and fears and responsibilities. The towns and the fields, the steady thrum of the tracks and the constant patter of the train operator over the loudspeakers, all of it together, was making her tired and sleepy.

She didn't want to read anymore. She didn't want to do anything. But her aunt was sick and needed someone to help, and Netsuko needed a home, and everyone agreed it was the best for everyone. Everyone but Netsuko. She didn't know what she wanted. She tried, but she couldn't feel anything. How weary she was. You weren't supposed to get so tired when you were young, were you?

She'd come a long way, Kyushu and the south were already another world, another existence. And Hokkaido lay over the horizon, a longer journey yet. She missed her father. All she had left of him, after the funeral, was a picture and a letter. Everything else had been sold. Her aunt's house wasn't all that big. She was lucky to have that. That's what her aunt said, that's what her family had said.

Another, more official voice reminded her that Morioka station was approaching, transfers to Akita and to the Sea of Japan coast. She was going to that coast, but farther north. Much farther north. Where all the world was white with snow and cloud. She looked at the inside of the train. The bullet train had been expensive, but she'd paid for it herself. All her small savings. She wanted to get the travelling over with as soon as possible.

She looked around out of the side of her eyes. White ceilings, white walls, bright white lights, she felt as if she were travelling on the inside of a long, oblong egg, shooting across fields and towns at dangerous speeds for an egg. Eggs get broken easily. Lots of things break easily. She should know. She was already broken.

She had a few minutes before the she had to change trains and go under the strait through the tunnel and onto Hokkaido. She felt restless and wanted to do something with her hands. She used to be able to sit still. Now she couldn't, or wouldn't. Pulling out the book, she found herself turning the pages back and forth, and reading backwards, the wrong direction was making her eyes hurt and her head dizzy. She felt a little sick.

She leaned back in the chair, feeling the upholstery wrap around her head, confused and troubled by the constant feeling of irritation she felt nowadays. It never stopped. It made her feel upside down and inside out - she'd fallen through the rabbit hole, like Alice, like Wonderland. That was a strange book. This book was confusing too, stories about planes and lizards and Russian winters and young men coughing in empty rooms and girls on trains to white nowheres. She didn't want to think about it anymore. She didn't want to think about anything.

She closed the book. Running her hand over and over the smooth serpent on its fuzzy green cover, she looked out the window and watched far-off foothills leapfrog towards her.

Leap-frogging foothills. Hmmm. Japan and Australia, Russia and Argentina. Hmmm. The book itself leap-frogged around a lot. All kinds of different stories. Different people. Hmmm. Making the humming sound felt good in his chest in a kind of painful, slashing-and-cutting kind of way. Like scratching an itch. Hmmm. He knew he shouldn't be doing it.

Damn. He felt a huge tickle starting up from way down deep inside. His chest felt jumpy. Then more than jumpy. This couldn't be good. The hum, no matter how good it had felt, had obviously been an error in judgment. As in – a big mistake. It was turning into an earthquake – this humming kept on going, building, growing on its own without him even trying. It morphed into tremors and ripples of convulsive gasping that began to work their way up his diaphragm. They hit his throat. Then, his head, which started bouncing off the pillow, he was hacking so much. His oxygen tubes exploded right out his nose. It had officially started. Basically he'd stopped breathing. Now he was a pale, pasty-white, coughing machine.

Nothing new. But he couldn't say he was having fun doing it.

He was forced to close the book with a series of coughs that wracked his whole frame, and just wouldn't stop. It actually scared him a little this time. He was really out of breath. It was an epic cough, this one, it was. He had, what? maybe five percent body fat now, he was ripped, and his abs were working it as if they were rows of muscular air compressors, bulging impressively each time he so dramatically and unsuccessfully tried to suck in air. Too bad he'd never make it to the beach again. He'd be ready. With a tan and a board he'd be... well... he'd be....

He looked amazingly similar to an anatomical drawing from an anatomy textbook. Maybe a little too much like one now. He should know. He'd been pre-med in college down here. And he was a surfer-maniac. It had been nip and tuck, which one would win out, the pre-med or the surfing. He'd loved them both. Like having two girlfriends. One of them would have made him drop the other. But... Been. Was. Had. All past tense, now man. Past pluperfect. As in, very past.

It took a good five minutes for him to get his breath back. He waved away the nurse when she came in to check on him with a questioning, not unkind look on her face. The waving, it didn't do any good. She came in all the same, re-inserted and checked the oxygen tubes to his nose, held him as he hacked and spit trying to cough his lungs up and out of his throat. His face, even whiter and paler with the effort, and streaked with slime was a mess. She helped him clean up with a towel.

Afterwards, he lay back and closed his eyes, letting the well-used and torn book with the green fuzzy cover fall down between his pillows. The nurse retrieved it, punched the pillows a few times, helped Derrick to sit up straighter and with a severe look and a nod – a warning not to try anything foolish again like using his lungs to breathe - she went off down the hall to answer another patient's buzzer.

He drew some tentative breaths anyway. It was breathing, but from underneath a sitting elephant. Or a sitting cement mixer. He'd been brought up in the city, not out in the bush, so elephants, water buffaloes and giraffes were as familiar to Derrick as mountain lions and rattlesnakes were familiar to urban dwellers of Phoenix. As in, not. Not very. Derrick was a city boy. Always had been.

Cape Town at the tip of Africa, South Africa of course was his home. The place he felt he really was himself. He couldn't explain it. It was just the best place he'd ever been. He'd been born in a tidy, domesticated suburb of London, travelled through America, Australia, even worked for the Saudi's for a year. But now, False Bay, Boland, beaches all over the peninsula, wherever there was a swell, wherever there were decent waves, and a board to ride - that was where and how he lived.

That was also pre-AIDS and pre-pneumonia and pre-hospital. Pre-everything that kept him stretched out, tired and wheezing on this bed, breathing, living the way an old man breathes and lives. Now he spent a lot of time thinking about next week, next month, next year, when he'd be better. But, he was beginning to suspect, in the middle of the night when he was alone with his thoughts, in those long fits of hyper-rational quiet that fell upon him at four in the A. of M. - fits that wouldn't go away, no matter how hard he tried to focus on the trivial, on the superficial - that it was very possible, in fact it was more than likely, that next week, well, basically, next week might never come.

Not to mention next month or next year. And he wasn't sure how he was going to handle that one. He hadn't figured that one out yet. Although he really didn't have a choice, now, did he? Nope.

How do you do that? How do you ride your last wave?

Nikolai realized he'd just read the last sentence "How do you ride your last wave" five times and still had no idea what it meant.

Quite abruptly he'd had enough. Enough of this apartment and enough of this bed, and definitely enough of this useless book and if anyone was listening, enough of everything that looks good but gets you nowhere fast, and enough with love and enough with desire and enough with Alexei. He was done. He was through. He punched the book off the bed. He wanted to be caught. He wanted to get it over with. He wanted his old life back.

Narrowly missing Alexei's head which was buried under well-worn blankets, the book flew off after a manner, a new species of bird, pages flapping, bindings pumping the air, arcing away from their bed and away from Nikolai and Alexei and out into open space. Nikolai tried, dispassionately, as a University student should, to predict where it would land. It should have been easy for him, it was a practical vector force problem in his Physics class - but the book jerked and flipped - it was a wild thing – it didn't want to be the object of anybody's predicting – and it moved with a primitive and dangerous will of its own, flying and twitching and making noises as if it were trying to raise an alarm.

Then the book hit the bare floor...

ABOUT THE AUTHOR

Anders lives as does Thoreau's mass of men, a life of quiet desperation - sometimes less quiet, sometimes less desperate, but a life nonetheless. That's what you have to remind yourself, when you least believe it, that you are, actually, living your life, and that it is quite the accomplishment, in and of itself, and that you should give yourself a pat on the back occasionally for doing it as well as you do, for as long as you have.

There are many who never will make it as far as you've gone, and none who have lived what you have lived, so every once in a while, remember, it's no sin to celebrate yourself, and give the desperation a rest. It will always be there. You can pick it up and shoulder it anytime you want and start walking again. Setting it down doesn't mean you're getting soft. It just means you're setting it down. Try it, you'll see.

But maybe, one time, at a point of self-celebration, you'll put the desperation down, party, pick yourself up afterwards and start walking and realize you have more energy and more (to use a four letter word) hope - that you're walking with a spring in your step and you won't know why and you don't want to know why. It won't even dawn on you that you've left something behind, that you lost something you thought you were going to have to lug behind you for the rest of your life – yes, your desperation. You won't be desperate and it will feel strange – until you remember where you set your desperation down - and you go to retrieve it - but, with any luck you won't remember – and never will – and from that point onwards, or at least for a while, without your desperation, you'll no longer be one of the mass of men, you'll just be you, yourself, a woman or a man who is alive, in the universe and walking about, here and there. And that's all

That, at least, is the goal of Anders. Living in the first, frantically social and riotously connected decades of the 21st century, where the desperation flows as easily as the texting and maybe even easier, and is almost as unstoppable. Almost.

www.ingramcontent.com/pod-product-compliance
Lightning Source LLC
Chambersburg PA
CBHW060155260626
47160CB00001B/278